P9-DHB-210

DECADENCE

Also by Eric Jerome Dickey

The Education of Nia Simone Bijou (e-book)
An Accidental Affair
Tempted by Trouble
Resurrecting Midnight (Gideon series)
Dying for Revenge (Gideon series)
Pleasure
Waking with Enemies (Gideon series)
Sleeping with Strangers (Gideon series)
Chasing Destiny
Genevieve
Drive Me Crazy
Naughty or Nice
The Other Woman
Thieves' Paradise
Between Lovers
Liar's Game
Cheaters
Milk in My Coffee
Friends and Lovers
Sister, Sister

Anthologies
Voices from the Other Side: Dark Dreams II
Gumbo: A Celebration of African American Writing
Mothers & Sons
Got to Be Real
River Crossings: Voices of the Diaspora
Griots Beneath the Baobab: Tales from Los Angeles
Black Silk: A Collection of African American Erotica

Movie—Original Story
Cappuccino

Graphic Novels
Storm (six-issue miniseries, Marvel Entertainment)

ERIC JEROME
DICKEY

DECADENCE

DUTTON

DUTTON
Published by the Penguin Group
Penguin Group (USA) Inc., 375 Hudson Street,
New York, New York 10014, USA

USA | Canada | UK | Ireland | Australia | New Zealand | India | South Africa | China

Penguin Books Ltd., Registered Offices: 80 Strand, London WC2R 0RL, England
For more information about the Penguin Group visit penguin.com.

REGISTERED TRADEMARK—MARCA REGISTRADA

LIBRARY OF CONGRESS CATALOGING-IN-PUBLICATION DATA:

Dickey, Eric Jerome.
Decadence / Eric Jerome Dickey.
pages cm
ISBN 978-0-525-95383-8 (hardcover)
1. African American women—Fiction. 2. Self-realization in women—Fiction. I. Title.
PS3554.I319D43 2013
813'.54—dc23 2012043098

Printed in the United States of America
10 9 8 7 6 5 4 3 2 1

Set in Janson Text Lt Std. 55 Roman
Designed by Leonard Telesca

PUBLISHER'S NOTE

This is a work of fiction. Names, characters, places, and incidents either are the product of the author's imagination or are used fictitiously, and any resemblance to actual persons, living or dead, business establishments, events, or locales is entirely coincidental.

For Dominique

This novel takes place during the Penguin Special

The Education of Nia Simone Bijou.

Just thought you should know that.

—The Management aka EJD

We might be through with the past, but the past ain't through with us.

—*Magnolia* (1999)

The woman who follows the crowd will usually go no further than the crowd. The woman who walks alone is likely to find herself in places no one has ever been before.

—Albert Einstein

I held his lingam, suckled the part called the meatus. The glans. Licked his foreskin. Suckled the shaft. At the same time I felt his mouth and tongue on my sex. On my mons pubis. Clitoral hood. Labia majora. He painted from my glans clitoris across my labia minora to my meatus. He pushed his tongue inside of me, inside of my orifice, licked up and down, across my perineum and almost to my anus. Then my lover held me by my ankles, had me on my back, on a soft hotel bed overlooking the docks. His erection remained profound. The color, the texture, the evenness. He wanted me to see its muscularity, its veins. The way testicles were attached to his tool, and it was indeed a tool, was nice. His foreskin didn't extend beyond the end of the penis. His lingam was worthy of being plastered and molded and sold in adult toy stores. He pushed my ankles toward the headboard. My knees bent and he denied me his lingam, eased his face between my legs, extended his tongue, parted the lips of my yoni, then his tongue stiffened and moved deep inside of my sex. My hands grabbed the white cotton sheets, clawed and pulled.

I looked across the hotel room and saw my second lover.

I nodded, told him to come to us, told him to come help please me.

I told him to come give me pleasure.

He eased inside of my body and settled in.

I wasn't in search of the lies that came with romance.

I didn't want to be a slave to my heart.

I needed more than simple pleasure.

I was back home in Trinidad. Land of the Hummingbird. The island of the Trinity. Where the majority of the population was East Indian and black, where many were of combined heritages, and where all others were minorities. My lover was beyond handsome, beyond exotic, dressed very hip, very sophisticated, looked *Trinizuelan*. We had met in South Trinidad in the area called Philippine during the first night of a wedding celebration, a three-day Hindu fête that was being thrown at the prime minister's extravagant mansion. I had crossed Trinidad's velvet rope and was placed at a white-tablecloth table with a few other Trinbagonians. We were introduced by the minister of transportation; all of us at a party for those who had either status, positive fame, or deep connections on the island: politicians and powerful men and women who had so much familial money that they made the American rich seem as if they were paupers struggling to become middle class. But from the poor to the rich, men were men and women were women, even when they were prim and proper and in high heels and a long skirt.

All had carnal desires. All had needs.

After the beautiful prime minister had entered wearing a beautiful golden-and-red lehenga-style saree, she walked the receiving line, then made her rounds. The affair was standing room only and soon we relinquished our table that was on the fringe of the Indian singers and live band. We exchanged smiles as we moved and stood by the crowded bar and talked about the religion of greed and hubris, the biggest threat to our economic and social order. Much eye contact. Transmitting. Receiving.

Restless. Once again I lived in a season of restlessness and desire.

My carnal craving revealed itself in my eyes. The message was clear. He was in need. I was in need. I was always in need.

With a man who was so handsome that it was startling and that left me open to whatever. He made me itch. I craved many positions. And at times I craved many lovers. I imagined being fucked inside of the prime minister's home, on her bed, in her office, then at the beach. In a parking lot. At church. In the kitchen. Inside of a movie theater. I wanted to be fucked inside of the bathroom at Rituals. I wanted him to make me taste him while people pushed grocery baskets around us in the frozen food section at Hi-Lo. I wanted him down my throat. Deep down this throat. I wanted to try anal again. I wanted him to spread open my chocolate star and give me that pain and pleasure. I craved it all, moaned a small moan and imagined all of that naughtiness, even the sacrilegious parts, without apology or shame.

I smiled at him. He smiled in return.

The party was outside underneath an amazing white tent that made the enormous tiled patio feel as if it were part of the interior of a home, the night air warm, humid, tropical, like the prelude to an astounding zipless encounter. I had been a jagabat, a wajang, a wabean, a woman of questionable morals, one who haunted the steamier side of life, a nocturnal female. As there were nocturnal men. As there were male whores on the prowl. One thing had led to another and he had extended an invitation to change our setting, and I had accepted. Then we had left the party in his car, driven the curves and narrow roads and roundabouts and highways and passed by people partying into the night and liming and selling oysters and doubles and fruit and coconut water as thumping music poured from innumerable drinking dens. He drove us back north, a forty-minute ride with us passing countless Digicel billboards, bMobile billboards, BP Petrol stations, and M. Rampersad, touching each other, my hand in his lap, his hand pressed in the V of my skirt, pressed so deep that it felt like his fingers were inside of me, massaging where my legs connected, rubbing me as I stroked him. The fire roared. I undid my seat belt, leaned over, and kissed him. My kiss was so intense he almost ran off the road. I kissed him as we sped down a highway as wide as parts of the 405, as insane as the Georgia 400 in Atlanta. Cars whipped by us. Horns blew. Then he parked. We kissed for a while. The intensity was amazing. As we sat in his car with the air conditioner on high, we were as warm as the night. Then I held his erection as he drove away, stroked him and touched myself as he zoomed by traffic, as he drove at twice the speed of the posted fifty-km/hr speed limit. I gave him my fingers, fingers that possessed my sweetness. I was a rebel. Breaking rules. Breaking the law. That excited me. That danger.

Swerving from lane to lane was orgasmic. I stroked him in slow motion. Made him grow. Once near the Queen's Park Savannah we were in insane late-night traffic, the traffic of partygoers and revelers, and he drove the two-mile loop of the world's largest roundabout, an area that used to be sugar land and now had cricket, football, and rugby matches, passed by the Botanic Gardens, Emperor Valley Zoo, National Academy for the Performing Arts, and the Magnificent Seven as I continued to masturbate him.

He swallowed. I told him to keep driving the world's largest roundabout.

The third time around, after being masturbated for six miles, he couldn't take it. He pulled over in front of the US Embassy. He threw his head back and made sexy sounds. I adored his arousal. I took him to the edge, and then backed away, to the edge, backed away. Watched him breathe like a dragon, hard, deep, heated. Watched him suffer as cars zoomed by, as horns blew, as people almost sideswiped each other, as people passed us walking the Savannah, as homeless people sat and slept on benches in the park. He had moved from the embassy, could barely drive and almost sideswiped a car, then almost ran into Tony's coconut stand, made a sharp turn here and there, frustrated as I laughed, passed by Flair, More Vino, Players, moaned and turned and turned, and parked in the McDonald's parking lot near Club Aura. I took my hand away and stared at the monument between his legs. It took a while, but he calmed enough to be able to walk, and we moved from bar to bar, mixing with people with roots in India, Venezuela, Serbia, island women from St. Kitts, Jamaica, Turks and Caicos, and Trinidad. Women wore short dresses, much flesh showing. Men wore trendy shirts and jeans and sexy shoes. We cruised from nightclubs to lounges and liming spots, drinking, touching, kissing, whispering, teasing, then left again, sat in his car kissing like lovers-yet-to-be, like lovers-destined-to-be. We headed toward the clubs and bars on Ariapita Avenue, The Avenue, his hand between my legs. As he drove by Mau Pau casino, he eased two fingers inside of me, finger-fucked me. I let the seat back and closed my eyes. He took me to the edge. I smiled at his game. We gave up the idea of getting back out of the car and mixing with the crawlers at Club 51 Degrees. The need to orgasm had become unbearably strong, the foreplay had been too much, his need to orgasm and please and come and please again had become just as strong. I begged him to take me to his hotel, kissed him and sucked his tongue and told him that we could stop hopping from small limes to big fêtes and make a fête of our own, a naked fête, a fête of moans and hands pulling sheets and orifices being intruded, nerves being ignited, the sensations bound to be unreal. I unzipped his pants, leaned over and gave him oral sex, sucked him, and made him shudder.

His pre-come was sweet like guava, tamarind, mango, five-fingers, Portugal, and cherry fruits. I couldn't wait to make him come, to have his taste fill my mouth. He asked me my fantasies. Asked me what did I dream of doing, what type of loving did I want to make, and told me to trust him, begged me to trust me, told me that he was here for my pleasure, that he wasn't inhibited, that he would do what it took to please me. His words made me want to come. I told him my desires, my latest fantasy, my abnormal want. As I sucked him, as his hand massaged my hair, I told him. Whatever I needed, he could make happen. He sped by roadside watering holes and rushed me to a penthouse suite inside of the Hyatt, his bird's-eye view of the island facing the Breakfast Shed. He was distressed. As was I. It was time for pleasure. It was time for him to feel my heat and wetness, time for us to amalgamate as I felt the hardness of his lingam and the softness of his tongue. His suite overlooked the Gulf of Paria. Now with my ankles in his hands, my legs open wide, his tongue painting my sex as if he were Michelangelo and my sex the Sistine Chapel, he re-created the masterpieces *The Creation of Adam*, *The Forbidden Fruit*, his lips on my sex, his teeth on my sex, I was his captive, his prisoner.

It wasn't enough. He knew that. He had asked me my fantasies. They were beyond this.

I desired the abnormal. I'd lost my taste for regular things, a tofu sexual life didn't appeal to me.

Then my second lover entered the room. A man twice as handsome as the first.

I didn't want vanilla sex. My other lover undressed and stood nude, feet away, masturbating, watching. My eyes met his. I nodded. *Yes*. He came toward us, toward me, eased onto the bed, his heat powerful. My mouth opened and I licked my lips, hungry, ready to become a three-headed beast.

He blessed my taste buds with the flavor of Portugal, tamarinds, five-fingers, of many exotic fruits. Then he took out lubrication, used his middle finger and filled my chocolate star, and prepared me.

I was nervous. I was excited. I was ready. Mind, body, and soul, I wanted what I wanted.

My physical self had a demanding, ferocious appetite. Like a war between darkness and light, my yin and yang battled like Horus and Set.

I understood that my inner adversaries weren't polar opposites, weren't as simple as dark and light, weren't manifestations of good and evil, but were interconnected and gave rise to each other. Yet they battled, remained in perpetual conflict, a never-ending war within my soul. Everything, everyone had yin and yang. Darkness could not exist without light, and without light, darkness had no definition. It was about balance, not about good or bad or dichotomous moral judgments.

My lovers. Each the perfect fit, as if each orifice had been designed with that particular lover in mind. And the way we danced, each the perfect rhythm.

They had me. They both had me at once. And I had them. I owned them because anything that was inside of my body belonged to me. I had them but all I could do was hold on and come, come, come, come, come, become the grunts to my heavy breathing as I became the *oohs* to their *aahs*; it was like love. They filled me from front to back, they kissed my skin, bit me, sucked both ears at once, said sweet and vulgar things, praised me, challenged me, and it felt so good that my guttural moans probably startled the birds and aroused the destitute around Brian Lara Promenade, probably paused the traffic on Wrightson Road and Maraval Highway; then we were intense and my screams of orgasmic pleasure could be heard in San Fernando, maybe as far as the shores of Venezuela. Being filled felt so fucking good.

The want of pleasure, the need to dance inside of the sexual fire in the pursuit of physical gratification, to embrace what was taboo, have carnal delight, the need to be satisfied, have all senses fulfilled until I was trembling and light-headed and dehydrated and was left as limp as a rag doll, to come until I cursed like a fiend, to have a powerful orgasm draw out this heat that lived within me. When I breathed, desires danced and I saw their colors, saw my own energy. I wanted the raging, savage force inside of me to be set free.

A third handsome man entered the hotel room. With candles lit, the shades drawn, the lights from ships out in the Gulf and the streetlights edging in, a third nude lover watched us from the shadows.

As I was being relished, as I existed on the edge of orgasm, I nodded, gave him my permission. And while one lover took the anterior position, as the other took the posterior, the third lover climbed on the king-size bed. Again, as I was filled, as I felt orgasm live and bloom inside of me, I tasted exotic fruits. There was no rush. There was no hurry. It wasn't fucking. It was love.

At the same time three lovers roared; at the same moment three lovers held me tight.

Energy poured into me, ignited me and as they thrust, I exploded.

Like savages, the violence of orgasm consumed us and we all came together.

ONE

When I stirred from my erotic dream, from the sex dream I couldn't remember, I woke up lubricated, lips swollen, the sweetness of my own honey dampening my thighs. I touched where I ached. I touched moistness. I had had an orgasm. I had had a wonderful orgasm and the fire was alive. I rubbed fingers over my inflamed lips and honey. Then I held two fingers there. Felt myself pulsating.

I was engorged as if I had a powerful female erection.

My cellular rang and I jerked as if I had been caught touching myself, as if someone in the shadows had seen me tasting myself. Skype. It was the most annoying, the ugliest, most irritating ringtone ever invented. Eerie. Almost paranormal. Someone was Skyping me in the middle of the night. It was Hazel Tamana Bijou. It was my mother. I grappled for the phone and accepted the call. Her beautiful face came up on the screen. It was impossibly early in Beverly Hills, California. Her hair was pulled back into a ponytail. She was letting it grow long again. She had on glasses. No makeup. She had on a sweaty T-shirt and shorts. She had been in her gym lifting weights or running, maybe both. My energetic mother. Last year she had moved from her three-level home in View Park and returned to the home that I had grown up in, the estate that had become hers when she married my stepfather. She was once again living in luxury in a sophisticated yet charming stone French Provincial reminiscent of a vineyard home that should be in the South of France instead of on Mulholland Drive.

For a moment I missed home. I missed that house. The good times. For a moment I was a little girl running around that yard again.

I clicked on a light and in a voice that hadn't normalized said, "Yeah, Mummy, wha?"

"Yuh wake up, Trini."

"I go to bed Trini craving Crix and I dream I Trini wearing red, white, and black and I dream I eat doubles and bake and shark and pelau and I wake up singing the Chimok Bakery song and craving a roti like a true Trini. And I have Benji on my ringtone. Lord, I jus dream I was in hotel in Port of Spain."

She laughed. "Doh forget yuh interview."

"You in real trouble, wee. Wake me over that. Jus another interview."

She was in the kitchen putting kale leaves, a cucumber, celery stalks, two green apples, lemon, and a piece of ginger on the counter, a cutting board and her overworked Jack LaLanne juicer at her side.

She said, "All interview important. Doh forget nah. I know you, Miss Bijou."

The juicer kicked on. I wanted to scream.

She said, "During the interview talk bout de film and make sure tuh mention Trinidad as much as yuh can. If they think yuh is American Black yuh get less respect, so let 'em know yuh is Trini."

"Bye, Mommy. Ah gone. Love you."

"What yuh think about us buying a condo on the properties behind The Falls at West Mall? It will cost about a million and we can lease it out to a diplomat long-term."

"Mom. Ask me when I wake. I real damn sleepy."

"It's on a high floor that faces the sea. Three bedrooms. It will cost under a million."

"US or Trini dollars?"

"One million US. That would be about six-point-five million in Trini dollars."

"Yuh mad? How you going to call me in the middle of the night asking for a cazillion dollars?"

"I bought you a new car. I just bought you a brand-new BMW."

"I didn't ask you to. My roadster is fine."

"It's too small. You need to be in a bigger car."

"If you like the new car so much I'll send it back with a thank-you note."

"We can lease the condo out to a diplomat long-term and it go pay for itself. It's on the side of the island with all of the private schools and expats, so they will be willing to pay ridiculously high rent."

"Mom. Geh your hand out of my money. Ask me again when I wake. I real damn sleepy."

"Swear jar."

"Whatever."

"Go sleep. Call me after the interview. And mend your cacology. No slang. You are a Hampton girl. A USC woman. Represent."

"I shall speak with perfect diction and make my mother proud."

"And reconsider doing the television interview in Atlanta with Jewell Stewark."

"How many times do I have to tell you that I don't like her?"

"The Jewell of the South, or whatever they call her, she does a great interview."

"Why are you still talking? Mommy, please. How many times I tell you I sleepy?"

"Why don't you like her? She's an island girl."

"Wait. Hold on, wait a minute."

"I'm hanging up. Go to sleep and wake up with a better attitude, which I doubt."

"Mommy, don't play with me. Get in the light and let me see something."

She laughed as she moved in front of the Viking appliances. "What are you trying to see?"

"You know what I am trying to see. Oh my God. No you didn't."

She laughed harder. "Was wondering when you were going to notice."

"You dyed your hair? How dare you dye your hair."

"There is only one mother in this conversation."

"And she is behaving like a child. What color is that, Mommy?"

"It's a color called ecru."

"You dyed your hair and you didn't tell me? You didn't ask me my opinion?"

"You like or is that a stern frown of disapprobation?"

"It's beautiful. You let you hair grow long. Now you color your hair super light brown like you a teenager. Look at your body. No fat. Yeah, I disapprove of it all. Now you look younger than me. I hate you. I want my mommy to look like a mommy. How you get your hair dyed and not ask me if I like the color first? Then call me at this early hour just so I can see it? That mean you just had it done today. So evil."

"Nice to have haters. You're nobody if nobody hates you. Now tell Siri to remind you to call your mommy and tell her how much you love her when you wake up and have some sense in your head."

I hung up and dropped my iPhone, licked the inside of my mouth, expected to taste exotic fruits. The world was silent. It was the piceous hour just before dawn. Smyrna, Georgia, was gentle at this hour. This was the hour for suburban refucks, for the second round of making love. This was the time of night made for reaching for your lover, it was the time for second rounds, for refucks, for middle of the night orgasms. The storm was strong outside of my windows. All I could feel was the storm inside of my body. I thought that I had danced my heat away last night. I had spent the evening in town in the Old Fourth Ward on Edgewood, had danced to house music, African salsa, and jungle music from eleven P.M. until two in the morning. I had come home, showered, crawled in bed.

Dancing hadn't been enough. Three hours of dancing hadn't burned away the fire of need.

Last night I should have driven to Decadence. I had joined, but I hadn't found the bravery to make the four-hour drive and venture into the unknown alone. There had been a hellified series of interviews followed by an arduous and expensive screening process that required recent medical records. The last interview had been in NYC at Trump Tower. I guess that it was there because of their international clientele. The club also required up-to-date blood tests of its current members. The club did its best to ensure that all patrons entered this world disease-free. After being screened for all transmittable diseases known to man, I had passed with flying colors. And like everyone else, I would have to be screened on a regular basis. They offered many services, the best of everything that money could buy.

I hadn't found the courage to make that drive.

Maybe because I felt like I would be betraying Prada. Or maybe I used Prada as an excuse. Seemed like forever since I'd seen Prada. Since I had met him in Trinidad, his businesses had expanded over the last few years, businesses that were scattered from Jamaica to Trinidad, radio, television, real estate, retail, and now his businesses and empire were marching across other parts of Europe, attempting to do to Europe in some ways what Walmart has done to America and a few countries beyond, only on a higher level. He who owned media shaped the world and its values.

My libido didn't care about business. My yoni craved the sweet intrusion of lingam. Six weeks had passed. Six weeks of not being touched. Six weeks of being ablaze. Six weeks of celibacy was starting to drive me as mad as a woman in solitary confinement.

My arousal was as distressing as it was perplexing. My arousal was part of me, part of my humanness that I had tried to explain, to comprehend. Nude, I took the elevator upstairs, too turned-on to walk up one flight of stairs, went to my office, an office that also had unpacked boxes of books all over, sat in my leather chair, turned on my laptop, and began typing. As a side project, one that I took on in between working on the script and ghostwriting, I had been journaling my life, had been writing the unexpurgated version of my existence, the version of my life that was unbowdlerized. I was a long way from being done writing the novel that would be my greatest labor of love. I had much living to do. *Abnormal Desires*, by Anonymous. I only worked on that novel in spurts. No one knew that I was writing about my life in detail, the good, the bad, chronicling my lovers, not for the sake of counting notches on bedposts, but as a way of being able to look at myself objectively, if that would ever be possible. The eye couldn't see itself. But it was all there, without shame, without apologies. The parts that were erotic—such as the run around Stone Mountain, the remembrance of wonderful lovers—each time awakened the sexual fire within me.

And enemies.

I touched my neck where a knife had been, and I remembered.

Still haunted by the fragments of my dream, I stared out at the darkness, wishing. No matter how I positioned myself, or what I did to distract myself, I tingled. I remembered the dream. A man's hands on my ankles. Me on my back. His tongue inside of me. Taking on two lovers, as I had done in the past, as I had enjoyed being made love to then. Taking on three lovers, as I had never done. Decadence. The interviewer that had conducted the final interview had planted that seed.

I typed fast. I typed faster. I typed as fast as I could.

Then I stopped, sat shifting in my chair, inhaling, exhaling, nipples hard, moaning softly, rubbing my neck, bouncing my leg, chewing my bottom lip. I stood up, kept my hand on the back of my neck, and walked in circles, danced in circles. I needed maintenance. Day in and out, I stayed busy, but at times I was severely lonely. Even though I preferred to live my life unfettered, lately I had been craving a male roommate, someone less than a husband, a lover who was not quite a boyfriend, but more than a booty call, a man who would quell that loneliness and feed my need for perpetual pleasure. This was my only need. Could be worse. Could be addicted to a dozen pills, or a food addict. My sin now as it had been for the last few years, as this body aged and hormones remained aflame, was the need for pleasure. My sensual hunger was always present and invisible to all. My hunger for orgasm was in every breath and unseen, hidden behind an Audrey Hepburn smile on Caribbean brown skin. But it was more than sex I wanted. Most days I was jeans and running shoes, but sometimes I was girlier than I wanted to admit. Sometimes I needed to be pampered and treated in a special way by a man. Sometimes I had moments when I wanted to be protected and taken care of, despite my independence, despite my feminist streak, despite my obsession with self-sufficiency, despite my battle with the laws written by men, for men, the laws that oppressed and stymied the progress of women. I wanted to have permission to be lazy. I needed someone to have my back so I could take a breath, relax, and close my eyes and dream the dream of a well-protected queen. But I worked. I worked hard. The need for intimacy had never interfered with my job, and the pursuit of fantasies had never done me any harm, no more than a few emotional scars, so that told me that I had no addiction, just desire. In the battle with human nature, I remained the victor.

TWO

By late morning there was a break in the storm. As soon as I finished the interview, my cellular buzzed with a text.

TWENTY MINUTES?

I responded in the affirmative. I changed, stretched, and hurried out of Ivy Walk dressed in black workout gear from head to toe, including my winter gloves and cap. Clouds over Smyrna were like one unending layer of dirty cotton. With a frown and a few unkind words to the makers of the storms, I jogged through the security gates, my eyes still monitoring the skies.

The distance from his bed to mine was no more than five minutes, ten minutes if there was traffic. He was five foot ten with skin that always looked like it had been kissed by the sun. His name was Bret. I had no idea what his last name was, only that he was former military, drove a Mustang, dark blue convertible. His music was bumping, but not too loud. Country music. Brantley Gilbert, "Country Must Be Country Wide." Bret and I had met last summer, after I had returned to the States from my season of travel. We were in Virginia Highland at a bar. There he was, dressed in simple Wranglers, brown cowboy boots, and an AC/DC T-shirt that showed off his rock-hard arms. A few drinks later we were barhopping from Ponce de Leon to North Highland to Glen Iris Drive, laughing and flirting and dancing. That night he had been a zipless encounter. Probably the best zipless encounter that I had

had to date. It had been like a romantic BFE—boyfriend experience. It had been a summer night of need, both physical and emotional. I would have preferred to be with Prada, but he lived and worked across the pond. But I was a neighbor with Bret in a big small town called Atlanta, where country music, gospel, and crass hip-hop ruled the airwaves.

I had had a one-night stand with a man who loved fishing, hunting, and baseball.

I said, "Hey, Bret. Thought that you would've passed on running on an ugly day like today."

"Anytime I'm not where it's one hundred and twenty degrees, not almost six thousand miles from home, not dressed in full uniform and carrying eighty pounds of gear and worried about driving over a bomb, it's a good day. Men in Afghanistan and Iraq are begging for weather like this."

He owned a soft accent that echoed South Carolina, his bucolic place of birth.

I said, "Streets. I think we should skip the Silver Comet Trail and run the streets."

"Some parts might be flooded. I want to run, not swim."

"Aren't you the man who loves to do mud runs all over the South?"

"You should come with me on the next one. It's in Florida."

"How far?"

"Only a five-K."

"When a man asks a woman to run over three miles in ankle-deep mud, she has arrived."

"Anyway. We should drive five minutes over to the Silver Comet Trail."

I looked up at the sky, held my hand out with the palm toward the sky, as if I were gifted with the powers of meteorology. The Silver Comet Trail started about five minutes away, a fully paved trail that began in Smyrna and extended sixty-one miles to where it connected with the Chief Ladiga Trail and ended ninety-four miles later in Anniston, Alabama. I'd biked most of the trail twice in the last year.

It was a state trail. There was no traffic. It was safe. But today I wasn't feeling the trail.

I said, "If we start at mile zero and run eight or nine miles out on the trail we'll probably be somewhere near Sailors Parkway. Look at the clouds. That's too far out and if the rain returns, we'll have to swim back. This way we won't ever be more than three or so miles from here. I'm thinking. Hold on. If we run the loop to Cumberland Boulevard the entire run, we'll have plenty of places to duck for cover. Gas stations, fast-food places, even the mall or Costco or Chuck E. Cheese."

"True. If we get beyond that we have Home Depot or Starbucks, even the Cobb County Sheriff's station, that's if it starts to come down hard by the time we're on that side."

"So we are in agreement?"

Bret nodded in agreement. He wore black running tights, Nikes, a sweat top, gloves, cap.

He said, "Are you serious about going on the mud run?"

"You know me. I'll try anything once."

He nodded, convinced. "How did that place turn out?"

"Which?"

"When you flew up to New York to have that chat. The interview at the one-of-a-kind place with the steep membership fee."

"It was fine. Not supposed to talk about it after at this point."

"Sounds like it's better than the place you had contemplated, the place off Fulton Industrial. I don't care for that part of town."

"Oh yeah. Decadence is at an entire other level."

I told him that I had never made it inside of Trapeze. I told Bret that I was afraid that I would run into my former lover, or my former lovers, if I had gone there. I didn't want to run into the identical sins. They were my past. There were many more swingers clubs, many more institutions that made it possible for the adult lifestyle to thrive in Atlanta, in the heart of conservative Bible thumpers: Venus, Tina the Swinger, Swinging Atlanta, Luxuria, Club Desire, Atlanta United Socials, 2Risque. Too many to count, some congregated in mansions out by Lake Murray in Lexington, South Carolina, and at some meetings they were still old-school, they still dropped keys in bowls and left with a random sex partner.

That told me a lot. I knew that my spirit was out of control, but I was not alone in my journey.

Bret said, "You're going to do it. The place called Decadence."

"I'm a member. At least for the next year I'm a member of that adult-themed country club."

"Trapeze would have been a lot cheaper, based on what you told me."

"How would you know how much Trapeze would cost?"

"Was curious. Looked it up online. Besides, they advertise in *Rolling Out* magazine. I guess that means the locals go there."

"Yeah. If I do get up the nerves to go, I definitely don't want to run into my next-door neighbors. They are not attractive, not at all."

He laughed a little, then he nodded. I grinned. He was a former military man who understood the concept of Need to Know.

He knew that I was interested in joining a club that celebrated being an adult. He hadn't been judgmental, just nodded and smiled a smile that was indecipherable, yet felt mannish. He told me that I was a queen, a ruler, a sensual goddess walking amongst mere mortals. The same words that he had told me the first night we met. The man could dance and that was a turn-on. He danced all night like he was at Carnival. Soon one thing had led to another, the moon was high and I was a sensual vampire, in search of nourishment. Kissing in the parking lot. Kiss after kiss after kiss until I told him that we needed to stop or get a room. After the one-night stand we had run across each other again at Home Depot on Cumberland and Paces Ferry, right up the road from my new dwelling. Seeing him again, seeing him on my side of town, that was a surprising moment. He was with his two kids, a son and a daughter, ages seven and ten. He was in daddy mode. While I bought lightbulbs and cleansers and he had duplicate keys made and selected paint for a bedroom, we talked as if we knew each other, as if that night of sex at a hotel in the heart of Midtown had never happened. People assumed that we were a family. I told him my real name, gave him my cellular number, and within three days we became text buddies. He hasn't ever called me. Only sent texts. Never mentioned that night.

We had gone to a Wednesday WindDown at Centennial Park and when that fun and dancing was over we went to a movie at the independent theater near Piedmont Park at the Midtown Promenade on Monroe. Had watched a Norwegian film, *Turn Me On, Dammit!* After the film that I loved and he was ambivalent about because it had subtitles, we had stopped at Après Diem, sat at a candlelit table outside the sexy restaurant—sexy because of it being nighttime, sexy because we were surrounded by couples who were so into each other. We talked and talked and talked. In the middle of the conversation he reached over and grabbed my hand.

But he let it go and never tried to hold it again. I wondered if I had done something wrong.

When we were done eating, drinking, and talking, he walked to his car and I headed to mine and we drove in the same direction for a while, then he continued past my exit at Atlanta Road.

Part of me had hoped that he was stalking me, following me home to take this yoni.

We'd gone out a dozen times since, had always met at the location of the event, but he had never tried to seduce me again. A dozen times I had wished that he had tried. A dozen times I had been weak for his sexual healing. Including last night. He had been my dancing partner until the crack of dawn. We had shared that energy for hours.

For him, with the moment we had shared, with the wine, with my mood, it wouldn't have taken much to have me again.

I wondered if it was because he knew that Prada existed. He knew that Prada wasn't my boyfriend. He'd known about Prada from the first night. I had mentioned that I was seeing someone. I always did. It helped keep the zipless aspect of what I needed in perspective. He knew about Prada.

Just as I knew that he was about a year into being divorced. A horrible divorce.

Fiscally Bret knew that he was the opposite of Prada, his polar opposite at the bottom line.

Prada was an established man, good in bed and perfect on paper, the type who sent men like Bret to war to die for their profits. And based on how we met, Bret knew there was a heat simmering beneath my cool façade. He knew that during this season of my life, I was distracted, that I wasn't a loyal woman.

When we met to run, he was never invited inside my gates. I always came outside.

I'd never let him inside of my world and I'd never been invited inside of his.

We took to the sidewalk on Atlanta Road, headed up the incline jogging at an easy nine-minute-mile pace. The wind pushed into our faces, but not enough to make me want to surrender. It made me stronger. Soon we had passed where Paces Ferry ended, had also passed a series of new developments that ranged from $300K to $700K. When we passed

Campbell High School, the school that Julia Roberts had attended, I was warmed up. Bret picked up the pace, pushed me, made me run faster than I would if I had been running alone. Less than three miles later we were moving down Spring Road breaking a seven-minute-mile pace, that area being lined with apartments, older properties of lesser value and an area that had changed from Caucasian to Black and now was rapidly becoming Asian, African, and Latino. The train tracks, the Farmers Market, and Deeply Rooted natural hair salon all went by in a blur. Bret took that route to Cumberland Parkway and turned right, looped back over the I-285 overpass toward the Cumberland Mall. I spotted a billboard that featured the local superstar anchor nicknamed the Jewell of the South.

Memories came like a thunderstorm.

With a grunt I spat at her face and picked up my pace.

He said, "You always spit at anything with her face on it."

"Leave it alone."

"You look at her like you want to cut her throat."

"You're good at reading me. Too damn good at reading me."

"What does that mean?"

"Means I don't have to explain what I feel to you."

Cool raindrops mixed with my warm sweat. The storm was about to return. It always returned. The calm never ruled for long.

Bret asked, "You're okay with running in the rain?"

"Are you okay with running in the rain?"

"Weather enhances the challenge of the run."

As Bret played country music on his MP3, I jammed Sy Smith, "Fast and Curious." I ran on Bret's heels, made him my rabbit for the next nine miles. The rain worsened. So, we decided to cut the seventeen-mile run short, headed back in, took Cumberland Boulevard and its rolling hills past condos and luxury apartments. Near the end, after we had passed the Cobb County Sheriff's station, I moved by Bret, took the lead, and pretended I was running Fatuma down and beat her to the tape in the LA marathon. Lungs on fire, legs aching, I stopped at Atlanta Road. Ten seconds later Bret stopped near me, hands on his hips, panting. He was a gentleman, always let me win whenever I sprinted at the end. By then cold rain fell with a steady rhythm. A moment later, chest still heaving, I checked my time, checked it for each mile. My best mile had been six minutes and one second. The last mile was six minutes *and two seconds*. Disappointment rose.

I caught my breath. "What do I have to do to break a freaking six-minute mile? *Fuck*."

"It's raining, it's cold, your clothes have weight, and the wind slows you down."

"Six minutes and *one fucking second*. Might as well be a seven-minute mile."

"You'll break six."

"I know."

"When Kobe learns that basketball is a team sport, you'll break six minutes."

I cursed him. He laughed. He was a Hawks fan, a Miami Heat fan, despised all things Lakers. I was a blue state girl and he was a red state man. Chest rising and falling, sweat raining, I ached and it was a good pain. The anxiety from being in need of pleasure, for now, had been diminished. A harder rain had returned by the time I cooled down.

He said, "You've dropped a few more pounds."

"Have I?"

"Your raw foods and juicing diet is really working."

"I just have to make sure that I'm getting enough protein."

For a few moments I stood with my face to the sky, mouth open, allowing heaven's cool orgasm to fall on my tongue. The winter rain here made me miss the summer and warm showers of Trinidad.

Bret watched me. When I realized he was staring, watching me with my mouth wide, swallowing, he moved his eyes to his sports watch.

He said, "I have to get back home."

"No time to eat or grab a spot of tea at J. Christopher?"

"Next time."

"My treat. Want to thank you for getting my hair wet."

"Would love to, but today isn't good for me."

"Whoever she is, she must have you on lockdown."

Bret waved good-bye and jogged to his car. His engine started, rumbled like the muscle car it was, and right away I heard Eric Church singing "Springsteen." I was learning about country artists. Windshield wipers came to life. Headlights woke up. Bret tooted his horn. For a moment there was a gaze in his eyes, a memory, an acknowledgment. Then he was gone, flying down Atlanta Road, turning right and blending with traffic heading toward the East-West Connector.

No one would ever think that we'd had a shared sexual encounter. To country music. Now country music was a soundtrack to memory. Country music told stories about first loves, about memoirs, about the feeling about the past and loves you'd never have again. It might have a twang, or be religious, might have a redneck feel, even might have a Confederate flag, but it was intelligent, it was passionate, it was music you could play in front of your friends, family, and children. And when he hung out at places that played country, there might be a fight from time to time, but nobody was shot, no police were called because they fought man-to-man and the loser acknowledged his loss and went on his way, sometimes even buying the man who whupped his ass a tall one before he left the bar. That was how Bret felt about it.

I respected and admired that. Hip-hop only had fuck songs and R & B barely had a pulse. Maybe it was hard to be romantic in a culture that didn't portray itself as romantic, not in more than three decades.

The former solider named Bret had pleased me. He was meek but his sex was remarkable. My inner thighs, my neck, he had done things to make me unleash the beast.

When intromission had changed to intermission and his lingam had turned flaccid and I was ready to raise my right hand in a fist so I could scream and declare myself winner of that never-ending session of lovemaking, he had taken two washcloths and cut four-inch slits in their centers. While I lay on the bed naked, in rapture, simmering, barely alive, barely awake, shifting and wondering what he was doing, he filled a bowl with hot water. He let the towels soak. He kissed me awhile, touched my face, then had me recline, put me on my back with my knees bent, legs open. He wrung out one of the steaming washcloths. Bret looked at it, turned it until the cut was vertical, like the slit of a yoni. He put the washcloth on me, put it on top of my sex, lined the slit from the washcloth up with the opening that nature had given me. I moaned. The heat from the towel felt amazing. Bret leaned forward and put his tongue through the slit of the towel. It was mind-blowing. It was the best tongue massage I had ever had. Like fingerprints, everyone's tongue print was different. His was unforgettable. He ate me and stimulated my nipples, made my body surge with oxytocin, enough to drown us both. I died. Over and over I saw more than one hundred billion galaxies, saw a billion stars, and I died.

When the towel cooled down, he put it back in the bowl and took out the other warmed towel; wrung it out, lined it up, and again gave me his tongue. His tongue went so deep. The heat from his mouth, the heat from the towels, indescribable. It was the best oral orgasm I'd ever felt. He had left me spent. I was a sweaty Trinidadian rag doll with a sensitive clitoris and nipples and reddened skin and a satisfied smile. There were forty-five miles of nerves in the skin of a human being. He had kissed every inch of mine.

He had told me, "I've never been to bed with a woman born in another country."

"Is it any different?"

"Maybe because this scenario is new to me. You're amazing. Both of you are amazing."

Then we had looked over at her. The woman we had picked up while barhopping. We had found her partying at Rooftop 866, enjoying the spectacular view as we swayed to the rhythm of the house beats. She had looked like a good girl, like Carrie Underwood, but she was a tourist, a Vancouverite in town for a weekend of fun, the whiskey in her blood sending her to us, making her join in as we had danced, making her smile that smile of debauchery. Bret had told her that she was sweeter than a Krispy Kreme doughnut when the HOT light was turned on. The hue of her skin, her nice frame, and the electricity that ran when she touched us, it had caused Bret to look at us, try to understand if he had to pick one of us, but when I had asked them if they were good at sharing, when she had smiled, then when Bret had smiled like he was the luckiest man on the planet. It had been a three-way at the W Midtown. We had been in an unscheduled ménage à trois. He had taken a warm towel to her, pleased her as I squeezed and kissed her breasts.

We had participated in the abnormal. And what was abnormal, to me, felt so very normal.

Bret had handled me well. He had handled me as if he were a cognoscente, a connoisseur, and an expert in the art of pleasure. The man formerly employed by Uncle Sam had handled both of us so very well. I had watched Bret with the Vancouverite. Their lovemaking went to a new level of intensity. Strangers in a rented bed. He had her legs wide, an ankle in each hand as he stroked her. She pulled sheets and lost it. I lay on the bed with them and watched until I witnessed her screaming orgasm. She was loud, so loud that I had to clasp my hand over her mouth. For a while, as Bret stroked her, I held her neck, choked her. She loved that. The way he sexed her aroused me. The way she came and came and trembled and said things in her Canadian accent aroused me. Bret was on something. Jack Daniel's. L-arginine. Saw palmetto. Tongkat ali. Yohimbe. Something damn good kept him filled with power. Soon I had let her go and I moved behind him, kissed his neck, sucked his ear, and gave him a new level of stimulation. Then he strained, stretched, took her with one of her legs over his shoulder. I sucked her toes and Bret made his skin beat hers and she screamed. He was lost inside of the Vancouverite. She came again. Bret kept stroking her and I moved and sat on her face, let my yoni muffle her lewd screams and cries, made us into the perfect triangle, kissed Bret as she ate and sucked on me. We were like that until she trembled and moaned and cried out that she couldn't breathe. I moved away from her and her mouth became a letter *O* and she quaked from crown to corns. Since my Sunshine days, I had watched a lot of women come. It was a fetish. Seeing the pleasure in others turned me on. Bret tried not to, but he came, his release powerful and copious. I watched his face as he came. I stroked his chin as he lost control. It was spiritual. The energy. The primal, barbaric grunts. Watched him transition from madness, strain, become fire and rock, and release, then watched him return to peace. He could barely breathe. She was barely able to breathe. It was like she had been killed, then resurrected. When he was done he didn't withdraw from her. He kissed me as he was inside of her, and when our passionate kiss had finally eased, when it had ended, he looked down at her, asked her if she was okay, sprinkled soft kisses on her dank face. She smiled and they rubbed noses.

An hour after she had arrived, she had orgasmed many times, and then fulfilled in both pleasure and curiosity, she showered, gave us kisses, and with her hair wet and back in a ponytail, she called a taxi and left to head back to the Four Seasons in Buckhead, reconnected with her Canadian friends. It was Bret and I the rest of the night. Until the break of dawn. It had been one of those nights when my need was so high it terrified me. I wanted to fellate, suck lingam because it turned me on. I wanted to suck because sucking made me feel good. I wanted to be fucked hard, wanted my ass smacked, wanted bites on my neck, wanted my skin sucked, wanted my nipples pinched, wanted come in my yoni, mouth, wanted come in my ass and on my skin, wanted a hard and unapologetic session, wanted to fuck a man the same way, wanted to fuck a man senseless while he fucked me without mercy, wanted to be lubed and fucked in my chocolate star after my yoni and mouth had been fucked. I had wanted Prada, he was familiar, he was tied to my emotions, we had known each other for many seasons, and we were lusty and cerebral together, our sex amazing and intense, romantic and lovey-dovey. Romantic and lovey-dovey was good, holding hands and flirting was good, but I was liquored up and hormonal and wanted strange; I wanted hot and hard, wanted hard and at that moment, wanted it nasty from a new lover, from a mystery, from a man whore who would be added to the zipless count, and the nastier the better. Then as Rascal Flatts played on the radio I had crept out of the room, purse over shoulder, shoes in one hand and my jewelry and car keys in the other, left him sleeping, my trademark red heart and smiley face drawn on the mirror in lipstick the hue of lust and love. I had been tempted to do something that I never did, leave my name and phone number, but I didn't.

But we had run into each other again by happenstance.

Then on the Fourth of July we had hooked up at Lenox Square and run the Peachtree Road Race. We had been sharing heat in a different way ever since.

As rain fell, I smiled and imagined that some lucky Southern bitch was waiting for him now, probably had a bowl of cheese grits, sausage, and eggs sunny-side up waiting for him at the table. While he ate his cheese grits, she would probably be underneath the table sucking his balls as she stroked his lingam.

He was distracting without trying to be, despite how convoluted my life had become. I was glad that he was my friend. Or whatever we were now, I was glad. I enjoyed the energy of a man in my world.

My situation with Prada, if it was a situation, was more than enough at the moment. Still Bret lived one exit away, no more than two miles, two moments from my bed. I took sharp breaths, tried to have power over what was beyond control, and swallowed. If we had continued being lovers, maybe I wouldn't feel this fire that I felt right now. But it could have also ended up being a disaster.

That was my track record.

Once abnormal desires became the normal longing, not only was it incurable, it became preferred. I craved the absurd. I suppose that it was that way with men after they had gone to Brazil and had fun with many gorgeous women at once. After a few days as a sexual god, after hedonistic nights, returning to their wives and girlfriends and monogamy, it was no longer inspiring; it had to be less than remarkable, too normal. Normal was as flavorful as boiled tofu. The same for the randy women who went to Jamaica or Italy and experienced ménage à trois with handsome foreign lovers, then returned to dull husbands and boyfriends, to one-on-one loving, pretending that the sin-filled lovemaking that they had experienced hadn't changed them. But all came home ecstatic, yet depressed, some already planning the next escape to Brazil or Italy.

It was physical, but for me—even as I treaded in my own hypocrisy—it also felt spiritual.

Each time I took a lover, I wanted to learn more about life, about me, my humanness, wanted to find my own limit. I wanted to cross so many lines. What I wanted no one lover could do alone. Years before Bret I'd been with two men and the ménage à trois had taken me to a new altitude, then a woman was added to the awakening and it became a *ménage à quatre*, a beautiful four-headed beast, that matter between four had made me realize that there was more. I wanted love and the beauty of sex. I demanded it sinful yet classy, loving yet raunchy and vulgar, the smells of my lovers and me combining into one unique fragrance that should be bottled and sold by someone as famous and stunning as the provocative actress Regina Baptiste.

That had come to an end, but that was an ending I had mastered, an ending I had controlled. In every relationship that I had had, in all that had failed, I was the least common denominator. We were all the least common denominator in all of our miseries and pain.

Still, as needs persisted, they made me want to have a local lover. If I did have a capable lover within reach, that ache would be satiated more than intermittently. Maybe my mind wouldn't be on Decadence. For Bret, to explore him for a while, to continue to pick up a third lover, to have had fun in that preferred way, I would've delayed joining. It would have only been a delay, for I was on that road.

No man would be able to stop me from doing what it was in my destiny to do.

THREE

Drenched in sweat and rain, I hurried back inside of my garage. Next to my ten-year-old Z4 was a sparkling new 6-series BMW. My mother bought that for me as a congratulations on my first major film project. She hated my roadster. She wanted her daughter to be in a safer car.

Unpacked U-Haul boxes were still all over my townhome, pretty much on all four levels, most of my life still sealed since the recent move. I had been here two months and I wasn't in a hurry to unpack.

Seemed like yesterday that I was ready to quit ATL, was ready to sell my old townhome inside of Park at Oakley Downs after affairs had gone bad, but the real estate market tanked and had left me trapped in what felt like a bad marriage with a stubborn and hateful bank. A little more than eighty days ago I found a foreclosure in Smyrna, five minutes from my old townhome, this one more modern; with much better amenities, tucked behind the gates of a much-desired area. It remained a bad time to sell, but a great time to buy. So I had to lease my old place to balance out the cash flow, had to lease the place where insanity had occurred, and I was able to cover the mortgage and association dues and pull a profit. I stopped and looked at my disorganized home, a cluttered and bewildered home that reflected my inner feelings.

Boxes, boxes, everywhere. My home was a minefield made of U-Haul boxes. Out of habit, I began opening a box the moment I stepped through the door. I guess I was unpacking one box at a time.

It was a smaller box, unlabeled, and heavy for its size. But it had been left near the dining area. I assumed that it was dishes. Or cutlery. Something for the kitchen. But the box didn't rattle like dishware.

When I ripped up the flap I saw that it was a box stuffed with pictures. No one takes Kodak photos and gets them developed, not anymore. At first I smiled, thought that maybe it was the box of photos of my mother when she was a child in Trinidad, the photos of her and her mother dressed in magenta salwar sets, or maybe the misplaced photos of me as a child along with my mother, both of us back on the island dressed in kurtis, duatas, silk sarees, and wide-legged pants. Actually I had hoped that it was the missing photos that we had taken when I was a teenager and we were home for Diwali. I had hoped that I had found the photos of us lighting deyas, our hands painted in henna.

I was wrong.

The worn box contained photos, but they were photos of someone else. For a moment I lost my breath and my heart ceased to function. His face caught me off guard, his sea-green eyes bored into mine as if he were here. Chris Eidos Alleyne. *Eidos*. His father gave him a middle name based on a concept in Plato's Theory of Forms. It felt like Chris *Eidos* Alleyne was inside the box in my hands, waiting on my return.

In one photo I was standing in front of him, on my tiptoes, kissing him, my hands pulling his long dreadlocks as his hands held my ass and pulled me into him. His best friend had taken that photo.

Rigoberto had taken that photo, the sun behind his head, his shadow falling across us, almost between us.

Underneath that was an eight-by-ten. Chris in his Hampton U football gear. Signed to me. With love. As I was his yesterday, his yesteryear, during my college days he was mine. Maybe not mine, because ownership, even in love, was an illusion. No woman owned any man and no man owned any woman. He was tall, muscular, articulate, a Mensa, and athletic. Copper skin. Bronze dreadlocks.

His photo looked so real. Underneath that eight-by-ten, all of the photos looked too real.

We'd broken up abruptly, violently; no wind down; no debriefing; no good-bye. The most painful good-byes were the ones that were never said, never explained. Good-byes without closure left open wounds. Memories rose. These memories were earthquakes. And as I stared at his face I breathed fire.

It was a box of lost memories from a part of my life that had happened more than five hundred miles away from here, from when I was in college. We were at Busch Gardens. Shopping at Coliseum Mall, outlets in Williamsburg, Patrick Henry Mall in Newport News. Peninsula Town Center had replaced Coliseum Mall but nothing had replaced the memories. In countless rolls of Kodak photos we were standing on the edges of the Atlantic Ocean. There were photos and cards and letters and newspapers from when I attended Hampton. There were hundreds, maybe thousands of photos of my ex from days gone by. And there were just as many newspaper clippings from the first man that I had loved in an adult way. Hundreds of sports section articles. Like I was an obsessed fan. A groupie. There was a journal that I used to write corny Love Is sayings in every day. I wrote one every damn day. *Love is drinking green tea in the morning as the sun rises. Love is early morning phone calls. Love is hours spent IMing each other. Love is sweet nothings and beautiful promises. Love is waking up before he does so I can watch him wake up.* There were also at least two dozen brochures regarding wedding dresses. *Love is sappy and sappy is good.* Guess I had done everything but hired a wedding planner and booked a wedding on the Chesapeake. I had longed to be engaged and married to him. I would've marched across the stage, received my degree, and while I was still wearing my cap and gown, walked up to a minister on the other side of the stage and married him ten seconds later. Without pause. *Love is kissing his photograph.* As Jane Austen had said, a woman's imagination was very rapid; it jumped from admiration to love, and leapt from love to matrimony in a moment. And from matrimony it leapt to reproduction and white picket fences.

That was who I was then.

Hundreds of photos. There were photos of Chris.

And Rigoberto.

My Dominican friend. I could see the plantain in his face.

He had been Chris's best friend.

There were countless photos of Siobhán and me.

In countless photos, from summer wear to winter gear, we looked like we were the best of friends. She would have been one of my bridesmaids. And there were photos of my roommate, Mona Marshall. We called her M&M. She would have been another bridesmaid.

M&M was the only good memory in that box. Rigoberto wasn't a bad memory, he wasn't a horrible memory, but he wasn't a neutral memory. His desire for me had complicated things as much as the way I had been betrayed by Chris. In photos I saw me, Chris, and Siobhán. In one, she was standing between me and Chris, his arm around both of us. The irony. Mona Marshall was the memory I could handle.

She had been my sister.

She had been the closest thing that I had had to a sister.

I hadn't heard from her in forever.

I remembered the night that we had double-dated.

I was with Chris.

She was with the man who impregnated her.

She had dropped out of college.

She had gone home to have a baby.

I'd never called her. Not once. I never sent an e-mail.

I'd become so consumed with my own life, with Chris, with the battles with Siobhán, that I had never reached out to Mona.

I had abandoned her.

That was how it felt at this moment.

During the roughest era of her life, I had abandoned her.

I thought about my mother.

When she was alone and pregnant with me.

I should have kept in touch with Mona Marshall.

I would have to look for her on Facebook.

In a trance, in the past, I stared at the photos for a while.

FOUR

Not long after, I was showered, had made a food run to the Nam Dae Mun International Farmers Market in Smyrna on Spring Road, and was back on the fourth level of my too-large townhome, once again alone in my writer's cave, using a fork to eat slices of mango and pieces of Jamaican jackfruit, coolie plum, nesberry, and red apple. I ate while ghostwriting smut on a MacBook Pro that rested on an antique wooden table, an antique table that rested on a ragged rug. Smut, even bad smut, made me anxious, made me shift in my seat, made me damp with need. I sucked a slice of mango; let its juice fill my mouth.

On my wall was a poster I had bought at a seminar, a poster that motivated me.

A STORY IS NOT INFORMATION
STRUNG INTO A NARRATIVE

BUT A DESIGN OF EVENTS THAT
CARRIES US TO A MEANINGFUL CLIMAX.

—ROBERT MCKEE

Today the part that stayed with me was *meaningful climax*. I wanted to be carried into the depths of a *meaningful climax*. On my desk, staring at me was my membership to a private club called Decadence.

Soon I went online to read the scheduled events. One of the sexier, bolder events caught my eye. I would need amazing new shoes. I RSVP'd and used my American Express card to pay the entry fee for that night. It had to be paid in advance. Then I checked the box *WATCHER*. I would play it safe and register as a voyeur. I would watch. Even though I wanted to fulfill all fantasies, I wasn't ready to commit to the unknown, wasn't ready to once again take on two at once, or challenge three, wasn't ready to unleash the abnormal need that ran hot in my blood, so I left the box *DOER* unchecked.

My cellular rang with the ringtone that I had assigned to the man called Prada.

With a wide smile I answered, "Please tell me that you're back on this side of the pond."

In his wonderful British voice he replied, "Sydney. But I'd rather be in North America."

"When are you back in America, so we can repeat our amazing, fucktastic lost weekend?"

He laughed. "I'm regretting being on yet another business trip. I feel the same passion for you."

"What's on your schedule after Australia?"

"China and Dubai are next. Meet me there. I'm staying in a suite at the Burj Al Arab."

"Wish I could. My mom and I had a great time there. Could have more fun with you."

"I will have meeting after meeting, but you could wait for me. I want to make love to you."

"I don't require words like those, Prada. I want to have sex with you too."

"It's been forever since we've seen each other."

"Sex weeks. I mean *six* weeks without sex. Seems like forever."

"We're finally disembarking. Full flight. They're moving slowly."

"Oh, your flight had literally just landed at Sydney Airport."

"As soon as the wheels touched ground, you were my first call."

"Oh, well. If only you had a layover at Hartsfield."

"How would that work out?"

"I'd rent a van and come to the airport in nothing but a trench coat. Parking-lot sex."

He laughed. "You're incorrigible. Absolutely incorrigible."

I imagined that he had his phone up to his ear as he finally retrieved his carry-on.

He said, "Nia?"

"Yeah, Prada."

"Never mind. Now might not be the proper moment."

My heart raced, the anticipation of bad news.

I asked, "What, Prada?"

"It's nothing."

"Tell me."

"We never discuss your love life."

I paused. "My love life? What are you asking me, Prada?"

I anticipated him asking me if I had other lovers, if he was the only man I was sleeping with.

In French he said, "*We talk about profound subjects, religion, philosophy, existentialism, or we joke, or make love, but we never talk about you in depth. I feel as if I have told you much about me, as if I have revealed my deepest emotions. I was wondering, when was the last time that you were in love?*"

His words became serious and he changed languages so the people around him wouldn't understand. When he felt intensely, when he was more than serious, he spoke in French.

Again I paused, then in equally passionate French, I answered, "*Define love.*"

"*Define?*"

"*Love is a word that has many definitions and is a beast of varying degrees.*"

"*Can't-live-without-each-other kind of love.*"

Again, as my breathing slowed, I hesitated. "*Codependency.*"

"No, love. *The kind of love where you can see yourself with me forever.*"

I asked, "Where is this coming from, Prada?"

He hesitated, something he rarely did. "*Do you lust after me?*"

"*I'm lusting after you now. I want a repeat of our lost weekend.*"

"*In a way more than needing sex. Are you ever consumed by wanting me to be in your life?*"

I stood up and rubbed the back of my neck. "*Why do you ask, Prada?*"

"*Because I have a never-ending hunger for you.*"

I didn't answer. I couldn't answer. Fear robbed me of my vocabulary. Fear felt like anger. Phone in hand, I paced. Like a dog on a short chain,

I moved back and forth. My emotions were strong, for Prada they were strong, as they were strong for Bret, only in a different way. What I felt for Prada was powerful. I could tell him that I was in love with him. That would be easy, it would placate the moment. And it wouldn't be a lie because there were so many different types of love. I could tell him that I loved him and mean the same way women loved their shoes, the way men loved their cars, the way a fat kid loved cake.

When the silence became unbearable, in English Prada said, "No worries. I have to go now."

"Prada—"

Then he returned to French. "*It seems that after knowing you for these months, for so many months, after the meals we've shared and conversations we've had, after things that we have done in private, after feeling as if we had established a solid connection, I've crossed a line. And I apologize.*"

I sat back down, leaned forward, my elbows on my knees.

In English, each word almost an accusation, he asked, "How is your friend?"

I knew whom he meant, and again frustration expanded, still I asked, "Which friend?"

"The one you run with. The American soldier who texts you through the night."

I paused, offended by his asking. "Bret? Honestly, I have no idea how he is. Why?"

"You haven't seen him?"

I chose to lie to Prada. To punish him by lying. I have given him the truth, had tried to be honest and give him the real me, the convoluted me, only to have that pushed back into my face.

I ask, "Am I supposed to see him? Was there a message from you to him I need to deliver?"

"There is no message."

"Then how did Bret find his way into this conversation?"

"You talk about him from time to time."

"I mentioned him once. I said that we ran together. He's helping me train."

"Is he someone that you are interested in?"

"Prada, he has two kids. As far as I know he doesn't have a job. I don't know the man."

"Didn't mean to cause you to raise your voice."

"Why are you asking about some other man that I hardly know? He's not your concern."

"I love you and want to scream it to the world, so I apologize for my frustration."

"Prada, there is no need to be frustrated."

"I noticed that you haven't changed your status on Facebook."

"My Facebook status?"

"It still says that you're single. Is that still how you regard and present yourself, as single?"

"This is a joke, right? You're confronting me about my Facebook status?"

"Mine says that I am in a relationship. Should I not have done that? I don't want to make a fool of myself. Or maybe I should change my status to say that it's complicated. Many have that as a status."

"Prada, sweetheart, baby, man who I can't wait to see again, to fuck again, to suck and swallow again, until I am married, I am single. Until you marry, you're single. Nothing complicated about that."

I took a breath. I imagined his expression. His frustration. Pursuing a woman for this long, and not being able to tame that wildness in her, being invited inside of her bed but not inside of her heart.

I said, "I saw Bret this morning."

"Did you? What was the occasion?"

"We ran together. We ran, then he hopped in his car and went back home."

"Okay."

"Anything else that you need to know? Do you need to know if we fucked? No, we didn't have sex, Prada. Have we ever fucked? Yes. Once. Before I slept with you. After I had known you, yes, but not since I have slept with you. Does he know about you? Yes, he does. Now we're only friends. Bret isn't rich, isn't a reader, isn't a movie lover, and couldn't care less about philosophy. He doesn't compare to you, Prada. Now, does that make you feel better? I know nothing about the man. He is mysterious, but he isn't shifty, isn't sneaky, isn't a man who asks me a thousand questions. We run together, that is all."

"You were with the soldier after you met me, but before we were intimate."

"Six months ago. I met him when I was at a bar, when I was alone, when I was lonely, when I decided to have fun. Do you need more details? Because I will give you every detail, from the first smile to the first kiss to the insertion to the moan to the orgasm if that's what you need to hear. One time. And don't you dare judge me. I met you at a bar. You tried to bed me the night we met, Prada. You cruise bars looking all dashing and debonair and confident and pick up women all over the goddamn world. You sent me drinks before you knew my name and eased your way over and did your best to seduce me."

In a calm tone he said, "There is a particular tone that you have when you speak of Bret."

"And what tone is that?"

"The same tone that I have when I speak of you, when I tell my friends about you, when I tell my parents about you. We have many differences, Nia Simone, but love can overcome all obstacles."

"Tell me about the women you have fucked, Prada. Tell me about the ones you met in bars and sent drinks and took to your room and fucked the way you fuck me. Tell me about them all. Especially the ones of late, the ones you have bedded since we have met. Cover the last four years. Tell me about every women you have fucked and I will open my diaries and tell you about every man I have fucked."

"You're angry."

"You want honesty, I will give honesty, but I want honesty in return. I can give you honesty the way I give you head; brutal and you will have me begging to stop before you cry. You become honest and I become honest and we take it from there. No walls. No bullshit. No pretending to feel what you don't."

"You are very angry."

I said, "Prada, I enjoy you. I enjoy us. Don't make the honeymoon be over."

"The honeymoon never has to end, Nia Simone. It could go on and on and on."

"No, it doesn't, but I don't think that the honeymoon you fantasize about is the same as the one I would desire. Mine is fun. Mine still allows you freedom to be whoever you are when you're not with me, Prada. You gave me a good fucking, as many men have given me a good fucking, as you have given many women a good fucking. I've seen you *once* in the last six weeks, Prada. Once. Not enough. We have had one magnificent weekend in the last four years. Not enough to satisfy my needs, Prada."

"You say terrible things to me when you are drunk, and things just as harsh when you are sober."

"I know. I apologize. It's my defense mechanism, Prada. It makes me speak that crude way."

"It's abusive."

"I apologize. You don't deserve to be talked to that way. You've done nothing wrong."

"I think that you misunderstand my being a gentleman for being a weak man."

"You do something to me not many men have been able to do."

"It's not about quantity, Nia. It's about quality. And once again, I am not a weak man."

"Those orgasms have faded, Prada. Yesterday's orgasms are yesterday's meals. Again I hunger."

"It's a new day."

"Yes. It's a new day. And every day I wake up hungry. Every day I need to be fed. I need you."

I had almost told him then, almost told him about Decadence, about the next phase of my pilgrimage to find my inner self, about my joining, about the adventure that I was preparing to embark on alone, without anyone's permission. I almost told him about the powerfully erotic interviewer at Decadence. Enough damage had been done. What was confessed couldn't be erased.

Frustrated, head pounding, in French I whispered, "*Be safe, Prada. Be safe.*"

"*I love you, Nia.* That's all. *I love you and I want to make sure that it's appropriate.*"

"*I know. And I appreciate the sentiments that you have toward me. I really do.*"

With those awkward words I ended the call. I was always the first to hang up.

Then I set free a therapeutic high-pitched scream that spread itself from my office to the garage three levels below me. I screamed like my mind had been raped, screamed as if my mind had been fucked.

Yet there was an extravagance, an excitement that came from our frustrations and conflict. If Prada were dull, if our conversations were emotionless, if he didn't challenge a particular part of me that needed to be challenged, that needed to be confronted, if I didn't see the reflection of me in him, if I didn't feel like he was some aspect of me, an answer to some desire, he would be of no value to my spirit.

On my desk inside of a glass were keys from hotels. Each key was a decadent memory that had happened before I had gone to bed with Prada; a couple since I had had a one-night affair with the soldier named Bret. I wasn't ashamed, but I didn't broadcast it. Bret had been a well-built, powerful, potent, astonishing, beautiful zipless fuck. If I had met him at the LA Times Festival of Books, at the DoubleTree Hotel in Bakersfield, at the Clift Hotel in San Francisco, at the W Hotel in San Francisco, at the bar in the Hotel ZaZa in Houston, at the Holiday Inn in Killeen, in Las Vegas at the Monte Carlo, at the Hilton in South Carolina, even at the Swissotel in Amsterdam or Myhotel in Central London, he would have been my first choice for companionship those nights, for nights when I would have suffered from a mean sleep, for nights when the quicksand of loneliness pulled me down, nights when I had the morals of a man and misbehaved as a man. Prada had been just as wonderful in bed. Maybe I should've bedded Prada the night that I had met him. Maybe I should have left a lipstick heart on his mirror. Then he would have been a key amongst keys. A key to a door that had been reprogrammed, a door that he would not have the power to reopen.

Inside of one of those unpacked boxes was a newspaper article that spotlighted a nineteen-year-old Trinidadian woman, a UWI student who used to play netball and ran track and played soccer, then went home and washed all of her clothes, all of her family's clothes by hand because there was no washing machine. No washer, no dryer, no dishwasher, no hot water, no vacuum cleaner. In the article by the *Guardian* she was a pregnant teen. Probably a shame to her family, to my Caribbean family, to her church. Another woman-child to point a finger at and spread gossip. Her boyfriend had been murdered the night before and with tears in her eyes and on behalf of his family, on behalf of the unborn child in her belly, she pleaded to the people of Trinidad, begged them to donate money so that the father of her unborn child could have a proper burial. Her name was Hazel Tamana Bijou. His name was Derren Liverpool. His mother was in Tunapuna Village and his father was in Santa Cruz. I never met them. And I rarely spoke the name Derren Liverpool. He was my blood father. I didn't know him. The man I never knew. His full story remained a mystery to me.

A year later my mother met Francois Henri Wilson. She was still grieving, but life moved on. When you had a newborn, you didn't have time to rest, had to keep moving forward or become a failure.

I've never known the details of how they met, only that they met and fell in love and married.

In those boxes were copies of her wedding pictures. A small wedding on Catalina Island. She had been a Caribbean Cinderella.

Fast forward past thousands of photos and smiles became frowns. The affair. The other woman. The younger woman with the European accent. Once upon a time, my stepfather had divorced my mother. I guess he had a new lover and had deemed my mother as being redundant. Within ten months, he had remarried. He had destroyed my mother's fairy tale. Had destroyed mine. Maybe that had damaged me. Divorce, like death, damaged everyone that it touched. Only the pangs from divorce never diminished.

Francois Henri and Hazel. The only father I have known. And my Trinidadian mother. They had looked inseparable, invincible, but they had failed, the honeymoon eventually ended. Then I remembered the box of memories. I remembered Chris Eidos Alleyne. The breakup in college had been my heartbreak, my bitter divorce without a judge.

FIVE

I stared at Facebook, tempted to change my status to COMPLICATED, but they didn't have the level of complicated that I needed. I needed a COMPLICATED AS FUCK AND FRUSTRATED AS HELL option. Soon I returned to the information about Decadence. The paperwork that I had signed explained the club rules, the language of sex, and assured that many congregated there to play out their fantasies.

I whispered as I read, "'To serry and taste what was forbidden, as what was forbidden tasted you. To touch one lover or be touched by many. A woman's heaven. A paradise for the feminine.'"

It still sounded like it was the perfect place for me, a woman who felt like Anaïs Nin was her alter ego. I was a Caribbean woman who too felt like the virgin-prostitute, an accidental whore, a perverse angel who wore the two faces of Gemini, one side saintly and the follower of rules, the other side as mysterious as my desires. Over the last four years my desires have become darker, as I have become bolder.

As I rested on my belly kicking my feet, I smiled a nervous and excited smile.

I remembered the questions that she'd asked during my last face-to-face interview. My fifth and final interviewer was a petite Cuban woman. An island girl. She wore a Lady Datejust Rolex, True Religion jeans, the identical Hermès Birkin handbag that Francesca Eastwood had burned like money, Rampage pumps, that and a T-shirt that read SLUT (noun): A WOMAN WITH THE MORALS OF A MAN and a silver necklace, Jesus on the cross. I wore a necklace and colorful bracelets, skinny jeans, black heels, my hair down. When I entered she shook my hand, greeted me in Spanish. I reciprocated. Spanish and French were listed as the languages that I spoke fluently. She barely looked twenty, resembled actress Shari Solanis when she was in profile.

With a satisfied nod she returned to a stack of newspapers that were on the desk. *Granma*. A paper published by the Communist Party of Cuba. *Juventud Rebelde*, published by the Union of Young Communists, and *Trabajadores*, the newspaper published by the Centre of Cuban Workers.

So, Miss Bijou—

Nia is fine.

I am acquainted with quite a few Trinidadians. And I love the way the people from Trinidad speak. I love your singsong voices. Yours is very mild. It's as if people from your country have their own dialect.

We have one of the most fascinating languages on earth. Trini isn't broken English. Those are the white man's terms, his political spin used to put down the languages created by non-Europeans.

I see. And to a certain extent, I do agree.

She motioned to an armless chair facing her desk. She was comfortable with me. I had passed some test. I sat, leaning away from her, legs crossed. I wouldn't sit without being offered, not even if there were a thousand chairs. Etiquette. She sat. Next she offered me bottled water, antioxidant rich, which I accepted out of manners. She dug a thin file out of her one-hundred-thousand-dollar purse, my file, and eased on her frameless glasses, then sipped alkaline water and skimmed a few pages in silence. Silence was unnerving. I was being judged. It made me feel as if my heart would explode, as if I had Chagas disease.

With the casual tone of a professional she asked, *Ideally, how often would you like to have sex?*

How often?

Yes. How often?

Every day. I say that, but I don't think I would want to every day. I think that in reality I would like to have that option. Like having a refrigerator filled with food and you could eat whenever you chose.

She nodded.

I said, *Would love to please and be pleased every day. But I rarely do have sex, actually. For me it comes in spurts. No pun intended. I have long, dry seasons of famine. Then I feast, become a glutton. I have fantasies, some ex-*

treme, some violent, some loving, and I act on them. Sometimes I need a day where I have a lover and all he does is please me. I have days where I really need to fuck a man, ride, suck a man. When I'm having sex I feel so alive, the world, my existence feels so wonderful. Sometimes I want the friendship of a man but other times I only want his passion. Friendship can be false; passion never lies.

She nodded.

I sipped my water. It felt like I was unemployed and on an important job interview.

She asked, *How would you feel if someone were interested in your mate, but not in you?*

I don't have a mate. I checked the box for single, never married on the form.

Yet you paused.

I do see someone, but we're not a couple. Not officially. It's a very gray area.

Hypothetically.

I prefer realism.

A fiction writer who prefers realism?

We're all hypocrites in some way. But the work that I take the most pride in is unpublished. It's the story of my life, my journals, my diaries, my truth, my struggle, my flaws, my humanness.

Humor me. What if you did have a mate? What if someone became your official partner?

I would be fine with that. Especially if I could watch. I enjoy watching others. Seeing them interact, studying how they are intimate with each other. I would study him. His pleasure would be mine.

If you weren't invited to watch? What if the other woman wanted to be alone?

Then I would be free to roam the compound alone, find new pleasure on my own.

What if he objected to you seeking your own satisfaction with one or more lovers?

Then he wouldn't be there with me. That night I would probably be kind, wouldn't cause a scene, but I'd know that we would be done as lovers. He wouldn't fit in that extraordinary lifestyle, not with me. I can't allow any man to set the agenda for my existence. I can't allow anyone to oversee my soul.

What if you witness people of opposing religions sharing a sexual experience?

That would be better than witnessing them bombing the shit out of each other.

Seriously.

I am serious. I prefer sex to violence, but many are more comfortable with violence on television and in books than sex. Watching opposing religions do and share the one thing all cultures have in common? That would be beautiful. Everyone on this planet, we exist because two people were in pursuit of pleasure. That is one thing all races, religions, and cultures have in common, the pursuit of pleasure.

Or power.

I agree. Or power.

Have you ever had group sex?

Yes.

Size of group?

The largest has been four. Few three-ways, but the largest has been four.

How did it turn out for you?

It was beautiful.

What made it beautiful?

It was spontaneous. It was naughty.

Go on.

The sharing. The lack of selfishness. Probably the best sexual experience of my life.

Why did you engage in group sex?

It was a fantasy and when the opportunity presented itself, with the right partners, of course, I gave myself permission to explore. I wanted to learn more about this body, this soul, this sexual spirit inside of me. For me it was about the senses. One lover can be wonderful, but can only do so much.

Explain.

A man can't kiss you while he sucks your toes. He can't suck your ear and eat you out at the same time. Or you can't kiss him while he eats you out. You can't suck him while he rides you doggie. You can't ride reverse cowboy and give him head. With more than one lover so many needs can be met, so many senses can be stimulated. It can be beautiful with the right people. It was for me. I learned a lot about myself. Did things I never thought that I would.

Double penetration?

Enjoyed it. Never knew that I could orgasm anally.

Triple?

Define that for me, please.

Vaginally, anally, and orally, all at once.

Never tried it. But you have planted a seed. The thought is blooming in my mind now.

Noted. Additional terminology will be posted on our secure website.

Vaginally, anally, and orally all at once. Challenging. I wonder what that would do for the senses, which additional nerve endings would be set on fire, how hard could I come while filled that way.

I've seen a woman take on five men at once.

Five? Wow. Sounds like she's a professional.

She is a shy professor at a prestigious college on the East Coast. The youngest in her profession. She looks so innocent, so well-spoken and demure, but the sensuality of Sasha Grey lives inside of her.

What did she do, put one inside of each ear?

As she took on five as she engaged in triple-P, she gave two of the gentlemen hand jobs.

I'm not that coordinated. Nor am I that ambitious. At some point it becomes a circus act.

But the triple penetration interests you?

As of this very moment, it's officially on my bucket list. Maybe I should call it my fuck-it list. A woman has the right to be amalgamated or integrated with the lover or lovers of her choice, assuming all are consenting adults and are there to share and experience pleasure and make the woman feel good.

I see.

Low on the list. But if I ever meet triplets, triple penetration will be moved to the top.

Interesting.

Any triplets belong to Decadence? One would have to have a small penis.

I'm not allowed to say. I said too much when I spoke of the shy professor. That was unprofessional of me. I must ask that you keep that between us.

Wait, would two guys and a girl count? In that case I've done that once.

Not sure. I think that they mean three men on the form. Penetration.

Then, no.

Two guys and a girl.

Long time ago.

And you had no problem with that sexual activity?

I'm telling you things that I've never talked about, not with anyone.

Not to worry. Everything is confidential.

It was fun. Was incredible. Addictive. More stimulation than I had imagined I could handle.

For you it seems to be all about the stimulation, not the act itself, but from the sensations.

For me it's about the indulgence of the five senses. And the release. My body needs the release.

Afterward, psychologically, did anything change about your perception of sex?

Only that I had learned that vanilla sex no longer appeased my appetite.

Guilt?

None.

What are your limits?

No idea. It may not mean more people, but something different from what I am used to.

Golden shower?

Not interested in any water sports or anything involving bodily functions.

Tell me how you perceive love and sex.

Apples and oranges.

Explain.

Love is for the soul and sex is for the body. Both cry out for satisfaction.

Interesting.

I've learned that I can be in love with someone and not have sex with the object of my affection.

Interesting.

I've also realized that I can need sex and not be interested in being in love.

I know you're joining alone, you're single, never married, but in a future setting, hypothetically, how would you feel seeing your partner obtaining lustful satisfaction with another person?

Didn't you just ask me that?

Some questions may sound repetitive, but they are in some ways different.

This is a psychological evaluation. Like having a conversation with Kinsey or Freud, or both.

How would you feel? The man you love is with another woman. A beautiful woman. He's having the time of his life, maybe even enjoying sex with her more than he does with you.

It would turn me on, but I wouldn't have to be included. And hopefully he will feel the same. Every man makes a woman feel good in a different way. No two dicks or yonis are the same.

Have you been with a woman?

You already asked me that.

Please, Miss Bijou. Would you mind answering again?

Yes.

Yes, you would mind answering or, yes, you have been with a woman?

Yes, I have.

More than once?

Uh. Yes.

You paused.

It was a complicated answer.

So now, after consideration, there seems to be a different answer.

Asking me again, it sort of put my mind in a different place.

That's why some questions are duplicated. So there was more than one woman?

It happened so fast. The second one . . . my situation, back then, was very complicated. You're making me remember that rainy day, that storm, the thunder and lightning.

Why haven't you tasted a woman?

Pleasing a man comes naturally, is instinctual, but I wouldn't know what to do with a woman.

It's easy. Just pretend. Pretend that you are the man and you're pleasing yourself. Pretend that you are doing the things that you want a man to do to you. Do that and being with a woman will be easy.

Pretend to be a man.

Pretend that you are pleasing yourself, if you could please yourself in that way. Female version of autofellatio.

Do you masturbate?

Of course.

And when you please yourself, do you imagine that a man is pleasing you?

I do.

At times do you imagine that you are the man who is fucking you?

I guess that I do. It becomes some sort of out-of-body experience.

In your mind, if that helped, yes, you could imagine that was what you were achieving.

Is that what I do? Imagine that I was a man and I was eating myself out?

It was what I did at first. Now I simply enjoy tasting the orgasm of another woman.

You make it sound so simple.

Will you require vitamin B or testosterone shots?

Testosterone shots?

Wait, sorry, that was a question for the men. Ignore that one.

Testosterone?

Give a man a testosterone shot and Viagra and he's a Ferrari in bed. He'll go all night and into the morning. We also offer love potions, natural aphrodisiacs to enhance the libido the natural way.

The secrets of men.

Women take pills and imbibe love potions that make them change from quiet and shy to sexual Lamborghinis with porn-star aspirations.

More questions were asked, two more hours of what-if scenarios.

Miss Bijou. We need to see you naked.

Why?

Well, some women who apply weren't born women.

Oh. You're concerned with gender reassignment.

We don't allow chicks with dicks.

Transvestites have tried to become members?

We have to be sure. A lot of powerful men and women who belong to the club arrive from foreign countries; actually most are from abroad, which is why we prefer to interview in New York and London. Occasionally we interview in Buenos Aires. Tokyo. Chicago. London. Paris. Osaka. Mexico City. São Paulo. Los Angeles. Philadelphia. Abu Dhabi. Ankara. Morocco. Johannesburg. Madrid. It varies year to year. This year it is in New York. We cater to clientele of a specific nature and appetite. We have nothing against transvestites. For many men and women, transvestites are their fantasies.

I opened my blouse, eased my skinny jeans down, and as she watched, I undressed for her. She inspected my genital area, looked and didn't touch, then she smiled. Her pupils dilated.

You're very toned. Your stomach is flat. Small waist. Nice bottom. You're in great shape.

So are you.

Years of ballet. I danced my way out of poverty in Cuba. Danced into the arms of an American. Now. I want you to see exactly the type of place Decadence is. You will not get there and find yourself in the company of unattractive or old or basically people you would not want to see nude or making love or make love with. We reserve the right to not admit anyone without giving cause.

But they also look clever, remarkable, imaginative. Never saw anyone do sixty-nine in that way.

Only the chosen make it this far. Only the special make it to an actual interview. Very few make it to the fifth interview.

So, you discriminate. Like Hollywood you engage in the art of lookism.

We choose to think of it as being selective.

The people were the epitome of beautiful. The sexual videos inspired and ignited me.

How do you feel watching the videos?

Lots of sharing. Lots of orgasms. Very passionate. Lots of living in the moment. The sex looks incredible. I'm sure that you're showing me the best of the best. Wow, she's coming so hard.

There are eighteen ways to stimulate the clitoris during sex. We teach that skill to the men.

Eighteen ways.

We teach women that as well. If a woman desires to learn, we teach her. Or if she is more traditional we teach eight ways to give fellatio. But the one that most seem to love is mastering the clitoris.

Really?

I took that seminar several times. If at any time you want to sign up, send me an e-mail.

I touched my face, swallowed, then rubbed the back of my neck, my tell, a habit I needed to break. But I also heard the voice of Anaïs Nin, the voice that lived inside of my brain as blood coursed through my veins, as if she were an unseen goddess, watching over me, yet allowing me to make my own choices. I heard her talking to her cousin Eduardo, asking him if the desire for orgies was one of those experiences that one must live through, and once achieved would those desires eventually extinguish themselves, or become never ending, if this was another layer of my life, another layer of my rebellious instincts.

Miss Bijou? Does anything that you have seen offend you?

No. I don't object to anything you showed me.

In case I forgot to mention, we do offer classes in oral sex. You have to bring your own partner. The men are trained and so are the women. They learn to please their partners. It's our most popular seminar. Also, we have classes in Kama Sutra and BDSM, if you are interested in expanding your horizons.

Heat rising, I took a sip of my trendy water and nervously asked, *Do many people need instruction?*

No matter how good one thinks he or she is, there is always room for improvement.

I know. Each new lover is like a different instrument that plays a different song. Each lover may make me sing the same notes, but every chorus is unique, as will be every refrain.

I like that. Mind if I write that in my notes? Miss Bijou?

Sorry. What was that? Was caught in watching the video. This is . . . arousing. Wait a moment. That clip that went by, was that you?

It is. I can rewind it. If you want to see me, I can rewind. How far back shall I—

There. My god, you're flexible. Very, very sexy . . . and competent . . . who is the one behind you?

That's my husband. The others are a few of our new friends, and me at Decadence.

Wow. You're amazing. And inspirational. You make triple penetration look so easy.

My slumbering arousal awoke, the heat spread from my center, my nerves tingled like fire.

Again I throbbed. Again I was swollen. Again I was moist. Again I was in need.

I was given a code and password to access their most intimate pages on the website. The code would be good for a month, then I had to e-mail a request for an updated code. Then she handed me a bag of books. A large, heavy bag. I put the books on the table.

Hot Sex. The Anal Sex Position Guide. Joy of Sex. Sexopedia. Sexual Intelligence. Marathon Sex. Spectacular Sex Moves He'll Never Forget. Oral Sex She'll Never Forget. Spectacular Sex Moves She'll Never Forget. 50 Wild Sex Positions You Probably Haven't Tried. Quickies You'll Never Forget. Erotic Massage. Threesomes. G Spot Orgasm and Female Ejaculations. Clitology. Sex Toys. Kama Sutra Erotica. The Sex Bible. Ultimate Sex Positions. How to Make Love Like A Porn Star. Fetish 101.

It felt like I was entering college all over again, this my freshman-year reading materials.

Any questions, Nia?

I have one. Are you brutally honest with everyone about your lifestyle?

No. And I will never be.

Thanks. I'm pretty much the same way.

I don't see the point of disclosing all that I feel or do.

We are all entitled to our secrets.

By then it was after two in the morning. Minutes later the interview was over. But the effect of what she had shown me remained.

Miss Bijou? Nia Simone Bijou? Are you okay?

The club . . . amazing. Everyone seems so supportive. It feels as spiritual as it is sexual.

As for me, I am craving my husband, but I wouldn't mind tasting the orgasm of a woman.

I'm craving to be tasted. I love being tasted.

By a woman or a man?

By both.

My interviewer, with the same casualness that she had employed when she had asked me if I desired a bottle of water, asked me if I wanted to make out with her. She wanted to experience my energy.

Pupils dilating, voice husky and soft I asked her, *What is your name?*

Pupils dilating, breathing heavy, with a grin she whispered, *Anaïs. My name is Anaïs.*

The five senses of the interviewer Anaïs, the woman named after the Cuban Anaïs Nin, remained with me as I soaked inside my Jacuzzi bathtub. My iPad sat in a chair, the videos of the people at Decadence before my eyes. Venturing into the unknown, the dangerous always excited me.

Maybe that was why I had been drawn to an occasional zipless encounter.

The risk.

The adrenaline.

I knew that pleasure wasn't happiness, but pleasure made me feel happy, if only for a while.

As it had done when I was being interviewed, the sexual videos inspired and ignited me.

I watched.
I touched myself.
I envisaged being loved by three stunning men.
I fantasized about being a four-headed beast.
I came.

SIX

A demon of restlessness continued to govern me as I moved beyond the main entrance of the plush establishment. Wonderful fragrances seduced my sense of smell as I took in the crowd of tony sensualists outfitted in rich and sumptuous clothing.

Waterfalls and the sounds of running water blended with mild chatter, as if this were a mainstream function and not a palladium of the secret desires of libertines. Haunting and relaxing music by E. S. Posthumus played, a score that was cinematic and classical and fused intertwined drumbeats. My heels joined the chorus of other heels that were clicking and clacking across marble floors. A woman puts on high heels and she feels like she is living inside of a brand-new body. Everything changes. Everything lifts.

Extremely handsome, chivalrous, and gallant men opened doors for women, and those women thanked those men for opening doors, social graces that had all but gone the way of the dinosaur in the outside world. Already I was impressed by the architecture, the soft scents, and the sounds. The male species was courteous and attentive to the ladies—and every woman carried herself as if she were a lady.

There was an area that was a dance club. Tailored suits. Dresses. Congressmen. Supermodels. Chemists. Architects. Engineers. Archaeologists. Musicians. Professional athletes. Many were dancing in couples or groups, laughing, kissing. More than impressed. Seduced. Three of five senses had been captured, the first impression remarkable.

There was a sign that indicated this unfamiliar road that I walked was the direction to the undressing area. Underneath that sign was a quote.

BEAUTY WHEN MOST UNCLOTHED IS CLOTHED BEST.

—PHINEAS FLETCHER (1582–1650), *SICELIDES*

I walked behind a group of graceful women dressed like they were at a political dinner party. All wore stunning shoes. Victoria Beckham no-heel boots and Louis Vuitton. They were drop-dead, marry-me-now gorgeous. They probably had super-handsome husbands, were super-rich, and made pretty babies. Wearing a backless black dress, I strolled with rhythm. Music eased into my blood. Sexual needs took a deep breath and a soft prickling sensation washed across my flesh. Arousal journeyed up my spine. I kept Need on its short leash.

A brunette asked a wonderfully shaped blonde, "So if Alfredo puts his cock in some sexy woman's mouth and rams it down her throat the way they did Obamacare, you going to be okay with it?"

"I'd better have picked the woman."

More laughter came from a group of women who smelled like Scripps and Bryn Mawr collegiates. I turned left, right, then stepped onto a glass elevator. The elevator was held as a dozen more enchantresses got on, all in heels, some walking, some trotting, some with a sexy canter, others with a sensual gallop. Filled with bubbling enthusiasm, a strawberry blonde hurried onto the lift last; she pulled a black carry-on like she was a flight attendant.

She chuckled to her friends, "Speaking of swallowing, men love that new study."

A redhead said, "Doctor Conroy, you're saying that women who swallow on a regular basis, I think you said once or twice a week, can reduce their risk of breast cancer by damn near forty percent."

"That's what the study said, Doctor Norton. It's in the medical journals now."

"And you say that the study was done in North Carolina."

"A lot of cocksuckers in North Carolina. They should know."

They surrendered sophisticated, conservative laugher.

They exited the elevator first. I followed them.

Dragging carry-on luggage and laughing like they were staunch Republicans on a vacation in the Hamptons, they walked ahead of me, confident, excited. I slowed down and took in my new surroundings.

My heartbeat was fast. I was nervous.

The interior was dazzling, sexy, reeked of pomp and money, should have been on the turquoise waters off the coast of the Emirati capital. When I entered, the handsome workers up front had given me chocolate made by the legendary chocolatier Paul Wittamer, chocolate imported from Brussels, Belgium, and a glass of moscato cupcake wine. The chocolate plant's botanical name was *Theobroma cacao*, which means "food for the gods." The chocolate was as mouth-watering as the people looked. Each nibble was orgasmic. Each taste made me moan as if I had been blindfolded and a lover was licking up and down my spine, his mouth filled with ice. The drink was another level of foreplay: It was liquid pleasure and held bright flavors and finesse, reminded me of a pineapple upside-down cake. I had to finish my arousing offerings before I left the changing rooms and went to Eros. Excitement and nervousness shaped a sensual dance, choreographed a passionate ballet inside of me. The next set of opaque French doors led to a beautiful and astounding section with the wonderful dance floor and a vast buffet with delicacies fit for kings and goddesses. I walked behind quidnunc women, relaxed women drinking chocolate martinis, margaritas, or cognacs with ginger ale and cherries, sipping their drinks as if they had sex in a glass.

On the big screen they were playing celebrity porn. Not in an ex ploitive manner, but to demonstrate that the most famous of us were human, had needs, had dark sides. Regina Baptiste, her face in rapture, her orgasm apparent, her lovers come all over her hand. I knew her. I had shaken that same hand during a business meeting. Then it changed to a man and two exotic women. I recognized one of those women. She was Miss Trinidad. The other was Miss Japan. The man asked Miss Japan if she wanted it in the ass. His language was coarse, direct, exciting, like Henry Miller. She looked back at his erection and smiled, the room dark, and then she turned the light on. She laughed, a giggly, girl laugh. A woman pretending to be a naughty girl. She was facedown on a tan sofa, on her stomach, her legs together, and the camera moved and showed him giving her anal sex, her moans immediately sharp, and as he stroked her, the camerawoman, Miss Trinidad, reached in and finger-fucked Miss Japan at the same time. Miss Japan screamed, the stimulation intense. I didn't want to watch, but I watched. I watched Anya share her man. He made love to Miss Japan as Anya watched. She smiled, enjoyed being a Watcher while he was being a Doer.

A woman next to me said, "Isn't that the sexy girl from *Project Runway*?"

I nodded.

The crowd stood like passengers on a subway, silent, and watched that segment. When the next segment started, no one moved.

"I'll have to try that upside-down blow job with my husband. That's hot."

Soon bits from other celebrity videos played and were celebrated. Tyson Beckford masturbating. Colin Farrell and Nicole Narain. Sasha Grey. Kim Kardashian. Jayne Kennedy. Paris Hilton. Daniella Cicarelli. Pamela Anderson. Spears. Lohan. Lavigne. Keeley Hazell.

Recording was an act of vanity, a foolish act of vanity, performing for self, the eye of the camera the ultimate voyeur. That was arousing. The eye could not see itself so we needed the camera to be our eye, to allow us to see our faces of arousal. It allowed us to see our own reactions. See how intense we were. See self during a thousand little deaths. Then watch ourselves return to life, feel that awareness, that shame that came from being so primal, and smile, giggle, laugh as amazement painted our faces. The ultimate act of being a Doer.

When I glanced above my head, once again I was in awe.

I was walking underneath a glass floor.

Sixteen feet above our heads, in another stunning hallway decorated with Kama Sutra art, as I paused in the crowd of women, we saw handsome, well-dressed men heading into their undressing rooms. Above us, the men looked like gods in Italian suits, business suits, adorned with Rolexes and Montblanc watches, each god in well-shined shoes. Women could come alone, but men could only enter when they were with a woman; so there were no stragglers, no perverts in search of a night of sex, not like in a strip club, not like at any other club on a Friday night. The male species had to pay four times the amount that women had to pay to join, and the same ratio for the nightly admission. Renting yoni from a renowned madam was much cheaper than a membership here. A few of the men paused and looked down at us. A few smiled down at their lovers. Some waved and flirted. Women paused, looked up, smiled at the well-dressed gentlemen, and did the same. The aesthetics were breathtaking and reassuring that this was not a lurid place where one came to cheapen his or her existence. It was opulent and elegant as if Tomas Pearce had been hired to come down from Ontario, Canada, on a private jet to design and build this exotic and stimulating space himself.

Underneath the glass floors, I paused and read one of the colorful, playful signs.

WE BELIEVE THAT SEX IS BEAUTIFUL.

Along the walls was erotic art by Frenchman Édouard-Henri Avril. Lovers in standing positions. Missionary. Woman on top. Rear entry. Socrates and Alcibiades. Fellatio. Male masturbation.

And on display, as if it were in a museum, was a Bible. Not the standard Bible but the Wicked Bible, sometimes called the Adulterous Bible, or the Sinner's Bible. The collectible version that had been printed by the royal printers in London back in 1631. It was probably the most famous misprint in history. I'd seen one of the Bibles when I was in London; saw it on display at the British Library, opened to the misprinted commandment. The word *not* had been omitted from Exodus 20:14, giving new meaning to the seventh commandment. The Wicked Bible was opened to that same misprinted commandment.

Thou shalt commit adultery.

That scandalous version of the Bible was worth close to one hundred thousand dollars. For a regular King James Version of the Bible to have that value it would have to be signed by Moses, Jesus, and God. The Bible had distracted me more than the art. That knowledge-seeking part of my brain was being stimulated. I was unaware. He probably saw me then, from above, through the glass floor, caught a glimpse as I paused and read. He had a bird's-eye view of a woman in six-inch heels and a black dress, her hair straight, her Trinidadian features more mature, and that well-earned maturity decorated with enough makeup to make me look as if I were going to a fashion shoot. I no longer looked collegiate. I think that he had seen me and memories came, but had dismissed it, then memories dissipated, dismissed his past long before I had seen him.

If I hadn't been distracted by the chatty women, I might've looked up and seen my past from sixteen feet away, would've seen him paused over my head, through two feet of glass. Maybe I wouldn't have recognized him right away. Not in the smart shoes and suit of a businessman. Years ago he had lived in clichéd football jerseys or fraternity clothing and worn long dreadlocks. Time had changed us all.

Purse over my shoulder, winter coat underneath my arm, sipping a libido-enhancing liquid mood modifier, I walked down a corridor that didn't have a mote of dust and passed dozens who were drinking their poisons of choice and flirting. Some danced in groups. This was their carnal carnival. Several couples were engaged in sensual kisses and erotic foreplay. Slow, soul-stirring romantic kisses. Some engaged in three-way kisses. Movement was over my head. I looked up and saw that I was below the glass bottom of the Olympic-size pool. More than a dozen nude couples were at the bottom of the pool waving at us all.

I whispered, "This is fucking amazing."

So many naked bodies swam by as if they were mermen and mermaids in the London Aquarium.

Some were making out, kissing and playing in the pool. From where I stood I saw what appeared to be the makings of a bunga bunga, a marvelous orgy where people had sex, made love underwater.

There was nude volleyball going on in the upper level too. Already I was in love with this lifestyle. From the moment I had stepped across the threshold, I felt that this was where I was supposed to be. There were statues of Bacchus and Dionysus. The Roman with the Greek. Maybe it was a metaphor for no cultural boundaries, no sexual boundaries. That paused me as if I were in the Musée du Louvre. I loved mythology. Loved history. I walked a few more feet and once again was in awe. There were three statues of the type of satyrs called sileni, art that depicted men with huge erect peens, some with erections that went higher than their heads. I touched each, ran my fingers across each erection the way contestants at the Apollo ran their hands over the stump known as the Tree of Hope for good luck. Provocative movies were being projected onto the walls, onto almost every wall. I walked into the projection of Abi Titmuss's celebrity sex tape. My silhouette and I paused. A dark-skinned girl tasted her, sucked the magic button. The scene changed and Abi reciprocated. I reached to touch Abi's face, my silhouette becoming part of her sensual experience. My clit owned a rapid heartbeat.

My cellular buzzed and I lost my breath as if a probing tongue were touching my ache. It was a text message from my forever-working mother, Hazel Tamana Bijou-Wilson.

Awakened, incited, out of habit, a habit that I was struggling to conquer, I patted my legs, licked my lips, felt like a wayward daughter and the dark side of Gemini cursed as the light side laughed.

My mother had called ten minutes ago as I was checking in, placing my index finger into the fingerprint scanner and entering my secret code, and I hadn't answered, so now she was texting.

I read the message.

YOUR NEXT SCRIPT. OFFER CAME INTO MY OFFICE. THE BUZZ ON THE NEW MOVIE IS AMAZING SO WE WILL BE ABLE TO ASK FOR MORE MONEY UP FRONT AND ON THE BACK END. GOING OVER THE PROPOSAL.

Even when she texted for business, I knew that she did it because she was my mother, and at times was worried. And even when I was in the pursuit of pleasure, I'd never forgo business.

Pleasure was wonderful, pleasure was needed, but pleasure paid no bills. For some the freedom that money allowed was one of the most powerful aphrodisiacs on the planet.

I typed,

HOW MUCH IS THE PRODUCTION COMPANY OFFERING?

$50K FOR 12 MONTHS, APPLICABLE TO PURCHASE. $50K FOR AN ADDITIONAL YEAR, NOT APPLICABLE.

CHANGE IT TO $50K AND $50K, NEITHER APPLICABLE PURCHASE. HAVE THE SECOND YEAR REDUCED TO SIX MONTHS FOR SAME PRICE. MAKE THESE CHANGES AS WELL: PURCHASE PRICE—2 1/2% OF BUDGET. TALK SOON.

THIS TEXTING CRAP IS FOR PEOPLE WHO HAVE NO TRUE SOCIAL SKILLS. FACETIME OR SKYPE OR CALL ME.

I responded,

BUSY WRITING. DON'T INTERRUPT.

DAUGHTER, THAT WAS RUDE. DO YOU THINK YOU ARE THE MOTHER OF ME?

I LEARNED FROM THE BEST. ☺ TALK TO YOU TOMORROW AFTERNOON OR EVENING.

IN THAT CASE I WILL CALL YOU. LEAVING FOR AMSTERDAM IN THE MORNING. AND BY THE WAY FRANCOIS HENRI LEFT A MESSAGE AT MY OFFICE. THE FRENCH HAVE SILENTLY BLACKLISTED BLACK FILMS, SO HE WANTS TO GET AHEAD OF THE RACIST MACHINE, LET IT BE KNOWN THAT YOU ARE HIS DAUGHTER, SPEAK MULTIPLE LANGUAGES, HAVE YOU DO INTERVIEWS IN FRENCH AND IN SPANISH PAPERS, LEAD THE ARTICLES WITH THE FACT THAT YOU ARE LITERARY AND HAVE AN ADVANCED DEGREE, ARE WELL-TRAVELED SO YOU WILL BE GIVEN RESPECT AND TREATED FAVORABLY. I KNOW THAT ALL OF THAT SOUNDS HARSH, BUT HE'S THINKING ABOUT IT FROM A PUBLICITY PERSPECTIVE.

WOW. DAD SAID ALL OF THAT? AND YOU ONE-FINGER TYPE FASTER THAN YOU TALK.

I'M BUSY PACKING.

THAT WAS RUDE.

LET ME PREPARE FOR MY LONG JOURNEY.

I nodded.
And let me prepare for mine.

SEVEN

More French doors led to the anteroom, the lounge before the changing rooms. It was a pristine area of marble, carpet, red leather sofas, chandeliers, and endless floor-to-ceiling mirrors. Sections were decorated with fresh-cut flowers and fruits, scented candles—the luxurious aroma of an exclusive spa in the mountains of a foreign country. Subtle physiological changes occurred in my body as it responded to the effect of the accumulated erotic stimuli. I wanted to be here, I craved to be here, yet I paused as if I were on the 5 Freeway in San Ysidro. This was my metaphorical last US exit, my ultimate chance to turn around before I crossed the border into a new lifestyle. I wrestled with needs and fears. This was the buffer area, graced with a beautifully lettered sign that spelled out the mantra of Decadence:

Rule 1: Never touch without asking.
Rule 2: "No" always means "no."
Rule 3: Observe proper hygiene: shower, brush your teeth, and gargle between sex partners.
Rule 4: Progress at your own comfort level; there's no pressure to do anything you don't want to.
Rule 5: To experience hysterical paroxysm is wonderful. Enjoy as many as you like.
Rule 6: Every time a woman has an orgasm, an angel gets its wings.

Troubadourish moans lived over my head, the sounds like a church bell calling all worshippers to service, to pleasure. The language of sex filled the room, each syllable part of a sermon to the brave.

As did the attention of most who were in cahoots, my eyes went to the television. On the big screen, a Spanish man and a Latina made love. He took her on all fours. Another striking couple took to the same mattress. Skin slapped against skin and echoed like a drum beat. It echoed like a calling. Soft, slow, sensual kisses. My hand went to my neck and I hummed a kindling tune.

Thick Portuguese brogues caught my attention just as two nude Brazilians bumped by me, without apology, then paused in front of a row of floor-to-ceiling mirrors and prepped themselves. Both had long hair, super-long eyelashes, and wore diamonds that spoke of wealth and heels that looked like eight-inch pedestals. Those heels made the petite women look like *moko jumbies*, the stilt walkers back in the country of my birth. As the conceited South Americans stood touching their hair over and over, as they had love affairs with themselves in the mirrors, they prepared themselves as if they were carnal hunters.

A deucedly pretty and bald woman in extreme high heels, silver Lady Gaga fetish heels that added seven inches to her height, came toward me. Top-shelf alcohol was burning through her veins. A pink DECADENCE towel was low around her waist, yet high above her colorful garter; with the exception of miles of suntanned skin decorated in glitter lotion, she wore sensuality and nothing else. Her breasts were exposed, free; her areolas were beige, thick as a pinky, and erect.

She stopped in front of me and with an Amber Rose smile said, "Good fucking."

I looked up at her, saw teeth whiter than white, and said, "What was that?"

"Good fucking. That's what we say here. Good fucking."

"Oh. In that case, the same to you."

A smile uses anywhere from five to fifty-three facial muscles. Hers used all fifty-three. Mine used half as many. Her breath owned the sweetness of at least one Long Island iced tea, top shelf, and her voice had both articulation and authority. All legs and breasts. Her shoes and jewelry told me that she was both a shoe whore and a spendthrift.

She said, "Your mouth is so sexy. Heart shaped, full with the promise of good loving. Lovely, full as the lips of a beautiful and aroused vagina. Bet you could suck the accent out of a Mexican."

"Wow. That's . . . that's . . . wow. Caught me off guard with that one."

She looked familiar. She was famous in some arena. But I didn't want to ask her for her name. I only hoped that she wasn't part of the business of Hollywood, hoped that she didn't know my name.

She asked, "You here for a swapportunity?"

"My . . . my boyfriend . . . this is my first time here and . . . I came alone."

"Watcher or Doer?"

"Watcher."

"Too bad. You're very hot."

She waved her fingers and her bipedal stride took her away, skin shining from her glitter lotion, and joined a nude woman who wore pearls and Ferragamo peep-toe pumps with an origami bow. The woman she was with was as tall as she, only she looked to be Serbian.

Seeing them side-by-side, I recognized the one who had flirted. She was Canadian, a professional basketball player who played in the Turkish women's basketball league. Six foot four and wearing Lady Gaga heels, so she was at least seven feet tall. And her friend, I recognized her as well. She was another member of the Fenerbahçe basketball club. Naked, in extreme heels, makeup done, toned and tall, they were almost unrecognizable, but their heights and physiques made them incapable of looking anything but super extraordinary.

The Amazons sashayed toward the playrooms, where moans would rise like praises.

She was famous, a recognizable face, and she felt comfortable here. She was bold. It was obvious that this wasn't her first day sampling this lifestyle. Her energy told me that this was her way of life.

I recited the definition: "Swapportunity—the opportunity to swap lovers. Fair exchange."

The Amazon would've taken me to her lover and placed me at his feet as if I were an offering.

My boyfriend. Jesus. I had actually called Prada *my boyfriend.* I needed to check myself.

My cellular hummed again and I jumped.

It was another text message. For the last two weeks it felt like I had been receiving text messages every other second. This message was professional, from one of the actresses I had befriended months ago when I visited the set. She had sent a text to the producers, the director, the cast, and the crew.

> IT WAS AN HONOR TO BOTH MEET AND WORK WITH ALL OF YOU ON THIS AMAZING PROJECT. I LOOK FORWARD TO CELEBRATING WITH YOU ALL AT THE PREMIERE. UNTIL THEN, ALL THE BEST. LOLA MACK.

Before I finished reading that text, another came. It was from Bret. He wanted to make sure I had made the state-to-state drive without incident. I told him I had and thanked him for looking out for me. As soon as I hit send another text came. This one was from Prada. His message spoke of never-ending desire, of love, of lust that came from love. Tonight, in order to enjoy myself, I needed to be free of him, of the significance of him. That last conversation with him had left me feeling uneasy. Maybe I should simply stop returning his messages. I'd done that with lovers before. When I was done with them, or when something had broken inside of me, in defense I had simply gone AWOL, vanished, had stopped returning calls, e-mails, faxes, and texts.

But Prada was different. He affected the light in me. A surge of strong emotions came and sent a sweet, warm shiver up my spine. It was the warmth of guiltiness. The goody-goody, holier-than-thou, pious part of me fought to protest. As I became mentally prepared to take this adventure to the next level, as I prepared to be unfaithful to the man who wasn't my boyfriend, Prada refused to leave my mind.

I saw Prada as if he were standing in the room. Slender with golden-brown skin, always immaculately dressed. His boyish, infectious smile had stolen my heart when I had met him during a trip back home to Trinidad. His muscles, his skin against mine, it felt so good. The sensation of my senses being magnified and satisfied. The moment he slid beyond my fleshy folds. The moment his weight was on me and he sank inside of me was unforgettable. He was Kama Sutra. The man could make love. The man could fuck. He owned a stroke of many temperaments, one that made me crackle and glow with electricity, made me want to claw and climb the wall as I writhed and shuddered and moaned. Three chocolate martinis were in my system. I welcomed the power and relief of hysterical paroxysm, the liberation that came from orgasm. Once I started to come, it was as if the Hoover Dam had broken. It had been too long since I had been with a man, too long since I had had hard lingam. My body trembled with joy and I came, I came, I came, I came so goddamn good. I had been trying to be reserved. I was the daughter of Hazel Tamana Bijou. Was trying not to show all of my naughtiness at once, was hoping that he would show me his naughtiness before I revealed my hand. He thought that I was a reserved woman; I tried to live up to that lie. It was the equivalent of a brilliant woman allowing a man to think that he was smarter by lessening her vocabulary, only on a sexual level. My sexual range was far-reaching, erudite, profound.

He told me, "It's you, Nia. You are my stimulation. Cannot get enough of you."

"Liar."

"I want you with me all the time. More than in a physical way."

"It was religious. I opened my legs like they were the doors to a church and you made me call God and Jesus and moan like an old Baptist woman on the front pew at a backwoods Southern church."

"I want to be with you. I love you, Nia."

I ignored his sentiment, but my heart skipped.

Prada said, "I bet that you would look stunning in a wedding dress."

I surrendered to silence. Pretended that I didn't hear him say that pandering remark. When a man said things like those a woman felt as if he were planting seeds. Words were only words.

He had said three small words that had a huge meaning, three words that implied a huge responsibility, one that most couldn't live up to; it was their Peter Principle. I felt chains, I felt shackles, I felt the weight of monogamy crushing me. I didn't reciprocate the emotions.

I asked, "Have you been in love before?"

"Those were girls. You are a woman. I was a boy then. Now I am a man. What a boy wants from a girl is not what a man needs from a woman."

I wanted him to ask me if I had had one-night stands, if I had been with more than one man at once, if I had experienced the touch of a woman, if I relished it all, if I desired that perversion all right now, if I preferred excessive behavior, if I preferred what was deviated as opposed to what was considered orthodox or normal. He asked no questions. I sighed. After a while, all conversations seemed like repeats of earlier conversations. Different men, different voices, different scents, but in the end it was the same music, only with a different dance partner. Very few men would come along and make that same old two-step seem brand-new. Each encounter with a different man was unique in its own way, but very few would make sex seem new. At some point, for many, the conversation before the dance seemed pointless. The metaphors mixed in my head, but the meaning, the emotional content was clear. No matter how good a woman looked, someone somewhere was tired of her shit. And the same for men. The same for Prada.

I should've offered him other women, ménage à trois, all the wicked things I desired. But what I felt for him, even while I was inebriated, had made me behave like a coward.

No. Not like a coward.

I had behaved like a man. A man who couldn't bear to tell a woman the truth for fear of breaking her heart and never having access to her pleasures again. I had been as selfish as men were bred to be.

What Prada gave, any normal woman wouldn't ask for anything more, wouldn't need anything else. When Prada was making love, he was as magnificent, as passionate as one man could be.

As *one* man could be, that was the problem.

EIGHT

Thoughts of Prada faded and the magnificence of Decadence reappeared.

Like the majority of the women in the room, women with dramatic hairstyles, jewelry made for queens, and perfumes that would seduce all men, I'd bought new shoes for this night. It was fuck-me-pumps night. And the most astonishing shoes I'd ever seen surrounded me. B Brian Atwood. Chie Mihara. Chloé. McQueen. Wang. Giuseppe Zanotti. Gucci. Choo. Givenchy. Diane von Furstenberg.

Opulent shoes were to women what luxury cars were to men.

I had worn black heels, a pair of sexy Louboutins, but the ones that I had brought for this occasion were Burberry. Red heels. Beaded platforms: The colorful beads hung around my ankle.

After I found my assigned locker, a locker that was six feet tall and more than three feet wide, I undressed, put my clothing on wooden hangers, put my black heels inside of my locker, and, barefoot, my Burberry box at my side, I stood as unclothed as the rest.

To my left a woman with a corpulent build, her raven hair shaved on one side, her heels high, her body a canvas for a thousand colorful tattoos. She asked another woman of equal size with a remarkably curvaceous shape, "What's on your agenda this evening, Jillian?"

"Guy I brought is very attractive. Generous, liberal, and ambitious. You might want to meet him in an alcove. Swapportunity?"

"Think he can handle me?"

"Give him a try. He's full service too."

Two nude women paused as they passed by. One needed to readjust the straps on her shoe.

With sincerity, one woman asked another, "Why don't you enjoy fucking your husband?"

"Having kids changed everything. Took away the romance and now we're in the business part of parenting and being married. We joined a few swingers clubs, met some very nice and very interesting people, even did activities like hiking and movie nights with them, and it did spark it up for a while."

"This making it any better at home?"

"Some."

"Made it better at home for me and Ted."

"Swapportunity?"

"Works for me if that works for you."

"Let's check with the boys."

"They don't get to choose."

"It's just nice to make them think they have a choice."

A multitude of perspiring women entered from the French doors that led to Eros, the most sacred part of the building, their adytum. Shoes in hand, they were cheering, zealous, and reveled in their nakedness. Diamonds and pearls. Skin flushed. Foreign accents. They'd engaged in consensual affairs, had shared husbands and boyfriends, experienced woman with woman, and were heading for the marble and glass showers to have more fun without the presence and needs of men. At the locker behind mine was a leggy woman with bold streaks of balayage in her hair. Colors had been painted onto chunky sections of her mane to lighten her hair, and her hair color blended well with her sun-kissed skin. She heard the zealous women talking about how great the sex was tonight, and she grinned, became overexcited, but the woman at her side, a sun-kissed woman with hair that was shaded like a gradient, the roots dark brown while the rest became light and lighter, looked very concerned, intimidated, and unsure. The gradient favored diamonds by Cartier. Both had on cowboy hats, the kind that were sold over the counter at Dairy Queen. The leggy balayage wore too much jewelry from Tiffany.

Balayage adjusted her cowboy hat and whispered to her gradient friend, "Look, decide if you're here for soft sex, hard sex, or no sex at all. If you are not here for sex, then I'd advise you go wait in the lobby or go up front and dance until I am done with my fun."

She wrinkled her nose before she asked, "What's soft sex?"

"Jesus Fucking H. Christ, Vanessa."

"What, Barbara Millicent Roberts?"

"Don't come here with me and turn this into a bad time. I've spent too much to have a bad time. And I gave myself an enema so that I can finally try double penetration. Maybe triple. Don't mess it up."

"You're seriously going to let some man fuck you up your ass?"

"It's my goddamn birthday."

"Don't say God-d no damn more. You can say eff and em-eff all you want, but no God-d."

"And don't look at me like that. Don't judge me. God's not done with me yet."

"Let me get this right. God finished the world and the universe and all known and unknown in six days, and you're twenty-six . . . twenty-six years and you claim that He's not done with you yet?"

"Hurry and get drunk. You're no fun when you're sober. No goddamn fun at all."

A different woman opened the locker to my right. She'd just reentered the room. I think that she had been in the salon section, where women could get their hair touched up, eyebrows done, or a full manicure and pedicure. Her waist was small, her breasts remarkable breathtaking globes. Her vagina was like a pitted peach. Her sex looked beautiful, well cared for, a work of art she was proud to display. She saw me admiring her nakedness. She smiled an appreciative smile. Then, as I opened a box that had been inside of my big bag, her smile widened and she complimented me on my brand-new shoes.

I asked her, "Which wonderful fragrance are you wearing?"

"It's called Anaïs Anaïs."

Hearing that name, hearing the name of one who had inspired me, again I paused, felt as if this were my destiny. I didn't believe in destiny, yet in that moment I subscribed to that foolish notion.

She asked, "Which scent are you wearing tonight? Your fragrance smells very lovely as well."

"Ce Soir ou Jamais."

"Your scent is as delicious and as eatable as you appear to be."

I smiled at her wonderful body, at her curves. "Love your red shoes. Those are stunning."

"Stuart Weitzman's wonderful creation. Special made."

"Weitzman? Then those are real rubies."

She grinned as if to say *of course*. "They were a cumshaw from my wonderful husband."

"Very nice present. Were they for a special occasion?"

"Sort of. We had great sex one night. Actually two nights. One night, the first time I had the balls to let go and do what I wanted, was at Sushi-Hiro. Best sushi in London. I gave him a moment of oral sex inside of the restaurant. It's a tiny restaurant, mind you."

"Sounds daring."

"It was daring. Blame the saki. Had always wanted to give a blow job in a restaurant. Then, after I had sucked him and aroused him, I looked around the room and held on to his wanker. As he sat next to me in the restaurant, I kept my hand underneath the table. I was sipping my saki as I masturbated him."

"You must have wonderful coordination."

"Practice makes perfect. Anyway, I put the half-empty glass of saki under the white tablecloth right before he was about to come."

"Wow. Bet your husband wanted to remarry you after that."

"I told him I wished he had put his special sauce to my dragon roll. He was shocked."

"Sounds like an exciting marriage."

"Another time we were at the Fat Duck. I was tipsy and begged him to take me inside of the men's room. He did it, but afterward, despite his orgasm, he didn't approve of my behavior. He's a modest man. A wife and a mother should not behave that way, so he says. We have to worry about what others would think of such low-class behavior. I must be proper. Respectable. You never know who's watching. He's a famous man across the pond, a man who wouldn't be willing to do much in public. All said and done, after those wonder escapades, despite his complaints, these shoes were my tip."

I laughed. "Wow. Awesome. You pleased him in public. Twice."

"As always. Unfortunately that river runs only in one direction. He's good, just not great. Great provider, decent lover. It is hard to find someone who knows how to keep the romance in a relationship. Sex.

Love. You always think that you want one more than the other, but in the end you need both."

"Sorry to hear that. Think I overheard another woman here with the same problems at home."

"We seldom marry the man who fucks us the best, but we are lucky if we marry the one who loves us the most. But that man who fucked us senseless, fucked us often, he will never leave our memory."

"I know."

"And on those days when we need what we need the way we need it, we do tend to think of that old lover. We do miss the great lover."

"Question."

"Yes?"

"Just to be clear, did you imbibe the elixir after you made your husband come in the saki?"

"Of course. Never waste saki. That would be beyond rude."

As chatter and the sounds of orgasms echoed in the area, we shared a laugh and we bonded.

Then the Brit grinned and asked me, "Did you bring someone to play with this evening?"

"I came alone."

"Coming alone is called masturbation. And you're too pretty a woman for that."

We exchanged naughty grins. Her wedding ring sparkled, caught my eye. She raised her left hand and showed me. Her pupils dilated as she stared at me, and she caught her breath when I touched her hand.

I said, "Sorry, didn't mean to—to—break the rules."

"No, it's fine. Your energy is strong. I could feel so much of your remarkable energy."

"Yours is very strong as well." Words caught in my throat. "I was just admiring your ring."

"Archduke Maximilian of Austria gave the first diamond engagement ring to Mary of Burgundy in the fifteenth century. That set a precedent. Since then every bride-to-be has wanted to be like her."

"I've never seen a ring as spectacular as yours."

"Ten carat. Radiant cut diamond."

"Jesus. In the United States that would be a two-hundred-thousand-dollar wedding ring."

"I am guilty of envy and gluttony. We all emulate and try to outshine all others."

"I must admit that I'm impressed. The ring has the eye of every woman in the room. So does your footwear. Not all of us get to be a real-life Cinderella. Not all of us get to meet a real-life Cinderella."

"Cinderella's slippers were originally made out of fur."

"Really?"

"Squirrel fur to be exact."

"Had no idea that Cinder wore the cousins to rats on her feet."

"Without the glass slippers, the fairy tale would have fallen flat. All about the shoes."

"Yeah. Definitely not as sexy wearing rat fur shoes to the ball."

"The story was changed and that folk tale retold so many times it seemed the truth. There were over three hundred versions. A Chinese version with shoes made of gold thread with golden soles, French version with the squirrel fur, on and on. The original one did not have a pleasant ending, mind you. It was a bloody massacre at the end. Since I'm talking fairy tales, in the original 'Sleeping Beauty' the prince opened her legs and raped her while she slept."

"Good thing that was rewritten."

"Not so sure. The prince was pretty hot. Oh, to have a hot sexy man appear in my bedroom. A lot of us have that sort of fantasy."

"Speak for yourself."

I smiled at the Brit. She was under thirty, maybe twenty-five.

At the moment, everyone in the undressing room definitely looked under thirty. Ivy League. I couldn't have imagined being here when I was in college. There were many things that I couldn't have imagined doing back then before I was forced to face a fork in the road.

The Brit nodded. "I'd best finish preparing myself and go and meet my favorite pilot."

"Your husband is a pilot. Kudos."

"A lady like me wouldn't bring her husband to a place like this."

"Oh. Got it."

"I have spent and still spend most days being the veriest good. That requires so much time and so much energy. And it's boring. Every now and then a woman has the right to be the veriest bad."

"Understood. So you're here with a friend who appreciates your need to be your veriest bad."

She made the corners of her deep-red lips rise. "My pilot friend, they call him Quince Pulgadas."

I laughed. "If that's true either you're a brave woman, or one of remarkable depth."

"I'm profound. But I'm not that deep." She winked and grinned. "This will be our first time."

"Maybe I can watch."

"Oh, I'll probably hide inside of a private room. Hope one is available. I like to do it in private."

"Aren't you excited?"

"I have a new lover and he has a big dick. I'm across the pond. I have no accountability here. I have no concerns here in America so I can pretend I am whoever I want to be and alleviate and make more bearable this full life that I lead. I am full of estrogen and wine tonight. That makes me a very bad girl who is anxious to be filled with dick."

"Maybe I should go to London where I have no accountability."

"Have to run. Would hate for him to get started without me. I wouldn't appreciate that. Happy wanking."

"In that case, happy wanking."

She abandoned her towel and left.

More women came inside. There was much chatter.

A shapely woman winked at me. "Hey, cutie. Were you here last month for Threesome Night?"

Her voice was very professional, very take-charge, very privileged, and very Southern all at once.

I shook my head. "Threesome night? Sounds intriguing. Where do I sign up?"

"You sort of remind me of this girl who was here."

"I take it that you're here a lot."

"No place I'd rather be on a Wednesday, Thursday, Friday, or Saturday night. My only complaint is that they're not open Mondays, Tuesdays, and Sundays after church—Lord knows that I hate Mondays, they're always bad in court. All of the weekend offenders wear me out, so after hearing case after case after case, blah, blah, blah, blah, blah, I need to get laid, and since I hate Mondays I'm stressed all day Tuesday and need to get laid. And Sunday, after sitting in church and listening to the preacher talk about all the depressing shit that God has done to his so-called children—the floods and killing first-born males and crucifixions and threatening people with eternal damnation and burning for eternity—I leave there so depressed I need a good fucking."

The room exploded in laughter like they were in an urban comedy club on blue humor night.

She was a judge. An adjudicator who came here to escape the judgment of others.

The adjudicator blew kisses, told everyone to have a great evening, and she hurried toward Eros. Her shoes caught my eye. They were Louboutins, black and double-strapped high heels. Fur spilled across the front of her shoe and rose to her calves, then exploded into a wonderful part that hung over the upper strap, reminded me of a pair of UGGs. I chuckled and imagined those were made of squirrel fur.

A woman leading a half dozen well-dressed, martini-sipping women came in and announced, "This is my goddamn divorce party. I'm going to have fun and catch up on all the sex I let pass me by."

The room applauded and glasses were raised as if Rihanna had said cheers, drink to that.

When I finished doing my makeup I barely recognized my face. Dramatic highlights. Dark shadows. High arching eyebrows. Sharp cheekbones. Smoldering eyes. Lips dark like desire. Soft red transitioned to soft orange to soft yellow to soft white. My mask. Caribbean skin painted with the hue of the fire that lived within. My body was heat personified and I had become the fire that lived within.

I found an unoccupied mirror, took in my reflection, modeled, wanted to see what men would desire, what the critical eyes of other women would judge. The red heel and the beaded platforms were stunning. My legs were toned, and the heels made my back arch more, made my bottom provocative, made me taller and more powerful, added to my already existent confidence, made me as beautiful as beautiful could be. In every spot in the room, on every woman, there were lavish shoes. I had to admit. It felt good. Getting dressed, or getting undressed, to defy convention, it made me feel superior.

Bret. I thought about Bret.

I tried to imagine his reaction if he were to see me this way.

Bret and I had run early yesterday morning, had completed a long run on the Silver Comet Trail. Fifteen miles. There was a moment while we were walking, drenched in sweat, that he reached over and grabbed me around the waist. I had lost my breath. It was a Tiffany-diamond moment. But he let me go right away. Then he waved goodbye as he drove away, country music playing, again no time to sit and chat and share a cup of tea or a meal at J. Christopher's. I had wanted him to hug me again, needed that more than I had desired sex. There was something that I felt each time he drove away. It was a burn. An emptiness.

NINE

Wearing a lavish, pink DECADENCE towel that covered me from my areolas to my yoni, I followed a dozen other loquacious fairy-tale queens and Rapunzels as they sashayed toward the sexual promises in Eros. Their walks were runway perfect, showy, meant to draw attention to femininity, but keeping near them made me feel safe. I had no idea what to expect once I entered this arena. I was aware of me. With each step I eased down a hallway filled with grand arches. A swanky red carpet led to the meeting area, where men waited for their dates. We exited the undressing room as if we were stars at a Hollywood premiere. The ceiling was ringed with soft lights as if we were in the mouth of luxury, maybe the Burj Al Arab Hotel. To the right was the mini-cathedral. That was where some came to marry. No wedding was scheduled tonight. Would love to see that type of wedding.

As I stood there and stared at a very handsome man, a woman moved by me, heels clacking on marble, and she walked to him, kissed him, and immediately he put her on her back, took her right there, on the floor. Her legs were apart and he held the heels of her shoes like they were handlebars. He rode. People casually went to watch.

Maybe my past saw me then, saw me as my heat distracted me.

I felt self-conscious. I felt aroused. I hurried away.

Dozens of lingams were on display. Short and thick, long and thin, like branches from oak and sequoia trees, that twenty-first digit of a man with more complexions than Baskin-Robbins had flavors, and each was unique, had its own texture, its own taste, its own aroma. They were nourishment for both the starved and the curious. The uniqueness in the shape of each fascinated me. Some curved to the right, some to the left, some hung straight, some were circumcised, some still had nature's hood. My spirit was as mesmerized with the boldness and nakedness and sex of others. Some were like collops, folds of flesh on the body, some with big outer lips, some with no lips at all, just a vertical slit that marked the gateway to a man's paradise. Most had been given Brazilian waxes, no triangles of pubic hair for the public to see and none at the opening of their chocolate stars.

There were dozens of oversize red leather sofas, each large enough to house a ménage à trois. Couples and trios flirted, made out. There were armless chairs and two women straddled their men as they gave each other soft kisses and chatted, shared laughter as they engaged in foreplay or fornicated like they were high on opium or wine. There were benches at the right height for women to be taken doggie style, or for a man to lie on his back while she rode him. And that was what women were doing. Watchers enjoyed the view from bistro tables and barstools. Mirrors lined the corridor.

As I strolled, men introduced themselves, or girlfriends or wives came over to make my acquaintance before they presented their boyfriends or husbands, all game for play. They asked to please me, asked to be able to learn me, know my body and all of its senses, relish in my flavors, made offers casually, their lust and desire held on chains, as if I were inside of their home and they were simply offering me a glass of ice water to quench my thirst. I was the new girl. The unconquered one. In their eyes I was the vestal virgin in the building. And that, in and of itself, made me an aphrodisiac in high heels. All offers were enticing, stirred the curiosity in me, but all were denied; I kept moving, had to keep moving, had to keep my lust on its chain as I enhanced my walk, sashayed through light and shadows, through the echoes of love and the heartbeat of lust. The club was spotless, smelled clean, smelled more of laughter and fun than of the aromas I had imagined would be endemic to places where people engaged in group sex. It smelled like Pier 1, so many wonderful and competing fragrances under dim lights.

I paused in front of a gigantic fishbowl filled with condoms. They had the Ramses brand, a condom named after the great pharaoh Ramses II, who fathered close to two hundred children, a man who obviously only sexed bareback. An assortment of pills to help with erectile issues was on display as well. Men chatted amongst themselves as they reached by me, as they took pills like they were jelly beans. Some popped more than one. Pills that might cause blindness, heart attacks, and death were being taken to maintain a man's ego.

More lingams had stolen my attention, as a good lingam should, but not until I moved my eyes did I notice that most of the men wore expensive watches. Tissot. Maurice Lacroix. U-Boat. Bell & Ross.

As random acts of love and lust took place feet away from where they stood, men and women chatted amongst themselves as if they were in suits and ties and standing in the hallway of a Fortune 500 company. With each step, as I drew closer, I stepped into a seductive den of foreigners. Without warning I felt a wariness, felt like I was an outsider. Sweat sprouted in the palms of my hands. I rubbed my hands on the towel that I wore, first aware of masculine eyes, then of semierect parts that defined them as man.

Across from that area was a library. A library filled with decades of erotica. I was a book whore. The nerd inside of me wanted to rise up and lead me to books, but my yoni pulled me away. Outside of the library there were glass aquariums shaped like the bodies of men and women, goldfish swimming inside.

I didn't know that his sea-green eyes had seen me then. Had no idea that my past was in my moment. Hormones guided me. I was too busy enjoying my heated gait and the powerful way my heels made me feel, too busy being a tower of sensuality and supremacy as I regarded all the colors, all of the designs of stilettos, all of the wonderful jewelry many women wore, and the nudity of aroused men before me.

My sexual aggravation overflowed. I watched a woman suck lingam. She had three very yummy lovers. She went from one to the next, smiling, this her game, this her fun. She focused on one. There was so much joy in her face, in her body language, in the way she fed her need. Soft gentle sucking, soft suction, and then suckling, suckling, suckling, moistening him with her saliva, stroking, suckling, taking the head, sucking, licking the length, sucking his balls as she masturbated him. I watched one of her lovers have an orgasm. It seemed so natural. I watched the one she fellated passionately come, watched her suck him in a beautiful manner, her oral massage rhythmic and done with ease, with a smoothness I'd never witnessed, as if she were in the bathtub, drinking wine as she listened to arousing music. She sucked him until he became hypersensitive. She looked up at him and smiled, and then she took him inside of her mouth again, now toying with his sensitivity. As he reeled from his orgasm, he found his balance, thanked her, kissed her, tongued her for a moment. Then when he stepped away, without hesitation or reservation she took the next lover, the one she had been masturbating, eased inside of her mouth. She licked him slowly. Brushed his lingam against her lips. Rubbed her nose against the tip. Licked each side in circles. He looked so high, as if she were taking his mind, body, and soul to a new place. A few women casually masturbated their men. Some were in conversation with others as they chatted and took to their knees and gave their men blow jobs, did that as if it were no big deal. More than a dozen began fucking in just as many positions. It was like being at a party and when music played, after one couple started to dance and broke the ice, the group joined in. Soon my hands rose, touched the towel over my nipples. I wanted to touch myself, see if I was wet, see how embarrassingly wet I had become. Then I returned to blinking, to breathing, returned to walking. I eased through the crowd and moved on, my legs wobbly, my clit swollen. Men smiled at me. A few women did the same. They knew I was aroused. Each smile was an invitation.

My heels click-clacked until I made it to a dramatic glass walkway. I swallowed and looked down. Below the glass walkway were countless bedrooms, half-dozen alcoves of lovers.

With orgasmic faces, Doers looked up, eyes glazed, saw their audience, then went back to each other. In one bedroom a woman rode a man reverse cowgirl as another woman blessed his face with her sex. The women looked and saw the crowd staring down at them. Then they leaned into each other, kissed as they used both the lingam and tongue of a capable man to their advantage. They had beautiful bodies, curvy, with broad noses and powerful features. Three of the brown-skinned women were doing the head-top, where they literally danced on top of their heads with their legs bent, body moving like waves of the ocean.

On their heads, effortlessly, they used their hands and legs to get momentum and slid across the floor like they were moonwalking and they did it upside down in diamonds and pearls and Manolo Blahnik and

Balenciaga pumps. They slid from lover to lover, from man to man, from waiting tongue to waiting tongue. Chills moved up my back.

I was overstimulated. Had to walk it off before I grabbed someone.

A man of average height came out of a private room—olive skin, hair short and dyed blonde, clean shaven, another man with colorful tattoos up and down each arm—and the door was left open long enough to see a woman on all fours, her head moving in a smooth rhythm, giving one man deep throat while another lover pleased her from behind, working in concert so beautifully. It was the judge, the adjudicator. Her face looked different now, as we all looked different when our orifices were filled with lingam. She had been comical in the dressing room. Now she was serious, severe, in deep pleasure, getting the bejesus fucked out of her, on the verge of giving an angel its wings.

The door to her private chambers closed. Her court was in session.

One alcove had its curtains apart. Inside, there was a group of about a dozen lovers. A woman of about forty was in there with them, in a chair, legs crossed, palms on knees, and she told them to slow down, told them to listen to the woman, feel her body, feel her response. Fucking looked so fucking good. Looked damn good.

She saw me and said, "Watcher or Doer?"

I swallowed and replied, "Watcher."

"Then watch."

As the crowd became shoulder to shoulder, I marinated.

Soon a woman approached me, attractive with plum lips and a genteel smile, nude in amazing golden seven-inch stilettos. Her face as mathematically perfect as it was beautiful: large eyes, full lips, high cheekbones. As she watched the lovers in session, she rubbed her fingers back and forth across her pearls, smiled, and eventually gave eye contact as she flirted, as she talked. Her English wasn't comprehensible, sounded as good as my attempt at German, which was her native tongue, but she also spoke decent French.

I said, "*I am fluent in French as well.*"

"*Really? Not many Americans speak two languages, let alone speak French.*"

"*My stepfather is French and we had French weekends in our household, that Romanic language the only thing we were allowed to speak for two days. Used to hate those days, but glad we had them.*"

She touched her hair, her pupils dilating as she moved deeper into my personal space. I didn't reject her advance. She touched my breasts. In response I traced my fingers over her thighs and derriere, and as the moans from the lovers in the room in front of us increased in volume, I stimulated the nerves that innervated the clitoris. She moved closer to me, made our breasts kiss. Her erect nipple touched where my erect nipple hid behind my towel and electricity surged through my body.

She said, "*I love man, but I like to be with woman. I eat . . . eat pussy with my mouth. Good.*"

She made *pussy* sound like the most beautiful word in the world.

I said, "*I love to come on a woman's tongue. Would love to come on yours.*"

With my response she lost her breath. A rush of excitement flooded her eyes. I cleared my throat and cleared my head, a mind that was filled with too much uncertainty. I declined her marvelous offer. Immediately I felt her disappointment, experienced an unpleasant visceral feeling of sorrow. Her shoulders slumped a little. She didn't make the cry face, but with her full, sinuous lips she pouted. A sexy lip pout that had probably disarmed many men. I imagined that she had been spoiled as a child and that treatment had followed her into adulthood. I mimicked her childish lip pout. She grinned like a woman who knew when her game had been exposed. Game recognized game. Still she held my hand, licked my palm up to my wrist, then she told me that the offer to join her party stood. Rejection increased my stock, had made me that much more desirable. She kissed my cheeks, then she sashayed away, stilettos and pearls making her as royal as Princess Grace, her womanhood strong and enviable, her confidence magnetic.

My honey flowed. She made me tingle. She made me curious. Not many women could motivate me in that direction. When it had happened, when I had submitted to that curious part that lived inside of me, it was beautiful. Women understood women. I rubbed the back of my neck, again a habit I needed to master. Watching the woman give passionate and profound oral sex, watching the Jamaicans dance upside down, all that I had seen, my body had become so sensitive that the wind from the ceiling fans titillated me. Sexual energy crackled in the air and I expected to see streaks of lightning across the ceiling.

I'd almost walked into him then. But the sounds. The rhythmic moans had pulled me away from the crowd. Years had gone by since last we loved, since we had fought, and he watched me walking away.

In another area, three couples explored one another. Slow road to rapture. Extremely lustful. Very loving. Big turn-on. Everything, every couple had been a big turn-on. Inspired, glorious envy.

This wicked lifestyle was a compartmentalization. We partitioned our existence with others. We never gave anyone all. Not our mothers. Our fathers. Our lovers. We engaged in segregation, hid our total selves, compartmentalized in order to simplify things, to keep from being questioned, to keep from being judged. Each compartment was a place we went to feel safe about that part of our existence.

This club was a compartment. The exorbitant membership fee was the cost of privacy and silence.

There were high-ceilinged rooms to the side, rooms with beautiful crown molding and sconces on the walls, those sconces with dim lights. There were rooms with doors, rooms for the inhibited, but their sounds and pious ejaculations permeated the club. I paused in front of a door, a room that failed to contain overlapping sounds of gratification, paused and heard so many audile and perverse sounds of pain and pleasure. A symphony of sex noises. One woman was a screamer. Another an enthusiastic moaner. Guttural groans. Caveman-like grunts. All of that combined with what rang out as the familiar hum of a vibrator.

The crowd rushed to see an event. Heels clacking, I ran with them, hurried to see the attraction.

A broad-shouldered, square-faced man of German stock, a man who sported a black Mohawk and had hundreds of colorful tattoos, colorful sleeves on both arms and on each leg to his ankles, made love to a woman with dyed white hair, a woman who had great cheekbones and a narrow chin, wore a big necklace of silver and faux emeralds, bracelets and earrings of the same, her lips ruby red, her makeup shellacked on her oval face, a face obscured by long, side-swept bangs. He pushed up on his palms, stroked her missionary style. He grunted at her in German, moving fast as she moaned, "*Fick mich hart, fick mich wie ein pornostar ein fach so, dat ist gut so, fick mich, fick mich wie ein verdammter pornostar.*"

The woman next to me shifted, stumbled, bumped into me, found her balance again and rubbed her palms up and down her arms as she chewed her bottom lip. Shivering, she clasped the back of her neck and squirmed, revealed how vulnerable she was. Severe arousal owned her. She squeezed her thighs, held them tight, moved up and down against her partner. With one finger, she pulled at her pearls, twisted them on her pointer finger. When she couldn't take it anymore, she let her pearls go, shook one leg as she bit her lip over and over, then gave in, touched herself, then she gave her fingers to her lover to taste her arousal, and as he sucked her fingers she whimpered, and then she moved back into her lover, bent over, bent her knees, reached back, pulled at his short and slender lingam, and as he held her waist, she slid him inside of her. Now I was shaking my leg as she had been. I lamented. His erection rested inside of her, rested across her clitoris, sat on the densest concentration of nerve endings of any part of the skin. She winced, clenched her fists as she raised her upper lip, set free erotic sounds as the muscles in her face contracted, as her eyes closed tight, as the bridge of her nose wrinkled. She released a shuddering sigh. Then she cleared her throat.

Pearls hanging, she lamented, "Fuck me. Fuck me right now."

As they remained in my periphery, they became exhibitionists as well as voyeurs. Watchers transitioned into Doers. He moved into her and she rocked into him and they moaned and watched the main show. She almost lost her balance, her hand reaching out. Before she could topple, her hand found my thigh and she held my leg, held on to me as he stroked her. As she held me for balance he made her bend and again he went back inside of her. She was wet. I heard her dampness. His power rolled through her body and coursed into mine. She held my leg and as she was being stroked I rubbed her back. I looked at her lover, looked at his handsome face, then I rubbed his hairy chest. My fingers traced his neck, traced his chin, moved to his face and across the fleshy parts that formed the upper and lower edges of the mouth, and he opened his orifice. He received my digits, sucked my fingers. I moved two fingers in and out of his mouth, moved my fingers inside of him as he moved inside of his woman, and finger-fucked his face while he fucked his woman. He closed his eyes and sucked my fingers one, two, three at a time. There are close to nine thousand taste buds on the tongue. I moved my hand from his mouth and my hand eased underneath my towel. I touched between my legs, felt my dampness, saturated my fingers, then I raised my hand, put my fingers inside of his mouth again. His sense of touch and taste were being stimulated. He tasted me and worked his woman that much better. She stumbled again, this time her hand gripping my leg, her nails pressing into my skin, that pain making me moan as if I were being penetrated over and over. I moved my hand from his mouth, moved my fingers back down his chest, slid it down and rubbed across her back again. She let my thigh go, then grabbed her own breasts, pulled at her nipples, pulled them hard. Pain remained. She had her balance. Our subtle three-way ended.

Beyond aroused, feeling as if I were in a state of coitus interruptus, the tips of my fingers moving up and down my throat, I returned to watching the main show.

The broad-shouldered German fucked his lover good.

He fucked her hard.

What he was doing, how he was delivering sex, every woman, at some point, wanted it that way, demanded it like that, needed it in that crude fashion because getting it like that was the only way to truly salve that aggravating itch. And for some of us, that itch ran deep. Our amazing, educated, outspoken, and loving mothers had had it like that. Our self-assured, beautiful, Jesus-loving, and God-fearing grandmothers had been taken by our grandfathers in that manner; our great-grandmothers had been fucked like that on Saturday night, then praised God on Sunday mornings. And our daughters, if we had daughters, would receive sex like that from someone's son, as would their daughters and the daughters of their daughters. Our souls required love. But our bodies required maintenance, required a good fucking.

Prada had given it to me like that.

Bret had given it to me like that.

Other lovers had done the same.

They had entered my body and gone insane with passion.

They applauded the German. The Sisterhood of the Engorged Labias encouraged him to keep stroking. He raised his head and his eyes caressed mine. He grunted and became relentless again. She yelled for him to come. She begged him to come. His skin beat against hers. He fucked her. I exhaled in short spurts. My knees almost buckled. I knew that she felt him growing inside of her, becoming engorged. And at the same time her yoni was opening, lengthening, doing its best to accommodate him as he grew, as he swelled, as his lingam elongated.

He grunted as if he were coming inside me. I absorbed his energy, felt myself opening up, and became damp as if he had spewed his pleasure, as if his come were rivering inside of me.

Compared to what I was seeing, what Anaïs had shown me during the final interview, it didn't compare. What she had shown were clips. Where I stood I absorbed the energy of the act, the energy of the crowd, was stimulated by fragrances, additional sounds, art, and images being projected on each wall.

Next to me the couple that had been inspired by them, the couple that had touched me as I had touched them, they shared an orgasmic moment. She came. He didn't come. But she came and she was loud. She laughed when she finished her orgasm. She stood up. Reached back. Kissed him. He wasn't done. He picked her up and rushed to the mattress. Laughter ended. He gave her hard-core sex. He pounded her and she cursed and moaned and made the most intense face and begged him to fuck her harder, to not stop fucking her like that, and over and over she told him that she loved him so much. Love. It was about love for them. Her expression of love was like watching musical notes rise.

A man bumped into me and apologized. He was behind me. He was erect. I didn't look back. I didn't react. But I swallowed and closed my eyes. That bump had felt good. My right hand moved back behind me. I moved his towel to the side and I touched his lingam. It was thick. It was meaty. I glanced back at him. He was very handsome. One arm was decorated with tattoos from his shoulder down to his elbow, the type of markings that could easily be hidden underneath a business shirt. He smiled. I smiled. Then I turned around and resumed watching the menagerie, my hand underneath his towel, manipulating his girth and length as if it were no big deal. Breathing deeply, I masturbated a stranger. Arousal modified behavior. Absolute arousal, absolutely. The crowd was absolutely aroused. I was part of the crowd. The power of the group determined what was socially acceptable underneath its roof.

After I caressed his lingam, when he was hard, I felt his ragged breath on my neck; he asked if he could touch me. I nodded. The stranger kissed my shoulder, traced my ass. Then his hand eased underneath my towel and he squeezed my breasts. He moaned. He pinched my nipples. I moaned. He rolled my left nipple between his finger and thumb. His hands were soft with edges of roughness, a self-made man who had risen to wealth. I bit my lips and swallowed a thousand moans.

Again I touched myself. Again I put my damp fingers inside the mouth of a strange man while I stroked him. Held him and stroked him slowly and watched the plethora of creative lovers. Breathing heavily, he touched me, touched my neck, my shoulders, my curves, the small of my back, the rise in my ass. He touched between my legs. He teased me. It felt wonderful. It felt romantic. It felt like romance for the sake of romance, the purest kind of romance, with no expectations. I needed to feel love. I needed to be teased as well.

He could've had me. If he had entered me, if a stranger fucked me now, if he took his fantasy, I never would have looked back. I never would have looked back as I closed my eyes and moaned and grinded and surrendered to a much-needed orgasm.

I glanced back at the man I was masturbating, stroking musically with my right hand. He had the body of a man, hard chest and arms, the body of a weekend warrior, but he barely looked twenty-one.

I controlled him, owned him, and stroked him toward resolution.

People watched us. People watched his distress. People watched him lose control on my behalf. This was what it felt like to be the center of attraction. As eyes turned in curiosity, as labored breathing rose, I felt the power. Felt its high. I owned all who watched. His strong hands gripped my soft shoulders and he fucked against the rhythm of my hand. His jaw was slacked. He quaked violently. In those final moments, when he was severely engorged, when he had grunted and told me that he was about to explode, I stopped masturbating him. He was forced to finish what I had started. He jacked off feverishly.

It was beautiful. Watching him masturbate was beautiful.

Stirred, Watchers witnessed the arrival of his orgasm. Women wanted to see him come. They leaned in. Some moved closer, their eyes fixed on his lingam, watching, waiting. Men watched as well, maybe to see his volume, to compare, see how they measured up. He shuddered and jerked and spewed into his black towel three times, three voluminous spurts. Then he milked it until there was no more. A Rorschach, art made of semen. His volume could have shot across the room. People applauded him. They celebrated his pleasure. I rubbed his back, touched his face, then placed my hand over his heart. Moments later he calmed. With heated breath, he thanked me.

Then he kissed my left shoulder. A soft kiss. A tender kiss. The kiss of a servant, a gentleman. I fed him three fingers of honey once again and told him, Good fucking and good night.

What I had done stimulated me. The fire that I fought to contain roared, cursed. Evocative music throbbed, a hammer tapping my swollen clitoris. The images on the big screens alternated among live sex throughout the compound, sex from dozens of alcoves, to provocative movies. It paused on the debauchery in this region, focused on the wicked menagerie of erotica. Lust was magnified on every screen. This was hell. I was in paradise and now it had become a living hell, a hell worse than Sartre's *No Exit.* As I burned, as I suffered, I had no idea that as I stood entranced, my past—the man with the build of a running back, the man with hypnotic sea-green eyes—stood right behind me. With one step, I could've backed into him right then.

Suffering, I brokc away, I moved in the other direction. I was ready. I was open. I searched alcoves, open areas, hurried from room to room looking for her. The exotic woman who had approached me, the sensualist with the plum lips, the hedonist who wore golden seven-inch stilettos, pearls, who I then, like a fool, like a poltroon, had rejected—now I desperately pursued what she had offered. I was determined to find her. I was ready to be inducted into her party, was willing to connect with her party, was ready to exchange fantasies and spice up their orgy with the singsong hallelujahs of a randy Caribbean woman. Every nerve was alive. I was on fire, yoni throbbed, flames leapt from my pores. She said that she loved to eat yoni, had asked me to become her sexual buffet. I was ready to let her dine. I needed her tongue.

I ended up facing the elevator, in a crowd, again kneading my neck, again tapping my thighs, blood rushing away from my brain, struggling, unable to decide if I wanted to search one floor up or down.

Then all heads turned when we heard extreme moaning in the land of the morally unrestrained. The moans came again. Musical moaning, sweet sexual torture came from a woman with a delicate, beautiful voice. Many hurried toward the moans as if they were a seductive chant, a call to a religious service.

Someone was at the main altar of Eros putting on a show.

I eased into the crowd of excited worshippers, moved by erect lingams and stiff nipples, my skin touching the skin of unembarrassed nudity as I tried to hold my towel and see. A man and a woman with a magnificent wedding ring were on a giant mattress. His lingam laid to the side, covered his thigh like a snake growing from his groin. His face was between his lover's trembling legs. I witnessed the pinkness of his tongue swirling in and out of her yoni. Her back arched, her intake of air was sharp. Everyone had rushed to Eros to catch sight of his lingam. It was bronze, the veins like coils, pulsating wires spiraling from the head toward his testicles. It was a fucking amazing tool of yoni destruction. As people whispered, I swallowed. He sucked and lapped the pinkness of her sex. Her wetness was a mushy sound. The woman that he was pleasing, the woman who uttered beautiful sounds and called us all to hear her sermon, I had seen her earlier. Her eyes opened for a moment and she panted, expression severe, painted with orgasm as she took in the crowd. Then he opened his mouth wide and consumed her sex, and she tensed and moaned loud enough to rouse and disturb sleeping gods before closing her eyes again. Her back arched again. Once more her dramatic moans reached the four corners of the pantheon. My spine tickled with warmth. Frantic, she gripped his head again. She wore luxurious shoes adorned with rubies. Her hair was the style of a flapper. It was the high-society British woman I'd engaged in conversation in the dressing room. The unfaithful Brit was with the pilot, the conquest that she had nicknamed Quince Pulgadas.

Quince. Spanish, for the word *fifteen*.

Pulgadas. Spanish for *inches*.

TEN

The Brit's well-endowed partner held her backside, gripped her like he owned her. Quince Pulgadas nibbled her and when the bed rotated it gave me an unblocked view. Like everyone else, I looked at his phallus. Women *oohed* and *aahed* and excited whispers permeated the room. It was amazing. Saint Patrick had not run all of the snakes out of Ireland. A woman near me whispered that she wondered what it would be like to experience a man so blessed. I wondered the same. Another woman said that when a dick was that large it wasn't attractive. She shivered in fear. But she didn't walk away. She was like me, curious. I marveled and wondered how much my yoni, my womb, could handle. Wondered what it would be like to be opened so wide, to be filled so deep.

Watchers moved closer. Body heat permeated me like an electric blanket left on a high setting. Everyone was still chattering, evaluating, judging, whispering as the oral sex gala ensued. When the Brit and Quince changed positions, when she took over, she caught her breath, pulled her hair back away from her face, her glorious flapper hairstyle now undone, licked the sides of her lips, playfully stretched her mouth as if to say she had a serious task in front of her, and as a few chuckled she went to work, moisturized him, then growled and sucked and stroked his phallus. Women applauded and cheered her on, told her to swallow that sword. The wet, greedy sounds she made echoed. Her partner pushed up on his elbows and watched her, watched his impressive erection, the ingress and egress into her orifice used for speech, watched her become artistic and tongue-paint up and down his meaty shaft, watched her stroke him and stare at him, own him, control him. When she was ready, after she had raised her head, taken in the crowd, and regarded her spectators with a slick smile, she lowered her oval-shaped face and sucked the head. While he begged, as he pleaded, she gave him the most profound deep throat. She could only take half of what he offered, but it was still amazing to watch her master the gag reflex. She did it in slow motion over and over. His lingam was her toy and she had fun. She played with his sex. A long way from the UK, this was a room filled with foreigners she'd never run into as she walked Piccadilly Circus or Leicester Square with her family, with her husband, with her children, with her parents, with her cute little dog. In America, she could be the lover she'd always wanted to be.

That had been me the night that Bret used the hot towels. With Prada, the weekend that we had been together, that had been me then as well. But that had been me many nights; the hotel keys in my office the notches on my bedpost. Many nights, yet not enough nights.

She turned and they were in position ninety-six. He licked. She sucked. Her British accent made it sound extremely sexy. Waywardness always sounded more enticing with a foreign accent that created exotic moans, moans that were so damn provocative. With each stroke of his tongue, with each greedy whimper, Quince Pulgadas made her quiver. She begged him not to make her come again. Then when she started to come again, begged him not to stop. The Brit no longer practiced restraint. Everything that had been upper crust about her had vanished. Orgasm erased all that was false, suspended all manners that had been learned and practiced. We showed the savage that lived inside. We were savages. Seeing her draped in all the trappings of the privileged and acting like a common whore was very hot, sexy. In rapture, she was someone new, so unlike the woman I had chatted with. I glanced left, then right. It was a large room, a room of many beds. They were on the largest bed, a bed in the center of all of the sensualists, a bed made to hold at least ten lovers, a circular bed that was two feet off the ground and rotated in slow motion. It reminded me of the beds that they used in live sex performances in Amsterdam.

A handsome man came to me, smooth brown chest, the subtle smile of a great lover, nails manicured, no visible hair on his body, very nice build. When you are sexually attracted to someone, when aroused, when sexually awakened, your pupils dilate. His dilated. As did mine.

I said, "Your accent."

"What about it?"

"You're not American."

"Not exactly. You?"

"Trini."

"Island girl."

"Damn right."

He grinned and told me that he was a fusion of Surinam and Bonerian. Light brown eyes. As we stood and watched oral sex, he told me that he found me attractive. I nodded and my soft, feminine expression, the way I repeatedly touched my face and hair broadcast that I found him very sexy as well, and that I did admit to him, then reminded him that practically everyone in this building was sexy beyond belief and reason. Pulled away by the noise, the moans, the sucking sounds, blood pressure rising, I returned to watching the Brit's oral sex. As my nipples became thumbs, the man from Curaçao kept talking; his voice was deep and provocative, each word stimulating.

Next to Quince and the Brit, an Indian man led his woman to the mattress. They were the perfect Bollywood couple. They crawled onto the rotating bed. The woman with him, her skin was beautiful, her hands and arms painted in henna as if she were prepared to celebrate Diwali. The henna was astounding. Her hair was coal black; her eyebrows arched thin, and no hair was on her genitalia. She was as beautiful as Esha Gupta, Lara Dutta, and Trisha Krishnan, had that girl-next-door look. Her shoes were beautiful, of course, but the decorations on her body made her stand out. The attention of the men went to her brown skin, to the forbidden Indian girl, her exoticness extreme here, where it was a rarity, where she stood out in the crowd.

She opened her legs for her lover, and he mounted her in a hurry. He regarded the crowded room, then looked at her and stroked her with clumsy motions. He wasn't skilled at the art of massaging yoni with lingam, made love like this was his first time, or maybe he couldn't handle so many nude women watching him, so many judging him.

Compared with Quince's, his phallus resembled the penis of a child. Yet the Indian man continued as if his diminutive lingam rivaled King

Kong's. His technique, the way he moved, how he made his woman feel was now public record. He kept stroking, stopping, looking up, watching others, and eventually restarting his awkward stroke, disturbed by the number of onlookers who were salivating over his woman. She was very pretty, worthy of lust. A very handsome man offered to join them. She looked at the man and yielded a nervous smile, a positive smile of anticipation. Her husband touched her face, moved her eyes from that man, shook his head. He would not share. That was not the fantasy he would give his wife. But so many men looked down on her beauty. A glint in his eyes said that his ego couldn't handle the moment. He finally found a rhythm and moved in and out of his woman, strained, pushed inside as hard as he could.

The good-looking island man who had stopped next to me rotated his face toward me. I revolved my face to gaze into his eyes. As I stood alone in Eros, as my breathing told of my sexual distress, he read me. Read my craving. Read me in this weakened, sensitive state.

He asked, "Would you care to join the party?"

My mouth said, *No, thank you*, but my tone, my dilated pupils exposed my true sentiments, the eye contact I gave him in response to the eye contact that he gave me, my grin that matched his, the way I twirled my hair and shifted from high heel to high heel, the scent of my pheromones that overruled the aroma from my lotion and perfume, my words were negative but my eyes were a flashing green light.

With his mild accent he followed and said, "Would love to introduce you to my wife."

"Where is she?"

"Swimming. That or playing volleyball and making friends."

"Oh. Bi-curious or bi?"

"For you, the way you look, I'm sure that she'll be whatever you need her to be."

"How considerate."

"We'll treat you right."

His eyes massaged my breasts.

Mine moved lower, imagined his lingam.

A man wanted to be successful with all women.

A woman wanted to be victorious with the man of her choosing.

My concentration returned to the British aristocrat in ruby slippers.

The moisture from her mouth, the sucking and slurping continued to give me goose bumps. She wasn't rushing anymore. She had cooled him off, took him away from orgasm, teased him. I closed my eyes. She savored him noisily. She was so turned on. My mouth wanted lingam. My mouth wanted to feel phallus, wanted it down my throat, wanted to swallow orgasm. When I opened my eyes I was close enough to touch her. I licked my lips as she exercised her power over him and controlled him as if he were her slave, her love slave, bound by his pending orgasm, not shackles. The Brit's lover couldn't take it anymore, pushed her away, panting. She laughed at him. With zeal and a grunt he pushed her back down on the mattress, the rubies in her shoes sparkling in the room's faint light, forced her on her back and opened her legs wide. She laughed until his tongue touched her clit and moved like gyres of warm wind coming over the Pacific. She lost her breath and shivered. Her lover consumed her yoni. Her hands clamped on his head, held him, no more laughter.

I felt different eyes on me.

That was when I saw her cerulean eyes for the first time.

Another woman was fascinated by my existence.

She was beautiful, in a simplistic yet extraordinary way. She owned a combination of sensual qualities; her complexion as erotic as it was mysterious. She saw my subtle reaction, saw me inhale, causing my breasts to rise. She swallowed, blinked a hundred times. And since she didn't look away, since she held my stare with more blinking, she was curious. Again I licked my lips and swallowed, nervousness rising. I was taken aback by her directness, her lack of shyness, her coming across, in that instant, as being bold and uninhibited. As we stared, I lost my breath at the sight of her outstanding natural beauty.

Smile broad and friendly, she walked to me, her steps slow and measured, testing me, and said, "Cowabunga. You're attractive."

"Thank you. As are you. You have killer eyes."

She reached to me, undid my towel, and with a coy little wink, she pulled it away.

As I stood nude in high heels I said, "Rule number two."

"I hate rules. Everybody is here because they hate rules, then they give us rules."

Part of me wanted to protest, wanted to scream at her, but I grinned and she smirked. She took it away from me as if she were removing me from the safety of a cocoon. As if she were freeing me.

She smiled. "Much better. Everyone wondered what you looked like butt naked."

"Everyone?"

"Remarkable legs. Breasts to die for. Look at that little waist. Oh, I'm jealous. Don't hide that beautiful body behind a drab little towel."

"I wasn't ready to show any more than I was showing."

"Oops."

"Yeah. Oops."

I reached to her and removed her red DECADENCE towel.

She laughed and handed me back my pink towel, put the end in my hand. Her body was amazing. Simply amazing. I returned her red towel as well, grinned at her naughtiness, shaking my head.

She smelled like fresh rain, so clean, and her physique was beyond astounding, so very feminine. Her aroma was simply clean, not overdone with scented chemicals. She didn't put her towel back on. She stood, as she was, towel in her hand, proud to be a nudist. It was a challenge. As if we were both playing chicken. I accepted the dare. I let my towel hang to the floor, swallowed and looked to my left, glanced to my right. Smiles met me in every direction. People admired what I owned, but no one leered. They acknowledged, nodded, then returned to watching the performance. They were all too busy watching both the Brit and Quince or adoring the East Indian couple. I looked at the bold, audacious, naked woman who had removed my towel without asking. Her nipples were as distressed as mine. Her breathing just as ragged. She held her legs together, did that as if she were trying to stop her sex from shouting. I stood and I was damn near doing the same thing.

She said, "My name is Rosetta."

"Nia Simone."

"Nice to meet you."

"The pleasure is mine."

Her hair was wet, skin clean. No makeup was on her face. She had just showered. That meant she had just finished sex. I hadn't seen her in action, so I assumed she had been behind a closed door.

She said, "Cowabunga. She is getting the tongue real good."

"He is an expert at the art of cunnilingus."

"I wish he would fuck her again and get it over with."

"He fucked her?"

"He did. They had stopped right before you entered the area."

"That's why she was so loud."

"Bitch was screaming."

"Wow. He fit?"

"About half."

"Half?"

"Might have been more. Couldn't see for the crowd."

"She's so nice and curvy, like she could make it all vanish."

"A nice ass and a full figure don't mean that the well runs deep."

"True. Like big hands and big feet don't mean a thing."

"You can look around the room and see that's a lie."

"This guy here is the exception."

The Brit was crazed, almost deranged, and the room saw another angel get its wings.

Rosetta said, "You've garnered an audience of obsequious admirers. And I am not ashamed to say that I am instantly one as well. If you don't mind my saying so, you're an excellent specimen."

"It's the shoes."

"Babe, the women love your shoes. Those are so fucking hot. But the men, well, as far as the men are concerned, we are all barefoot."

I said, "I'm watching the show. How can people carry on a conversation and watch this?"

"Right now I have to talk to keep from engaging in public masturbation. At this moment I'm so heated up that I'd come so hard I'd probably squirt across the room. I'd skeet like a man right now."

We laughed.

I playfully bumped into Rosetta and she playfully bumped back against me. She was aroused. Her flesh against mine was exciting.

I asked Rosetta, "What do you do? Are you an instructor here?"

"Not even. Program coordinator. Simplified job title for a complicated job. Economic development. Human rights. My job is very stressful, political. Lots of traveling. Cameroon, Ghana, Kenya, Nigeria, South Africa, and Uganda. Taking some time off. Enjoying my life. I come here and take all of those hats off and get rejuvenated."

"You're a bold one."

"You'd be surprised to see how boring I am in the real world, how reserved I am, how people perceive me—as a stick-in-the-mud."

"Your husband? What does he do?"

"Hedge funds. Babe. Nia Simone. She's watching you."

The Brit's eyes locked on mine. Prickling danced across my flesh, waxed and covered me with tickles of fire and electricity. The spotlight was on me. Every one, all eyes had followed her gaze toward me. She wanted me to come to her. The invitation was clear. In rapture, she raised her left arm, lifted her delicate limb and with one finger she motioned toward me as if I were an old friend and she had a secret to tell, if only I came close enough for her to whisper. Fantasy lived in her eyes, as it had lived in the eyes of the Vancouverite on that hot summer night. The Brit desired to have a stranger come to her, touch her, make love, be made love to, never knowing who she was, as if God had sent a brown angel in high heels to satisfy her carnal needs.

Rosetta whispered, "Go to her. Help her wrestle that anaconda."

Then, without warning, he penetrated our conversation, changed a chat between two women into a verbal ménage à trois and told me, "Upgrade your status."

The handsome man from Curaçao remained on the other side of me. The last comment was his. He studied my unclothed body and hummed. It was cute, comical, and it made me smile. As I chuckled, I pulled his towel away. He didn't object. He had shaved away all of his pubic hairs. His nice, dark lingam was many shades darker than his complexion. It looked strong. It looked as delicious as chocolate.

I asked, "May I?"

He licked his lips, then, with a lump in his throat, he nodded.

My finger traced it, felt how warm it was, and then held it in my hand, stroked it a half-dozen times before I sighed and let it go. He tried to act unaffected. The truth stood up. His lingam rose. He made it do that. Made it bounce the way a bodybuilder moved his pectoral muscles. It was smooth, the veins that ran along its length thick and powerful. It was smooth, clean, no baby botts.

Eyes were on us. I felt the attention. I felt the energy.

He touched me. He traced his fingers around my distended nipples, used both hands, and outlined both of my erections at once. I wanted to moan. But I didn't surrender. I clenched my teeth. My hands became fists. I sucked my tongue. Then he leaned in and kissed my neck. Sucked my neck. Pulled me closer. Pulled my hair back and sucked on my ear. My breathing caught in my throat. So many eyes were on us. Sex was before their eyes but our foreplay teased many of the Watchers. What he did, how he treated me was very romantic.

We kissed and made out and touched each other.

Like we were teenagers.

A thousand soft moans later I pushed away.

Naked, revealed, I whispered, "Rule number two is now in effect."

He nodded. He had left me light-headed. If he touched me again, I would've come. I fought not to squirm where I stood, in torture, and watched his lips as he talked, as he stopped talking, as he pulled them in, as he squirmed where he stood, his arousal very pronounced.

We stared at each other. A moment later, he put his towel back on and he left, fascinated, erect, disappointed, but with a grin. I was so wet that I imagined my honey moved stealthily down my legs.

Rosetta stayed next to me. I looked at her and imagined her as my lover, imagined us in that way, alone, just us, and her smile said she imagined the same. But she didn't make a move and neither did I.

She asked, "Who was that guy with the nice towel rack?"

"No idea. Just another one who wants to be the next one."

Again I glanced at the Indian couple. Finally her passion ignited. She moved in sensuous motions, owned the rhythm of Odissi, Bharatanatyam, Mohiniyattam, Kathak, Manipuri, and Kathakali.

But the Brit was nasty and dynamic.

She forced her lover onto his back and again she took as much of him as she could inside of her mouth. Once again her eyes met mine.

She was calling for me.

I was put under a spell.

Naked.

Beyond aroused.

Needing to come.

My moment had arrived.

The erotic architecture. The exotic scents. Imported chocolate. Moscato. The stimulating art. The provocative videos. Being a Watcher.

Touching and being touched and having my flesh kissed by a handsome stranger. The sexual excitement that surrounded me at this moment underscored all of my senses. I had endured so much foreplay.

As I inhaled lavender, licorice, chocolate, pumpkin, and the hint of what smelled like doughnuts, as I breathed in scents that increased arousal, my DECADENCE towel slid from my hand, fell to the floor.

I abandoned my pink cocoon.

The confident didn't need a plush security blanket.

The self-assured vixen that lived inside of me, the dark side of Gemini took control, ignited and rose inside of me. It rose up inside of me as my past watched me, head tilted, his eyes wide, his mouth open. He stared at the woman with a face made up like fire.

He stared at a woman who was on fire.

He swam in his memories and he stared.

The man with the sea-green eyes stood nude.

Unseen by me, he stared.

He watched me move as if I were in a sexual trance.

I moved through the crowd of Watchers and went toward the aristocratic woman with the hairstyle of a flapper, took slow steps, and walked toward the foreign woman decorated in the ruby heels.

ELEVEN

Libertines applauded.

It was a thunderous clapping as if they had been watching me all night long, eagerly waiting for me to enter the stage, as if I had been part of an Asch conformity experiment and I had finally submitted, as if social influence had won. I couldn't lie; I felt it. My identity shifted, brushed aside internal conflict. I was no longer in search of justification for what I was about to do. This felt right. Peer pressure, the influence exerted by the group, their decadent energy encouraging me to succumb to their attitudes, to adopt their values, to conform to the group, to be more than a Watcher. It held hands with my internal heat, with my ongoing internal struggle, with the dark side of Gemini, and helped to guide me. Not all peer pressure was negative. As the Brit masturbated her well-endowed lover, I eased behind her, slipped into her personal space. It was like a powerful form of foreplay as I felt the cool air in the room breeze across the warmth of my sex, across the heat from my engorged sex, felt myself open up as I squatted over my glorious heels.

I breathed on her damp neck, blew a stream of air to help cool her, but it only stoked the fire. She trembled and cooed. I cooed along with her, put us in a state of harmony. Nervous, excited, under the eyes of many, I pulled her fallen hair back and blew more air on her skin. She shuddered and began to utter feeble plaintive cries. I caressed her with five fingers, dragged my fingers over her soft skin. I was fire but she was hot coal. My warm hands absorbed her radiance.

Her lover looked at me hungrily.

I acknowledged him, his magnificent lingam, and smiled.

I rubbed her arms, her face, and then squeezed her full breasts. My brown hands squeezed her beautiful alabaster breasts. That taboo thrilled me. Her breasts felt so soft, so malleable. Like the women I had seen earlier, I imitated them, took on a free-loving persona and I pinched her nipples. She tensed and shivered against my body. She stopped moving, like she was overstimulated. Then she smiled another heated smile. She stroked her lover harder, faster. Now she was too excited. I reached for her hand, made her slow down. I didn't want her to hurt him. Lingams were strong, but at the same time, very delicate. My hand was on top of her hand as she masturbated her lover. He looked at me. Amazed. Like I was a cherub. I became her masturbatory assistant for a while. Soon she moved her hand away. I took over. A second man I didn't know, had never met, I held his power and stroked him. He was thick. He was long enough to move from my yoni and tap my heart. His lingam was amazing. It was heavy. The veins were like ropes. I ran my finger down one, made it give, traced its path toward his testicles. It excited me. Touching him. Studying him. Feeling this part of him excited me. The Brit sucked my breasts as I manipulated her lover. I held the strength of another man I'd never met, the hardness of a different stranger, stroked him as a foreign woman sucked my sensitive breasts, sucked one breast and pinched the other nipple, did that until she made me bite my bottom lip, made me tremble, and my surrender added to their moans. Without warning, the Indian man grunted and I sensed that all eyes left us and went to that handsome couple. As the Brit tasted my breasts, as I masturbated her lover, I watched the Indian man march toward orgasm. He glanced and saw me spying on him. We were both bonded by our exhibitionism and voyeurism. Our eyes locked. He smiled a little. I did the same. His chi connected with mine. His muscles tensed. A quickening of his pace and a few short thrusts as his lover gripped his back, patted his back, reassured him that it was okay to go deep, to go mad, to give her his passion the way she liked it.

She moaned, "*Nekni ana sharyaana. Neekni sahrawi. Neekni sahrawi.*"

His partner wanted more, had let loose and turned fey.

The British woman's small hand moved between my legs, her fingers rubbed, massaged my lubricated and enlarged clit. Her hand on my sex, the suddenness of her hand on my sex surprised me, made me as fey as the Indian woman had been. Tingles spread. I felt it rising. Orgasm called my name. I fought it. Pushed it. But her fingers, the musical way she strummed, the perfect way she massaged, it made me set free blissful moans, made me sing so damn loud, made me float, made me lose control. As I moaned, I masturbated her lover, I used my own saliva and burnished him, consoled his erotic agony, and he lamented a coarse song, moaned a potent British tune that felt powerful inside of this love chamber, relished and sang for me, like a well-heated teakettle. He sang and I felt the heat and humidity rise from his pores. And as I massaged the lingam of a liberal stranger, as the assembly watched us, I turned and gave eyes to the Indian man, then to his lover, wanted to see her ascend. She had become used to making love to him in this forum, in a room of people, in a room where she was being watched, evaluated, fantasized about, a little bird spreading her wings, ready to fly away and be free, told him what she wanted, but he pumped a few more times, without rhythm, without urgency, without depth, pumped as a man did after he had shot his load and wished a woman would be still so that he could rest, and he stopped moving.

He was finished. Breathless and done. She wasn't. He had left her in a bad place, a place of desperation, a place that could only be fixed by a balsamaceous orgasm. She moaned and held him, panted, strained, her fire fully ignited. Her lover had come. The faulty design of man had once again intruded upon the pleasure of a woman. Our refractory periods are short, allowed multiple orgasms, don't refrain us from continuing, unless we were truly overstimulated. He slowed, entered that state of drowsy contentment, that state of kef that had him looking as if he had smoked hemp leaves; her hips were still powerful and moving urgently into him, grinding into him as she tried to resurrect his lingam, her yoni begging for her itch to be scratched. She strained, made orgasmic faces, desperate faces, she buried her face in his shoulder and twitched, but I wasn't sure if she came at all. But he had busted his nut.

The British woman, she caught me off guard when her tongue joined in with her fingers. As the bed rotated for all to see, as the room was given perfect views of perfect carnality, I cursed and called out to God. I held her head. She sucked and I gasped, sighed, wailed, screamed, cried. When I caught my wind, I giggled, ashamed for being so vocal, aware of being watched. Others in the crowd giggled too. The Brit was super-sexual. Intimidating. She ran her tongue from top to bottom, licked the length of my sex, found the button again and she sucked it so damn good. Sounds rose. It was a massage on my sexual center. My button was being sucked, each lick making me sing a singsong note. I masturbated a stranger and stared at the Indian couple. I made eye contact with her. But my lover passed her tongue over my flesh, drew her tongue over my engorged clit, moistened me where I was already moist, stroked me with her tongue, tasted me, ate me.

The Indian man, he needed to study me, see how good I felt, see what my lover did to send me to such a state of madness, observe us, learn, see what the fuck he needed to be doing to his beautiful woman, and learn to satisfy her. He needed to study the aristocrat, see how she had let go, see how she was willing to cross so many lines, and learn what only a woman could teach a man about loving a woman. Men should read fiction and handbooks penned by lesbians and learn how to make a woman feel. It took a long time to make some women come, took a lot of foreplay, physical and mental, and he had delivered none. His woman watched me too. Her lover had stroked her, but it was as if it did nothing for her. She watched, suffering version of me, wanting to trade places. She wanted what I was being given. We made eye contact. She stared at me as my connoisseur of yoni showed techniques that she had mastered, as she gave the gentle licking, the simulation to my labia, the way she licked my entire genitalia, how she used the tip of her tongue. She employed slow movements, then fast moments, adjusted to my singsong moans, staying with the chords and riffs that were the strongest. Her tongue stiffened. Men shifted, cursed, more aroused by watching the Brit and me. They were more turned on by our lovemaking than by watching a man and woman. What was taboo excited both the brave and the poltroons. Abnormal desires were life changing.

I stopped stroking him and pulled at the Brit, controlled her, forced her to lie on her side, made her back into that robust lingam, held it and put it inside of her. She caterwauled and the room applauded. That was what they wanted to see, that big dick inside one of us. They wanted to see the absurd. She succumbed to the pressure of the assemblage, to the pressure from her own internal desires, and tried again. Quince Pulgadas didn't move, but she did, she rocked against him, took in only five inches, maybe six, then backed away and eased back into him, making it to about seven inches, tried again, took in a good nine inches before she patted the mattress in absolute surrender. With his girth, with his length, she was done; she was in pain, yet she wiggled like she felt so damn good, like she felt waves of electric tingles blending with a bottomless fire. He had enough left for me to touch, enough to fill me up, so as she moved against him, I held his power, his pride, and I masturbated him from his balls to where they were connected, did my best to enhance their sensations. The position was awkward, so I pushed her away, made Quince get on his back and she squatted over him, again only taking as much as she could handle. Rosetta came over and held her arms, held her so she wouldn't fall and impale herself. The Brit moved up and down, barely taking more than the tip, and as she did, as I had been doing before, I masturbated him, used both hands and massaged up and down his length, the angle perfect for me to stroke him the best that I could. Soon the Brit had had enough, had come again, and she fell away from Quince, crawled back to me, parted my legs with her hands, licked me, sucked me. I reached for Quince Pulgadas again, felt his slickness, felt her juices, and with both hands I masturbated him very fast. Rosetta touched his face, whispered nasty things to him, excited him with the sound of her demure voice and the mental images that came from her provocative words. He pulled at her legs and she didn't resist, she eased up and sat on his face. The Brit ate me and as I masturbated Quince, he ate Rosetta. But not for long. Rosetta stood up, aroused, but struggling to control her fire.

She trembled and stepped back into the crowd. She left me on my own. I looked up and saw me. I saw my face on the screens. I witnessed this scene, watched in awe. I stopped masturbating Quince Pulgadas when my own orgasm demanded my full attention. Leg shaking, I gripped my lover's head, held her head the same way that she had held her lover's head minutes ago, held her and rolled my hips into her face as I fell into habit and once again bit my bottom lip. Quince Pulgadas was now holding his lingam, stroking himself, eyes glazed over, watching us. We smiled at each other. His arousal grinned at mine. He imagined being inside me. The wickedness he saw turned him on more than the blow job he had been receiving.

Quince Pulgadas cursed and inhaled and exhaled with such power that my body absorbed his energy. Electricity was alive in my body. I tingled head to toe and my yoni jumped and cried, sent my eyes back to him. He made the ugliest face. She moved away from me. That aristocratic bitch left me throbbing, abandoned me with my legs shaking, left me with the edges of my voluminous orgasm holding me down, left my yoni screaming for the return of her tongue, and she rushed back to him. She betrayed me, left yoni for lingam, took him inside of her mouth, took as much of his big dick as she could while she stroked him with both hands. His lingam made her dainty hands look like the hands of a child. So many eyes were on me, so many watched me squirm in my misery, my sex open and tender, like a flower bloomed. Eyes. Everywhere I saw eyes. Blue eyes. Light brown eyes. Gray eyes. Dark brown eyes. Sea-green eyes were there too. They had been there the entire session, only I didn't see them, couldn't see him in the wealth of the crowd. Everything was a blur. Underneath this lighting, eyes became shining stars. In the dimly lit room I heard faint house music, but all I saw was a constellation of lust-filled eyes. And the prettiest and most hypnotic pair of eyes stood over me.

The handsome man from Curaçao watched me. He held hands with a gorgeous woman, tall like a model, at least six feet of woman wearing skyscraper heels, black bondage platform sandals that made her taller than the handsome man. She was the hue of eroticism and elegance. Her Afro was as large as it was stunning. I reached for her husband. I reached for him in the desperate and demanding way the Brit had reached for me. Energy magnified the experience in the way of a drug called ecstasy. I understood her frustration, understood how deep she was in her pleasure. I understood how absolute arousal had made anything possible. As eyes looked down on my misery, as my energy radiated, I reached. He looked at the woman at his side, at his wife, sought permission, and she let his hand go, encouraged him toward me.

TWELVE

He dropped his black towel and revealed his nakedness. The room stared as he came toward me. His lingam swayed, had swagger, and was so full, so enthusiastic to become wooden, so alive and eager. Applause accentuated the moment. Suddenly I became a poltroon. The light side of Gemini was afraid. Not of him, but frightened of my powerful itch. The room applauded. With my chest rising and falling, my sexual distress pronounced, my eyes went to his wife. She was a blurred vision, yet in my covetousness I tried to read her. I wondered if she would rebuke me, reel in her husband, refuse me what my body needed, become outraged and spit in my face. When he was so close that his energy added its fire to mine, his desire to mine, I no longer cared.

He took to his knees, crawled toward me, pulled my shoes away and kissed my feet with warm lips. He took five of my toes inside his mouth. Bosh sounds escaped me. I had forgotten how sensual, how good it felt to have my toes sucked. So many nerve endings resided at the end of the foot, nerve endings that sent erotic signals directly to my brain. He sucked my toes, licked my foot as if it were a clitoris, and then sucked each toe as if it were a tiny lingam. My body danced.

He released my foot, licked my shins, moved his tongue across my thighs. I saw shooting stars. The texture of his tongue grazed my sex, painted my sex. I couldn't breathe. He kissed my belly. Mouth opened, I panted, gazed down at him. Licked my lips and stared down at his smile. His expression told me that he would be kind with my body, wouldn't abuse it, would praise my body as it deserved to be praised. I nodded for him to go on. The world felt wonderful. He licked between breasts that felt heavy and full, put his warm lips on breasts that were swollen. My hands touched his soft, curly hair, grateful to have chosen an experienced, patient, unabashed lover to cross these waters that separated voyeurism from exhibitionism with. The crowd no longer mattered. We all had the same religion. We were an audience, all of the same mind-set, of the same surreptitious society. I pulled his hair, encouraged him toward me. His breathing was thick and we stared. So beautiful. So fucking beautiful. I broke my gaze and without a kiss I pulled his weight on top of me, pulled him to the slick shores, pulled him onto the exuberant, fierce place where my legs intersected.

I hated being out of control, yet I never felt more alive, never felt freer than when I achieved this level of madness. My hand reached for his lingam, rubbed him across the lips of my yoni, slid him inside. I inhaled sharply when my lips spread. We merged. He was inside me. I had become his cocoon. He filled me. My insides molded to his shape. The mushroom of his lingam spread me wide. My mouth became an O and I admitted defeat, tried to swallow my sounds, but I surrendered many moans, ashamed because I didn't want him to know how good I felt. My back arched and I sighed when he slipped beyond my lips, spread me, widened me, and crept inside of me. Once inch. Two. Three. Four. He was polite and paused. Looked into my eyes. His expression assured me that he was here with me. Breathing ragged, leg quivering, I nodded. He slid. Again he paused. He took a deep breath, regarded his wife for a moment, then his eyes returned to mine, and he slid.

My right leg wouldn't stop trembling. Orgasm tapped at the door.

He moved slow and steady, slow and steady, slow and steady.

He managed to whisper, "You feel amazing."

I couldn't talk. My response was a primitive grunt.

We had become a two-headed beast. He pulled back out to the mushroom and entered me again, gave it to me hard, moved inside of me until his hard belly touched mine, stroked me, stoked this madness and stroked me until my body caught fire. He matched my rhythm, rode my rugged waves, was almost capsized by my rise and fall, but he held on, found his balance and gave me the dance and rhythm of Curaçao.

There was more to him. He grew, hardened inside me.

My insides purred, stretched to accommodate, and again my lover put his tongue on my left breast, sucked my nipple. I absorbed the warmth from his well-built body. His skin spanked my skin. He moved in and out of my grotto. As I nibbled his shoulder and dug my short nails into the skin of his strong back, I experienced the shakes and trembles and loss of control that was the prelude to being overwhelmed by paradise. He had the weight and skills that it took to handle me.

Some members eased down on their haunches. I was being evaluated. Commented on as I had commented on others. That was surprising and terrifying all at once. But more than anything, I found it very arousing.

Yes, this is how I make love.

This was the animal within.

Watchers again lined the walls like apprentices of love. A handsome man fucked me without shame, fucked me as if he owned this yoni, as if the wedding ring that he wore was inspired by his love and devotion to me. I came and before I could calm down, I lost control and immediately I spiraled into the mouth of another nirvana again. Orgasm would not let me go and I refused to set him free. It hurt so good. I was imprisoned, but he was my captive. Again I was almost there. I never left from feeling like I was almost there. I wanted more. Needed more. But I didn't move because I was afraid of losing the sensation.

He took me missionary, the position that gave the man the most control, only I had him as much as he had me, my legs wrapped tight and anchored around his ankles. Then he had me close my legs tighter, and with him inside me, he rode me that way, rode me with his hard lingam rushing directly on my button. He opened my legs again, took one ankle over his shoulder and fucked me. I was gone. He had me pinned down. Couldn't move with him. He had my leg pushed so far back he was able to suck my nipples. He took both ankles and placed them around his neck. That position was dangerous. That angle always made me come, and my yoni didn't care if I was with man or vibrator.

Panting, dizzy, I managed to whisper, "Are you okay?"

"Oooo it just feels sooo fucking gooood."

He found his control, pushed deep, held it there for a moment, then started over again, took it from the top and slowly worked his way back to the pace of sweet violence. I pulled him into me over and over. I grunted as he grunted, and moaned as he moaned. I wanted it harder. Deeper. Faster. I grabbed the back of his dank neck like I was angry with him. I cursed. He gave. He gave. He gave. Each time I received and like a boomerang I rolled and threw it right back at him.

I opened my eyes, looked through my sexual haze and saw his forgotten love. She licked her lips, folded her arms over her breasts, held her thighs tight and rocked and shuddered like she felt each stroke.

I had forgotten about the others.

Until he set free a bear-like grunt, I had forgotten.

Quince Pulgadas tightened his buttocks, tensed his sphincter, began to surrender to momentary madness, and revealed his weakness, his vulnerability, the growls and grunts from his voluminous pleasure resounding from wall to wall. He sped up, pumped, fucked the aristocratic Brit's face as if her mouth was the orifice he craved.

As my lover moved in and out of me, and he rolled his hips, what I saw as he gave me pleasure excited me that much more.

Quince Pulgadas became a lion, roared so loud his anguish could be heard a mile away. Women cheered the Brit on and applauded. They loved a lover who was vocal, not a man who orgasmed silently. The Brit struggled to keep up with him, to not let the snake slip from her mouth, a mouth that was stretched so damn wide. He was coming. He cursed and announced that he was coming and all eyes went to them. My lover didn't stop moving, maintained a pleasing rhythm, but he looked to them as well. The Brit consumed copious amounts of orgasm as if she were imbibing on the sweetest of the sweetest of alcohol. Eyes closed tight, Quince Pulgadas jerked and thrust and her eyes widened like she was surprised by the amount of love and lust that spewed from his engorged erection. She stayed with him, sucked and swallowed and consumed him. Her nostrils flared as she looked at him, as she monitored him, as she struggled, as she consumed him like she was feeding on his energy, absorbing his strength, his power. Too bad angels only received their wings when a woman came. It was too fucking bad. The room applauded like thunder. The members were alive with interminable, unsurpassable energy, as if we were all at a Roman colossus. We were all connected on an unseen level.

The Brit smiled, opened her mouth so the room could see that her viscid smoothie had been ingested. A bleb of orgasm as thick as callaloo remained on her face, but she wiped her chin and swallowed that smidgen of zinc, fructose, potassium, and free amino acids as well. She savored his semen as if it were honey. The libertines clapped, the women praising the loudest. They approved of her valorous act.

Many touched her. Hugged her. Kissed her cheeks. Some shook Quince's hand. The behavior of the group was always more daring than the individual. The social status here, the interaction between the members of this collective, the companionship, the encouragement, it was beautiful.

Then my lover resumed stroking me, wanted my eyes back on him. I complied. I heard our shared wetness. I reveled in his strength and manhood. I was in a state so intense that I was beyond reason and self-control. Emotional, rapturous delight had pulled me into a trance, into the warmth of an electrical happiness. And as he lived inside of my sweetest orifice, as he gave me his enthusiasm, as he became frenzied, he was exultant. The dark side of Gemini sheltered and controlled me.

Then as my moans rose and pervaded the room, the building, the world, his wife's eyes remained with mine. She leaned forward. Her body language told me that she was waiting on her invitation to come and feel as beautiful as I felt. She needed what I was receiving. She was waiting for the applause that would bring her into this arena. I was supposed to share this as she had shared this man with me.

But as tears of pleasure clouded my vision, I closed my eyes and drowned in my sensations. No woman's husband, no man should be able to make me feel that fucking good, no one man, not alone.

My orgasm diminished, but *orgasmus* didn't extinguish because a new orgasm started as soon as that one ended. He lost himself inside of me and grunted. I sang. He convulsed. Gave me more power. I sang louder. My lover gave me what belonged to his wife, felt his girth expand, felt his lingam elongate, felt his desperate strokes, felt each ingress try to reach beyond my womb to my heart, but I sang and put my nails in his side, made him not go so deep, his stroke delicious as the crowd watched, as the British woman watched in astonishment, as the Indian woman watched in admiration, as Rosetta watched in awe. His stunning wife watched him lose control, watched him as he went insane inside of another woman. And as he went insane, so did I.

His legs tensed, his arm tensed, his buttock tensed, and I felt his power, was given his energy as he strained to empty himself. His handsome face became ugly. It looked like he was about to drool. He had traveled beyond the point of no return, and with hard, primal grunts he surrendered. He spiraled over the edge. My lover grunted again as he strained, as he clenched his buttocks, as he thrust, as I tensed and made my yoni grip him tighter, as he gave me beautiful aggression and made me start to scream and come again, as I held him and danced my dance, as he became more passionate than any man I had ever experienced, as he started to jerk and come in squirts. I felt him continue growing inside of me, felt him become harder, felt him giving me all of his power, all of his marital energy.

THIRTEEN

And in response I grinded against him; grinded hard enough to reduce him to fine powder.

He held on to me like he wanted to spend the rest of his life inside of my body. In time he slowed. Beads of sweat on his flesh. Beads of sweat on mine. Our skin sticking together. His sexual diatribe, his sexual discourse arrived at its conclusion. It seemed like it took minutes for him to come, to shove and exhaust inside of me, but it was only seconds. His orgasm, the way he had swollen and thrust inside of me, his dominance, the way he had given me his energy triggered another orgasm inside me. When he was coming, when he had become mean, powerful, and tempestuous I had had an apoplectic orgasm. I ascended, trembled. Shook violently. Driblets of sweat fell down my neck as I rode contractions, as I climbed, as I soared. Held him tight. Wanted more. *More*. My body wanted him to keep going until the end of time.

Sweat draining down my neck, orgasm diminishing, I looked first at the Watchers, then at his lady in waiting. She was anxious, uneasy, as if all of a sudden the skies were dark and the rain was in her face.

I had displayed a personal moment, a private moment, a moment when I was the most vulnerable. Suddenly, despite the tingles and warmth that covered my body, despite the adrenaline high, despite the endorphins, I was uneasy as well. Fear rose. There was no need to be ashamed of my body as I had been taught in America, no need to be ashamed of sex as I had been brainwashed by culture; there was no reason to be afraid behind these walls. I had paid handsomely to be able to enjoy this type of freedom. Yet the battle remained. As reality cooled my skin, calmed my senses, I felt self-conscious, I felt guilt, I felt shame. I expected finger-pointing, maybe even laughter, or snickering. Intellectually, I attempted to process this moment, but it was impossible to do while I existed in this moment, while my energy was part of the energy of the group, while I was in a den of modified social behavior.

Again there was the echo that came from applause, this time in honor of a stranger and me. So many eyes were on me. Men and women wished that I had chosen them for that journey.

Winded, I touched the side of my exotic lover's dank face. He had worked hard, pleased me in a wicked way, his sex as powerful, as moving as the letters that Henry Miller wrote to Anaïs Nin, and my body wanted more of him, wanted to allow body and spirits to reconnect, and I couldn't move my eyes from his. He sweated as if he were in the full sun, in the high temperature and humid air of my personal rain forest. He glowed. My dankness, the heat that covered my flesh told me that I had visited his jungle as well. The warmth of my overworked body, my dampness, told me that I radiated satisfaction.

I panted, swallowed, caught my breath and said, "Thanks."

"I can do more. Won't take me a minute to get hard again."

I moved my hand from him, moved my hair from my face. "No, that was all I needed. Always save the last nut for the wife."

The Watchers gazed at us, but most grinned and moved on, went to see others, hurried away in search of more entertainment, more orgasms. We had come. Our credits had rolled. The show was over. All were happy. I had crossed another line. Had redefined myself.

My lover was amazed, smitten, enamored. My flesh smoldered, smelled of his flesh, his of mine, his lingam of my yoni, and he was sprung. Years ago I would've mistaken that physical, that spiritual release for true love. I craved the attention of a man. I craved raunchiness to rise and satisfy my carnal desires. I pushed away from men and yet I craved the affection that came from a man. I craved sex. I craved love. Neither craving would ever die. But now I wanted that attention, that praising, that lust, when I could be in control. When I didn't lose me. If a woman lost herself, then she was nothing more than a log in a man's river, owned by his currents. The man before me was smitten and already destined to try to smother me. I gave him the smile of a respectable writer, a smile that told him I was glad that he was married, and I respected that, as should he. My smile told him not to judge me by sex, because judging me by carnal knowledge would only leave him swimming in the cesspool of ignorance. This bold moment was not the sum of my existence, only a paragraph, maybe an incomplete sentence in my life thus far. Don't judge me by my weaknesses, not when your weaknesses are the same; don't label me by my desires, as most hypocritical men would judge and label women.

I looked up at the tall woman with the Afro. I saw his wife. She made me feel nervous. For a moment she looked upset. Her man had enjoyed a fantasy moment a little too much. She had wanted him to have fun, but not like that. Her eyes held her insecurity. Her man had entered me and made her feel less than invisible. She hadn't been included. She hadn't been in control. Still, I should have invited her.

I looked at the beautiful woman. Her man. Me. Her. We were close enough to start a war. My smile told her that I didn't want her man beyond this fantasy. I was done with him. The affair had ended.

I said, "Thanks for the ride. You helped me arrive at my destination. Exit to the left."

I said that with kindness, not as if I were giving him the cold shoulder, not as if he had been my female dog. At that moment, the other side of Gemini that lived inside me, the light side, could've held him a million years, but the dark side patted him on his head as if he were a child on an adventure in my playground. Underneath nervous eyes, as I released him sans embrace, his wife's smile broadened.

The Brit and her lover applauded the longest, then waved and walked away, hand in hand. She could barely walk. She looked drained. Her yoni was swollen, tender, each step echoing the pain. The married aristocrat and her pilot from British Airways held on to each other, he too a stranger in a strange land. He took steps as if he were tipsy. He had been drained. The snake had been pleased for the moment.

He would travel back across the pond with a wonderful story about a nameless brown-skinned woman. No, about two beautiful women, me and Rosetta. Plus the Brit. Three women. His tale would sound like the ultimate fish story. My lover rose and staggered, light-headed, and the crowd laughed a little, made jokes about not being able to control me. When he found his bearings, he reached down and helped me to mine.

Again I looked at the Indian girl. Looked at her well-managed anger and disappointment. Her lover had left her in need. She should've made him suck his worthless come back out of her temple.

I retrieved my heels, slipped my colorful Burberrys back on, and hoped that passion hadn't damaged the shoes or the beautiful beads. I wrapped a towel back around my body, hand combed my hair and with a kind smile and pat on his ass, I took my nameless lover's hand and took him to his nameless woman, told my unexpected lover, told my zipless fuck to enjoy the rest of the evening with his wife.

He wanted a discourse after intercourse, but that was not the course that I desired. His wife stared at me in amazement, her jealousy heating her beautiful skin, this infidelity seared into her brain after she had watched her husband plummet into an abyss of pleasure. During our affair, she'd disappeared from his life. But she stared like she understood. Something about me, my moment of boldness, how I had been in that heated instant, astounded her. She was changed. Or maybe it was he. Something had happened between them, in their marriage, that led them here. Unhappiness in the outside world always drew people toward a metaphorical Disneyland. All that mattered was that, through my eyes, as I interpreted her reactions, she understood me. Not all would. Not everyone would try. Just the generous and unselfish ones like her. Or stupid like her. Some would not see her in that warm, colorful light. Some might think that I was as foolish as she. I chose to see her as being benevolent. Myself as being audacious. Only a few understood humanness, the need to fulfill curiosities without the desire to own or give harm, to be selfish with self and generous with love and never possess the lover, the ache to learn and give without being bought or imprisoned by the rules of others.

I kissed her cheek, whispered, "Thank you. Sharing him, allowing him to take me away from the agony that I was feeling, that was very kind of you to help me in that way. I'm forever indebted to you."

It only took a few words to disarm someone. Only took a few words to soften a heart. Women didn't always know what to do when another woman showed them an unexpected kindness, especially when they were still trying to define which box to put that woman in. The box of competition. The box of foe. The box of friend. The box that said the other woman meant nothing.

She touched my tousled hair, used her fingers to comb my mane, did that with a caring gesture, one of concern, as if she were making me presentable to the world. She winked at me. Then she ran her hand down the side of my face. Her soft gestures broke the fourth wall and humanized us, womanized us. We were sisters in solidarity, if but just for a moment, united in ensuring the satisfaction of a comrade. She gave me a tender hug, and when she released me I touched her amazing Afro, put my fingers into soft cotton and told her how beautiful she looked, told her how I admired the strength in her hair, that moment making me just as personal with her as I had been with her husband.

She too had met me out of context.

I needed her to know that there was more to me than this.

She smiled at her husband. "You were amazing."

Exhausted, he said, "Lucky me. I have the best wife in the world."

"I've never seen him that spirited. He gave it to you good."

I nodded. "I'm sure that he gives it to you much, much better."

He chimed in, "My wife is an amazing lover. Best in the world. Especially during a threesome."

She smiled. "Now who has the wickedest wife in the world?"

He kissed her. The taste of my skin, of my flesh, of my sweat had permeated his tongue and he kissed her, shared remnants of me with her. When he finished, she kissed him, her smile still fractured.

Tongues danced while I watched. It was very romantic, like it was a night for the renewal of marriage vows.

She was sexually stimulated, heated to the point that she couldn't be still, kept crossing her legs tightly and clenching the muscles in her long legs, creating pressure on her clit, trying to calm her yoni.

She asked me, "Are you done for the night . . . or . . . ?"

"I'm exhausted, sweaty, satisfied. It didn't last as long as the war between Zanzibar and England, but like Zanzibar I surrender by waving the white flag. That was very intense, more than enough."

She said, "Hopefully we will see you again."

I nodded. *We*. The woman with the beautiful Afro and skin gave me undeniable eye contact and said *we*. Then she stood close to me and rubbed her hand over my flat and firm stomach, my swollen breasts, then moved her hand south, eased between my thighs and touched my damp yoni with her fingertips. Two fingers touched me, massaged where I was swollen, where I was the most sensitive.

I asked, "Are you a regular here, or only on occasion?"

"My husband started this. He loves to put me on a mattress and get me hot and bothered and show me off to the crowd. I'm not dumb. Other women see how he fucks me and want to experience the same."

"But do you like it?"

"I was a prude. Now I am open to many experiences."

She licked her fingers and tasted our permitted sin. As the woman behind her moaned and rode her companion, my lover's wife's pupils dilated. She rocked, licked her lips again and again, inhaled, her nose flared when she exhaled, and then she smiled. I brushed my wild hair from my eyes and smiled a fatigued, intoxicated smile in return.

I said, "You're in a serious mood."

"He fucked you well. That has left me very, very jealous."

"I feel the heat coming from your body."

She smiled. "You have made me yearn to know you better."

"I'm flattered."

"I would love for a woman as remarkable as you to be responsible for my climax."

Her husband stood behind her. He held her. She stood forever tall in her sky-high bondage heels, those skyscraper heels making a statement, as all shoes made a statement. He touched her breasts, breasts that were a wonderful, natural C-cup, but looked small on her height. He nuzzled her, licked her, and sucked her ear. Her eyes stayed on mine. As her husband playfully bit her, and he kissed her simmering flesh, she lifted her chin, leaned her head backward, exposed her long neck and shoulder blades, studied me as he molested her, invited me to join him as he molested her, and her eyes said that right here, right now I didn't need to shower away the scent of her husband, that three could have much more fun than two.

She asked, "How are you with a woman?"

"Inexperienced, for the most part."

"As energetic as you are?"

"Certain things are new to me and require practice."

"A class on orally mastering the vagina starts in about twenty minutes. You could shower, or we could shower. I could join you."

"Not tonight. I'm leaving soon. Long drive home."

"You're a hot little Mandinga. You reek of sex and sensuality."

I smiled in return. "Mandinga. I take that as a compliment."

Again I leaned to her, kissed her cheek, but she held my face, touched my face, stroked my hair, moved it from my eyes, then leaned in and she gave me her tongue. I gave her mine as a sweet solatium, something to give her in compensation for her inconvenience, for loss, for my stealing her husband's orgasm. She tasted remarkably sweet, like a combination of wintergreen, vanilla, and cassia. That tender kiss made me purr. Made my flower want to open and bloom once again.

With regret I said, "Would love to be your next. Just not right now. All of this is new to me. I came in as a Watcher, and all of a sudden I have changed status."

"Maybe I'll leave my information at the front desk."

"That would be nice. This is my first time here and I will definitely be back to play."

"Tell me your locker number."

"My locker number?"

"The locker number that you've been assigned is tied to your finger scan for the night. It's your identifier, of sorts. In case you didn't know, your locker number will be different each time you come. Some people here prefer to remain anonymous. We do, for now."

"That's good to know."

"They don't use the names or membership IDs here. Many prefer to remain anonymous. And I respect that. I'll give them our information to pass on to you at the end of the night. I hope to hear from you."

"I'll call you."

"But here's the rule. You've had my husband. And you can have him again. After we've become better acquainted. It can be you and me, or he can be included. But I want you first. That is all that I ask."

"I'm indebted to you. I look forward to paying that debt."

I walked with them a few steps. Not far. I was being kind, trying not to dismiss her as I would an overenthusiastic man at a club. I kept looking back at the Indian girl. The Indian girl studied me as if I were a goddess, breasts swollen, her eyes remained dilated as well. I moved past a woman engaged in double penetration. My lover's wife looked at the couple, then winked at me, a notification of a sensual debt.

She said, "Good fucking."

I replied, "Great fucking."

They laughed. He kissed me on the cheek. I kissed his wife on the cheek. Then she took her husband's hand and headed toward the other side of Decadence. His erection was still strong enough to please her, to help erase her heat. Our surreal and out-of-control moment had come and gone. Yet I felt him inside of me. He looked back at least twice. Each time he looked back, that sensation of love made my heart race, made my breathing curt. He was Caribbean. Caribbean recognized Caribbean. We felt the connection. It was in our blood.

Women who were near me touched me, told me how beautiful that was, complimented me on the way I moved my body, told me that they wanted to see me on top so they could study my gyrations. A woman slapped me on my ass as if I had scored the winning touchdown for our team. The German woman, the one with blond hair that was short and sassy and standing like spikes, she walked her golden seven-inch heels toward me, smiling. She and her international crew came and touched my dank back, touched my tousled hair. I had crossed the burning sands and was being welcomed into the Sisterhood of Doers. Then, as my body still felt electric tingles, smiling and confident women surrounded me. I wasn't their leader, but I was one of them. Part of me couldn't believe what I had just done and was ready to flee this building.

The Indian couple remained on the mattress, the man now watching others, self-absorbed now as he had been from the moment he brought his lover into this forum. Now he was all but invisible, all but in the way of the Doers. Despite the sexual congresses, the ongoing carnal knowledge around me, I looked at the Indian woman, concerned. Her lover watched others, but did nothing to give her satisfaction. He had emptied himself and turned away, as a dog does from a bitch. A moment later her lover stood and helped her to her feet. She stumbled. She could barely stand. I imagined that she was weighted down by embarrassment. Her fire was still blazing, her body suffering from coitus interruptus. In heels she was four inches taller than he was. Her body curvy, yet small, almost childlike. He was a tall, thin man. She was delicate. They stood holding hands. He kept her close to him.

She was a fetching woman, who scowled at her mate as if he were her nemesis, then gazed at me, adjusted her body language, and yielded a much softer, very respectful and evocative expression.

She said, "Your moment was truly enviable. Your companion, outstanding. You sexed well together. He has a gift and so do you."

"Too bad your session didn't last longer, at least as long as my session, with the same results."

She read my body language. My disappointment wasn't concealed.

She said, "Please. Speak your mind."

"You're gorgeous. Powerful. We accept the love that we think we deserve. You shouldn't calibrate your desires to the limitations of anyone else. Live the best life that you can live. Always."

My eyes told her that she deserved better. Again her expression changed, as she was very expressive, and her unspoken language told me that she was grieving for something that she had never had, and that something, again, was more than lingam inside of yoni. My eyes told her to engage in succession from unhappiness. I had been miserable before. She paused, looked like she wanted to confess something.

Instead she nodded. Then she hugged me with one arm. She hugged me tight, breast to breast, her skin connecting with mine, flesh sticking because of our dankness, and she kissed my cheek before she let me go. Now I smelled of her. Her sweat, her perfume, her essence was now a part of me. I smelled of her lover as well. His sweat and cologne had permeated her skin. And now due to transference his aroma had stained mine.

She repeated, "I'm beautiful. Entitled to the love that I deserve."

"And you should define what that means to you. Let no man define your needs. A man should accept you as you are, or watch you as you go on to a better and more satisfying life."

No longer watching others make love, with impatience her lover tugged at her small hand. The Indian woman clenched her teeth, made defiant veins rise in her neck, and resisted. Her attention had shifted to another session. Two men were taking a woman. Her lovers had her suspended. One took her from behind, had his hands on her hips, as another lover stood in front of her holding her by her biceps and triceps. The Indian girl looked at the woman being fucked. Her eyes said that magnificent sex was what she craved. Her lover pulled her hand again. She resisted. People noticed. He was angered. Tension rose. Again, eyes colored with envy, the Indian woman gazed at the orgasmic woman living in pure euphoria, in a heat that rose like her soft moans, existing in a high better than any drug, watched the beauty of what she saw and heard, saw how the muscles were being worked, flexing, releasing, the agility, maybe love addicts sharing severe pleasure, a race in which whoever finished last was the champion of this sport. Her lover, he blinked a thousand times, looked shocked, humiliated, overwhelmed. Because he knew that once her desires crossed the line, and abnormal desires became her norm, then there would be nothing that could satisfy her, definitely not him, and definitely not for long. Her lover pulled her hand, spoke to her in their native tongue, and this time she followed, the submissive wife. They moved through the crowd. They disappeared among the people, inside of the many moans.

Rosetta stared at me, her cerulean eyes wide as she whispered, "Cowabunga. That shit was hot. Especially when she was sucking him while you were jacking him off at the same time."

"Yeah. Cowabunga. Wait. Did we do that? Jesus. I was in a zone."

"Big-dicked bastard made me come so hard it scared me."

"Really?"

"Yes. In under a minute. So I really had to get away from him."

"Damn."

Rosetta said, "The Indian woman got the short end of the stick."

"And she got the short stick too. I think I'm suffering from some sort of orgasmic guilt. I felt so good and she was robbed."

"Dude with the woman in red shoes, my lord. Never have I seen a penis like that. It was perfect."

"Quince Pulgadas. His nickname means 'fifteen inches.'"

"The dong was long, but it wasn't a foot long plus three. Maybe if you add girth to the length."

"I bet if all of that was inside of you, it would feel like two feet."

"It would go in my pussy and come out of my mouth."

"Yoni. If you're going to hang with me you have to call your temple your yoni."

"Temple? Yoni? Well, excuse me, Gandhi."

I said, "Hope that I didn't make a fool of myself."

"You looked so nervous then . . . like a little innocent girl . . . then you . . . damn . . . you rocked it. His wife used to be an Olympic swimmer. And you took her husband. It was so incredibly passionate."

"She was in the Olympics?"

"Just a bronze medal. No one ever remembers who came in third. Latecomers thought that the random guy was your husband."

"His profligacy . . . my own profligacy . . . my solecism . . ."

"You and your vocabulary. *Profligacy.* 'Reckless extravagance.' And *solecism.* 'Breach of etiquette.' I bet you know twenty-thousand words in English that don't sound like they are in English."

"I'm a word slut. Book slut too. A movie and theater slut as well."

"Most of us are just plain old sluts in high heels and makeup."

I said, "I really need to head to the showers and go freshen up."

"Offer you a glass of wine after you get cleaned up?"

"Wine? You are really trying to be my new best friend."

"My husband and I always leave a bottle of Domaine de la Romanée at the bar. French red Burgundy."

"I want to watch you get laid. I want to see sexy Rosetta in action. I want to see you on your back with your yoni filled with lingam."

"Told you. You missed me earlier. I had fun and showered and came back out to watch. Quince licked me good. Damn. Now I need to go shower again. I'll bet my husband saw me on the monitor."

"Uh-oh."

"That's what we're here for. He's a cool guy. Love him to death."

We eased by the erotic archipelagos that offered more than sixty-nine styles of physical gratification. Rosetta yanked my towel away from my flesh again, my skin scented by nameless lovers. She walked in front of me as fast as she could, hips moving side to side, twirling our pink and red towels. Naked and in high heels, as this microcosm that I inhabited moved from being incomprehensible to prehensile, as fantasy became reality, I laughed and held my exposed breasts and chased her toward the bar, imagined so many eyes on me, as my eyes had been on their bareness and sex. I felt liberated. I had stepped outside of myself. I had done wrong and what was wrong had felt like the breaking of chains. It was invigorating. But that victorious feeling was short-lived.

My past.

I saw him and my mouth fell open as my jovial pace came to an abrupt halt. His orphic sea-green eyes assaulted me and I changed from being confident to demure. Blind optimism abandoned me and it felt as if the floor were about to fall from under me. He had escaped the tattered box in the closet in my townhome and followed me here.

I cringed.

I had come to a halt in a crowded area. Some had seen me perform. Now that I had stopped my playful run, some were still trying to chat and befriend me. I was an instant celebrity. And as I stood in a herd of nude strangers, again my past announced my name, said my name, a name that I didn't want to share with this world. This compartment could never mix with the life I lived beyond these walls.

Chris Eidos Alleyne was here. The man who had been legendary on campus. The man who had been mythical. The man who had been a phoenix. Double take. Triple take. Blinked. Blinked again. As haunting music played, as sexual videos surrounded us, as couples near us exchanged soft sex and hard sex and a violent BDSM *Fifty Shades of Grey* inspired sexual fantasies for a crowd of curious beings, my smile collapsed. The lover that had abandoned me had had dreadlocks that hung like a cape. No more. Even with his magnificent mane gone, I knew his eyes. A powerful leopard with eyes of that hue was unforgettable. The color of his eyes made him unique, the tint made it almost impossible for women to look away without being affected by what stirred inside of him. I knew his circumcised lingam. Remembered how it curved to the left and upward. Knew that he suffered from cryptorchidism; his left testicle hung lower than the right. The right one had never descended properly. Intimate memories rushed at me, same as when I had opened the box filled with memories of him. He used to enter my sacred place and cause hallelujahs to rise inside of my body. I saw his face and was reminded of deep-seated nightmares that I wanted to forget. Memories latched on to a feral horse and dragged me back in time.

Then, like an idiot, my mouth creaked open and I said, "Chris?"

He nodded as if to confirm that it was indeed him.

Again I said, "Chris."

Again he nodded.

I was frozen. As if Jesus had caught me shoplifting.

In a kind voice he asked, "How have you been?"

Without another word, I lowered my head as my hands became fists and I bumped into his rock-hard frame and moved by *him*, made my way by my admirers, moved by the talkative women and their words and smiles of praise, moved by men who applauded me like I had achieved some coveted status in this clandestine arena. My heels clacked across marble, then lost that powerful sound on the plush carpet. While dozens of women cheered, I seethed with rage and hurried past them at pace with the throbbing music. Jarred. My blood pressure dropped. I became weak, nauseous, and instantly my sweating increased as anxiety accosted me along with agitation and confusion.

Rosetta held my forearm. "Are you okay?"

"Fuck."

"Nia?"

"That was my ex."

"What? That was your ex-husband?"

"An ex-boyfriend. He's an ex of mine from college."

"He was in the crowd when you performed."

"That bastard stood in the crowd and *watched me*?"

"Better an ex than your parents. A girl had joined and she walked into Eros and the woman performing was her friggin' mother. The girl was twenty-one and her mother was thirty-nine. Watching your mother in the middle of triple penetration, that was what I would call traumatized. Well, at least one of the guys was her stepdad. He looked over and saw his stepdaughter naked and in super-high heels. So compared to that traumatizing event, running into an ex, don't sweat it."

"*How have you been?* How the *fuck* do you think I've been?"

"Calm down, sweetie."

"He watched me. Are you sure that he watched me?"

"He walked in the room right after you did."

"He followed me?"

"Seems to be that way. His eyes were on you the whole time."

My orgasmic mood had been short-lived and now fear rode my nerves. Happiness abated and now I was terrified. My mother. Imagined her finding out. I massaged my temples, took a deep breath, and picked up my pace. Only now it felt as if I were fleeing through the moans and sex of the huddled masses. Rosetta did the same. There were more than three-hundred-thousand inhabited places in the world, close to two hundred recognized countries in the world, almost twenty-five-thousand miles around the world, seven continents and more than two million islands existed on this third rock from the sun, and he was here.

I had been blindsided and I was angry at my reaction to him.

Being where what society deemed as bad behavior was seen as being natural, if not an entitlement, then running into someone that I knew had left me in shock. Seeing Chris Eidos Alleyne appear out of nowhere had all but paralyzed me. For a moment I regressed, was no longer an adult, no longer a liberated woman, but I was a young girl, the daughter of my mother. I felt my mother's gigantic shadow. I panicked. But my mother was in Los Angeles and with the rising of her sun would be leaving for Amsterdam. Then I thought about everyone I knew, stared into the crowd and looked for other familiar faces. Which was ludicrous. My stepfather, I couldn't imagine him being here. He was under fifty but still too seasoned, even though the women whom he preferred, based on the trophy woman he left my mother for, would fit in seamlessly. Relatives from Trinidad wouldn't dare partake of a place this hedonistic. Now I was ill tempered and paranoid.

Before I made it deep inside the undressing area, to add insult to injury, I found myself staring into the bright eyes of a woman who wore a seven-carat marquis diamond ring, oval shaped, maybe like a football. Chris's wife. My former friend. He had married the woman he had betrayed me with. I had been her tutor and she had proven to me that there was no version of Hippocratic oath between women, that we didn't have a true sisterhood because we were unable to keep the promise to do to each other no harm; we didn't behave ethically and honestly. We were hunters. With smiles, charisma, cooked meals, uxorial behavior, and the pleasures of sex, we attained what we desired.

We were face-to-face, practically nose-to-nose, as we had been during our fights. My emotions boiled. She told me, "Good fucking," then kindly stepped around me, her breasts bouncing, her hips swaying like she was measuring time, her wedding ring sparkling as she kept going. She kept going as if I were nobody, as if I were nothing.

FOURTEEN

After I showered, I had taken a million deep breaths. Twenty minutes passed. Twenty minutes of disbelief. I wasn't angry, but I was not unangry. As I dried my skin, Rosetta came back to where I was. She was nude. Her makeup redone. The stylist had given her a quick and dirty hairstyle.

"Are you okay?"

"He watched me in Eros. He followed me and watched me."

"Are you leaving?"

"My ex . . . after the way we broke up . . . that's . . . humiliating."

Rosetta asked, "Was he your first?"

"He might as well have been."

"First true love."

"The one who fucked it up for everybody else."

"So he might as well have been."

I blinked as if I were coming out of a trance.

My eyes had been opened so long they had become oval deserts.

She said, "His wife?"

"We were friends. Me, her, and my college roommate were like the Three Musketeers. I tutored his wife, taught her how to cook."

"Your bestie robbed you of your first true love. Some deep shit."

"Yes, indeed. We had so many fights. Was almost kicked out of college."

"Sounds like it's not over. This can get ugly. Walk away."

"Not walking away. I walked away then. Not now. Not tonight."

I went to the women who assisted the members and paid to have my makeup redone, had them do an outstanding job, lotioned my body. Then, with Rosetta in tow, I went to revisit my past. We walked the compound, hunted for them, and then we saw them on the multiple screens. I wanted to know how he ended up at Decadence. But I knew the answer. The answer was where our truths intersected. Religious people of the same faith ended up at the same churches. Screenwriters ended up at seminars; salsa dancers at the same clubs. Swingers. It was its own world. The word would spread and libertines would end up at the same institutions for adult behavior. And a subset of that subculture, the ones who would pay for extreme privacy, ended up at Decadence.

My ex. His wife. They were being featured. They were being applauded, were starting. Just getting on an oval-shaped bed, one that rotated underneath dim lights. He was naked. His wife. Siobhán. The woman I had tutored. The woman who used to dress in ragged jeans, tennis shoes, and wore a flower in her hair. She was stunning. Nothing like she had been when she was at Hampton. I don't recall ever seeing her in high heels, not once. Had never seen her wear a nice watch.

Chris was a Doer.

He had always been a star, the BMOC, the man in the spotlight.

This was his arena.

I wanted to see his intimacy up closer.

I wanted to violate his space as he had violated mine.

I followed the crowd.

FIFTEEN

As carnal enthusiasts crowded into the smaller room and watched him, as his raging pheromones rose and stimulated practically every clitoris bearer in the room, as he too moved his hips and stirred his wife like a Caribbean man, I was right there. His dreadlocks were gone, his face now clean shaven. When I closed my eyes I recognized his every moan. With eyes opened I recognized, remembered his every move.

He was very handsome. She, gorgeous. Beauty attracted, as did skills. Everyone loved to see a beautiful woman with an oral fixation.

She massaged his lingam, this their sensual moment that started off as if it were a ceremony with her honoring his penis, not trying to arouse him, but praise him, recognize him as a man. She nurtured him. They were connected. Him inside of her mouth. They were one, amalgamated as lovers, as husband and wife. It was like watching his heart beat, then her heart beat in response. She massaged his testicles, then she sucked them, masturbated him. She changed, sucked him, massaged testicles. She licked down to his root, licked from his root to his hat.

He panted, "Yellow. Yellow. Yellow."

She slowed down and grinned. That meant that he was about to come, but had delayed it. She glowed. She was a crowd favorite.

Soon, in a calmer breath, he whispered, "Green."

While she sucked him, she did a handstand. He reached up and helped her balance herself. With her mouth filled with lingam she did a one-eighty, had started with her back to his face and with his help, turned until the front of her body faced his, and he eased her down, brought her sex down toward his face, and performed sixty-nine.

Women whispered, "Damn."

Men whispered, "Damn."

People bumped into me. Bumped Rosetta into me.

The room filled with couples, with men who loved to watch a beautiful woman suck cock, with women who loved to watch a Mandingo lick and suck on clit. Soon she mounted him. Then he turned her over. As my ex loved his wife, he watched me, found my eyes and stared at me, dared me. He fucked her and she sang an epithalamium and gave an angel its wings. My mouth was drier than Saudi Arabia. When I inhaled, his sex pheromones were strong, had been just as powerful in college. It was like smoking a joint, inhaling his scent had that effect, made women light-headed and hungry for his come.

In college, I used to sleep in one of his T-shirts, used to sleep inhaling his scents, pretending he was in my bed. Pheromones stimulated, made victims of us all, a trick of nature on the human species. I'd never lived in Trinidad full-time, but the Caribbean culture was in my blood and her men were my sin, my weakness, as if some lust or need for them had been preprogrammed into my soul. With eyes of jealousy, a heart of pain, and a wicked smile I inhaled the sweetness of his wife's elegant perfume. Her scent was soft, angelic, perfect, probably only detectable by my memories and me. I listened to the positive comments from the poltroons known as Watchers as I watched my past make love to his wife. It was truly a creative, romantic fuck session. I saw what she had done to move his heart from me to her in college. Passionate. Uninhibited. She was high on wine and maybe more. It was like being in his bridal suite on his honeymoon night.

Most of all, as memories resurrected, as old wounds opened, I saw how he had been with me. They moaned like Protestants. It was indeed like watching a religious experience. Dozens more congregated, more than had come to watch Quince and the Brit, or me and the Brit and Quince, or me and my lover from Curaçao. As my past made love to his wife, he took her through a gallery of positions, advanced positions, kinky positions that ignited the fires in others, some done sitting down, her diamonds sparkling, her heels looking amazing, her breathing deep and husky as they did positions that complemented each other, lustful positions, reverse cowgirl with her long shiny hair flowing to the floor, her riding him as I had ridden him when he had been mine, her sucking him as I had sucked him, massaging his lingam with her mouth, her breathing technique enviable, various versions of man on top, of woman on top, with her legs opened wide and spread into a split as his muscles flexed in dominance. She sat across him, their bodies in an X, and she took control. It was remarkable. Applause from the Watchers. My hands became dank fists. As they continued their give-and-take, as their pleasing harmony aroused many, my arms remained folded across my breasts. He pinned her ankles up behind her neck and stroked her. She sang. He pulled her into him over and over and over and over and over. He fucked her as he used to do me when we were in college.

Rosetta stared, shivered, trembled, mouth opened in amazement, hardly breathing. She watched him in his most sensual form, in his athletic prowess, nude and naked, saw the original alpha male in congress. Her nipples were strong. She rocked from foot to foot.

I said, "Rosetta."

"Yes?"

"Blink."

She took a deep breath, her eyes rapidly opening and closing, and broke free from her stupor. She had been mesmerized. Embarrassment tinted her skin as indecipherable emotions tinted mine.

She whispered, "Sorry. He's . . . he's . . ."

"I know."

Rosetta shuddered like she had the chills, as if electricity had been turned on inside of her body and in a jittery tone said, "You've seen enough. We should leave now. Let's go watch other couples."

"I'm not leaving. Not yet."

"Nia. You are standing here looking like you're about to explode and that is not good."

"I'm not ready to leave."

"Why not?"

"Because I want his wife to acknowledge me."

Siobhán witnessed my emotions; saw lack of praise, unhidden disgust, and her voyeuristic smile became uneasy. My eyes left her, settled on him. I smiled. I exposed him, spoke his full Christian name. That caught his wife off guard. Saying his name had had the shattering effect of a high explosive. Siobhán looked at me. She squinted. Leaned toward me. Squinted again. She asked me who I was. I didn't answer. She asked

Chris. No response. She asked again. She grabbed a red towel and covered herself. She felt uneasy. Now she was anxious.

I moved closer, squatted down next to her, close enough to speak at a normal tone so she could hear. I said, "We were friends; at least I thought that we were since we broke bread every time we met. Siobhán Kline, stop pretending that you don't know who the fuck I am."

She whispered, "Bijou? Oh. My. God. Bijou?"

"My favorite cheerleader. Still as flexible as a contortionist and, Siobhán, you can suck dick. Not much on moving that little ass, but you could suck the yellow off a banana. Kudos. Same to you, Chris."

She said, "Nia Simone Bijou. Oh. My. God."

Fear. Abrupt fear showed in her eyes. She felt threatened.

Smile on my face, I stood up. I stepped back into the crowd.

Rosetta and I turned and left.

In times of madness, a woman was always bolder with a friend.

Old feelings rose from six feet under and followed me, each as attractive as a corpse on *The Walking Dead*, each just as rancid. Soon I felt my legs. Soon I could breathe. It wasn't me who had lost it and had a fit. I existed outside of myself. The person that had done that suffered from PTSD and was a person of diminished capacity, a ticking time bomb that had taken years to detonate. I had seen him, watched him, and relapsed. He was the origin of who I was today. If only bad memories could be created on an Etch A Sketch and when they were too much to bear, shake, erase, and start with a clean slate.

After that explosive moment, once we were on the other side of the compound, I had shaken it off. Every nerve ending came alive. My arms and legs shook, teeth clattered like I was nude at the South Pole.

Rosetta said things, but I was unable to hear a single word.

I returned to flirting, to making friends, to being touched, mild making out, to expressing myself as lovers made sounds as if they were at a nighttime prayer meeting to worship Dionysus or Orpheus. I returned to being bad, and I wanted him to see me be bad, wanted him to see others admiring me, lusting after me, wanted him to look at the monitors and to see the top-shelf option that he had missed out on. I could've been his wife. Maybe this could've been our world.

In the hallway at Decadence a man who looked like Idris Elba had sat on a red leather sofa as Rosetta rode him reverse cowgirl. I stood in front of his face, and as Rosetta rode, he ate me. Rosetta was feeling good and leaned her back into his chest and while he moved in and out of her, while the man who looked like Idris dined, I reached and rubbed her clit, strummed her sex, and sucked her breast as he led her into the mouth of an orgasm. I had sat on that man's face moving up and down and grinding and winding and she rode his strength and did the same.

Chris watched me. His wife violated me as well.

She stood at her husband's side. She stared. We made harsh eye contact over and over. She remembered how she had betrayed me.

She remembered what I could never forget.

Beyond its pearly gates, heaven had some hell within its walls.

SIXTEEN

As the chandeliers brightened the club, many headed toward the showers. On the way to the dressing area Rosetta and I, heels in hand, stepped over the members who would have sex, the ones who would still be making love when the workers started running vacuum cleaners, the members who would sleep or fornicate on the furniture until someone in management was sent in to politely ask them to stop making love and call it a night. I found the Indian woman who had been in Eros at the same time that I had been, I found her inside of the undressing area. She was sitting on a pink DECADENCE towel that had been placed on a red leather sofa. She was alone in a crowd of excited women. She looked woebegone as she drank wine and wiped tears from her eyes. Instantly, I saw me years ago. Her lugubrious expression trumped whatever I felt at that moment. It was the way I felt when I had broken up with Chris in college. Heartbroken. Shattered. My anger, my rage that had begun to drive me, was placed in neutral and parked.

I went to her, cautiously, and asked, "Have you been here alone all evening?"

She tried to change her dismal expression. "A while."

Her mood made all of the joy and frolicking around her spleenful, almost callous. I sat on her left side. Rosetta sat on her right, her face also painted with concern. It was then that the Indian woman ran her fingers across her henna, drummed her fingers on her thighs, took a few breaths. She struggled to pretend that she was fine. She lost the battle. Tears fell and the Indian woman wiped them away.

Eventually she nodded and said, "Yes. We went to swim. After we made love we went to swim. Then I came here. I sat down. Alone."

"Did he make love to you again?"

"No."

I sat next to the Indian woman, consoled her, hugged her. The women in the room turned away from her as if she were less than worthy. I befriended her. She told me that she was from a matriarchal society, where the men were uninspired, insignificant, and emasculated.

She said, "Add up those things, all that produces, for the most part, is a very immature and selfish breed of men."

The lights flashed three times in rapid succession.

I said, "The club is about to close."

"I know. This is the last hour. He will be waiting for me."

"You are not happy."

"I have never been so unhappy in my life."

Soon she went to the shower. She was going to the shower, frustrated and disappointed, and would use a water head to seek orgasm. As she went, she looked back at me, and smiled a sad smile.

I went to claim the shower next to hers. Minutes later, her body still wet, she had come to be with me while I showered. I didn't ask her to. She just came. Stood outside of my shower door.

She said, "You are angry."

"I am. I have had a lot of fun, have had many orgasms, but I saw someone . . . I'm tense."

"I can help you to relax."

"What is your name?"

"Chandra Maharaj."

"Chandra, I'm Nia. Nia Simone Bijou."

"It's a pleasure to meet you."

I pushed my glass door open and with a nod gave her permission to come and join me, then with a second nod gave her permission to touch me. With a nod she gave me the same permission.

Chandra said, "May I give you a very loving massage?"

"You may."

"Breathe through your nose."

"Okay."

"Breathe deeply."

"Okay."

"Relax and I will massage you."

We inhaled and exhaled together. We connected.

She put her hand on my chest, over my heart, then came closer, put her other hand over my ass, covered my buttock, did that as hot water covered us, as steam rose, and made me feel as if I were breathing through my yoni, as if my yoni were inhaling and exhaling. Her hand covered my yoni. She touched me. Studied me as I received her touch, as we breathed together with heated water bouncing from our flesh. She gave me her physical blessing, her chakra, and even though I had thought that I was done making love for the night, her touch awakened a deeper part of me, energized me, and forced away bits and pieces of the negative energy Chris had delivered into my world. It broke up the energy that came from once again seeing and being in the same space with Siobhán. It was more healing than sexual. Chandra massaged me as if we were in an ancient ritual, touched me as if that part of my body were the most beautiful place on earth. My sexual energy was in her hands. I let down my walls and fell into a state of arousal.

I said, "Your lover wasn't this good with you."

"No."

"His mind is not open to many things."

"No."

"He won't take classes?"

"No. He'd never do that. He thinks he knows it all."

Rosetta was outside the shower door. She watched.

Chandra smiled.

As she shifted, as she said she was leaving, I stopped her.

I said, "You deserve to be pleased by someone."

I asked her to show me the same, how to make her come, how to give her relief, how to massage her yoni, her spirit, until calmness returned. Shuddering she had put her hand on my hand, led my finger to her spot, and directed me, showed me how to move two fingers in circles, where to apply pressure, how to vibrate my hand.

Rosetta stepped inside of the shower.

Chandra said, "Hello."

"I'm Rosetta."

"I watched you earlier in the night. Amazing."

Rosetta asked Chandra, "May I?"

Chandra smiled and nodded.

My fingers rapidly strumming her clit, I watched them as their energy intertwined. Rosetta lapped Chandra's breasts slowly, admired them, squeezed them, sucked on Chandra's dark nipples and touched her damp skin. Chandra's hand found Rosetta's yoni. As she had done me, she massaged Rosetta. Rosetta's mouth opened like a guppy and she panted. I slapped Rosetta's ass as she moaned and she sucked Chandra's breasts again. Watchers. Women stood at the steamed shower door and watched our ceremony as we gave healing to our frustrated sister, as we all healed one another, I had helped Chandra give an angel its wings. I massaged Chandra as Chandra massaged Rosetta and Rosetta massaged me. Chandra had a wonderful, spiritual, leg-trembling release that told me it had been a while. A long while. That night her frustration ended. She had needed to come. She had come wonderfully. When she was done she turned to Rosetta and went down on her, her tongue giving gratitude. She made Rosetta come as I massaged her soft breasts. That evening Rosetta and I had become a team, or maybe more than a team since she knew me in ways no one else did. It felt like we were instant best friends.

After we finished, Chandra dressed and left before we did, sans makeup, as her husband had been waiting for a while.

Siobhán appeared, stepped into a shower as I was getting dressed. When she exited the shower, she stood four lockers away from me. We made eye contact a few times, but not a single word was said.

Rosetta left with me, she too dressed in business attire, looking like an exhausted CEO. We mixed with the lethargic crowd as it took the elevator and returned to the main lobby.

It was a grand lobby, just as dramatic as the rest of the edifice.

Messages were waiting for me. A woman named Margareta had left me her information. Printed photos were attached with messages. Margareta was the Brit who had been with Quince. She and Quince had left a while ago and she asked me to call her if I was staying in the area. Tomorrow she was flying back to the UK. The other message was from Ricardo and Yesenia. Ricardo had been my lover from Curaçao, the man who had pleased me and taken me into many orgasms as my ex had stood in the room and watched me. They had left their number.

Rosetta said, "You have had one helluva night."

"Like no other."

"Do you have a room somewhere nearby?"

"All I need is coffee. I can make it. Have a lot to do today."

"Look, hardhead. Let me give you my cellular. Call me and we can talk while you're driving."

We hugged and while I stood in the long line at valet, Rosetta took her large purse and headed toward the section for those who wanted to catch taxis. Inside, I had been bold, sensuous, angry, ravenous, arrogant, and obnoxious. Now, removed from the world of fantasy, a wave of shyness washed over me.

Removed from the energy that was inside of the club, removed from being caught inside the waves of a tsunami of sexual energy, everyone remained beautiful, but expressions were different. We stood in front of a building built like Château d'Esclimont in France, a site that sat on one hundred and fifty acres. There were a dozen lakes in the distance. Members could come here and horseback ride as well. Outside, many sipped on cups of cappuccino, coffee brought by servers, along with pastries and fruit.

Chris Eidos Alleyne and Mrs. Siobhán Kline-Alleyne exited.

They saw me.

I had stood where I would be visible. I wasn't hiding.

I saw them. She turned away from my eyes. Intimidated. Pissed off. Couldn't tell. She held her husband's hand and they moved beyond valet and stepped inside of a stretch limo that was waiting for them in the private car section. That reminded me of the aftermath of our horrible days in college, when I would see them walking across campus, or hear about them at an event that I had refused to attend. It was happening all over again. Back then he carried her books and now he was pulling her carry-on luggage. It looked weighed down. I guess that she was one of the women who brought dozens of pairs of shoes and more makeup than they had at the Mac counter.

I stood stunned. Jaw tight. Chest heaving.

From the inside of her taxi, Rosetta caught my attention, waved as her rented chariot pulled away. Her face was colored with worry and concern. As soon as she drove away she sent me a text.

> IF YOU DON'T CALL ME TONIGHT I WILL CALL YOU. I WON'T BE ABLE TO SLEEP WITHOUT KNOWING THAT YOU ARE OKAY. AND I PROMISE THAT I WILL ALSO CATCH YOU ON THE WEST COAST. AND BTW, WHAT WE DID ON THE LEATHER SOFA WAS HOT. AND ANOTHER BTW, SEND ME A TEXT EVERY THIRTY MINUTES OR SO UNTIL YOU'RE HOME.

Then someone touched my shoulder. It was a strong hand with a soft touch. It was my zipless lover from Curaçao and his wife. He was in a dark gray suit, she in a beautiful red dress. Her figure was amazing. They looked like the covers of *GQ* and *Vogue* magazines side-by-side. They smiled. I was surprised. Then I smiled too.

I said, "I thought that you had left the building a long time ago."

She said, "We were leaving, then we decided to go swimming again. I could swim all night if they let me. Then we played upstairs."

"Oh."

He said, "This is my wife, Dr. Yesenia Watson-Quirindongo."

"I am Nia Simone Bijou."

Yesenia said, "Nice to meet you, Nia Simone."

"Likewise. And what is your name?"

He said, "I am Dr. Quirindongo. Ricardo. Just Ricardo is fine."

His wife raised a brow. "Sweetheart, no. Don't tell me that you hadn't introduced yourself?"

"No. We hadn't exchanged names."

"Where are your manners? You don't put your dick in a woman without saying hello."

We laughed.

He said, "Allow me to introduce myself. My name is Dr. Ricardo Juliao Quirindongo and I was born in Curaçao in a suburb north of Willemstad and east of Bonam. Is that better, my proper wife?"

"Yes. Much better. Don't believe you put your dick in a woman and didn't introduce yourself."

I asked her, "Are you from Curaçao as well?"

"Oklahoma. But one of my grandparents on my mother's side is Haitian and Anguillan."

I smiled. "You are an island girl."

"Not really, but I guess that in some ways you can say it's part of my heritage. I have never visited Haiti nor have I gone to Anguilla."

Yesenia said that she was born in Geronimo, Oklahoma. They had been married for five years. Seeing someone every day, sharing the same roof and walls, it changed everything. Her husband held her hand and agreed. They split for a few months before reuniting, before rewriting their vows, before opening up their marriage. First she had opened herself to women, did that because he wasn't fully comfortable being penetrated by another man, and she wasn't sure if her husband could really handle seeing her being penetrated by another man, even though he had no problems penetrating women. She had enjoyed her one-on-one with other women more than she had imagined. Being with a woman was new to her. Had felt natural, she said. She still wanted to experience my femininity. And she wasn't shy about her desires with her spouse. That aroused her husband. They said that they loved each other more. The only thing missing was a unicorn.

She asked, "If you might be interested, let us know."

"I'll definitely let you know."

"We're going to Hawaii soon. Would love to take you with us."

"I'll consider the proposition, something new to try for a while, to see if it fits my lifestyle. To be honest, it would definitely fit my needs. I would be free to come and go, wouldn't be smothered, right?"

"You would be."

Chris Eidos Alleyne and his wife's limo pulled away from the magnificence of this edifice. Again it felt like he had left first. I had wanted my car to arrive sooner. I had wanted to leave first, put him behind me. When his limo had disappeared, when he was no longer a part of my truth, I exhaled and felt calmer. Ricardo and Yesenia's town car appeared to carry them to their hotel. We kissed like lovers. She urged him to kiss me. I allowed him to give me his tongue. He urged her to do the same. We stood in the crowd and shared a girl kiss, one that made the people in our area applaud. We did a group hug thing, faces close, three tongues painting one another, kissed like lovers.

Then they were gone.

If possible, I would have gone with them, woken up as a unicorn.

Again my phone rang. It was my mother. The woman never slept.

My mother said, "Nia?"

"Yes?"

"Where you?"

I put on a strong Trini accent, did that so the people standing next to me chatting and flirting wouldn't understand one word. "I'm leaving a club. You're not going to believe this. I ran into Chris."

"Chris Pine, Chris Evans, or Christopher Darden?"

"Chris from Hampton. The football player."

"Did you kill the sonofabitch?"

"No. Caught me by surprise."

"Where are you?"

"At a club with a girlfriend from . . . from one of the social groups that I belong to. I turned around and he was looking at me like I was naked. Didn't recognize him at first. I was shocked, to tell the truth."

"And what he say?"

"The moment I realized who he was, I walked away. Didn't recognize him."

"You didn't recognize him at first?"

"His ras gone and he have a Procter and Gamble look now."

"He's clean shaven. Is he attractive?"

"Not to me."

"But he did say something to you?"

"He was with his wife."

"Same bitch?"

"Swear jar. Yeah. Same bitch."

"What she had on?"

"Not much. She had on nice heels. I just remember the shoes."

"Look, I'm just calling to tell you six more interviews have been booked."

"Mommy. Serious? How many interviews will I have to do?"

"Now. One more thing. We need to talk about the counteroffer from The Production Company."

"What's the problem?"

"They don't want to give you a fair ceiling."

"Insulting. They make their profit and they refuse to pay the writers accordingly. James Thicke has ranted about that so many times. I can't deal with it, Mommy. It's a bunch of crap. Work your magic when you counter. Just let me know the outcome."

"You okay?"

"I hate this shit."

"Swear jar."

"Still hate it. If you weren't a coproducer I wouldn't be a part of this. I would have done one film. One. Then I would've gone back to being invisible like J. D. Salinger. Pay me, then let me be who I am."

We ended the call.

Seconds later I texted Rosetta, told her that I was fine. Ended the text with six happy faces.

Four hundred miles, countless counties, and one Southern state later, exhausted, I took to my sofa, surrounded by boxes, and curled up underneath a blanket, lost in the reminiscence of my secret rendezvous, of the good and bad that had happened in that secret place.

I could not get Chris out of my mind.

The moment that I closed my eyes and felt sleep attempt to take over, my phone chimed. It was a text from Bret. I was tempted not to read it. But I had made a promise. I had to go meet him.

> BE READY FOR THE MUD RUN IN THIRTY MINUTES. WILL PICK YOU UP IN FRONT OF J. CHRISTOPHER'S.

Trying to count how many times I cursed would be like trying to count the drops of water in the ocean. Before I dressed, I went to that dusty box of memories, and once again I looked inside.

There was a letter underneath Chris's photos, three pages long, folded. It was from Rigoberto. The man who had been my lover's best friend. His *tigre*. Rigoberto's words. We had danced closely, intimately, with very little movement, occupying a single tile, as he had held me and allowed me to cry over another man, his best friend. This letter was Rigoberto's confession of love. Another memory rose from the dead.

I took a quick shower and grabbed my bag. Again my phone chimed. I cursed again. I rushed to see if Bret had sent me another text.

It was a notification from Facebook.

Chris Eidos Alleyne had sent me a friend request.

SEVENTEEN

After I crawled into the big pickup truck and we pulled away from the parking lot that housed J. Christopher's, driving toward the East-West Connector, Bret said, "You okay this morning?"

"I'm fine."

"We didn't sleep in the same bed last night, did we?"

"What?"

"Did we wake up in the same bed?"

"No. What do you mean?"

"Good morning."

"Oh, I'm sorry. So rude of me."

"Good morning. That's what we usually say when we see people in the morning."

"Good morning, Bret. How are you?"

"I'm fine." He laughed. "Here's the brochure. Printed it out."

I had on a heavy coat and sweats. No makeup. No lipstick; only lip gloss. Trainers. Hair was pulled back. I looked nothing like the vixen who had been in the halls of Decadence a few hours ago.

The Florida mud run was going to be insane. Bret had said that it was a 5K, but it was a 10K with more than thirty military-style obstacles along at least six miles of filth, muck, and, of course, mud. I didn't complain. We stopped by Walmart Supercenter on East-West Connector in Austell and stood in line behind a lanky redneck wearing a tattered coat, golden Jesus on the cross, and a T-shirt that read 49% MOTHERFUCKER 51% SON OF A BITCH. He was buying drain cleaner, camp fuel, and Lime Out stain remover.

Bret said, "Somebody's cooking meth."

"Those are meth ingredients?"

"Those are the ingredients used to produce meth, a Southern pastime as American as apple pie and baseball. Dumb ass. He's buying everything at one store. And he's using a credit card."

I yawned, rubbed my eyes, and looked down at my phone again.

The friend request stared at me.

That sonofabitch Chris Eidos Alleyne wasn't qualified to become my *friend*, not even in cyberspace. But now he wanted to become my *friend* on Facebook. At first I had wanted to open every window and scream, *Hell no* north, south, east, and to the west, but I added him.

I added him because I wanted to see his life, wanted to satisfy a burning curiosity, the curiosity that came with being a creature built on a foundation of feelings, wanted to become a Watcher and walk through all of his pictures, wanted to take a stroll through his postcollegiate life and see him and his wife, their wedding, wanted to see their life together, wanted to see what happiness they had shown his true friends on Facebook over the years. After I added him, as I stood in line in Walmart with Bret and rednecks who were stocking up for their meth factories, within five seconds Chris sent me a message composed of ten digits. Area code. Exchange. Number. Ten minutes later another message arrived, this one composed of words. He asked me to call because he wanted to make sure that I was okay.

Bret said, "You okay over there?"

"I'm fine. I'm running on fumes, but I'm fine."

With Bret I was not a woman, but a girl. A girl who loved to have fun. A girl who wanted to express her sexual fantasies.

Repressed sexual tension ebbed and flowed between us.

I bought non-cotton pants, thin calf-high socks to prevent arch strains, water-friendly hiking boots, and layers of cheap T-shirts so I could pull them off one by one as they became too heavy, because the mud would stick and soak into cotton and add as much as ten pounds. With my exhaustion, I was in no shape to take on a challenge made for gods and fools. But I had promised. Bret had shown up in an F-250, a vehicle made for the environment, and he said that he'd let me sleep as he drove down I-75 into gator land.

I browsed Chris's Facebook page. Thousands of pictures of him and

Siobhán. There were photos of them in the snowy mountains in California and on the warm and sunny beaches of Florida. In other photos they were in Northern Italy, in Venice, standing in front of beautiful canals, sipping champagne and riding gondolas through the waterways, each picture more romantic than the one before. Palazzo Cavalli. Venetian Palace. Then Florence, Italy. Fijian islands with the in-laws. Tahiti on a beach. Napa Valley. The Bahamas. Hawaii. Rome. Uluru-Kata Tjuta National Park in Australia. Outside of St. Helena Lighthouse on Lake Michigan. Kensington Roof Gardens in London. Baja, Mexico. Hundreds of photos of his wife doing mission work. She still fed the poor. I found the section I wanted. There were wedding pictures from when they married in Bali, Indonesia, an exotic beach wedding, the same place they had their honeymoon. I knew that they had married. I knew when. I had been so fucking distraught that day.

Bret said, "You okay over there?"

"Stop asking me that."

"Then stop looking like you're stressed out and preoccupied."

"Geesh. Now what's the problem?"

"I'm here with you and you're on the phone. That's pretty rude."

"That's what society does nowadays. We have no etiquette."

"I do. Put the phone away or I will throw it out the window."

I put my phone away. Made myself stop the madness.

I said, "Crank up the music. Let's burn down this barn."

For a while Bret played music by Brantley Gilbert and I joined in as he sang and I became his dashboard drummer, then when I caught on to the lyrics, I sang along. I tried to sing the ball of fire out of my system. We were loud and had become a country rock band. Then that country soul number "Who Says You Can't Go Home" kicked on and he was Bon Jovi and I was Jennifer Nettles. I didn't know the lyrics, but I faked the funk. Bret was just as silly. I'd never seen him act silly. It kept my mind occupied. Chris. His wife. Prada. My mother. The movie. My life. Things from the past. Hopes for the future. I was able to suspend thoughts of it all and live in the moment. A wave of exhaustion washed over me. The next thing I knew I had my trainers off, feet up on the dash, and was sleeping with the angels.

Five hundred miles later, on the fringes of Tampa was where we connected with military warriors and career runners. Marines, US Air Force, Navy, as well as groups from the police forces and fire departments, hick chicks, country divas, rednecks, brown necks, black necks, yuppies, buppies, muppies, civilians of all backgrounds had registered. Most of the vehicles had bumper stickers that let me know that they were either marathon runners or participated in triathlons. I was glad to see that at least half of the participants were women. We all smiled and nodded but we knew that in our hearts this would be about female competition. In that group of three-thousand-plus adrenaline junkies, there were a lot of kids amongst the ultra-athletes too, a lot of preteens and teenagers, again both boys and girls. This was their passion. After I had greased up and coated my toes, inner thighs and nipples and any other place that might blister, Bret and I connected with three more couples. We were all on the grass stretching and momentarily we became a team. As soon as we were corralled and the gun sounded, we took off racing, running, climbing over six-foot walls, slipping on sludge and gravel, sliding and crawling through swamp-thick mud like we were in Vietnam. As a collective, we were panting and spitting out damp earth and trudging through muck. It tried to suck my boots off my goddamn feet. I was out of breath by the time we had to use our upper-body strength to balance on a rope so we didn't fall into a muddy lake. Then we were jumping over bars as people screamed out encouragement. The part I hated the most was when I was on my belly swimming underneath some contraption that rose out of the ground like a snake, dark brown water splashing in my face and up my nostrils. Mud didn't scare me. I was from Trinidad, so earth mixed with tears from heaven didn't send me into a panic. Earth was part of J'ouvert, the days before Ash Wednesday, when we were baptized by the new dawn, mud and music being part of the celebration. I just had never run in the muck. It was beyond exciting. A great challenge. Bret encouraged me to keep my knees up and helped me keep my pace as we jogged through knee-deep muck. It felt like the ground had swallowed me. It was an obstacle course that made strong men surrender, weak women cry, and caused me to curse and swear and growl and grunt and lose my given religion. I finished second in my division. Exhausted and pushing it, I had finished before a lot of the military men who were built like Thor and He-Man. Nameless, mud-faced women hugged me and with broad smiles they congratulated and welcomed me. When we were done, Bret congratulated me too, smiled and patted me on my ass two times. That simple contact stoked my fire, a fire that never fully went out, its pilot light always aflame, but I didn't let it show that my secret garden had wanted him again since our zipless night had occurred. Agony assaulted me from head to toe. Every hair on my body cried. In the end we all had to stand close to be hosed down by the fire department, so while we were on the pavement in the group shower, as music blasted from gigantic speakers, we danced and it became a gigantic wet T-shirt contest. The firemen loved that part, especially the girls with the big tits. The women loved that part as well. Soaked, many of the men had removed their shirts and when their pants were soaked, you could see the bulges from the packages they carried. Bret looked sexy as hell. A couple of the women who had aerobic bodies had worn tights and had muddy camel toes. By then I was down to a sports bra and the running tights, discarding all that I had worn as I was running. Mud remained caked inside of my ears and my hair was slicked to my head, begging for shampoo and a deep conditioning. My manicure was destroyed and filth was wedged underneath my nails. I used more than a half-dozen towels trying to get clean enough to feel comfortable. Then I used another half dozen trying to dry myself off. But there was so much dirt and slush and swamp on me that I didn't think that I'd ever be clean again. Soaking wet, bottled water in hand, Bret and I sloshed over and looked at the photos. At the finish line I had looked like Miss Swamp Thing. Soon I was sleep-deprived yet energetic, high on adrenaline in a crowd of revelers drinking beer, eating barbecue. The power of the group. For a moment, I saw all of them naked, covered in orgasmic mire. I imagined them copulating in the sludge. I had only gone once, but Decadence was in my blood now.

Bret held my hand as we walked back to the muddied truck.

His touch refocused my attention.

I said, "You said that there are mud runs all over the country."

"Pretty much. Why?"

"This was fun. Epic pass."

"You looked so angry."

"Not angry. Came in second and I'm pissed because I didn't finish first in my group. Someone was better than me. Number two is not a winner. Number two is just the leader for the rest of the losers."

"You're too hard on yourself."

"Which war have you heard of where second place was praised? Life is about winners and losers. Life can be hard. Life is hard on us all, especially hard on the living. Becomes one thing after the other."

"That's true. That's so fucking true. Life beats us up and tries to wear us down. Don't knock yourself. You did a great job."

I blinked Siobhán from my mind. "But you're right. I did it. On little sleep I ran six miles. Makes a beach run look like nothing."

"You're amazing. Honestly, you're the only woman I know who will run in the rain, then get down in mud and crawl like she was trying to break out of a prison located in the middle of swampland."

"Your . . . your kids' mother . . . did she . . . did . . . does she work out with you?"

"Never had much in common. I like fishing. NASCAR. Going to the Redneck Resort Mud Park in Sweetwater, Tennessee. Jet-Skiing on Allatoona Lake. Doing five-K runs for autism or pancreatic cancer. She thought pretty much all extracurricular stuff like that was a waste."

"The mother of your children, if it's okay to ask, what does she do for a living?"

"She's back in Macon, Georgia. She lives in the old historic district with her parents. She works part-time three days a week at The Fresh Market on Forsyth Road. That's Macon's version of Trader Joe's and Whole Foods. The nights that she's off she's sitting on her tush at her parents' home, watching reality television half the night. Can't live without VH-One. Or Bravo. Says she's going back to Mercer and finishing up her law degree at some point. It's all talk. Nothing but her pipe dreaming. Unless they offer a major in dominoes or spades I don't see her going back. So I make a lot of drives back and forth to Macon."

"Macon, Georgia. We just drove through there to get down here."

He nodded. "I was going to college up in Chattanooga, UTC, when I met my wife. Ex-wife. We met up in Nashville at a blues club in Printers Alley. Bourbon Street Blues and Boogie Bar. She was going to Mercer in Macon. She was with her friends and I was with mine. Downtown Nashville is like Bourbon Street in New Orleans on a Saturday night. Lots and lots of drinking. We all started dancing, drinking, then went to another bar, think it was the Wild Beaver Saloon, then after that we ended up at another bar, can't remember the name, but we did karaoke and she rode the bull for the first time."

"Okay."

"I was in my first semester, got her pregnant not long after we met, carelessness on both of our parts, but I liked her and married her at the courthouse as soon as I found out, dropped out to get into the military so I could get a steady check and benefits. It all happened pretty fast. Yeah. So it goes. We met up in Music City and seems like not more than a couple of months had passed before we were getting married at the courthouse and I was on the way to boot camp. Had another baby two years later. I spent most of my marriage deployed, so I barely knew her. We barely knew each other in the end, outside of dancing."

"Sounds like a pretty exciting relationship."

"Not even close. She went Carrie Underwood. Court stuff, she didn't take too kindly to that. She wouldn't let me see my kids. I tried to be nice but ended up going to court and exposing how unfit she is to be a parent. She rode up in the middle of the night and took keys to a four-wheel drive I had back then and showed the world how bad her spelling really was. Spelling like that, she never would've made it out of law school. While that was being repaired, she came back and beat the headlights on my rental with a bat and slashed the tires. Yeah, Carrie Underwood jacks up your truck and Reba McEntire blows out your eardrums and Miranda Lambert shoots you and Taylor Swift slanders your name and Laura Bell Bundy drags you naked and Kellie Pickler lets you get hit by a bus. Country girls. Ain't nothing like 'em."

Lips pursed, I left that at that. Bret had never pried into my world, had never asked questions, and I didn't want to become the type of woman who felt like she needed to unravel his mysteries and secrets. Even though I wanted to tell him about Chris, about that part of my past, about that unforgettable season, about Siobhán, I didn't want to end up trading horror stories, or war stories, each of us trying to convince the other that we'd been to a deeper part of hell. But still. Curiosity owned its own power and it had slain many inquisitive cats.

I asked, "Did she get arrested?"

"Didn't press charges. Couldn't do that to the mother of my children. But I did let them pick her up and take her down and let her cool off and let being fingerprinted scare the bejesus out of her."

"Where were the children when she was acting out like that?"

"In the window. Saw it all. I had gone out there to try and stop her, but I wasn't going to put my hand on her. She'd turn it around if I did.

So I stepped back while she screamed and cursed and made threats and let her have a fight with my truck. She has terrified my kids."

"She sees them?"

"Supervised visits. I don't want them to *not* see her. She's their mother, good, bad, or otherwise. I know that if it were reversed she would cut me out of their lives and take as much of my money as the government would allow, call me out of my name all day long, but my heart ain't . . . *isn't* . . . evil like hers. Yeah, I know how to pick 'em."

"Printers Alley. Music City is rocking like that?"

"Nashville is probably the best city in the South. Nothing better. I'll never go that way again, that's for sure. Never again in my life."

"Bet she was passionate in bed."

"She was. A wild woman unchained. The crazy ones always are."

"The crazy ones."

"Present company excluded."

"So you do remember."

"I remember what is unforgettable."

"What do you remember?"

"We were no-holds-barred. Me, you, and the girl from Montreal."

"Vancouver. She was from Vancouver."

"All the same to me. She was good. But you were something else."

That was his first acknowledgment of our passionate night.

I said, "You were something else too. Towels. Hot towels. That was nice. I'll never see towels the same way. Hard not thinking about that every time I see you. Hard not wanting that again."

"Same here."

He smiled. Sexual tension existed between us. It was strong.

I said, "You were in college. What's . . . what was your major?"

"Electronics. That's behind me now. That was another me."

"Amazing how one person can change your life. One person can turn your world upside down."

"Sure is."

I asked, "Was she your first love?"

"Nah. She wasn't my first love and I wasn't hers. She let me know that more than once and I let her know that more than twice. She went back to dating her high school sweetheart for a while. Probably saw him while I was deployed. Being gone a year at a time has a lot of us standing in divorce court. Lots of marriages fall apart while men are fighting for the country. Wives stay home, get antsy, and have affair after affair and soldiers abroad are lonely and doing the same."

"The government doesn't issue chastity belts?"

"You're funny. I like that. You make me laugh."

He opened the passenger door of the oversize truck and helped me climb up inside. I compared myself to him. We were so different.

I was Kipling and Tolstoy, Ruskin and Lewis Wallace, Anaïs Nin, Plath, Steinem, Rand, Alison Hinds and Rihanna and Minaj and carnival and *moko jumbies* and Lady Young Road and boat racing at Pigeon Point Beach in Tobago, and I was a child of Los Angeles, a child of Hollywood, a West Coast baby as well.

He was *Sports Illustrated* and ten-dollar haircuts and guns and Brantley Gilbert and Tim McGraw and AC/DC and Toby Keith and Sugarland and four-wheel drives and Southern drawl and boot-stomping country music being played on a gravel road that led to a riverbank and his choice fishing spot.

Bret asked, "You sure that you're okay?"

"I'm fine, Chris."

"Wrong guy, Nia."

"Sorry, Bret. Wow. I'm so sorry for that."

"You seem distracted. Been that way since I picked you up."

"Tired. And I have to do a phone interview in a couple of hours. Girl from the top newspaper in Trinidad calling. Anxious about that."

He paused. "Who is Chris, if it's okay to ask?"

I shifted. "Ex from college."

"He must be on your mind."

"He had just sent me a friend request on Facebook, that's all."

"He sent you a friend request. He must be looking for you."

"I wonder how his wife would feel about him sending a request."

"Depends on the definition of friend. She might not like it."

"She wouldn't." I almost grinned. "She wouldn't like it at all."

Bret popped in a CD; Bruce Springsteen, *Born in the U.S.A.*

This time yesterday I was en route to Decadence.

It seemed like a dream.

Most of it had been beautiful. With Chris and his egotistical, humanitarian wife being there, part of it had been a nightmare.

EIGHTEEN

When we made it to the Sheraton Riverwalk Hotel, Bret paid for two rooms.

Disappointment rose, but I kept it at bay, maintained a poker face. I should not want the company of a man, not after yesterday; I should be satiated, but it was a new day, and this was a different man.

At check-in they said that our rooms connected. That was fine. We would be on the same floor, one wall away. Each room cost close to one hundred and fifty dollars. I offered to pay for both, since he had driven and paid the race registration fee, but he kindly refused.

He said, "I invited you. When somebody invites somebody somewhere, they are the guests."

"There are exceptions to that rule."

"Not in my book. I invited you. I pay. End of story. I know that some women will invite a man out to dinner and expect him to pay. They invite a man out to lunch and the man thinks that she's actually treating him and the bill ends up on his side of the table."

"I'd never do that."

"I've been out with you enough to know that you're not that tacky. That is something else that I admire about you. I wouldn't go out with that kinda woman, not two times. When a woman does that, she's not inviting the man out, she's inviting his money out. Women do that and wonder why a man stops calling or loses interest. No respect for a woman like that. Anyway, I invited you. Put your money away."

I didn't argue.

A man's ego is a fragile thing; as fragile as a woman's heart.

When we were upstairs in front of the doors to our rooms, he glanced at me. It was the same glance, the same lustful expression that was on his face when first we met. Again there was a long pause.

Inside every pause lived a contemplation.

He said, “Don’t forget about your interview.”

“I won’t. I don’t forget anything.”

He went inside his room. I went inside mine. His door closed. I closed mine. When I locked my door I walked to the door that separated both rooms. I imagined that Bret was inches away, imagined that he was doing the same thing, imagined that he was standing there with his hand on that door. Siri sang her alarm. I know he heard. She told him that I was on the other side of his door, listening.

NINETEEN

After I had taken a long, hot shower and practically used a bottle of shampoo to clean my hair, I dried my hair the best that I could with the small dryer that was in the bathroom. I did that with my iPad in front of me. Browsing Chris and Siobhán's wedding pictures on Facebook. I wrapped my body in a white hotel towel. It felt like I should have had on high heels. I took out information that had been left especially for me. Ricardo and Yesenia. Margareta's information was there too. I was tempted to call one, if not both. But there wasn't time. Work over pleasure. Pleasure was but a hobby. I fell into professional mode, checked e-mails. Mommy had squeezed in another interview and I saw the message just in time to make that call to a reporter with the *LA Times*. As soon as that twenty-minute chat was done, I took a deep breath, felt excited, and made the call to the interviewer back home in Trinidad. This one was the most important. At least it was to me.

I said, "You are with the *Trinidad Express*?"

"That is correct."

"And your name is Rae-Jeanne Quash?"

"Yes, Miss Bijou. This is Mrs. Quash. I have been assigned the task of interviewing you for the newspaper."

"This is my first interview with someone from Trinidad regarding this project. I am both very elated and honored to have this privilege."

"You are the daughter of Hazel Tamana Bijou. I have heard of her practically all of my life. Finally, I get to speak with her child."

I cringed like a wasp had stung me in my ego. My mother's shadow, it kept me cool, but at this moment it was unwanted. I was the writer. I had my own name. But I let it go. Just like that she turned me off and I tuned out, shifted and found other things to occupy myself.

She said, "They are really pumping up the film. The Bijou name is everywhere, inescapable."

"That's great."

"Your mother really makes things happen."

"She does. She is a daughter of the island and in her heart she will always be Trini."

"It doesn't matter if you are near the Caribbean Sea, Atlantic Ocean, Columbus Channel, or the Gulf of Paria, the film is being promoted all over the archipelagic island like it's carnival."

"That is great to hear."

"Let's see. Lola Mack's face is prominent on most of the adverts here. She has the prettiest brown skin."

"I love that. She's a wonderful actress."

"Is she from the islands?"

"She's African American."

"She's Black American. If she was not born in Africa, how can she be *African* anything? Americans don't move to Africa and have children and call them American Africans. It sounds ludicrous."

I said, "She is an American who happens to have brown skin. Each culture has its own rules. If that is fine, we'll leave it at that."

"If Miss Lola Mack has roots in the islands I would have loved to chat with her as well."

"Not to my knowledge. Anyway, so far as the interview, you e-mailed me a specific question—"

"I asked you about the imbalance in numbers between men and women and—"

"It's exaggerated in the film. Most films use hyperbole to make a point."

"It may be exaggerated in the film, to a certain extent, but it's pretty much the way that we women are now, often beguiled by love and left to feel disposable, to quote one of Lola Mack's lines in the film, only in the reverse. It's a man's playground. Your movie, interesting concept. I had never really considered the side effects or problems created from there not being a one-to-one ratio between man and woman."

"Most don't. But numbers don't lie. Ask the fact-checkers."

"So given the model of the church, meaning that for every woman there is a man, but there isn't, at least nowhere that I have read about, so many women will not have a man to reproduce with, will not give birth, and maybe not be seen fully as a woman by other women, maybe by the same society that creates and upholds those same rules, possibly will not be seen as a true woman by most of the world."

"Sounds like you connected to the film on some level."

"The backdrop of the film to me reminds me of the Laventille area in Trinidad."

"Really? My father was born there. He lived in Laventille."

"I know that area very well. I lived there when I was much younger. A very dangerous area. The police were up there shooting tear gas at the hooligans not long ago. Your father is there?"

"He was killed a few months before I was born."

"Your mother was pregnant when your father was murdered?"

"She has endured a lot."

She regarded her notes, then asked, "Your stepfather is French?"

"Yes. He adopted me."

"Your mother found a rich man and married for security."

"I would like to believe that she married for love."

"Do you mind if I ask for your stepfather's name? He sounds like a remarkable man. It would be great to mention him in the article."

"His birth name is Francois Henri Chevalier, but when in America, he changed his last name to Wilson, maybe to fit in. He maintained his business, his corporation under the name Chevalier."

"That's your stepfather? Your mother married Francois Henri of the Chevalier Group?"

"He's my stepfather. My legal father. He adopted me, so be sure to say that he is my father."

"So you consider him your father and not your father who was born in Trinidad."

"That could read bad in print. Derren Liverpool from Laventille was my father. I am of his Trini blood. But Francois Henri is the only man I have called Daddy. He is the only father that I've known."

"Lucky woman. The daughter of Hazel Tamana Bijou and the adopted daughter of the CEO of the Chevalier Group. Sounds like you have had a cushy life, compared to those who live here in Laventille."

"No matter where a person is on the socioeconomic ladder, life brings challenges. Money doesn't make love any easier."

"Chevalier."

"He uses the last name Wilson, rarely uses his true surname. He was actually born in a city a few miles outside of Paris. Forgot which one. Clichy, Yerres, or Le Kremlin-Bicêtre. Again, I am not sure. But he quit France for a while, moved to Los Angeles after he had come here to attend Princeton. He was in Trinidad on business, met my mother, love at first sight, and the rest is, as they say, history."

"How long have your mother and new father been married?"

"They are divorced now. He returned to France after the divorce."

"So your mother moved and became prominent in Hollywood."

"She did. I would prefer it if we could focus on the film."

"In one moment. Couple questions. The drugs and what have you in Laventille, was your mother part of the same dealing as well?"

"My mother never really gets into that part of her old life. But that's not my mother's style."

"Do you have more siblings here in Trinidad?"

"I'm an only child."

"Are you sure? You may be your mother's only, but men are village rams. My father was. Practically every man in my family was."

"There is a lot of static. Can you hear me, Mrs. Quash?"

"It is raining pretty hard here. Let me get back to the film."

"I think they did an excellent job casting the project."

"Hopefully you can arrange to cast Trini actors and actresses in your next project."

"So far as this one, I hope to see my project in the next Trinidad and Tobago Film Festival."

She paused and her tone turned cold as she asked, "Why?"

"Because I'm Trinidadian."

"You were gone before you could talk. You never live here. You never go to school here. You come here and go, visit like a tourist."

"I was born there."

"Well, I think you are American. I can't really feel you being a true Trini. At best you are what I call a pretend Trini. Not authentic."

"Are you gone mad? Iz a Trini."

"Ya Freshwater Yankee."

"What is your problem? Are you Tobagonian?"

"Me eh no Tobagonian. Don't you dare call me a Tobagonian. All Tobago has is better beaches."

"I was only asking. You seem to have a problem with me being Trini."

"You no Trini. I go to school here. From preschool, to primary school, to secondary school in Sogren Trace Laventille Community and afterward I work three jobs and pay my way through UWI. I go to school here. I work here every day. I live here all me life. Iz a Trini."

"*I born Port-of-Spain General.*"

"*You were born here*, true, but to be honest you have spent your formative years in the United States. And your film isn't Trinidadian. I mean, Nicki Minaj's video for "Pound the Alarm" was filmed here, used our people, so it's considered Trini. The festival will undoubtedly be searching for something that is uniquely Trinidadian and Tobagonian, with a Trinidadian and Tobagonian texture, a Trinibagan story and all that kind of thing. Your project was not filmed in Trinidad, it shows no Trinidadian characters, and there is no Trinidadian language such as creole. There is nothing about it that is not American. You depicted your postapocalyptic world as America does, as if America is the center of existence. In fact the director lives in America as well and all the characters shown are American. I truly can't see it being entered here."

Her words kicked me in my teeth.

She said, "But with your mother's influence I'm sure that an exception will be made. Maybe they will vote her the new goddess of wealth and replace Mother Lakshmi with Mother Hazel Bijou."

"Wow. What was that?"

She ended the call.

MOMMY, GUESS WHAT THE RAE-JEANNE QUASH BITCH SAY IN THE INTERVIEW?

SWEAR JAR, NIA. WATCH YOUR MOUTH. WHAT DID SHE SAY?

THE BITCH TALK DOWN TO ME AND TELL ME I'M NOT A TRUE TRINI.

SHE SAID THAT FOR REAL? OR IS THIS A JOKE? DON'T MAKE MOMMY VEX FOR PLAY.

NO JOKE. I'M ABOUT TO FILL UP THE SWEAR JAR. SHE TELL ME I'M NOT A TRINI.

YOU'RE BRILLANT. LET SUCCESS BE YOUR REVENGE. SHE GOES TO BED WITH YOU ON HER MIND AND TOMORROW SHE WILL WAKE UP WITH YOUR NAME ON HER TONGUE. HATERS ARE THE BEST AT GIVING FREE PUBLICITY. EVERY TIME SHE SPEAKS YOUR NAME SHE WILL UNKNOWINGLY BE YOUR CHEERLEADER.

TOMORROW WHEN I GET BACK TO ATL I MIGHT HAVE TO CALL THE NEWSPAPER AND COMPLAIN.

WHEN DID YOU LEAVE THAT HORRIBLE CITY? WHERE ARE YOU IF YOU'RE NOT IN HAPPY TOWN?

FLORIDA, MOMMY. TAMPA. DROVE DOWN HERE THIS MORNING.

WHAT YOU DOING IN FLORIDA?

WAIT. WHAT DO YOU MEAN YOU'RE TOO BUSY TO TALK TO YOUR DAUGHTER?

WHY ARE YOU IN FLORIDA?

IT'S THE MIDDLE OF THE NIGHT AND YOU CAN TEXT ME BUT YOU CAN'T TAKE MY CALL?

I'M BUSY.

MAN BUSY OR WORK BUSY?

WHY ARE YOU IN FLORIDA?

YOU'RE MAN BUSY. OH MY GOD.

☺

I put my phone down and stared at the door that separated my room from Bret's room. I heard him over there moving around. He sounded as frustrated as I felt. That interview with Mrs. Quash had left me disturbed. I wanted to go to Bret's room. I wanted to vent. I wanted his company. I had left my side of the door opened in invitation. A moment later I heard him talking on the phone. He was arguing. Then the argument ended. Silence. Silence was where the truth lived. It was also where lies went to hide. The questions that the interviewer had asked resonated and left me disturbed. Her attacks felt personal, more than an interview, coated with jealousy. She knew my name. My mother's name. My true father's name. The French man who had raised me, she knew his name as well. Another reason I preferred to stay anonymous.

This was what fame brought to the table.

I didn't want to be in a bed alone, but I closed my eyes. It felt as if I were trying to stay awake for Bret, in case he needed me, in case he wanted me. But exhaustion wrapped its arms around me.

TWENTY

When I woke and staggered into the hotel bathroom, sensual sensations dissipated, intense dreams were disremembered, yet the fiery tingles remained. I was wet. I had made honey. In my dreams I had once again made lady come. While I washed up and washed my hands I looked into the mirror. I saw edges of my biological father in my features. I saw bits and pieces, features of a man I never knew. Would never know.

When I left the bathroom I realized that Bret had opened the side of his door to our conjoined rooms. His television was on, down low, the screen glowing. That meant that he had seen me sleeping, witnessed my tossing and turning. He had been a voyeur. So I reciprocated and watched him toss and turn. I imagined that he had watched me, wanting to attempt to cool my uncoolable desire. And now I watched him wanting to do the same for him.

I crept inside of Bret's room, licking my lips, my sensual spirit all but begging me to accost a man, my body telling me that in a world that made women less than men, pleasure was a woman's entitlement, if nothing else. Then I saw documents were on the desk. Court documents. Child support. Custody battle. Ugliness, pain in black and white. Things to argue about. I read about his personal life. His ex-wife was behind on child support. He was suing her. His hidden stress came from his failed marriage and being a father two times over. I remained paused by the rough edges of Bret's life. I glanced at legal issues that I couldn't relate to. In the end, Bret's legal papers were a stop sign. A deal breaker.

Bret's information was laid out in front of me. He was no longer a mystery. Those papers reminded me why some lovers should only be zipless encounters. I decided to turn the television off, then hurry back to my room. Bret woke up when I turned the television off.

He sat up. I stared at him. I was as nude as I was naked.

His silhouette reached for mine. I wondered if he was dreaming, waking from a sex dream starring his ex-wife, maybe waking from a nightmare inspired by whatever was going on inside of his mysterious world, wondered if he knew that it was me, the woman he had had a one-night ménage à trois with and not the mother of his beautiful children. Wait. Not *the* woman he had had a ménage à trois with; I was but *one* of the women he had fucked senseless on that hot summer night. I licked my lips, swallowed, and nervously gave him my fingertips as if we were in some sort of ceremony. He pulled at me, pulled gently, pulled me toward the bed where he lay, the bed where moments ago I wanted to experience him again, just him and me, just the energy between two, what the light side of Gemini preferred. The dark side craved satisfaction as well. Both sides were simpatico because Decadence was yesterday's meal. Even when a woman found nourishment at the best buffet in the land, even if she had dined at Per Se or Alinea or Eleven Madison Park, by dinnertime the next day, maybe even by noon, maybe even by breakfast, she would feel the pangs of hunger again. No meal lasted forever. Even when Prada had come to America, when he had flown here to please me, after that forty-eight hours had ended and by the time he was boarding his flight, my sexual appetite had rumbled. Within days his touch had begun to feel irrelevant. I had gone into withdrawal. Now I felt that I was no longer addicted to him. Even if I were, he was across the pond and Bret was inches away. My famine remained strong, so strong I was light-headed. Like the unsatisfied East Indian woman had done in Decadence when her husband had pulled her diminutive hand, part of me wanted to pull away from Bret, to resist him, to deny him his power in that moment.

I inhaled Bret's pain, the hurt of many men.

If I had to choose, Prada would be the better choice.

Only Prada was not here.

Bret reached for me like he wanted to make love to me tonight, then fuck me in the morning. I ached. I always ached for this man.

I let my hair fall, took a deep breath, and inched onto Bret's bed, jettisoned my thoughts of a faraway king and eased into the disheveled bed with a warrior, a bed as messy as his private life, as tousled as my inner feelings. I was on the bed of a divorced man who had two young children. I expected him to mount me, to ride me, to exhaust his restlessness inside of me. I anticipated hot towels and a ravenous tongue. I anticipated an exchange that I would record and send to Rosetta, only my face showing, my passion filling her screen as I whispered her name and told her, *Shah mat, shah mat, shah mat*. But when I rested on my side he spooned against me. He was nude. So was I. For a long while we lay that way, my breathing beyond nervous, as if I were brand new and tonight was a night for cherry popping. I tried to be still, tried to not be restless, but as we existed in silence, I failed. The air con kicked on. Chilled the room. But it did not cool my desire. He shifted and I thought that he was about to make me the yoni beneath his lingam, but he tugged the white covers up over us and held me. Breathing in tempo, the warmth from his skin and pheromones permeating my pores, his chest against my back, his lingam smooshed up against my ass, as the sun appeared, he fell asleep that way.

Bret held me and in time I drifted to sleep, a fitful sleep, disappointed, thinking of another lover.

TWENTY-ONE

As Bret held me, I relived the touch of Anaïs, my Cuban interviewer, the sensual woman whom I had met not long before. Nude. She had been with me the way that I was with Bret. We had been together as lovers. Her head was on my belly. I played in her hair. She had been a good lover, very all-inclusive for a woman so small and feminine, very comprehensive. And truly a patient teacher.

Anaïs licked my nipples and whispered, "At times promiscuity is a rebellious act. When the male does the same it has no label. Or it is ironically revered as a man sowing his wild oats and each man sees men like that as the man to imitate. When we behave as the male, they hate, call us names, they become angered because we are challenging their hypocrisy. Brainwashed women will call us the same."

The intimacy had been good, I felt high, so very.

Speaking in English I said, "You said that you compile statistics on women and sex?"

"I have compiled lots of statistics, not that they mean much. White women with college degrees are more receptive to anal sex. Did you know that women who went to college are more likely to enjoy both the giving and receiving of oral sex more than high school dropouts? Women with a PhD are twice as likely to be interested in a one-night stand than those with only a bachelor degree."

"Amazing what we learn in college, most not in any textbook."

She asked, "Do you come while you sleep?"

"So much that I both look forward to and am afraid to go to sleep."

"The frequency increases as a woman ages, especially during her childbearing years."

"It will only get worse?"

"It only gets *better*. Many women are not able to experience the beauty of orgasm."

"Great perspective. So I will have many orgasms while I sleep. It will go on and on."

"It will. Men make seven million new sperm a day and we only have a limited amount of eggs. Men can make babies until they are in their eighties, if not longer. They have all the time in the world."

"Right now it's as if Mother Nature is trying to force my hand."

"When you arrive at Decadence, treat yourself. Let go. Celebrate. Be a rebel. Make love."

"I'm going alone. Should I look for you? Or would that not be appropriate?"

"Please do. Come say hello to my husband. Watch us make love. Or join us. I will tell him about us. Not many women are attractive to me. What attracts me goes beyond physical beauty. You have uniqueness about you. He will know that you are a special woman."

She gave me light kisses, her beautiful lips sticking to my skin, tongue-kissed my feet and sucked my toes, grazed my yoni with her tongue, used her hands to open my legs wider, sucked my inner thighs, navigated my hills and lingered in the warm valley of my sex.

She licked. Licked. Licked. Licked. Licked.

I pulled at my hair, moved my hips, started to die.

"I'm coming. Goddamn, I'm coming. You got me; you got me."

"Ride it. Ride it. You're so beautiful. Ride it to the end."

When the sensation died down, I caught my breath.

Then we laughed. We laughed like naughty girls.

While she continued touching me, we talked about men.

I said, "There is a man I am crazy about, but he's not crazy about me, not sexually."

"Then he is a fool."

She fingered me, played with me. As I trembled, she pulled her fingers from inside me, and then put them inside her mouth.

She whispered, "I. Am. Very. Very. Turned. On. Right. Now."

"Me too, Anaïs. This was unexpected. Totally unexpected."

"You want to learn the proper way to please another woman."

"I am curious."

She pulled my hair back, kissed my neck, sucked my ears. Soon she returned lower, held my ass, eased fingers in and out of me. I squeezed my breasts and surrendered singsong moans, she took another mouthful of my sex and sent me higher, made my body quake again. She turned around, eased her petite body one hundred and eighty degrees, first we were waist to waist, then yonis moved toward tongues.

She had done to me then what I wished that Bret would do to me now.

TWENTY-TWO

Late night in Atlanta, Georgia. Restlessness had me walking the floors, riding the elevator.

I found myself in my office, wearing a RADICAL DESIGN T-shirt, sipping on mango tea as I conversed with Margareta Liverpool via Skype. Margareta was the randy Brit woman who had swept me into her energy and given me enjoyment underneath the eyes of so many Watchers, the woman who had called me to the altar and converted me, I remembered her well, but my mind was on her well-endowed lover. Her lover-pilot's Christian name was Graham Anderson.

I asked, "Is Graham a Brit too?"

"Australian."

"And by the size of his lingam, of East African blood as well."

We laughed.

She told me that as they were leaving, many women followed them, wanted to touch his lingam, and more than a few wanted to take him on. She laughed that soft way British people did, a laugh that had no sound and was in the eyes and the corners of the lips. Her children called for her. So did her assistant, her husband, and other workers. It was as if no one could function, couldn't complete the simplest of tasks without her. I told her I could Skype her some other time, maybe some other day, but she wanted to chat. With a coy little wink she said that she wanted to talk to her old friend.

She had said, "My family can be quite loud and bolshie this early."

She walked around a large property. It was early morning and she was fully dressed. Seeing her in expensive, conservative clothes that aged her five to ten years, the same style that had made Princess Diana look older, seeing Margareta wih her hair pulled back in a tight professional bun, a hairstyle accepted by the masses, was like looking at another person. Didn't look like a person who enjoyed the pleasures of the flesh. Didn't look like she sucked dick, let alone clit.

I asked, "Where is your husband?"

"I think Tom went for a fag. He smokes too much. He'd better leave soon because yesterday when I was buying a Hoover I heard a bloke on the train say that today's trains would be delayed."

When she found a spot in the far reaches of an enormous guest bedroom, she took a deep breath and dropped the dignified façade. She told me that Quince Pulgadas was flying back to the United States that week and he wanted to see me again, at Decadence. She challenged me to take him on fully as a woman was designed to accept a man.

I laughed and shook my head. "It would feel like I was having a ten-pound baby in reverse."

"You said it intrigued you."

"So does the Statue of Liberty, but I'm not going to sit on it."

"Might help if you had a pint or two first."

"I'll never be that tipsy."

"What's the largest that you've had?"

"Stop it. You are so nasty."

"Tell me. I reckon you've had a pretty big one."

"Nothing that compares to that."

"Rubbish."

"You're one wicked lady."

"Tell me, tell me, tell me. I'll bet you fancy a big dick."

I laughed at her naughtiness. I had assumed that her conversation would be intellectual; if not highbrow then political, about their Conservative Party and Labour Party. I had expected and desired conversation that was challenging, and if it were challenging then it would be stimulating. But since she had met me in an environment of naughtiness and sex, that was how she saw me, as a woman gone wild.

She confessed, "In my youth, before my children, I've even been dogging a time or two."

"Be careful over there. Jack the Ripper and all that. Be careful."

"Oh, I'm very careful. If I were exposed, my husband would toss me from Tower Bridge. A WAG was thrown from the Tower Bridge a few years ago and I'm sure he'd want to do the same to me."

She cringed and closed her eyes, then her eyes became tight and she owned a crooked smile. The diligent housewife faded away and the badly behaved lady from Eros had returned.

Seeing her breathing changed, seeing her eyes tighten, I asked her, "Are you touching yourself?"

She nodded and stopped talking for a while.

I watched her make love to herself. She battled with herself. She held out, kept her orgasm at bay, stroked herself, slowed down, panted, squirmed, jerked, cooed, and then surrendered to pleasure.

She had me so aroused. Once again a woman had me aroused. It made me crave lingam, hard lingam, not the touch of a kindred soul in distress. My fingers touched, patted my dampness, patted the center of my energy, felt it spread. As she touched herself, as I touched myself, I told her what I rarely told anyone, confessed my occupation in detail. Part of me wanted her to know that I wasn't a slacker, that I was my own woman, that I was capable and no man financed my existence. In reality I knew that a woman like her would pity a woman like me for having to work like a man to obtain what men had. I wanted her to know whose yoni she had eaten, to know it was blue-blooded and royal in its own way. Again, like all others at Decadence, she had seen me both literally and metaphorically nude, had seen me caught up in heated moments, had seen me have sex, had seen me come, had seen me give angels wings in front of a choir of people as other women took on a gaggle of lovers, and she had met me out of context.

She said, "The beautiful Indian couple, did you meet them?"

"I did. Her name is Chandra and her lover was Dilraj."

"Dilraj was so horrible he was embarrassing."

"He is her husband of three years."

"A husband that lousy? That's utter bollocks."

I laughed. "He definitely could use some coaching."

"Three years of bad sex? That is insane. He should've gone down on her. She looked delicious. He should've slid her toward me."

"You slut. I'm jealous."

"There is enough to go around. She could've joined in."

"I think that she might have been open to what you have to offer."

"Really? What do you know that I don't know?"

With a wink, I yielded a smile at her from the screen of my iPad to the screen on her iPhone.

She said, "Someone has a secret. Tell me."

"Wait."

"Are you about to come?"

"Think so."

She smiled. "Tell me about your wickedness as you come."

I described the moment. The Brit swallowed, as I swallowed when totally aroused. Her arousal spread throughout her body as mine spread throughout mine. Sucking in air, jerking, panting, I struggled to tell the rest. Told her about Rosetta joining us. My rising orgasm covered my confession with a heart only a woman could understand. I relived that moment via my Skype conversation. I had come now as I had then.

Then I calmed.

I grinned that embarrassed grin that always came after orgasm.

Margareta said, "I'm going to see Quince again."

"At Decadence?"

"If not there, then I will have him at a hotel here. I would love for you to come over and be here when I do. I will fly you over. First class. You will be my guest and you can feel free to stay as long as you like."

"Let me give it some thought. Might be nice to spend time there."

The Brit told me that she had to start her day now.

I said, "We will chat again, not too far in the future I hope."

"Very soon. I wish that I lived as close to our special place as you do."

"It's as close as you driving to Paris plus another hour. Closer than Amsterdam."

She said, "Lucky bitch. Oh, how I envy you Americans and your freedom to fornicate."

"Quite a bit of fornicating is going on over there too. I watch Brits fucking on Youporn.com. And I have heard about London Swingers Club and the Limelight."

"You've been doing a bit of research."

"They are sort of like Decadence; at least I think they are."

"And there's the Limelight, you say? Where is that located?"

"Let's see. Online it says that the Limelight is located . . . mmm . . .

next to Barons Court underground station . . . in Central London. Ages forty-five and under, same basic club rules."

"But I am not allowed to have that sort of fun over here." She winked. "Have to run and be a good mother and wife now."

"Have a good rest of the morning."

"Happy wanking."

"Happy wanking."

"Prada? I'm surprised that you answered."

"Nia, my love. How are you?"

"I need you."

"Is everything okay?"

"Did I catch you at a bad time?"

"I'm en route to yet another meeting."

"I need you right now."

"Is everything okay?"

"I'm fine. In the middle of working and realized that I hadn't heard from you in a few days. Okay, I'm not fine. I'm feeling a little lonely. Missing you. Would love to share dinner and catch a movie with you. Then sex. Would love to sleep with your skin next to mine, then wake up and cook for you. Feeling girly. Need another weekend. Or a day. Any idea when we will be able to see each other again?"

"I have no idea."

"I need to see you. I really do."

"Likewise."

"You have no idea."

"One thing after the other continues to rear its ugly head."

"Can we Skype later? I'm very horny and I have a new toy and new lingerie."

"I have a long, long day today. After the meeting there is a dinner and an early flight. I'll try and look for you on Skype when I get in."

"No worries. You'll be tired. Get rested before your next flight."

"Are you sure that you're okay?"

"I'm fine. I'm about to get on the treadmill and burn some energy. Need to make a few calls after I put in a long run."

"I miss you. I love you."

"Kisses. Call me when you have a free moment."

The interviewer Anaïs had been on point. As I matured, as seasons changed and my body began crying out to have babies, as hormones that encouraged reproduction increased and forced me into carnal battles, I was always aroused. I needed to taste a man as a man tasted me, and then have him force me on all fours. I wanted a man to do what he wanted to do and when he was done to come down my throat. Then I wanted a refuck that would leave come running down my thighs. I didn't want to be fucking intellectual. I wanted the other side of me, the unintelligent side of my brain; I wanted my hidden side to feel pleasure. I wanted him to come on my breasts, give me a pearl necklace, open my chocolate star, make me scream. So very horny. Each day was worse than the day before. I wanted to fuck. I wanted to give him head. I wanted to close my eyes and feel lingam inside of my mouth. I wanted lingam inside my mouth up to his balls. Right here. Right now.

Bret lived minutes away, but wasn't interested in a sequel to our zipless night. Prada was über interested but he was an ocean and a million miles away.

Decadence was a four-hour drive.

For every problem life presented a simple answer.

I went online. Went to the website for Decadence.

Once again I registered.

TWENTY-THREE

There were hundreds of beautiful, colorful masks, each as unique as the libertine that wore them. Venetian masks. Italian masks. Costume ball masks. Half masks. Full masks. My mask was a Cignetta red, white, and black, a half mask with beautiful laser-cut swan and Austrian crystals. My heels were sky high and black with red soles. My dress was red, the color of power.

She was here.

The last bitch that I wanted to see on this planet was here.

Siobhán Kline was here with her sweet bread.

Maybe we had both been drawn here. We arrived at the same moment. She saw me when I pulled up at valet. She was holding her husband's hand, entering Decadence. She wore a red dress as well; hers like the one Jessica Rabbit wore. As fate would have it, in this moment of irony, we both had on the same brand of shoes. Just beyond the check-in, there was a marvelous dance club, an area that served as a place where people could wait for their friends, make friends, find new lovers, or dance and drink before proceeding to the undressing area. There were at least one hundred people dancing in designer gowns, tailored suits, and masks. Siobhán was dancing with Chris when I entered. Another woman was with them, laughing, her dress black and tight, and her skin as smooth as porcelain, her eyes tight, her skin as dark as her dress. A man who looked to be about twenty-one had asked me to dance. He was polite. He was from Seville. He owned a machine company that sold their products throughout Europe. He was six foot four, industrial-size, all muscles. From first impression he was a very cultured, very interesting man who loved the shape of my ass.

Delighted, he told me his name, then asked, "What do you do?"

"I'm an anpopisthographer, Giovanni."

"Sounds very interesting, Nia Simone. Sounds very intriguing."

"It's sort of like being an imagination engineer."

"Then you are good at what you do because as I look at you I am imagining things. We could make those things come true."

While we laughed and danced to a Motown record, I felt Siobhán's eyes on me. I was tempted to walk over to them and ask Chris why he had sent me a friend request on Facebook, then congratulate her on all of the lovely pictures that graced her page, but I kept on dancing and laughing. Even the intellectuals were entitled to petty moments. When the music changed, when they put on reggae, my soul came alive. So did the bodies of every woman, especially those who had spent time in the islands. Reggae gave way to soca. I pulled my dress up a bit and moved my legs like butterfly wings, wining my waist, twirling my head. Chris studied me. I felt it. So did the woman he had married. I tried not to look their way. But I did. I glanced their way. Siobhán did all of the Caribbean dances, but she was not nearly as good as I, not as good as the next woman she had befriended. The tartness of my face soured ripe grapes. My nose cringed as if I smelled a mountain goat. Siobhán was an imitator and my ancestors were the originators. I had taught her my dances in college. I had shared with her my culture and she had robbed me of my happiness. I blocked that from my mind and I danced the dollar wine, made my backside move left, center, right, shimmied with the music, made my bottom fling from side to side, did a jump and wine for a moment, changed and moved my neck and torso, made the dollar wine my dance, backed up and gyrated against my partner, wine and go dong and stick, then kept my upper body still while I wined from the waist down. When the record changed, I thanked my enamored partner, kissed him on his lips, and led him back to his Barcelonan girlfriend. I introduced myself and we shared a few words. His girlfriend was a bodybuilder, her figure incredible. They were interested in me. They were a beautiful couple, but the way Giovanni looked at me, there was something very *mamaguy* about his ways. I turned down an invitation to join them for the masquerade. Then I took my carry-on luggage and

I walked away from them laughing. I wished them good fucking; they wished me the same. I pulled my luggage on wheels behind me, jewelry sparkling, designer dress tight, did a wuk and wine to the music, walked and gyrated at the same time.

I moved with a flirty crowd, an international crowd of the advantaged, eating rich chocolates and sipping high-priced wine, chatted amongst hedonists and libertines, all in pursuit of a state of freedom from emotional disturbance and anxiety. Marquis de Sade had said that hedonism ended in ataraxia.

Bret was on my mind. My feelings for him. So was Prada. His feelings for me, mine for him had garnered another compartment.

Chris and Siobhán were in front of me. They kissed good-bye and he went to the elevator that led to the glass walkway and the men's secret area. Siobhán and I ended up on the same crowded elevator. We were separated by one chatty woman. Time slowed down. She breathed like she had claustrophobia. I gritted my teeth and battled the same swelling emotional paralysis. There was so much tension in the air. It felt as if fate were conspiring against me. Wanted to scream.

When the elevator door opened she couldn't get off fast enough, couldn't walk fast enough. I exhaled, took a deep breath, stepped off the elevator last. I walked the slowest, this time not noticing the art.

But when I was underneath the glass walkway, I looked up.

In the crowd of men going to their undressing room, I saw Chris. He stood there, his mask at his side, waiting, staring down. He waved at me. That seemed surreal. Unreal. Then he had the nerve to wave at me again. Old sentiments lived in that simple motion of the hand. Unspoken regrets, desires were heard. Years ago my emotions had lied to me. They had told me that Chris and I would be together until the end of the aeon. I tried to block the thoughts, but there were whispers in the back of my mind, whispers from every conversation we'd had when we were in college. Heard him whispering about misinterpreted astrological allegories. How he jokingly talked about what he called the invisible man in the sky with the special list of ten things he didn't want us to do, then engaged me in an in-depth conversation about religion and culture, how he looked at the world as a superstitious world. He gave astrological signs no power. He had said that constellations, the zodiac, have been redefined and personified and now the superstitious followed what other fools said were personality traits.

If nothing else, he had made me think in ways new to me. He used to make me laugh at what he believed, and laugh at what I believed as well. In the end there had been no laughter.

As a gaggle of women passed by me, head tilted back, I stared at him for a while. My ex. My rival's husband. Forbidden fruit.

I lowered my head and continued toward the undressing room.

After I found my assigned locker, I showered again. When I was done, I stepped barefoot past women who were talking, slapping asses, some making love. Disturbed by Siobhán being here, bothered by the idea that Chris had stood over me like a god and stared down, I stood nude at the body-length mirror at my locker putting on lotion. Siobhán was in the undressing area, naked, her body sleek, her hair in a 1940s style. As I lotioned my body, she was ten feet away, stepping into her extravagant heels. We were mere feet from each other while I prepared for the evening. She didn't say anything to me as she got ready.

One look from her, one side-eye, a word, even if it were a sweet word, one kind word and I would loose the anger that lived in my heart. As we stood naked in high heels and glitter lotion I would kindle the dead coals of war. I felt her inhaling and exhaling. She wasn't that close but I felt the heat of her breath, the energy from her skin. I didn't say anything to her. I had to take deep, deep breaths and suck on my tongue. She wore a Luna Baroque mask, a mask of blues, and a high silver leaf, varnished and waxed. Nostrils flaring, she left the undressing area before I did. But I caught her looking back at me.

My hair was in small, tight braids on both sides and a vicious Mohawk on top. Hennas covered one arm like a sleeve, the other arm from my shoulder to my elbow. This was how I felt inside. I had my makeup redone by the talented workers, had them do it extreme, as if I were a rock star, the rest of my skin covered with sparkling lotion. After imbibing wine and chocolate and putting on bracelets and necklaces by Coco Chanel, I took my Cignetta mask and explored another area, one exclusively for women. It was a quarter that I had overlooked, offering treatments to keep their backsides shaped and molded. Derriere photos were on each wall, screen shots from Mc Créu's videos, close-ups that showed not a single fault. Beauticians were on duty and there were thirty tables, most filled with women getting work done on their cellulite and stretch marks. Gregarious and loquacious workers and members chattered like sorority girls. High-tech machines were on hand and in that section the beauticians were all dressed in tight white slacks and wore BEAUTY MATTERS T-shirts.

"I want an awesome butt. A head-turning, traffic-stopping butt. I want to make all of the women jealous when their men can't help but look at me when I walk by in a short dress and no underwear on."

"You've been through a lot. Glad to see you back having fun."

"Chemo was a bitch. But we made it through. Hubby was right there at my side and didn't miss an appointment. He's the best of the best of the best. After the mastectomy I was worried about the do over, but they came out fine. It's time for me to live a little and love a lot."

"Make sure you research before you upgrade. I can e-mail you a few doctors to check out."

"Thanks. If I do get my buttocks enhanced, I will need the top and bottom to match. Would be great to take photos and be absolutely stunning. Want to make sure my husband stays attracted to me."

"Just don't use polymethyl methacrylate. That hardens and your ass will be as hard as a chair."

Beyond them was a room filled with bathtubs. Couples were in porcelain tubs bathing together. Women had their heads under the water, sucking off their lovers. Water splashed as others rode their men.

I put my mask on, took on a new personality, and entered the waiting area, again to a sea of nude men in expensive timepieces, all wearing long nose masks. Phallic masks. Venetian plague-doctor masks. Casanova. Checkered. Black. Whites. Golds. Reds. I paused and complimented a few on their masks, then moved on, filled with unbridled energy as I sashayed from room to room, saw sophisticated lovers hiding their faces behind masks designed like Farfallina wings, who wore vintage jewelry to match, lovers to lovers, level to level, a peripatetic lifestyle, then stopped at Eros, stood and watched a sex class. Men were being taught how to move, how to please, how to not come so fast, how to be better lovers.

Chris was in my periphery. He was in the crowd, without his wife.

I glanced behind me. Sea-green eyes were locked on mine.

My lips moved and formed the words, "Good fucking."

He nodded.

His sea-green eyes radiated leftover love.

Mine radiated a hurt that was yet to heal.

Chris walked away. Naked, lingam rising, he walked away.

I felt his energy fade as I pretended to be interested in the abecedarians of erotic love. I was aroused, damp being at a fête where sexual gratification wasn't forbidden for women. I was comfortable in that state. I embraced that sensation, my prelude to finding a handsome man, or men, or joining a couple and exploring, laughing, making love as we aided wingless angels. Bret hadn't touched me the way I had needed to be touched. Prada was nonexistent. So I was a woman who could manage her own needs. I allowed my sway to move me from room to room, speaking in English to some, in French to others, and conversing in Spanish at times. Again I was the new girl, the mysterious vixen, the single woman, and for many the desired unicorn.

While I watched lovers share pleasure, someone put a hand on the small of my back. I turned around and it was a suntanned, petite woman wearing a beautiful half mask, one that looked like the cut of a swan. I grinned. She put her hands underneath my breasts, made them bounce. We laughed. It was Anaïs. She was with her husband, a tall man, the nose on his mask so long it brought to mind the stud we called Quince Pulgadas. Anaïs wore golden stilettos, her golden mask, and a beautiful chain was around her waist, her earrings long. We hugged, breasts to breasts, skin to skin, and she kissed me on my cheeks.

On the big screens I saw Ricardo and Yesenia. The Curaçaoan did marvelous and loving things to his wife, while the woman from Geronimo pulled at the sheets and stared into the eye of the camera.

I asked Anaïs, "Which room are they in?"

"They are home."

"Really?"

"If you like you can connect via Skype and be broadcast live."

"Live streaming."

"They can't see the club. We wouldn't risk anyone recording us."

Anaïs had a large red purse with her.

I asked her what she carried.

She told me that I would find out.

Her husband grinned.

I followed them and we searched for an alcove, ready to give angels their wings. As we walked I saw Siobhán. She was with her husband, his mask was black, and its nose an erection.

Soon a luxurious alcove became available.

We left the curtains opened wide.

Chris and Siobhán appeared on the monitor. They had found themselves a glamorous unicorn. They had recruited a tall, modelesque woman who appeared to be East African, maybe Ethiopian, her skin the softest brown, hair wavy and long, her mask as dark as my feelings toward Chris and his egotistical, backstabbing sylph wife. I stared at the couple that had sponsored the rudest of rude awakenings.

Anaïs asked, "Do you want to watch them? We could join them."

"No. Your husband and you are all that I will need tonight."

For a while he sucked my fingers as she sucked my neck. He kissed my lips. She licked my breasts. Anaïs and her husband tied my ankles with colorful satin scarves. She put handcuffs on me, the kind that used Velcro to close. My heart raced. He removed my mask, he removed what hid me, removed the colors of my island from my face. He stared at me. Ran his fingers across my henna. The contact of skin. I tingled. I made more honey. I made honey as I had done with Bret. For Bret I had made honey that had gone untasted. For Bret I had made honey that I had wished Prada had been available to lick away. My breathing was heavy, anticipatory, nervous, excited. I was moist. Anaïs blindfolded me with a black silk scarf, one that still allowed me to catch glimpses of them and the outline of the Watchers, of the curious poltroons. She sucked my neck as her husband kissed up and down my thighs. Moaning and whispering in heated, aroused, intoxicating Spanish, Anaïs put her mouth close to my ear, licked my ear, sucked my ear and told me that she had a fantasy, something that she had never done and always wanted to do, wanted me to be her first. Delicately asked me if I would object to her using toys. Her husband's tongue danced inside of my yoni. As he sucked my clit, my back arched and I told Anaïs that I was hers for the evening, that if this was what she wanted, was what she needed, then I would be hers. She desired me. She didn't reject me. I didn't have to play a guessing game with her intentions. I expected nothing from her but pleasure and I promised to share with her my inner fire. She couldn't betray me. Her husband used the stiff nose of his mask, rubbed its smoothness against my yoni, then eased it in and out of me. Anaïs asked me if she could make love to me wearing a strap-on. If I did not want that, then she wanted me to make love to her with the strap-on that she had just bought at the store in the lobby. I swallowed. Trembled. Wanted to give an angel its wings. She gave me her tongue. We kissed. Her husband moved his mask away and put his mouth on my sex, put his tongue inside of my sex, and sucked me gently. Orgasm made me vanish from this world. When I regained control, as I rode on this high, as my appetite felt enormous, I told Anaïs that she could do whatever she desired, take me with her strap-on or I could take her. I could try and be the man, or we could take turns. It would be new. It would be my first time. Anaïs and her husband changed positions. Her tongue moved down my thighs and stopped at my fleshy folds as his tongue moved up to my mouth. Her husband moved his mask away, gave me his tongue. Slow kisses. He sucked my tongue as he had done my clit and in Spanish told me I was extremely beautiful. I tingled. Soon they turned me on my side. She ate me from the front as he ate me from behind. So much stimulation. Absolute arousal. Tears fell from my eyes. Anaïs came back to me, stroked my face, and as her husband sucked my clit again, as I came, Anaïs and I kissed. Women kissing fascinated men. Aroused me. Aroused other women.

The world disappeared. Hands bound, legs tied, they tortured me.

Soon Anaïs slid the scarf away from my eyes. She showed me her strap-on, oils, and butt plugs. I nodded, gave consent. I should've been nervous, scared, but I trusted her. I would be her mermaid. Tonight, as Chris pleased his wife, I would be Anaïs's nymph. She wanted to take me as if she were a man and at the same time I would give her husband oral gratification. I consented. Her desire was to take me from behind while I sucked her husband. To take me from behind while her husband took her from behind, to take me vaginally as he took her anally. She longed for me to take her from behind, become the woman releasing her masculine energy, and move my hips and massage every wall of her yoni, give her the full faux lingam as she sucked her husband and made him come. She said all of that in the softest voice, a tone that asked permission. She said it all in Spanish. Vulgar things always sounded better when asked with an accent.

I asked, "Can you make me come all night? Tame me tonight."

"We can. We can both fuck you at the same time."

The abnormal. She offered me the abnormal, and I needed the abnormal to get Bret out of my system, Prada out of my head, and Chris, he needed to be exfoliated from my heart for good.

I gave Anaïs my permission to please me and live her sexual dreams, to use her toys and husband and make fantasies come true, to make my back arch as I vanished from this world over and over.

Chris. Siobhán. I heard them. I felt their energy. Saw them on the screen. My mouth became the shape of the letter *O* and my eyes filled with tears. Pile driver. Siobhán was practically on her head, her knees pulled up to her face. Chris had sat on her and entered her from above. He was pile-driving her. Over and over and over. He did her as he had done me in college, intruded her as he had intruded me, forced himself inside of her as deep as he could. The sense of sight. The sense of sound. No sense of taste or feel, no sense of smell, not from them. Two-fifths of the senses were stimulated by Chris, the other three-fifths by Anaïs and her husband. But I did remember those three senses when they were from Chris. They were part of my past, part of my sense memory, part of me. On my tongue raised his taste, in my nostrils his aroma, at the tips of my fingers, along my skin, along every inch of my flesh, inside and out, was the memory of how he had felt. Siobhán came as I came. We came at the same time. We both sounded wild. We both had so much anger and envy inside of us. She stopped seconds after I stopped. But her concert didn't end. Anaïs and her husband took me the same way I had been taken during a summer in North Carolina, when his journey was only beginning. I could not escape my past. I turned my head, saw the screen beyond the parade of Watchers, the crowd of curious, the gaggle of libertines. Chris made a deep guttural sound, the sensual noise of exertion, of struggling to maintain control. He was fucking Siobhán with a glass dildo while their unicorn deep-throated his cock. A large crowd of Watchers was at their throne. They all wore masks. Minutes passed with me being pleased by my lovers. Chris's excitable murmurs, familiar moans, his sounds of submission and weakness, his pre-come grunts told me that he was beyond the point of no return and was being sucked into the mouth of orgasm. Siobhán wanted me to hear him come. His orgasmic sound rose and spread. As did mine. I wanted them to hear me living in a state of bliss. Our operatic moans danced. Watchers applauded for Chris, his wife, and their lover. Not long after, Watchers applauded for my lovers and me.

TWENTY-FOUR

That sonofabitch Chris had sent me his telephone number again and again and again and a-fucking-gain. Since we were members of the same club, I told myself that I was responding out of courtesy. I told him that it was okay to text. No calls. I didn't want to hear his voice. Not ever again. Then he had insisted that I call him. So here we were. The sea-green eyes of my past stared into my unfriendly face. We used FaceTime, the cousin to Skype, the big brother to texting and e-mailing.

In my most irritated voice I said, "I'm writing so make it quick."

"So brusque."

"Exactly what did you want, Mr. Alleyne?"

He paused and in a kind tone he whispered, "Long time since we actually had a conversation."

"Speak. Get to the point."

After another pregnant pause he shrugged. "Have no idea where to begin. A lot was in my mind, on the tip of my tongue, and now that I'm sitting here looking at you, I have no idea where to start."

"Say what you need to say so we can be done with it."

And there we were, thanks to technology, many miles apart, yet face-to-face. I wanted to flee this moment. But I would never run from anyone again. I studied his face. His chin. His nose. His forehead. His lips. His eyes. I studied him as if he were a photograph that I had just removed from an old dusty box. It was not what I had expected. When a man came inside of you, he never left. I had heard that many times. I had never truly believed that. Not until I sat and stared at him. We had not been alone, not since back in the day. Despite that ending, that horrible ending, I felt our intimate energy, even in this setting.

We said things about Decadence, again keeping the conversation safe as we spoke of the architecture of the establishment, the art, the sculpture, and then the Sinner's Bible that greeted all upon entry.

He said, "The Bible is nothing more than an astrotheological literary hybrid."

"Nice to know that even though you cut your locks, some things haven't changed."

He laughed.

I said, "Just to think I dated and fell in love with an Aquarius."

"And once again, as I have stated before and will again and again, anyone who wants to use celestial placements in order to explain the fate and behavior and destiny of people is a moron. No scientific evidence has ever been found to support astrology's claims."

"Aquarius and Gemini. That's what I get."

"I don't believe in astrology or any superstitions invented by man, but in this case, even with its falsities, I should've heeded that arrangement and all of the warnings that have precluded its union."

I understood his rambling, his going back to that familiar place, to that conversation. He was nervous. Our foundation was built on such conversations. And in that moment, in my mind, I was in a long-ago place, a faraway place, a place before the pain that interrupted pleasure.

I laughed a little. Rubbed my neck. My feet bounced. I exhaled.

He said, "The thing between you and Rigoberto didn't work out."

"Why would you think that it would?"

"Just saying."

"Have you seen your best friend since Hampton?"

"He's not my best friend, not any longer."

"Have you heard from him since . . . since your fight?"

"Not at all. You?"

"Not at all."

"All these years I had imagined that it had somehow worked out."

"Obviously not. Not the way it did between you and Siobhán. I was crazy for you. Rigoberto and I never had a chance at a real relationship. He was just being a good friend when I needed one."

"Siobhán was surprised to see you."

"Likewise."

"Very surprised."

"The first time she looked right in my face and pretended that she didn't recognize me."

"She didn't have her contacts in."

"Sure. Right. Whatever. I was two feet away."

"The makeup, the high heels, the late-night costume that all the women wore. I didn't recognize you in that extreme makeup. I was practically standing in front of you and I wasn't sure that was you. She had had a couple of drinks and you were the last person on her mind."

"I would've recognized her if she had been dissected into a hundred pieces, sent through a Jack LaLanne power juicer, run through a criss-cross shredder, and thrown into the James River."

"I wasn't sure that was you until I heard you moan. That was when I knew it was you. I'll never forget that sound. Delicate. Sweet."

"My moans."

"I don't recall seeing you in more than sweats back in the day. Big change."

"Well, if you must know, my collegiate attire, that is still what I wear most days. I work at home so I look like I do now most of the time, keep my hair pulled back into a ponytail, plain and simple."

"It's down your back now. Looks very appealing."

"I stopped cutting it a long time ago."

"It looks nice. You look really good. Amazing, actually."

"Can't believe that you chopped off your locks."

"They were down to my butt."

"Why did you cut them?"

"They had become pretty heavy, especially when wet."

"You had the most amazing locks ever."

"This is funny. My hair is shorter. Your hair is longer."

"As it should be on a man and a woman, let society tell it."

We stopped talking for a while. Had a hard time looking at each other. A heaviness rose up inside of me. My throat felt tight.

I found my center, took deep breaths, found control, and I stared at his clean-shaven face, so professional, that face of the Mensa and former football player, that look that had changed without asking for my permission, as I had evolved without needing his consent.

I walked around and asked, "How's marriage? Seriously. Not being facetious. I mean besides the obvious fun, besides the interesting sex. How are things with you and Siobhán?"

"All marriages are happy at the start."

"I heard that some are even good until after the honeymoon."

"You and that mouth."

"There are no absolutes in this world. You were a physics genius. You know about absolutes."

"True. Most are happy at the start. If they would end right at the I dos, most would probably be perfect."

"But?"

"Maybe it's the living together that causes the problems. Married people should be required to have separate residences. Would be a much better world if husbands and wives didn't cohabitate."

"That's called dating."

"And anything less than separate-but-equal habitations is called insanity."

"Wow. I guess that means that you and I never would have . . . nothing."

"What?"

"Nothing. That would have been off base, out of line."

"What?"

"You've never been one to complain. But that was a few years ago. And I guess when you view a person from inside of a relationship, with the eyes and heart of love, they are colored by your emotions."

"Maybe I have changed. I'm older. Have dealt with life issues. And marriage changes us all."

"The years change us. Awaken us. So far as marriage and its side effects, good or bad, I wouldn't know. Not sure if that is in my cards."

"Marriage will make a deaf man grouse in sign language."

I asked, "Where are you living?"

"Miami. Fisher Island."

"So, you're one of Oprah's neighbors."

"She sold her property. Where are you located these days?"

I said, "Outside of Atlanta in the suburbs."

"There are ten or eleven cities in the US named Atlanta."

"But there is only one that counts."

"So you're a three-hour drive from the club."

"Closer to four, traffic permitting."

"People fly into Charlotte, then drive the hour or so to get there."

"You and Siobhán?"

"That's what we do. Fly in, then take a limo."

"Impressive."

Chris said, "I imagined that you were back in Los Angeles hanging with the movie stars, maybe working for your mother."

"Will be going back that way soon. Just wrapped up a big project and my mother was the coproducer. She's trying to force my hand and make me a version of her. But I am resisting. Every day I resist."

"Your mother? How is Miss Hazel Tamana Bijou-Wilson doing?"

"She dropped the Wilson."

"Right, right. After the divorce. She's doing okay?"

"She's great."

"You're home in Atlanta now?"

"Pardon the mess. Just moved. No time to unpack."

"Did you just step inside of an elevator?"

I nodded. "Heading down to the kitchen."

"Looks like you're in a brownstone in New York."

"Your home looks stunning as well. Very, very posh."

"My wife put a lot of money into the place."

"The years have been kind to her. She hasn't gained any weight."

"Not as kind as the years have been to you. You actually look younger. And you're smaller than you were when . . . at Hampton."

"You and your wife. So much applause. She looked good nude, on her back, your lingam inside of her mouth, and draped in jewels."

There was no reply from him.

I opened my refrigerator, poured a short glass of juice, then rode the elevator back to the top level. The top level wrapped around, U-shaped. On the far side of the U was where I had an EFX machine, P90X CDs in front of a thirty-two-inch television, free weights, and a treadmill. The treadmill was folded up. I let it down, then placed the iPad on the lip in front of the controls and started a slow jog. Too much anxiety was inside of me. I had to run, had to get this energy out of me.

"You're working out. I mean you're still working out."

"I am. Sometimes two or three times a day. Short runs. Sit-ups. Push-ups. If I'm restless in the middle of the night, I will run awhile."

"You're definitely smaller. You're thinner."

"You're saying that I was fat in college?"

"You had a little more junk in the trunk."

"Well if my ass was spreading, it was because of you."

"Because of me?"

"Dick does a body good. Dick makes a woman fill out."

He laughed.

I laughed too.

We shared a laugh.

My cellular buzzed. I knew the ringtone. Prada was calling. He had earned his own ringtone. That told me something. It was like he had a drawer inside of my home. I didn't answer.

I ran.

Chris stared at me.

We talked as if nothing bad had ever happened. I didn't mention Siobhán again and he didn't mention Rigoberto anymore. His former best friend. As Siobhán had been my former best friend.

He said, "You were at Decadence with someone?"

"No. I was alone. I go alone."

"You're not married?"

With a small towel I wiped sweat away from my face. "Not married. Only one person in this conversation is wearing a ring. There is no tan line on my ring finger from removing the truth."

"Divorced?"

"Never married."

"Betrothed?"

"Nope and never have been and don't see being betrothed in my immediate future. I said that a couple of minutes ago. Pay attention."

"Kids?"

I gave him a face that told him he had lost his mind.

I said, "When you heard me say that I had never married, you knew the answer to that."

"Life leads us often not down the road of our choosing."

"True. We do have to adapt to new circumstances all of the time."

"I thought you'd have a family and some man would be taking care of you by now."

"I take care of myself. Other than my mortgage company, I am indebted to no man."

"You've been on my mind. Actually, hardly a day passes when I don't think of you."

"Wish I could say the same. Never expected to see you again before Judgment Day. Thought that I would be in that short line going north and look over and see you in that long line going south."

He nodded. "Strange the way we ran into each other."

I whispered, "You watched me. Jesus. You watched me have sex."

"I did."

"Pervert."

"You were damn good."

I pushed stop on the controls and the treadmill slowed.

I said, "Not as good as you and Siobhán. She was very creative."

"You were someone else, not the girl from college."

"I'm still that same girl. Inside, somewhere inside I still am."

"You watched me too."

"I sure did. As perverted as that was, I did. Your wife . . . she's awesome. The crowd loved her cute circus tricks. Good to see those gymnastic and cheerleading skills came in handy later on in life."

Then we shared another earnest laugh. A deep, deep belly laugh. A laugh of the ridiculous. I grabbed another towel and wiped sweat away from my face, my neck. Chris and I stared at each other a moment.

He said, "That was sexy."

"What?"

"Watching you just now. The way you were breathing. The way you ran."

"Chris."

"Yeah, babe?"

"Nia. Not 'babe.' "

"Yeah, Nia."

"This isn't Decadence. But there should be rules."

He nodded.

Chris said, "I have to leave soon."

"Same here. I need to shower and get dressed."

"Feel free to keep FaceTime going while you take your shower."

"Not gonna happen. Nice chatting. Take it easy, Chris."

"Nia."

"Yeah, Chris?"

"I've seen it all before."

"Smart and intelligent one moment, then so childish the next."

"I want to watch you. I want to masturbate and watch you."

I paused. "You're serious? You want to masturbate."

"Let me watch you. Let me be a Watcher."

"We're not at the club."

"Just me and you. No crowds."

"You said that you have to go."

"It can wait."

A long moment went by, a very long moment, a moment of inner battle, a moment where the dark side inside of me demanded servile behavior from other parts of me. In the end I stared at the man who had given his wife a seven-carat marquis-cut ring in the shape of a football, another ring that had followed the precedent set by the Archduke Maximilian of Austria, a ring that would never grace my finger.

I licked the corners of my lips. "I've never done that before."

"Will you?"

Part of me felt excited. Another part told me to maintain my commitment to emotional maturity. For whatever reason we had found each other again. And with each breath, I felt as if I were still in college. Maybe this was fate, kismet in action, and my destiny in motion. Chris was a married swinger. I had ended up in the same lifestyle, for this period of my life. He was far away, yet close. Memories of the five senses of him moved across my flesh.

I said, "Sure. If you shower at the same time."

"Serious?"

"Sure. Watch me and I watch you."

"Will you masturbate?"

"Why should I?"

"Fair exchange."

"Not exactly. Seems to be your fantasy at the moment."

"Why not spice it up a bit?"

"What do you mean?"

"Do you have a vibrator?"

"Chris. Seriously?"

"I bought you your first vibrator."

"Yeah. You did."

"Have one?"

"Jesus. Yes, I have a vibrator."

Chris walked through his elegant property, through echoes of his self-indulgent lifestyle, a home on an island. From room to room it was as pristine as a museum. He entered a bathroom of marble and recessed light, candles throughout, the touch of a woman. He put his phone at an angle, set it up to be seen. I watched him undress. Saw his physique flex as he pulled his shirt over his head. Memories of the first time that he had undressed in front of me rose. I'd been excited and terrified because I had known what was about to happen, knew we were about to make love. The way his broad shoulders moved, the V-shape of his upper torso, it was as if I had never seen him naked before.

By then I was in my master bedroom, the bottom drawer on my dresser open, a dozen vibrators and toys staring at me, begging to be chosen, begging to vibrate against my spot, begging to intrude me.

I said, "Surprise, surprise. You're already erect."

"Almost."

"Bigger than I remember. But the camera does add ten pounds."

"Watching you run . . . told you . . . that was hot."

"You were playing with yourself."

"I was. That's why I'm chubbed up."

"Maybe you should go put it inside of your wife's big mouth."

"She's not here."

"If you don't have horse, ride cow."

"You and that mouth. You're the one with the mouth."

"Shame on you. I was talking to you and you were jacking off."

"Shame on me."

"Didn't think that I was worthy of an act of self-gratification."

"You are."

For a long time I had missed sneaking away, spending the night somewhere off campus, and waking up beside him. A lot had happened over those years. I had missed him poking my butt in the middle of the night and feeling him grind against me. I had missed oiling his scalp. I had missed his smell. I had missed his taste. No one ever said our names separately, spoke them as if we were to be together forever.

Then I was naked, self-conscious of my nakedness, questioning of my appeal, inside of my shower, and he was inside of his shower, his big shower. I knew that I was beautiful, knew that beauty emanated from within, but I didn't think either appealed to him. I looked at him and maintained my poker-faced stare, as if nothing about him were arousing. Water ran over his naked body, over his muscles, over his frame. It was a waterfall shower and he stood underneath, his face wet. I wet my body as I stared at him, as I evaluated him, this version of him, a man I used to know so well. Then I soaped my body. Soaped myself slowly. With him watching, I didn't put a shower cap on. There were no fantasies that included shower caps. I had two of my toys, a rabbit and a dildo formed from the cast of a porn star's penis.

Chris stroked himself. As I watched him I leaned into the wall and pulled at my nipples and bit my bottom lip. At times I loved to masturbate. So I did. Today I loved making myself feel this way. There was a joy in self-loving. There was something erotic, exotic, and again empowering in taking responsibility for my orgasm.

He had known me in college. He had seen me at Decadence. He knew this side of me, as I knew this side of him. My sex drive was strong. I was proud of its strength, of hormonal influences.

Chris masturbated as if it were as normal as breathing.

He didn't deny his nature, didn't deny being a sexual being.

His breathing became shallow, thick, and deep as he wanted to be inside of me. I picked up the vibrator and eased it inside of me. I heard Chris moan. He moaned loudly. I fucked myself as he stroked himself. I made my rhythm match his, made it feel like he was fucking me. He called my name and in my post-orgasmic haze I watched him. He was about to come. As he growled, and masturbated harder and faster, as he milked himself, I closed my eyes, as it was impossible for me to come with my eyes open. Leaning against the tiled wall, I came. Then we stared at each other, panting, catching our breaths, returning to normal, both of us soaking wet, standing underneath waterfalls that were states away, cities away, miles away.

Naked. Warm water raining on us. Like Tarzan. Like Jane.

Soon he asked, "May I call you again?"

"Tell Siobhán that I said hello when she gets home."

I ended the session. I left him without a good-bye.

My cellular chirped. It was a text message. I stepped out of the shower and checked to see who had sent me a text message.

It was Bret. As I had done yesterday, I deleted his text without reading it. After the night in Florida, after he had dropped me off at the gates to my community, I hadn't responded to any of his texts. He served no purpose in my world. He didn't desire me. So I rejected him. Now I ran by myself. I missed running with him. Missed his company. But we had nothing in common. We didn't sex. He didn't read. He was basic. I would leave him to his children and divorce drama.

Then I stepped back into the shower. I took my mind off both the warrior and the king. As the shower steamed, I continued masturbating, continued fantasizing, my refractory period almost nonexistent.

TWENTY-FIVE

Via FaceTime, Chris called every afternoon. Like he had done at Hampton, he rang me every day. Sometimes I answered. I answered in time for him to reveal himself having an orgasm. I would watch him come. Then I would hang up. Work took precedence. I worked on the next screenplay. I ghostwrote. I ran. With Chris on my mind, with Decadence being part of my world, with Bret and Prada humming in the background, I wrote many, many, many pages of *Abnormal Desires*. I was beyond writing about twins and insane wives and storms and madness. I included my first night at Decadence. I included my second night there. I wrote of my nights without shame. Not bowdlerized. Explicit. And during my busy season I had many calls, countless interviews, some again using Skype and FaceTime, and each day I chatted with my overly ambitious mother about our upcoming responsibilities. Once again I talked to my wonderful, underpaid, overworked New York agent about possibly doing a novel using my true name, something that I was not comfortable with.

"Give it a thought, Nia."

"Then I would have to go out and promote."

"I think that you would be marvelous."

"Probably end up living out of a suitcase year round."

"Writing books with your face up front makes you the brand and when you are the brand your job becomes selling books, so then you will be in sales. Conventions, book signings, book clubs."

"Planes. Trains. Automobiles. Forgetting which city I'm in."

"Early mornings and late nights, if you are successful."

"I don't want to live out of a bag. I don't want to be up at four o'clock every morning to get to the next city in time for morning interviews. I don't want to eat hotel food and not be able to exercise. Sitting all day, a sedentary occupation is already unhealthy enough. That is why I work out. The writers that I have ghostwritten for, I have followed their careers, read their interviews. I just don't need to meet that many people. People are mean. They love to dish out backhanded compliments."

He said, "Times are changing. eBooks are sending a shiver down the spine of the publishing industry. I have no idea how the wind will blow, so it's a good thing that you're branching out into Hollywood at this point. Novelists are taking a hard hit, but I think that you can still do well. Many predict that eBooks are either going to be the saving grace for the publishing industry, or the final nail in its coffin."

"Books are dying. Bookstores are almost obsolete. I give it two generations."

"And then trees shall only die to make toilet paper."

"Unless they come up with an e-wiper."

He laughed.

I laughed too.

He said, "This is why you would be excellent as a touring author."

"The best that I might be willing to do, and that is a small might, is have my name on the cover of a novel that I have ghosted or worked on with someone. That and no picture on the back or inside."

"You're so beautiful."

"But I am from the wrong tribe. My face would not enhance sales. That's a reality. We have to do what works for the bottom line."

"We will talk about this some more in a few days."

"Make it a few weeks. The movie is coming up. Countless interviews. Too much on my plate and that is not top priority."

"I'll try to make it to Los Angeles for your premiere."

"I would love to see you there. But I know you have a sick wife right now."

And as soon as I finished that call, I looked for Chris on FaceTime. I looked for him. I called him. He answered immediately.

I said, "I'm about to shower."

"Let me get my lotion."

In a matter of days, after talking of our days gone by, we agreed to meet where our paths had crossed once again. We would meet again at Decadence. I had planned on going back very soon anyway. I had circled more events. The one that intrigued me was a Unicorn Party. I was ready to meet my lover from Curaçao and his wife, was eager to have him please me as I used my hands and tongue and pleased his wife, as attractive women had pleased me. Feeling greedy, I had told myself that I could be to her what the Brit with the wicked tongue had been to me, what Kiki Sunshine had been to me in the distant past. Fair was fair and a promise was a promise. I owed the woman who was born in Geronimo, Oklahoma, a debt of gratitude. As Anaïs had suggested when I was in my interview, as she had showed me during her heated moment, I would pretend that I was a man, and that the vixen I was pleasing was me, and as a man I would do the things to me that I loved. But the past wanted to meet. Everything inside of my body said no. But my unhealed heart said yes. That was new for me. Feeling for an ex, for an old lover, that was a new sensation. Not being wanted, being refused, maybe not being pursued, that was new to me as well. Yet it was old to me at the same time. Rejection was one of the least-desired emotions.

And Chris Eidos Alleyne was right there.

Wanting me as if he had never stopped wanting me.

After he had once again masturbated, this time via Skype, he said, "So we will meet at Decadence?"

"You want me there?"

"Yes. I can fly up and take a limo over."

"For what purpose?"

"We can be Watchers."

"Nothing more."

"Watch. And nothing more."

"If you want me there, you pay my entry fee."

"No problem. I will."

"And you will send a limo to pick me up, deliver me there, wait for me until the end of the night, and bring me back home afterward."

"I can arrange that."

"Serious. I'm not driving. And have the limo on standby to drive me back home the same night. There will not be an overnight stay."

"So, you're not spending the night at a hotel in the area?"

"And I want to be in a stretch limo with wine and peeled grapes."

"I can arrange that. But you might have to peel your own grapes."

"Send me the confirmation. Then delete it from your inbox."

"Okay. You're not going to stand me up, are you?"

Naked, orgasms done and faded, this sin completed, my expression once again dour, my vibrator fell from my hand to my bed.

"Guess you'll have to show up and wait and see, Chris."

I pushed the end button. I was a queen.

I wanted to regain my throne.

TWENTY-SIX

Laughing, competitive, Chris Eidos Alleyne and I had played nude volleyball.

That physical exercise had been energizing. When we were done, we had showered separately, then I put on red lingerie—it was lingerie night at the club. My past and I reconnected in the hallway, over the glass floors, and we stood and watched lovers do their thing. But I didn't keep my lingerie on very long. Within thirty minutes we were upstairs in the glass-bottom pool. Heated from watching sex, I needed to cool off. Again I showered. Then we met and walked to one of the bars in Eros. I wore only heels. He wore only a watch. We were both nude. We drank wine that he had brought along. I ate decadent chocolate. I felt good. A while later we came upon an empty alcove.

He said, "It's just been cleaned. Has fresh flowers and brand-new sheets."

"The maids just left. What's your point?"

"Let's claim this space before someone else does."

"Check the ring finger on your left hand. Why would we do that?"

He had looked at me and I was once again at college, skydiving without a parachute.

He said, "We don't have to do anything."

Music throbbed while stimulating adult movies were projected on the walls. Each wall displayed a different love affair, a different style of sex. All that showed on the wall was someone's fantasy, all that showed was someone's reality.

I told Chris, "If I did go in there with you, to talk, you know the rules of the club."

"I can't touch you unless you ask me to or give me permission."

"Remember that."

"Do you still believe that the only rational behavior is to pursue your own self-interest?"

"That's Ayn Rand."

"You used to quote her all the time. Her value system. Her radical, self-serving beliefs."

"Did I? Wow. Well, I guess you subscribed to her philosophy more than I did."

"Let's get an alcove. We can continue the discussion there."

"I'm not sleeping with you, so get that fantasy out of your head."

"We can sit. Be alone. Talk."

"What would we talk about, exactly?"

"We've talked naked before."

"In college. Many times. We were lovers then."

"And a few of those times we were high on weed."

"Yes, we were. We had smoked a tree and sipped wine. It's different now."

"Is it?"

"I don't know what this is. But you're a married man. You've moved on to new dreams. With the humanitarian cheerleader."

"Why do you keep bringing her up when I'm here with you?"

"She garnered the tiara. I tutored her. I hate her. She fucked you behind my back. After all the fights she was given the crown, the ring, and I guess I was Miss Congeniality. Well, I snapped, lost my cool and I guess that that secondary title was stripped from me as well. With you I had been a star, then this star collapsed. When a star collapses it becomes infinitely dense and creates a black hole. A black hole sucks in everything in its vicinity, destroys everything, and consumes everything. That is what it felt like I tried to do for a long, long time."

"What would you suggest?"

"I know that there is at least one couple here looking for a unicorn. I saw this woman in the undressing room. She's very hot. And you're pretty hot yourself, Chris. There are a lot of Siobháns here. I hear foreign women talk about their Mandingo fantasies so I know at least one

Russian husband here would love to watch you please his wife. Amazes me how men get off watching their wives fuck a man of another race or nationality. But the contrast is sexy. Getting to partake of the pleasures of a new country. We can go our separate ways and we can meet again in an hour, and maybe talk some more."

He smiled. "What if I just want to look at you and jack off?"

"That's grown old. We've done that enough." I smiled. "Siobhán has no idea that you're here. You broke a promise and came with me."

"She has no idea."

"You used me to be able to get in."

"And to be fair, at this moment, I have no idea what she's doing."

"Feeding the poor?"

"Beyond that."

"She's had sexual experiences beyond the confines of this marriage, surreptitiously."

"A man never knows what a woman will do given space and opportunity. She travels a lot. At times she's impossible to reach."

We commandeered an alcove. Watchers gathered. But I smiled, shook my head, and shut the thick curtains on curious eyes. When I closed the curtains, it was as if this other part of me opened up. I'd never imagined being alone with my past, not after the horrible way he had treated me at the end of our affair. Never thought that I would be able to look at him and not want to stab him in his heart.

I asked, "Where is the wife?"

"Lima, Peru. I'm joining her the day after tomorrow."

"Peru. Sounds interesting."

He said, "I really want you."

"That's direct."

"It's how I feel."

"We said talk only."

"I want you. I've missed you. I've regretted not being with you."

For a moment, I glared at him, at his weakness, a weakness that had been inside of him when we had been a couple, and I contemplated the power that I had over him, a power that he used to have over me.

I said, "You want to behave badly one more time."

"I want to make love to you. Like we did in college."

"We're not in love and we're definitely not in college anymore."

"I'm in love."

"No you're not."

"It sure feels that way."

"That season of insanity and youthful folly has come and gone."

"The smell of you, the taste of you, I'm back in college."

"Are you?"

"In my brain, in my heart, the way that I have longed for you every day and night, the way I hear old songs and think of you, it wasn't that long ago. To me it was only yesterday."

Memories joined us. Stood before me smiling.

He said, "I would leave her for you."

"Would you?"

"I would. I have always felt that way."

"Did she ask you the same? In college, did she ask you if you would leave me for her? Was it that easy back then?"

"If only you hadn't come by the dorm that day."

"But I did. Wish I hadn't. But I did. Was it easy to have me thrown out of your dorm and to watch me beg for you to take me back? I had walked in on you and her fucking and in the end I was the one crying and apologizing for my behavior. Chris, I was with you that morning. We had made love. I mean, was it really that easy for you?"

He rubbed his head. "It wasn't easy. I didn't know she was coming by. She popped up. Next thing I know, you're walking into my dorm room."

"What a moment. I opened the door and what a moment."

"Yeah. Every day I've missed the fun we had and shared. I've missed the love. The meals. The conversations. We were friends, Nia."

At last I whispered, "We did have good times. More than I can count. More than I want to remember. My sentiments were strong. I was uxorial back then. Like a wife. When it was good, it was fantastic. Can't deny that. I have a big box filled with cards, letters, and pictures. I look at those and see the smile on my face and I can feel it all."

"For old time's sake."

I searched for words, for a certain combination of words to be arranged in a specific order to tell him how I felt at that moment.

I said, "Eat me."

"What?"

"Crawl to me in slow motion. Beg me. Eat me."

I was no longer the naïve girl that I had been back then. I was a woman now. But in reality I knew that no matter how old I was, when I saw him, I would regress to being in college again. This was the part of me that had risen from the ashes of our failed relationship. Now I always sought out what wasn't available. I had been robbed, so I robbed others. This was nefarious, yet it felt comfortable; again my nature took the road less traveled, and pursued the unattainable.

He fell to his knees like a soldier surrendering to his queen, and he licked me. I placed both hands on his head, guided him.

Tingles rose. Ice melted. Anger dissipated. I stopped him, paused our battle when old feelings metastasized, infected my heart, and I started to feel light-headed, like an obsessed flibbertigibbet.

He backed away and said, "That's all I get?"

I made him back away as music throbbed, as I danced Caribbean dances, as I danced the Dutty Wine, as I dropped my ass, eased it back up, rocked my hips left and right and forward and straight back. I made erotic faces and danced the tick tock, did some downright provocative dancehall moves. Then I balanced myself on my head, used my hands for stability, moving to the beat in the background, moved in waves like the ocean, and I danced a raunchy head-top.

While blood rushed to my head and added to my high, while mixed emotions battled inside of me, he stood where my legs parted, held my ass and lowered his face, gave me his tongue, allowed his tongue to dart inside of me, to plunge inside of me, to paint long strokes, to write numbers as if he were writing me a bad check; and Chris Eidos Alleyne ate my yoni better than he had eaten me in college—not as good as other lovers, but he was decent—he was famished, proved to me that I was as esculent as his trophy wife, if not more. He had tasted me, then paused and looked at my response. After I had been on my head so long I felt as if I was about to pass out, he eased me to the floor, and where my yoni went his tongue followed.

I controlled him.

In college, he was so popular that many men were no more than his servants and would have extended to their running-back king the privileges of *prima nocta*, where a lord had the right to take a man's wife for himself on her wedding night. I wanted to kick him off his pedestal and make him less than a servant. I made myself the queen and I had sexual rights to the husband of any woman I chose.

I said, "Don't stop eating me. Don't you dare stop."

Chris Eidos Alleyne took the mouth that was meant for his wife, the tongue that was meant for her pleasure and tasted my yoni as I gripped his head and tried to push his face inside of me. Making him eat me, it was a hard-core rush, right or wrong.

It was about power. I found that rousing. It was invigorating.

I wished Siobhán had walked in. I would once again tutor her. It was not in my spirit to see another woman shattered, wasn't in me to do intentional harm but there was an exception to every rule.

Orgasm rose.

In college he would give me head, but never like this. He was a different lover now. I had to stare at him, this man who no longer had dreadlocks, this man licked me like he was losing his mind.

I said, "You've missed Trinidad, haven't you?"

He nodded, told me that he had missed my yoni, that he had missed my presence in his life, that he had dreamed of me so many times, had looked for me and found me online, but was afraid to send me a message. He had fantasized on the day he married that I would magically show up and ruin the event. But it had already gone too far. The dress had been bought. Everything had been reserved. Invitations had been sent out. Expectations were high. The wedding planner had been paid. Nothing was refundable. Four hundred people had taken vacation and bought plane tickets and rented hotel rooms.

He paused, softened his timbre. "I wish that I had married you."

"I wish that you had only been a zipless fuck."

"What is that? A zipless fuck?"

"A one-night stand."

"That stabs me deep."

"And I really want to twist the knife. You have no idea how badly I want to twist the knife."

He said, "I want to be inside of you again."

"When you stood in Eros spying on me, you liked what you saw."

He said, "I want to make love to you again."

"You want to fuck me. You want your orgasm to be your victory, your trophy made of spunk."

"Nia."

"The truth? Do you want me to tell you the truth?"

"Yes. Sure. The truth."

"After we broke up, even as I fell into rebound relationships, even as I was a bitch and mean to nice men who really cared for me, even when my heart had gone cold, I wanted you. I had sex and saw your face on their faces. And you invaded my fucking dreams. Nighttime was the worst. In some strange, perverse way, I wanted you. Everyone knew. Everyone at Hampton knew. They knew that you had left me for her. They knew about the incident. I was almost thrown off campus. My mother went off on me. I had almost ruined my life, my education, over you. My mother hates you. She hates your fucking guts the way Jewish immigrants hate the name Hitler. I did too. So if I saw you, I walked by as if you were invisible, or I just took another route, went across campus hoping not to run into you or your friends. I had to be strong. I always found something in my life to remind me of you. A T-shirt that you bought me. A cup that you left behind. A bracelet that you gave me. A scientific calculator you left. I threw it all away. Didn't help much. Everywhere I went, there were reminders of you. Your homies. The newspaper. Everyone treated you like a deity. And since I'm not the worshipper of pagan gods, or of any man, I put on my big girl panties and rode the heartache out. Cried so much, I still loved you, but I loved me more. That was when I became less outgoing at school. Not easy walking around with a scarlet *F* for *fool* on your chest."

"It was never my intent to leave you. Siobhán wasn't the endgame. You walked in on us and the best way I can express that moment, the most eloquent way that moment can be expressed is by saying . . . I fucked up and the shit hit the fan and you set Wilder on fire."

"What a fight that was. I didn't even recognize myself that day."

"I freaked out. I didn't handle the situation very well. Went to Becky's Buckroe Florist to order one hundred and one roses for you."

"Didn't get them."

"Didn't think you would accept them."

"You're right. And by the way, I hate roses."

"Since when? You loved them in college."

"One day you were my man, the next it was all over."

"We broke up abruptly. My wandering eye got the best of me."

"I learned a lot from that abrupt breakup. Almost as much as I learned reading Henry Miller."

"So did I. Learned more from our breakup than I did in any class."

"I learned about love's power but I've also learned about its downside. Love has too many side effects. I suffered them all. Nausea, lack of appetite, temporary paralysis, weight gain, vomiting, headaches, drowsiness, nose bleeds, diarrhea, constipation, unexplained rash, changes in moods, irrational behavior, anal bleeding, thoughts of suicide that lasted all of ten seconds, thoughts of seeing you and running you over in my car that lasted all of two years, irregular cycle and spotting between periods. I would have rather had cancer."

"Jesus."

"It was a living death. I used to pray that something bad happened to you on the field."

"Guess you got your wish."

"Not really. I wanted to see you carried off the field with a broken neck, paralyzed from the neck down. But I settled for a blown-out knee. Can't say that I was sad the day I heard that tackle had ended your football career. I popped open a bottle of wine, put on some soca by Alison Hinds, turned up the volume, and danced my ass off."

"Damn."

"What goes around comes around."

"Back then I wanted to come back to you."

"You're happy now?"

"She's my wife. She's a benevolent woman. She belongs to a dozen charities and supports a dozen causes, and is a churchgoing woman. But she's not my soul mate. You were my soul mate."

"When did you start believing in that soul-mate bullshit?"

"When did you stop?"

"The day that I broke up with you."

"When you were gone, I believed. When we were done, I realized that the concept was real."

"Whatever."

"I fucked it up. I knew that I'd never get over that one mistake."

"Healing a broken heart isn't easy."

"Neither is living with regret."

"Why did it turn out that way?"

"Please forgive me."

"There were a hundred women you could've chosen. Maybe a thousand women at the school would have loved to have you as their man. You chose the one you . . . you chose her. The part about her being tutored by me, her being my friend, didn't that matter to you at all?

"She was the outlier and worked her way into your bed. Somehow I ended up becoming the outlier. She stayed with you to prove a point and give the middle finger to her parents, the school, and society."

"I never saw you as an outlier. If anyone was, that was me."

"You chose her over me. You kicked me out of your dorm."

"Because you were going crazy."

"You made security escort me away and she stayed."

"I loved you so much."

"What type of love was that? If that's love, I'd hate to see hate."

A moment passed. "You made it known that you were done with me. You would've killed her if I hadn't had you removed."

"I would have."

"You would have killed me if I had let you stay."

"How many times had you fucked her before you got busted?"

He hesitated. "A few times. She would sneak by after her session with you, on the days you had another tutoring session right after hers."

"While I tutored other students, you were having sex with her?"

"She only came by a few times. At first it was to talk to me about making an appearance for a benefit. Something to do with raising money for starving kids in Africa or Haiti, can't remember."

"Keep it real. That means that you were with her a lot. Was she the only one? Be honest. We can be honest. Were there other women on campus? Were you having sex with more of the people I tutored?"

He said, "You know how they are, the groupies. They throw themselves at the players. They sneak into the dorms in the middle of the night. They show up naked, ready to have sex without talking."

"There were others?"

"Let's not go down that road."

"There were others."

"But no matter how many times I was with her, or anyone else, it was just sex. It was physical, never emotional. It meant nothing."

"Just another workout. Just another team on the field."

"Interesting analogy. But it was sex. Not love."

"Love me while you fuck other women."

"We do foolish things when we're young."

"What are we doing now?"

"We're adults now."

"This looks pretty imprudent to me."

He whispered, "You torture me. You shower naked. You make me masturbate. Now you sit in front of me. I can smell you. It's like I'm inhaling you. And this is nothing but torture. I taste you on my tongue."

"I'm sadistic."

"I guess that makes me masochistic."

"Why are you staring at me like that?"

"Just the tip?"

"That was how you seduced me in college. With the tip."

"Just the tip. Just let it taste you."

"No."

"Let it tell you how much it has missed you."

"Your lingam talks now."

"That mouth."

"That sweet dick. That fat cock. That magical prick. I had given it so many names. But in the end, I just called it lingam. My lingam."

"Just the tip."

A moment passed and I repeated, "Just the tip."

I looked at the multitude of memories that surrounded us in the alcove. I saw memories of the first flirt, the first phone call, the first date, the first hand-holding, the first kiss, the first laugh; flashbacked to the first time we did laundry together. Remembered going to the games and him waving to me from the field, remembered the first time that we studied together, the first time we had made love, the second time we had made love, recalled each time; and all of the warm memories ignited some false hope and I had become who I was then, a foolish believer, and I had surrendered to the pangs of an unrequited love.

I desired him. Part of me had never stopped desiring him.

We carried our past with us wherever we went.

He said, "Aren't you curious?"

"Forever curious."

"About us. To know what we feel like now."

"It used to be good."

"Better than good."

I whispered, "I'll want more than the tip. I'll want more."

"It that permission to enter?"

I whispered, "Just the tip."

"Just the edge of our memories."

"Like the beginning, when it was good, when I was mad for you."

"And I was mad too."

"No more than the tip."

"Just the tip, just the beginning."

"The beginning was amazing."

That was all he gave me for a long while, the mushroom of his lingam, the part that was designed to open a woman, to open a yoni that was lubricated from memories. Again I was in college, remembering the days before it all went to hell, swimming in the warmth of those feelings and promises. We were no longer like oil and water, no longer two mutually immiscible liquids. I took flight and the hands of time moved counterclockwise. I saw Homecoming. Spring Fest. I moaned like I was in the jazz ensemble. So did he. The mushroom, the hat, his head moved back and forth, became slick with my dampness. He teased me over and over. He teased me and teased himself. He became hard and I moved against his length, and he rubbed his length up and down my opening. Soon he gave me the tip again. Then a little more than the tip. Then a little more of the memories came to life. Saw us bowling at the six-lane alley. Roller-skating. Dancing in the ballroom. Sitting in the food court. He gave me more memories. Swimming. On Jet Skis. Boating on the weekend. I felt him opening me, easing inside of me. I trembled as he gave me more memories, memories that were as bright as yellow roses. We were back in the dorm. I expected to open my eyes and see that room. But when my eyes eased open, my past was staring in my face, unblinking, so much intensity, so much seriousness in his. He held my face and wanted to kiss me. I refused. It wasn't right to kiss a whore. Still, even as I tried to make him nothing in my world, he stirred those old feelings once again, and I lost my power and became fragile. I wanted more than just the tip. I wanted to go back in time and redo the way things had ended between us. I wanted to undo heartbreak. I wanted to undo hamburger fights and confrontations. I wanted to not let my emotions and needs and selfishness and desire for retribution allow Rigoberto between my legs. I wanted to not damage the friendship between two men. I wanted to remove myself from this trajectory of darkness.

He said, "I've missed you. I've missed you. I've missed you."

"I've missed you too, Chris. I've missed you so fucking much."

As a thousand moans filled the club, as I heard skin slapping against skin, as I heard laughter and celebration, his skin slapped against mine, and I held on to him, encouraged him to stroke me as my *oohs* blended with his *aahs* and we joined the chorus. He stroked me, pulled out, gave me his tongue, licked me, stroked me again, and licked me again. Then I sat on him, let him fill my insides, rose up and took him inside of my mouth, sucked, rode his face reverse, then turned and rode his tongue reverse cowgirl. Again I sat on his begging lingam and danced for a moment, then repeated, rose up from his erection, held it as I panted, confused, and I sucked him, tasted him, rode his face, did that over and over until he went mad and pushed me down on my back and gave my yoni his tongue again, tasted our flavors, growled as he made me come, come, come. I battled him, pushed him onto his back, sucked and sucked and sucked, and he held my head and strained as he came, just as I had held his head and strained when I came. The Watchers were outside our alcove, reduced to being Listeners of our sexual perversity. I know that they were there because as we finished, there was applause and whistles. Things were always different after the orgasm, when hormones had calmed, when reality stood tall, after that flaming and wretched need had been allowed to feed until full. When emotions and need were burned away, when lust was minimized, all that was left was the truth. We stayed sequestered in an alcove, the drapes closed, our sin hidden from the eyes of other sinners. He had been the first man I'd fallen in love with. I had had a high school love, but that was puppy love. And now he had been the last man to penetrate me. My first love. If I died right now, my last lover. There was madness in that poetry. The first man to break my heart in a romantic way had been the last man to break my skin, to widen, spread my fleshy folds and intrude me. When I was in college, when he had been but my second lover, I had wanted him to be the last man, the only man I allowed to enter me this way, for eternity and beyond. His familiar sting remained, his song just as beautiful, as familiar now as it had been during college.

Twenty-six minutes.

We'd left the present and taken a journey into the past. We had been together the way we used to be together for twenty-six minutes. It was the same. But it was different. Time had given both of us more sexual experience. His tongue verified that when I'd become his raspberry crème brûlée. My yoni quivered. Stomach pirouetted. Our sexual chemistry remained remarkable. He had matured in some ways. In sexual ways. He had sexual endurance now. Our connected bodies, our connected spirits had danced once again. The sex was good. The orgasm was more emotional than physical. It was like making love to a seasoned man, not to the boy he used to be. It was damn good. Because of emotions. Emotions had the power to make what was ordinary seem extraordinary. Emotions made what was wrong feel right.

I held his penis. Stroked it. Chris smiled.

He said, "I can't get it out of my mind."

"What?"

Then he lowered his head. "I'm sorry."

His expression changed.

I asked, "What's wrong?"

Chris whispered, "Rigofuckingberto flashed in my head."

"You're joking, right?"

"Now and then it hits me. You fucked him. You fucked my *tigre*."

"Rigoberto."

Mentioning his name changed the temperature in the room.

I let his penis go. I let it fall and slap against his skin.

I said, "If you must know, I didn't fuck him. We made love."

"You made love."

"It was emotional for both of us. We cuddled. We hugged. I cried. We even managed to laugh for a moment. We embraced. We didn't fuck. Not at all. Not once. We made love. It was for pleasure, it was for healing, the kind that I needed to numb a pain that could not be numbed, but like I said it was with deep affection, with passion. He took care of me."

"You and Rigoberto. It hurt me. It really fucked me up."

"That was my intent. I didn't want the fight, but I was glad for it. He fought for me. You had thrown me out and he fought for me."

"That was the worst time in my life. For me it was two deaths. One death was losing you, the other was losing a friend. I lost my best friend because of . . . back then . . . in the middle of all of that."

"No one likes to be betrayed. No one likes how that feels, being stabbed in the back. Rigoberto just took the knife that you had put in my back and returned it to its owner."

Chris whispered, "You slept with my best friend."

"I slept with my friend. I met him before I met you. I knew him before I knew you. He introduced us. Not for him, there would have been no us. Maybe he felt betrayed when you called and asked me out. Amazing how you leave out the part about sleeping with Siobhán first."

"We grew up together. We were brothers. He was my *tigre* and you fucked him without hesitation, as if you had always wanted to."

"He wanted me."

"Were there other men?"

"There was no one else. At Hampton I only slept with you, and when we were done, after we had broken up, after you had chosen Siobhán over me, then I was with Rigoberto. I wasn't with anyone while I was with you. Being with Rigoberto was a big surprise for me as well."

"My best friend. You could have gone to anyone but him."

"God, you have no idea how I wish that you would fucking stop saying that. After what you did, you sound so fucking ridiculous."

"You started hooking up with Rigoberto as if I wasn't a big deal."

"He came to me when you had me thrown out of your dorm, humiliated. I was practically on my knees begging you not to break up with me. Pathetic. I begged you in front of the entire football team. I begged you in front of Siobhán. I fucking begged you."

"The same goddamn day. You were with him the same night."

"Payback. The settling of scores. You humiliated me. I wasn't going to walk away without at least getting a few good blows in, physically or metaphorically or otherwise. I'm not that weak."

Voice trembling, I wiped my eyes.

The things we carried.

The unseen scars we carried.

The things that made us who we were.

Chris cried. Tears fell. Over losing me. Over losing his *tigre*.

He said, "God, I was angry. So damn angry. Back then, at first, I think that I stayed with her to piss you off. To prove a point."

"You lost your mind and went after Rigoberto."

"We almost killed each other. It took more than ten people on the team to pull us apart. Both of us almost lost our scholarships. Hell, we would have killed each other. One of us would have died. Over you."

"Again, it was about your ego. I was no one's prize. I wasn't human chattel. You had already acquired your trophy. You had the nerve to march her around campus, then attack Rigoberto at the dorm."

Twelve types of anger shoved good memories aside. The ones that refused to move, the stubborn ones, were stabbed. My nostrils flared. A dozen types of anger stood before me, naked, exposed, and doused themselves in gasoline. Then they doused me in invisible gasoline as well, saturated my naked body from head to toe. And without hesitation they set themselves on fire. A dozen types of anger burned like a bonfire. Chris took a deep breath, wiped his eyes again, took a red DECADENCE towel, cleaned me, and wiped away his milky white come.

He asked, "Are you okay?"

I could no longer blink. Jaw was rigid. Heat covered my body and I deflagrated at blinding speed, my mood becoming volatile instantly.

He said, "I'm sorry I brought that up. Forgive me?"

I remembered the notes that I wrote for him each day.

Love is early morning phone calls. Love is waking up before he does so I can watch him wake up. Love is kissing his photograph. Love is drinking green tea in the morning as the sun rises.

But most of all, I remembered the begging.

The humiliation.

Chris asked, "What's wrong, babe?"

The conflagration consumed me, and I breathed flames on him. "Don't you *fucking* call me *babe*."

There in that alcove, behind curtains, while I should've existed in the midst of an orgasmic high, I suffered a meltdown. I burst into tears. Chris tried to comfort me and I attacked him. It was now as it had been in college. He held my hands and I spat in his face. And when he reacted, when he let me go, I beat him. I attacked him as I had attacked his wife. As music thumped and skin slapped and women gave angels their wings and men grunted, my fingernails raked Chris's face and drew blood from the man I had once loved. He howled. I stood firm, waiting for him to become brutal, waiting for him to grab me, batter me, snap my neck, kill me.

It was in his eyes, the shock, the need to respond with brutality.

My scowl dared him as I whispered, "Hit me. Do it. Hit me. You know you want to hit me. I fucked your best friend. *Hit me*. I never should have gotten *involved* with you. You shouldn't've even been a zipless fuck then because you couldn't fuck worth a damn and you sure as hell didn't know how to eat pussy. You were horrible. Rigoberto was a *much better* lover. He was powerful, emotional, and erotic. You knew how to fuck for minutes, but he could make love for hours."

Now he sounded Belizean. "Bitch, you scratched my fucking face."

"Turn your back on me and this *bitch* will do the same to your back. I will put my nails so deep I'll leave marks on your bones."

"*You scratched my fucking face, Nia.* I'm fucking bleeding."

"Bleed until your heart stops beating, you sonofabitch. I bled for a long time. There was no tourniquet that could stop my heart from bleeding. My scars and blood were invisible. Get over it."

He held his face, a face dank with blood and sweat and saliva, and he backed away. Big man. Muscles flexing. Goliath scowled at David.

I stepped toward him and growled, "Tell Siobhán how I made you suck my clit like it was a dick. Go kiss her and tell how you sucked me and I came in your damn mouth like you were my bitch. *Runtelldat*."

He backed away, held his injured face and pulled back the curtains, stepped into the erotic music that pulsed outside the alcove, hurried through lovers in the throes and the sounds of orgasms. Naked. Lingam swaying. I closed the curtains. Twelve kinds of anger applauded, each clap sending flames and sparks from wall to wall.

The reality of what I'd done, it suddenly hit me.

My internal storm surged. I tried to hold it. I tried to prove my strength. I clamped my hand over my mouth as I sobbed, as I sobbed for this moment, as I sobbed for the woman I used to be, for dreams shattered, as I told myself that none of that mattered. I stayed hidden in the alcove. Orgasms echoed. Lovers applauded. People were making love. Copulating. Engaged in coitus. Chris had left. But Chris was still here. His energy was here. It spread all over me. It covered what had once been beautiful. I felt ugly. I felt the ugliness that he had left behind a long time ago. I felt the ugliness from what had just happened.

I had never felt ugliness so profound, so crippling.

I remained on the soft mattress, in the dark for the better part of an eternity. Nude, lying on my side, back to the world, tears draining, teeth clenched, heart beating like an African drum of war. I was entertained by enjoyment, sexual screams, chatter, and applause as angels took flight. I stayed that way, inhaling an old heartache that should've been thrown away, should've been burned with the photos from my college days, and never left inside of a dusty old box.

TWENTY-SEVEN

When it stormed in Southern California, it was as if dark clouds had been sliced open with surgical knives. As I sat in the backseat, as I once again felt anxiety raise its head, the downpour was like nowhere else in the world. It was cold outside of this town car, LA was winter cold, in the mid-fifties with wind blowing through shivering palm trees, but I remained heated by so many thoughts, by anger.

"*I love the Latina actress in the movie. What was that? Yeah, I love my job and yes, I am single. No children. Someday. Both. Yes, I am an early riser and a hard worker. I agree, my profession is of a high cultural level. True, very few are writers and fewer are good writers. Thank you for your time. Have a good evening. Bye.*"

I ended the call, finished the discussion with an interviewer who would place the talk in either *Alma Magazine* or *Cosmopolitan en Español* magazine. The phone rang again. I checked the caller ID. Chris's phone number. I put the phone down and exhaled, exhausted.

My mother said, "That went well. That went very well."

"Much better than the one with the bitch from Trinidad."

"Nia. Swear jar. Let it go."

"People can be so damn evil. Yeah, this one went well. Almost as well as the one for *Vanidades* magazine went *early* this morning. Anyway. What else is new on my expanding agenda?"

"*H para Hombres* magazine wants to do a blurb. That was who called me when you were chatting. But they will need a very certain type of picture of you, one that goes with the theme of their magazine. Their magazine is for the Latin man who is hip, cultured, and mischievous.

They celebrate beauty and covet women and prefer to expose them like they have never been seen."

"They want me damn near naked."

"Actually they want you naked, but tastefully done."

"Whatever."

"You're young. Beautiful. A body almost as nice as mine."

"Set it up."

"Already have. Photo shoot in two days. At our home by the pool. You should wear the white bikini adorned with gold jewelry."

Forty minutes passed and we moved through two traffic lights. I wanted to scream. From the 101 freeway and all of its accidents to the Highland exit and all of its fender benders, I remained trapped in a pensée as dark and gray as the skies covering the southland.

In her Trini dialect my mother said, "Nia, the condo will pay for itself. It's by the Canadian and other private school and is near West Mall. Hi-Lo and Movie Towne close. The unit is on the fifth floor and faces the sea."

"But you never sent de thing to de accountant."

"I'll have my people send it again. We have to move on this."

"Look at the high-rises. Shorelands Renaissance. Banks having problems there. Might be a better deal."

"The bMobile people want you to be a spokesperson in a two-year endorsement deal. Bus stops, benches, your face will be all over."

"How much they paying for me to endorse their phones?"

"An offer is on the way. If not, Digicel wants the same, but bMobile has the bigger celebrities."

"I know."

"Brian Lara. Machel. Anya."

"Iz a Trini. I know."

"Digicel has Destra. Kes. But bMobile is more widely used."

"Do you think I from outer space? Mommy, I know. I eat corn soup and roti like you."

"Either way, you, Anya, and Nicki Minaj will be the faces of the island that will be recognized worldwide, the faces that inspire the youth toward positive things and promote a little tourism."

Our accents were thick; enough to maybe keep the chauffeur from understanding our conversation.

My mother said, "This madness. This weather brings out the James Thicke in people."

"Oh, is that what Hollywood calls it now? Losing the plot is called going James Thicke?"

"When James Thicke is not around. No one will ever say that to his face. He offered to host the after-party for the premiere at his club."

"Club Mapona? No way. Great club, but it's a bit out of my price range. And I don't want to be anywhere rappers and fools hang out and fights get started and chairs get thrown and TMZ records it all."

My mother sipped her wine, then asked, "Why are you pouting?"

"Why does my day have to be the rainy day that summons all of the water in the world?"

She laughed. "In my mind and heart, the sun is shining."

"You've lost the plot."

My mother's shoes reminded me of the compartment I struggled to ignore. Her shoes were nosey platform pumps, coral with metallic and rhinestone detail. Footwear for the red carpet. Tonight mine were an exotic creation by B Brian Atwood. My mother had on a black dress, hers imported from Trinidad, only hers was a very sexy black outfit that also managed to be a power dress that remained occupation appropriate. I was clad in a black skirt and sheer top. Both of our outfits were one-of-a-kind creations by Trinidadian designer Anya Ayoung-Chee. Mine was more high fashion and artistic, like the clothing Anya wore on her Facebook page. I was the writer, could pull off intellectual bohemian, but tonight I looked like I was ready for *Project Runway*. Now my hair was ultra wavy, pulled back on the left side, that ear exposed, my earring long and matching my wealth of bracelets.

My mother studied the *LA Times* and read a review. "I love this. They say that your film—"

"Not my film. Studio owns it now."

"'It has such a strong narrative, built-in forward movement, compelling central character, outstanding secondary characters, almost as if Bijou has singlehandedly reinvented the postapocalyptic genre. A film for our times. For every unknown actor dying for a break, we predict that a speaking part in a Bijou movie is the desideratum, an essential step to making it in Hollywood.'"

"Stop reading, Mom. Please."

"Stop fidgeting. Stop complaining. It will be fine."

"No one is going to come out in the rain. Look at this traffic. Nobody will be there."

"If no one else shows, at least your number one fan will be there."

"Still wish that I could've hired James Thicke to doctor the script."

"Oh, my people need to call your people because *People* magazine called me. They want to do a feature regarding powerful women. They want both of us. And also I'm telling my people to tell your people to get in gear and get you on the cover of a few fitness magazines."

"Again they want me damn near naked."

"You have it, flaunt it, my dear."

"My mom, the Hollywood pimptress. That will be my next film."

She pinched my leg. "Horrible title. Sounds like one of those revolting urban books."

This was another compartment. The one of mother and daughter. The one of Hollywood. As we were chauffeured, I was about to ask my mother a personal question, a serious question about love and bonding, about romance, about why passionate love didn't last, about why what a man felt one day, three hundred and sixty-five days later, it had changed, and it had led him to seek to be between the legs of another woman, but my mother's cellular rang, a soft generic tone. She took an exasperated breath and looked at the caller ID, and cursed. I closed my mouth, returned my question to my thoughts.

My mother snapped, "Mocatta is going to call me over and over."

"Answer the phone. You'll be antsy all evening if you don't. You know how you are."

"What, do you think that you're the mother of me now?"

"Don't let that money end up on someone else's table, that's the phrase, right?"

She laughed, pinched my leg again, then answered and commenced talking business. While she did that, I wondered why some brilliant doctor, some scientist had never created an antibiotic for love.

My mother said, "Look, I'm with my daughter and we're on the way to our event. Oh, did I tell you what my daughter did? She bought me a new car two days ago. That convertible Mini Cooper that I always wanted. Of course I have to brag. No, it wasn't a birthday gift. She bought it because she loves me. I think I told you that she flew me first-class to Atlanta and we had a mother-daughter weekend getaway to Jekyll Island and St. Simons Island. She paid for it all. She's the best thing I've ever done in this world. We were bicycling and running and horseback riding and at the casino and doing dinner cruises and shopping and playing water games and touring the island and doing all sorts of things. Anyway. My new car is awesome. I'll be whipping around town with the top down as soon as this rain goes away. How are your wife and family and the grandkids? That's marvelous to hear."

Mother always initiated her calls on a personal note. She was an expert at befriending people. She had the heart of a politician. She would have been an excellent prime minister back home. I stared at the rain, counted raindrops as the conversation rapidly changed to business.

"I know they have made countless films exploiting the Holocaust. I'd love to be on board, but does a film about Uganda have an audience? I know that you are passionate about the project but do you really feel that a film about Uganda will have legs? A feature about the Holocaust will always do well here and internationally. Uganda? As an HBO documentary, perhaps. As a feature film? You put your name on it, that won't make the herd run to the theaters. It's still a black film."

My cellular buzzed. It was a message from Anaïs.

ESPERO QUE TENGAS UN BUEN ESTRENO.

Just as I finished texting my thank-you to Anaïs, my cellular buzzed with another text. It was from Rosetta. She said that she was en route. This was her first real experience in LA traffic. She hated it. Last night I had hung out with her and her husband and others crawling the Sunset Boulevard, most of us in jeans, hoodies, and trainers, hanging out at the Comedy Emporium and barhopping, then stopping at the Sunset Saddle Ranch to ride the mechanical bull. It was the type of thing that I bet that Bret would love to do. That was what I had thought when I was there. More than a few comrades from Decadence had come to town and everyone in the group was drinking and riding the mechanical bull, laughing and getting tossed to the side. Then we had all ended up at a strip club watching women who had amazing skills, skills that should be featured in the Olympics, performing like the women in the movie *Rock of Ages*, starring Tom Cruise. A few fondled each other's breasts, or rubbed nipples and breasts as they danced like oversize sprites. At the end of the night, the libertines went to the W. I had left them and gone back to my mother's place. I could only imagine how much fun they had had creating a satellite campus to Decadence. I gazed at my mother. She probably fielded eighty calls a day.

I inspected my nails. I had hurt my fingers that night with Chris. I hadn't realized that until later, until my adrenaline had lessened enough for me to feel my fingers throbbing and see my own blood mixed with his. They were repaired now. That had been a long ride back to Atlanta. I had no idea what Chris did about the damage I had done to his body.

It felt like a reprise of our silly season. I'd seen him and reverted to who I had been then, had returned to that era, to that epoch that had been marked by frivolous, outlandish, and illogical behavior.

My lovers.

The things that my lovers had in common told me more about myself than it did about them. They selected me, but I allowed them inside of my personal space. Many had been rejected, and even though I had allowed men to have me for a night as I had allowed myself to have them to salve my itch, I hadn't been open to every man, to any man, only a certain type. Strong. Intelligent. Self-made.

I forced myself out of my trance, forced myself to focus on what was in front of me. My mother pressed for closure in her negotiation.

Our driver looked in the rearview, saw my uneasiness, and asked, "Is the temperature fine?"

I nodded, answered, "It's fine."

"If you feel too hot or too cold, let me know."

I nodded, my eyes looking out of the windows as if I were a tourist.

My mother said, "What? Sure, but you can't sell the predicament without a star. Denzel would be great, but Denzel won't get out of bed for less than twenty. Same for Will. And you will still need to pair them with a white male, preferably as the protagonist, to sell it abroad."

I said, "Especially in France."

She nudged me, her way of telling me to say out of her business.

I pinched her. She slapped my hand.

It had been a long time since I had been in this large, yet claustrophobic compartment.

Again my mother touched my leg. Her motherly expression asked me if I was okay. I nodded, my expression telling her to handle her call. I wasn't a needy little girl.

When it rained in Los Angeles, nothing moved fast, all traffic came to a virtual standstill.

I took out my phone and sent Prada a text.

MISS YOU. HOPE ALL IS WELL ABROAD. OFF TO MY EVENT.

I was surprised when he responded immediately.

LOVE YOU. HOPE THE EVENT IS A SUCCESS.

I imagined that he had some exotic beauty in his bed, a woman who had the blend of all the ethnicities of that region, and he had left her pleased, had left her panting and sweating and mumbling gibberish, and he was across the room, in the window, perhaps inside of a bathroom, or right in front of her, held her in his arms because she spoke fluent Welsh, but wasn't able to read his messages in English.

I sent another text:

HOW IS LLANFAIRPWLLGWYNGYLLGOGERYCHWYRNDROBWLLL-LANTYSILIOGOGOGOCH?

KUDOS TO YOU. YOU ACTUALLY SPELLED THE NAME OF THE VILLAGE CORRECTLY.

CUT AND PASTE. EVEN GENIUS HAS ITS LIMITATIONS.

I'D RATHER BE WITH YOU. IT'S BEEN WEEKS.

HOW IS THE YONI OVER THERE?

I WOULDN'T KNOW.

YOU'VE BEEN OUT OF CONTACT THE LAST WEEK OR TWO. YOU'RE A BUSY, BUSY MAN.

FEELS LIKE FOREVER SINCE I'VE KISSED YOU. I'M DYING TO HOLD YOU AND FEEL YOU.

THAT WOULD BE NICE. ON A RAINY EVENING LIKE THIS ONE, WOULD BE NICE TO BE IN BED HAVING SEX.

IT'S STILL EARLY EVENING THERE.

AND IT'S GOING TO BE A LONG ONE. I'M WITH MY MOTHER NOW. SHE'S GOING ALL OUT FOR THIS ONE.

THERE IS A PARTY AS WELL, AM I CORRECT?

AFTER-PARTY AT THE W WHEN THE FILM ENDS. WILL BE NOTHING BUT INDUSTRY TALK, SO IT WILL BE BORING. UNFORTUNATELY I HAVE TO STAY AND SMILE UNTIL THE VERY END. MIGHT TEXT YOU LATER. GET YOUR REST. KISSES.

I LOVE YOU.

GOOD NIGHT. MISS YOU. THANKS FOR TAKING THE TIME TO REACH OUT, BUSY MAN.

I returned to staring at traffic and counting raindrops.

My cellular buzzed with a text. Again it was from Rosetta, my designated new best friend.

Her message said,

WE'RE ALL HERE. THIS IS AMAZING, NIA. I JUST HEARD THAT REGINA BAPTISTE MIGHT BE INSIDE. SERIOUSLY, REGINA BAPTISTE? HAD NO IDEA YOU WERE ÜBER FAMOUS. HOPE TO SEE YOU AFTER IT'S OVER.

My mother ended her call, leaned forward, and said, "Excuse me, driver?"

As we mixed with the madness of the traffic coming out of Hollywood and fought down La Brea Avenue toward Melrose Avenue, the driver of our sedan looked into her rearview mirror.

She responded to my mother, "Yes, Mrs. Bijou?"

"How far are we from the Regent? I mean, how long do you think in this traffic?"

"If there isn't another accident and if all the lights are working, ten minutes. We were stacked up so long because four lights were out and there were at least six minor accidents in the last mile."

My mother nudged me. "Just received a text. The paparazzi have arrived in full force."

Our driver asked, "Is that a good thing? Or should we slip you in through the back entrance?"

"We?"

"Oh, my partner will meet us curbside and open your doors, when you are ready. If there is a distance problem, if you prefer to not be touched or if you are uncomfortable when people get too close, we can handle that as well. We can play the bad guys so you still look good to the public. If there is anyone you prefer to not be in your space, we can intervene and make them back off. That's what we are here for."

"No, all is good. Tonight it's fantastic. Even with the paparazzi. Never thought that I would be happy to see them again. All press is good press, even when it's bad press, and I foresee no bad press."

I mumbled, "Other than that Rae-Jeanne Quash bitch in Trinidad."

Mommy pinched me.

The driver nodded. "Then I will park and let you and Miss Bijou out of the car at their feet."

I said, "In the rain? Thanks a lot. I should've worn flippers."

She laughed. "They erected a covering that extends to the sidewalk, and just in case, my partner has an umbrella the size of one they use on the beach. He will take you from the car one at a time."

My mother adjusted her black evening dress, and regarded herself in her compact mirror. She was here, in this moment, focused.

My mind was in so many places. I was back in college, at Decadence, trying to understand my needs, my fears, and the mental illness that many called love, the thing that made us all educated fools.

Returning to dialect, my mother asked, "What's wrong, Nia?"

"Nothing."

"I know what every expression means, and now you have something else on your mind."

"Mom . . ."

She whispered, "It's okay, chile. We alone here. Talk your mind."

I shrugged and swallowed. The need to confess lived inside of me. The need to understand. The need to know what restlessness was inherited. There were so many things I wanted to tell her about her daughter, but I knew that I didn't want to ruin her perception of me, of her perfect virgin-child, of maybe the last of this branch of our Trinbago family tree. Still I wanted to ask her about the complexities of love and all of its manifestations, from lust to insanity, and the way it waxed and waned, and why there was forever an imbalance, why it waxed and waned differently for both parties.

I asked, "Have you dated? Have you been in love with anyone since the divorce?"

She paused for several moments before she answered, "I've dated, of course."

"Have you been in love?"

My words, the seriousness of my question caught her off guard. My mother lost her look of power, her look of professionalism, and in that moment looked so vulnerable, so very young. It amazed me how my mother had moments when she ranted like a dictator, then others when she was a little girl.

I whispered, "Have you?"

My mother hesitated. My mother never hesitated, not even when she had decided to leave her birthplace. She was bold and brazen. Not a hesitator. You didn't conquer Hollywood by wavering.

But I also knew my mother in ways that Hollywood never would. I knew her as a woman, as a mother, as a real person. I have pictures of her when she was a little girl in pigtails, scars on her knee and mud on her face, when she was a precocious child living in Trinidad, years before she had met my long-deceased father. I have pictures of her during her youth participating in Carnival, partying with the revelers, drink in hand as she celebrated in the streets with men dancing up against her. I knew what was in her heart. She always read the last chapter of a book first or she always read the last fifteen pages of a script first. She wanted to know if it ended badly. If it didn't have a fairy-tale ending, she refused to read the book or was reluctant to touch the project. She knew what America wanted, but she also knew what she wanted as well. Mothers were women who used to be little girls dressed in Cinderella dresses.

I repeated, "Have you? Have you been in love with anyone?"

She whispered in return, "Why you ask?"

"Because you're beautiful. Because you're the best woman God ever made. You work hard, very hard, and you deserve love."

"Stop it before you make me cry. This makeup is expensive."

"Because I worry about you. The divorce was hard on you."

"Why you bringing up the divorce?"

"Guess it's on my mind. It was painful. More on you than me. You were angry at Dad and were rough on the world. Whatever you were going through you were all smiles and hug ups and kisses."

"You were angry too. It was hard on us. You were unhappy for a very long time. Even after he came to Hampton to fix that issue."

"I know. I was. But now, my worry is toward you. And your job. I worry about your status as well. You work at a heart-attack pace."

"It keeps me occupied. It keeps me from going home to that big empty house. And my job never let me down. It's hard, it's frustrating, but it has never failed me, never betrayed me, not once."

I paused. "Since the divorce, you ever had a real boyfriend?"

She touched her neck, then spoke in a soft voice, "I was . . . I was fond of someone at one point."

"*Fond?* So you were in love with someone since the divorce."

"I said fond. He was younger. It didn't last."

"When did this cougar thing happen?"

"Actually it was more than fond." She waved her hand dismissively, the same way I had done for years whenever I was asked about my past. With a thin smile she said, "Was a few years back."

"Who and when and why wasn't I informed?"

"It was over as soon as it started. We had a great opening weekend and fell off fast."

"That's pretty vague. So it wasn't a box office hit. Why wasn't I informed, Mother?"

"It was of no major consequence, Daughter."

"*Of no major consequence*? Really? Where is this mystery man now?"

"He's married."

"Oho. Was he married then?"

"No, he wasn't married then. He married after. You done cross-examining me?"

"He famous?"

"Not an actor, if that's what you're asking."

"He in the business?"

"Nia, stop macoing."

"He fell in love and married someone else and moved on."

"I guess . . . I guess that pretty much sums it up. So it goes."

"It's in our blood. After they date us, they marry the next girl."

"I've moved on. I pulled up my big girl panties and moved on."

I heard so much contradiction in her voice. I knew that tone of left-over love. I had inherited that timbre. There was a happiness that I wasn't sure I would ever achieve, but that didn't stop me from wanting that fairy tale for my mother. I could deal with my restlessness, my foolishness, my unhappiness, but not with hers.

I asked, "Are you seeing someone now?"

"I have a friend."

"Are you fond of this new friend?"

"It's nothing serious, mind you."

"Play dates? Sleepovers?"

She pinched my leg.

I laughed. "Mommy, I know that you don't suffer from ithyphallophobia, so you can stop pretending that you do."

She patted my leg. Mom didn't want to continue that conversation. I sipped my wine, let it settle in my mouth like a well-earned orgasm, like Prada's yummy orgasm, and after I swallowed I took my mother's cellular from her, read what she had posted on Facebook.

I said, "Sixty thousand followers. Impressed. Three thousand comments already. You have told the world where we are tonight."

Then my cellular rang. I saw that it was Bret. He'd never called. Surprised, I answered.

He said, "I just wanted to call, congratulate you on your movie and to tell you to break a leg."

"Bret, that means so much to me. How are you doing?"

"Well, I'm not going to complain. Anytime I'm not where it's one hundred and twenty degrees, not almost six thousand miles from home, not dressed in full uniform and carrying eighty pounds of gear and worried about driving over a bomb, it's a pretty good day."

"I appreciate what soldiers do, but I'm glad that I never enlisted."

"This is a busy time for you. Hope that I didn't disturb you."

"Was just cleaning the last of the mud out of my ears."

"Good. Glad to hear that."

"Thanks. This call is like a venti soy latte on a cold winter day."

We shared a few more soft words, promised to talk tomorrow, to actually talk on the phone and not text back and forth, and that had left me excited, and then with a smile on my end, we hung up. Again we talked as if a zipless encounter had never happened between us. Like old friends. Strange. Before I disconnected, despite all the *fuckedupness* in my life, the light side of Gemini almost told him I loved him.

My mother sipped her wine before she asked, "Who was that?"

"Just this military guy. One friend of many."

"'This call is like a venti soy latte on a cold winter day'? Seriously? How corny."

"Get out my business."

"Why you so shaky and secretive all of a sudden? This military man person has a name? He younger? Are you a cougar? Are you a DILF? I hope you still a virgin. I know that I am. We both should be."

"Wait. DILF? Oh my God. DILF? Did you call me what I think you called me? Does that mean *Daughter I'd Like to*... Oh my God. Mommy, no you didn't just call me a *DILF*. That was evil."

"Where is this Bret from?"

"He's from South Carolina, but he lives in Georgia."

"*Jaw-juh*. Isn't that how they say it in that godawful illiterate city? *I's frum Jaw-juh, suh*."

I leaned forward. "Excuse me, driver. What's your name again?"

"Cynthia Smalls, ma'am. But I use the name Panther, ma'am. I used to attend Clark Atlanta. Clark Atlanta Panthers. I kept that nickname to remind myself to go back home one day and finish getting my undergrad degree."

"Panther, I need you to pull over and put my mother out in the rain with the crackheads."

"Can't do that, ma'am. She's paying the bill. But unfortunately I can put you out if she asks."

We all laughed. I wondered how Bret knew what I was doing. I'd never told him. He knew who I was. I wondered how he had found out. I wondered how long he had known.

As we crept along in traffic our driver said, "Congratulations on your film, Miss Bijou."

"Thanks, Panther."

Then I regarded my mother. Again she looked so young. She had fallen into thought, was inside of some unseen abyss, barely blinking, as I had been when consumed by thought. She was somewhere else.

My conversation had redirected her mind, sent her on a journey, her road made of memories. She had opened the box that had been put away inside her mind and now she was traveling down a road paved with unwanted emotions. If not unwanted, then uncontrollable, *unkillable*. I reached over and held my mother's hand. She held my hand, squeezed my hand in return. Within seconds I was on my own road, a winding road that had many emotions.

Old lovers were the shadows that darkened my walls.

And old friends.

Siobhán.

I had so many memories of us as friends.

She had stolen from me.

She had stolen my happiness years ago.

And now I'd robbed her in return.

Like a thief I had broken into her marriage and burgled her.

I whispered, "Just the tip. Just the tip."

TWENTY-EIGHT

The Regent Showcase Theatre is one of the older art houses in Los Angeles, Hollywood-adjacent, a half block away from the world-famous Pink's Hot Dogs at Melrose Avenue where the Queen of Soul Aretha Franklin loved to pig out whenever she came to town, minutes away from the swank high-rent area that housed the Grove. It is a horrible area for parking in a busy New Yorkish–type of district, at least a hundred restaurants and wine bars and marijuana medical shops within its reach.

Photographers and the paparazzi were in full force.

"My God, so many people. You pulled it off, Mommy."

"All six hundred seats will be filled. SRO for the latecomers."

A section right outside of the entrance was set up with a backdrop from the film. It was far enough from the curb, so that area was dry and lit up like it was the set for a shoot. The photographers were stacked up front and the scum that comprised the paparazzi were off to the side at four levels, at least fifty of them stacked on top of one another, calling out the celebrities' names all at once, each trying to get the best shot. Controlled madness. Not only were the photographers and paparazzi in full force, but most of the patrons had out their camera phones and were taking shots and recording too. The posters for the movie showed toned, shirtless men, and three generations of exotic women.

Actress Lola Mack was featured on the advert poster here. When they sold it abroad, as they had done in so many movies, her blackness would be removed. A black face diminished sales abroad, retarded profits, so like they had done in the film *Couples Retreat*, as they had done with the adverts for *The Hunger Games* when it went to DVD, the black- and brown-skinned portion of the cast would magically disappear from all advertisements. After I had signed the contract, my work belonged to the system, as did the power. In the islands the Indian actress in the film would be moved closer to the star. In some parts of the world she would vanish. Actors of color were still begging Hollywood for integration. Begging for acceptance. Silently I hoped that I was part of the solution, and not another part of the problem. And if I weren't part of the solution, I hoped that I wouldn't be seen as part of the problem. That interview with the Quash bitch had rattled me.

Some of the male power makers were in stylish suits. LA kept it casual, trendy, smart. Of the four hundred people who were out front and in the lobby, people of color were hardly represented. The film was sold using white actors. A black sci-fi would still be sitting in my computer. Again, the politics of Hollywood. I had been taught that you had to work the system to beat the system. Hollywood was a business, not an extension of the Civil Rights Movement. I had learned.

My mother said, "What's that terse expression all about?"

"Was looking at the movie posters and . . . nothing."

"You grew up here. You know how it goes. Again, it's about the bottom line. Some say that it's a slow-changing system, but in reality, sadly, it's an unchanging system. Those who have tried to scream and shout and force integration on the system are blackballed in this business as if they were the spawn of Mel Gibson."

"This is a world that continues to choose Regina Baptiste over Regina King."

"Baptiste is talented. You can't take that away from her."

"So is King. If she were white, she'd be a superstar."

The theater was large with an art deco vibe from days gone by. Not even the forward-thinking people in Hollywood could let go of their past. The historic edifice was perfect for foreign or indie films, or tonight, a screening. It was like the theater that was used in the movie *The Artist*. Actually, I wouldn't be surprised if this was the actual theater they used during the shoot of the Oscar-winning silent film.

My mother told our driver to open our doors in thirty seconds.

Panther placed a call and said, "Driver. Thirty seconds. Are you in position?"

A powerful male voice said, "I'm standing right here at the back door."

My mother said, "Make that a minute. One more minute. They are cheering for someone. Never step on anyone else's laughter or applause. We could upstage them, but let them have their moment."

I said, "Lola Mack. They are cheering for Lola Mack. She's singing for the crowd."

Panther said, "Make it a minute, Driver."

"Copy. One minute."

I gazed at the controlled madness.

I gazed at a world that thrived on living in the realm of fantasy.

As a writer, there was bliss in creating, but there was no pleasure in this part of the occupation. I loathed insanity. I smiled at what my mother enjoyed. The madness testified that the fruits of her labor hadn't gone unnoticed. I didn't need the crowd or champagne or caviar. My paycheck was my reward. It had been that way since I was in college.

Ironically, I was more comfortable being nude at Decadence than I was fully dressed in this plastic world. Being gone so long, having lived in Virginia, Tennessee, and Georgia made this feel like a foreign country. Someone tapped on the curbside window and we jumped. I assumed that Panther hit the unlock button because the rear locks stood tall. The curbside door was opened by an Italian-suited tall, bald, well-built, and very handsome man who wore fashionable glasses. His skin was rich and dark as if he had been created from the finest of wood and rubbed with tung oil. He was a man made for pleasure and breeding.

Huge black umbrella in hand, he said, "Miss Bijou. Mrs. Bijou. My name is Driver."

My mother nodded. "You usually drive Thicke and Baptiste."

"I drove them tonight. They're already inside."

"Did Baptiste walk the red carpet?"

"She did. She posed for photos. She chatted."

"Wonderful. That will be great for publicity."

Driver the driver was going to see us through the ruck of boisterous people while Panther stayed with the car and waited for us. I exited first, to pandemonium, to overwhelming chatter. Driver held the umbrella up high. Rain pitter-pattered on it as he rushed me to the dry area. On the billboard I saw my name in sizable letters. It wasn't as large as the names of the principal actors, but by contract it was noticeable, it looked important. There was some applause. The chatter paused when my mother was escorted from the town car and stepped her dazzling high heels and Trinidadian high fashion onto the sidewalk. On this dank winter night we pretended that we weren't cold. We had taped down our nipples so they wouldn't betray us. I wanted a coat on so badly, but this was all about us looking invincible. The world cheered and applauded. Like libertines at Decadence giving approval, all applauded. I was no longer Nia Simone. I was the daughter of Hazel Tamana Bijou. Or at least, I was N. S. Bijou. That was the name I had used. I employed a neutral name that could be assumed to be the Christian name of a man. It also prevented lunatics from finding me on Facebook and Twitter and somehow getting my phone number. If they googled N. S. Bijou, what came up, for now, was N & S Bijoux jewelry and watches. That made sense, especially since my surname meant a small, exquisitely wrought trinket. Cameras and handshakes and kisses on the cheeks came and Driver guided us to the red carpet.

We moved through the crowd that had paused traffic that was Hollywood bound on La Brea, moved by women in short dresses and high heels, and right away I saw that most of the men who were in the business, most of the executives, were accompanied by youthful eye candy. Blondes. Brunettes. Tanned. Big kiss-ass smiles. We greeted people and passed by powerful men wearing pointed or box-toe shoes, skinny jeans and Maddens, even Converse. And I thought that I saw Quince Pulgadas in the mix, but the crowd shifted. I looked for Rosetta and Chandra. I followed my mother to the section beyond the velvet rope. All of a sudden I was overwhelmed, so very nervous, so many noises and faces. The photographers shouted commands as cameras flashed, yelled for us to tell them what we were wearing, and in unison my mother and I proudly spoke the name of our Trinidadian designer. We said it the same way at the same moment and we both laughed because it was unrehearsed. They wanted to know the details of everything from our clothing to our hairstylist to nail polish. It was intrusive, it was obsessive, but I smiled. The photographers competed for the best shots. We gave red-carpet smiles as hundreds of flashes blinded us, as a gaggle of energetic cameramen yelled out our last name: Bijou, look here; Bijou, now here; Bijou, Bijou, Bijou, look this way for me. Moments later most of the cast joined us for another round of photos. The predominant actress of color in the film, Lola Mack, stood next to me. She wore an adorable pink-cropped jacket, which she paired with jeans, bright blue Burak Uyan heels, and funky, colorful, futuristic, geometric jewelry. Her skin was a deep brown and her hair was a perfectly volumized blowout. I loved her complexion, and it looked better in person than on camera. She owned brownness that was coveted in the film by the men of all ethnicities. But her character had sacrificed herself for her two lovers, for twin brothers, and died early on. She came from theater and was struggling to turn herself into a Hollywood actress. My mother said that this was Lola Mack's first big role, but she had as much screen time as Rue did in *The Hunger Games*, her part equally as powerful. She was excited.

I said, "TMZ is here. I just threw up in my mouth."

"Publicity is publicity."

While we stood there I searched across the ecstatic faces in the crowd, sought out Rosetta in that multitude of parishioners of the cinema, I looked for other acquaintances from my hidden compartment. I'd find comfort in their faces. I even spied for my past. If Chris had shown up, it wouldn't have surprised me. The same for his wife; the same for Siobhán. In the middle of the crowd, beyond the shoulders of the cameramen I saw a pair of men watching me. Both had been waiting on me. The two men weren't together. Both were focused on me. Both loved me. Surprise registered on my face. It was too abrupt to mask. But I pretended that the flash from the cameras had blinded me, and used that as an excuse to look elsewhere. This felt surreal. When I looked again, both men were still there. This wasn't a hallucination.

One man was tall. In his very early fifties. French. Lean, six foot two, he too with a face that would make hearts swoon if ever it were on the silver screen, a man with the looks of Jean Dujardin. His silver-and-dark hair was cut short. The additional gray made him very distinguished and sexy. He wore an Italian blue suit, dark shirt, and dark tie. My stepfather. Francois Henri Wilson. The man who adopted me when he married my mother. This moment had brought him back to Los Angeles. I waved at him, blew him a kiss. My mother looked to see to whom I'd shown affection, and she almost lost her smile.

He blew me a kiss in return.

The surprises didn't end with my stepfather's unexpected presence. A different man smiled at me. His eyes were focused on me, on my every move. Hauntingly handsome, like an international model, clean-shaven, beautiful eyes, unblemished brown skin, he too in a dark tailored suit, his chic, as stunning as Billy Payne. He had flown at least twelve hours to come here and surprise me. I saw the mysterious businessman named Prada. I saw the well-learned man who told me that he loved me. I saw my lover, a compartment that I had done my best to keep segregated from this world. He held a dozen red roses.

TWENTY-NINE

Prada was here.

My distant lover had put on magical fins, swum across the pond, and braved this ridiculous winter storm. Unbearable tension rose inside of me, without warning, hit me with the force of a tsunami.

I waved at Prada, openly acknowledged him. Again, the ego of a man was as fragile as the heart of a woman. One moment that lacked something as simple as a kind gesture could prove to be so fatal, could commence the unraveling of a love affair. Just as appearing without notice could do the same. He was one face in a sea of many faces so no one would assume that he was my lover. But my face questioned him, my eyes questioned the tony industrialist who was only a few feet away from me, asked him what about his meeting in Llanfair-whatever-whatever, asked him why did he just play that game on the phone. Part of me, like Ayn Rand, hated surprises. I detested being tricked. When someone surprised you they assumed control; they had expectations. I disliked red roses, detested the stench and the memory they invoked, but I didn't let that show. I blew a kiss. He smiled and nodded and made his way through the gathering, but not toward us, but toward the doors. While the rain fell hard and flooded La Brea Avenue, as horns blew and chatter rose to an obnoxious level, he disappeared amongst the worshippers, moved deeper into the throng of Watchers and Doers of the movie industry. Sans invitation, he had entered my personal world. He had entered the place where I now worked. That jarred me more than the phone call from Bret. I assumed that my mother had seen him, had seen my startled reaction to Prada, so I whispered his name to my mother, nervously told her that he was an acquaintance from England. Said that I had gone to dinner with him a few times after meeting him when he was on a business trip in Trinidad.

But my mother hadn't heard a word. For less than a second her face had a serious WTF expression; WTF in bold letters, 100-point Verdana font. Then her smile returned, her Hollywood smile.

As cameras flashed she said, "Francois Henri is here?"

"He's my father."

"He has a lot of nerve. He betrayed the sanctity of family. And now he shows up to our event unannounced. Turn to the right."

"But he's still my stepfather. We have to be the bigger man."

"Him over me? Surely you jest. He's not your father by blood, only by paper. I can smear Wite-Out over his name and write in someone else who is more faithful, more committed, and more worthy."

Soon our time on the red carpet was done and other actors appeared. We stayed long enough to take a few shots with them before we moved on, passed the torch that signified fifteen minutes of fame to them and headed deeper into the lobby. We had to make our rounds, had to shake hands and acknowledge all who had come out to support us.

Another feeling washed over me. One that I understood. A part of my life that was yet to be written made the hairs on my arm rise. In that instant I wished that I had a child. I wished that I had had a precocious daughter to see this event, some new generation of us Trini girls to live in this proud occasion, a celebration that would arrive and leave so swiftly. Again, not a son. In all of my visions, in every fantasy that had come as of late, my child was a beautiful little girl. She would have Caribbean brown skin and look more like my mother than I. I wanted her here, now, at my side. Not to see what I had done, but for my child to see how wonderful her grandmother was. I would love for her to see her grandmother while she was this young, this powerful, this beautiful, this inspiring. Cloning myself was one of my mother's silent wishes. I knew her, so I knew that. Part of me wished that I had given birth to a child five years ago. Even if I had to do it on my own, I should have answered the fire that raged within, should've submitted to nature's calling. Besides, I'd never be alone, my mother my support system.

THIRTY

The followers and worshippers and hangers-on of the biased and profitable culture of Hollywood are like no other. When the movie started, the thunderous applause and cheering began and at times it was louder than an obnoxious graduation at a Southern high school or HBCU. They all had their mouths around the erection of Hollywood and would swallow until its nuts were dry. You would think that every film screened was the best film ever written. It was false. It was fake. No movie was that good, not even this one, and I did love this product. For the producer, the writer, for every actor's name that rolled by, for every name or position that went by there was deafening applause. And when the movie ended, everyone was applauded again. With the exception of Regina Baptiste easing out as soon as the film ended, probably to keep from creating a disturbance, no one else left before the final name scrolled by and the lights came on. Driver the driver escorted her out and kept anyone who was tempted to follow her in check. I loathed fame. Then one by one our names were called, the director, the producers, the writer, and the primary members of the cast. There was more individual applause as we took to the stage, then group applause as we all took a bow and blew kisses and gave thanks. We sat on director chairs and engaged in a question-and-answer session. I heard my stepfather clapping. I saw Rosetta's smile. I saw the libertines sitting next to her, all looking too professional as they gave praise. Prada applauded the loudest. At least it seemed that way. Onstage, I sat next to my mother. She was one of the producers. Questions came and went, some trying to get inside the mind of the writer, strangers always trying to be nosey and become personal as they remained unknown, but I was thankful that most of the questions were directed at the principal actors. Sitting next to my mother, we practically stole the show. Her fame in this zip code, the way we flowed when the spotlight was on us, even though inside I felt uneasy, how we finished each other's sentences and answered questions pretty much in sync, it all came across as natural. Someone actually thought that we were sisters. Many didn't know that my mother had an adult child. Laughter and smiles as nepotism lived. Prada was on the row immediately behind the section reserved for people in the industry. He had come to see my moment. He had come to celebrate. So professional with excellent posture. But I saw the lust shining in his beautiful eyes, the carnal need to orgasm inside of my orifices.

What he viewed as my achievement, as my success, seeing me on a stage, on a pedestal, aroused him. Power aroused, was orgasmic. But I was suspicious of this game he was playing. He was in my territory and that made me uneasy. I preferred seeing him on neutral grounds. He had come to spy on my world, see my life, see who I was around, friends and family, then to steal me away, to make me nude and render pleasure, if only for a few minutes, or fuck through the night.

He had never seen me in this light, as a daughter, as a writer being lauded, only as a lover. He had never seen me as a complete woman.

From my seat on the stage, sitting with perfect posture, hands on knees, I looked down on the royal court. It amazed me how everyone appeared affluent. Most were struggling. Most were one deal away from poverty, one deal away from losing Benzes, BMWs, Lamborghinis, boats and yachts, if not one paycheck away from being evicted from low-rent apartments and courting public assistance. It was a room filled with hustlers. The appearance of wealth was a four flush, a false claim in order to fit into this group. But with the credit checks that Decadence ran, that and background checks that rivaled applying for a government job, most of the people here wouldn't qualify. The clients at Decadence had to be bona fides; they had to be as they claimed, as their appearances dictated. Hollywood was filled with pretenders.

"A question for Lola Mack. Your performance was outstanding."

"Thanks. I have to give props to the director and the other actors for making me look good."

"Pardon me for never having heard of you, but I see that you came from the theater. How was the theatrical experience? And more importantly, how did you prepare for your love scene with the twins?"

People in the room laughed. Women sat with broad smiles, envious, applauding.

Lola Mack said, "We had a great script and great actors who were very giving."

"There was a lot of give and take. And in your big scene you gave it as well as you took it."

The room exploded in laugher.

"And, Lola Mack, your action segments, the way you used the gun was great."

"Well, I've always wanted to be an assassin or something. Maybe I've dated too many bad boys. It was so much fun training with the guns. Never know when I might have to shoot somebody."

They laughed.

Prada watched me. He studied me. I shifted and bounced my leg.

I inhaled, exhaled, rubbed my neck, inhaled, exhaled, patted my knees, inhaled, exhaled. My mother touched my elbow, that soft and discreet touch asking me if I was okay. I nodded. Adjusted my posture, took in more than twelve hundred eyes, more than six hundred Watchers.

As we filed from the stage, as people headed to the lobby, as some chatted us up, as Prada's eyes followed my every move, I thought of the way he had kissed my feet and sucked my toes. The way he fulfilled all requests. He was five-star, white tablecloth, all-inclusive. A sexual chef as well. I had experienced others since last we touched, tasted, smelled, and exchanged orgasmic moans. I wondered how many beautiful women that greedy lover had pleased since last he licked my clit.

I wondered how many orgasms he had had with me existing in the far reaches of his mind. As he had touched and pleased other women, I wondered if he had been haunted by my face, as his face had haunted me.

Rosetta and the libertines came to me. No friends and no one in the industry had left as of yet. That meant that the film was great. Otherwise they would have all left, maybe sent texts. In Hollywood no one wanted to be around a failure or associated with a bad product.

They were dressed nicely, all looked wholesome, like businessmen and businesswomen, some like the girl or the boy next door.

I said, "I hope that everyone enjoyed the film."

Rosetta said, "I'm impressed beyond words. My God, this is spectacular. You're a luminary, a person of great importance."

"Where is your remarkable and always-horny husband?"

"He went to swim to the rental car."

They were going to head back to the W in West Hollywood. The word was that the rain had stopped. The people from Decadence had wanted to drink, then sneak off to their rented suites and have fun in the tradition of the club we all belonged to, but I told them that with my having to stay until the very end, and also since my mother was here, along with my stepfather, and that a man I was seeing, a non-swinger, had arrived from abroad without warning, I might not be able to play.

Rosetta handed me a room key. Told me the room number. Then she winked. Chandra hugged me, kissed both cheeks. Dressed in an embroidered salwar kameez set of red, black, and gold, a brilliant outfit that sang praise to her culture, smiling, she looked so very different.

I asked Chandra, "How are things?"

She laughed. "I have run away from home."

"You have what?"

"I have left my husband. Your words inspired me."

"Wow. Are you okay?"

"For now. He is angry. He is very angry. But I am far away from him. I demand better. I deserve better. We will see. But we will not talk about that now. I am here to celebrate you, Nia Simone."

After I confirmed the directions to the W, as others came to shake my hand, they swam through the chattering crowd and headed toward the exit. Then I faced Prada. He handed me roses. Overpowered by the aroma, I kissed his right cheek, and then I kissed his left. We looked more like dignitaries greeting than two lovers many weeks removed. Two weeks ago I would've been thrilled to see him. Absence didn't always make the heart grow fonder. Most of the time absence was like rehab, diluted an addiction, especially when a new drug had been found to take its place. I tried to remain cheerful, to be appreciative of his effort, despite feeling my sphincter tighten as I inhaled the scent of the symbols of love and passion, despite feeling infuriated. My eyes didn't cooperate, but I forced my lips up into a professional smile. Then that professional smile softened. The heart defined whom we were attracted to. I was attracted to him, sexually, mentally, and maybe even spiritually. And the heart decided for how long that inner madness would last. *How long* was the variable in everyone's equation. The heart also defined what we were capable of doing. That same heart defined, maybe led us to certain lifestyles. The heart chose the lifestyle that we could endure. The heart controlled the mind. My heart had freed me from the delusion of monogamy; had changed me into a liberal woman, and I had evolved from that woman into a beautiful lady with the heart of a mermaid, a libertine. And at the moment, I had the spirit of a curious swinger. Yet Prada offered me something that I knew I would need long-term.

In French I said, "*Well, this is a big surprise.*"

"*You made a wish and abracadabra, poof, I am here with you.*"

"*I don't like being tricked or lied to. It's disturbing.*"

"*Apologies.*"

"*Never again, okay? I'd never show up in your life without invitation or warning.*"

"*Is not wishing that I were here an invitation?*"

I nodded. "*Yes. But. Okay. Okay. Shah mat.*"

"*I have missed you. I stopped the world and canceled everything and flew for almost twenty-four hours in order to be here.*"

"*That's not good business. As an industrialist, many people in the world depend on you.*"

"*Would hate for the guy you run with to move in during my absence. Did he come as well?*"

"*No, Bret isn't here.*"

"*You look dazzling. And you were a picture of perfection during the interview.*"

We stood staring at each other for seconds before I said, "I hope the film didn't bore you."

"It was amazing. Here in this theater, it captivated everyone as you have captivated me."

"Since both are glaring, let me introduce you to my mother and my stepfather."

"She is a very strong woman. Very opinionated, as are you."

We stared at each other for a moment. Once again the Horus and Set inside of me battled.

I whispered in French, "*I have to be honest. I'm pissed off but you look so handsome, so sexy, and I can't wait to suck your dick. Would suck you right now if I could. Would make you come all over your suit.*"

"*My angry queen, I can't wait to make love to you again.*"

"*You want to fuck me. Your hard dick made you come five thousand miles to fuck me?*"

"*My heart leads me. Not my dick.*"

Again we stared and stood motionless as celebrities passed by. We were separated a moment when the director stopped and wanted to take a photo with me. He handed Prada his camera phone. Then James Thicke stopped and congratulated me. He wore a very nice suit, tailor fit, and a T-shirt that read PORN IS MORE HONEST THAN RELIGION. He apologized for his wife's leaving so soon. He said that Regina loved the film and would be very interested in coming on board for the sequel, so her people would call the producers first thing in the morning. Then we shook hands, firm, very businesslike. When that was done, I took Prada's hand and moved. I had to keep moving. I was avoiding my mother. I was avoiding my stepfather. They were together, both wearing plastic smiles and undoubtedly speaking in French so that no one would understand what they were saying.

Prada had intruded and now there was only one way out. He had forced me into a corner. Any other woman, a normal woman would've been happy for a man to fly half the world to support her efforts.

I touched the side of his face. "*Prada. No one knows about us.*"

His smile lessened as his disappointment rose, became as apparent as my being pissed off. We both needed to adjust our expectations.

We both needed to accomplish the impossible.

"*Come with me. My stepfather wants to know whose hand I am holding. Mom is wondering who you are, especially since you brought flowers.*"

We were caught in a laudatory people jam. Lola Mack and her admirers had halted the traffic flow by being in one spot, talking and laughing. She smiled like she felt so sexy right now, her energy strong. I squeezed by Lola Mack. She stopped me and introduced her date, a man who resembled the Italian striker Mario Balotelli.

I whispered in her ear and asked her, "Your boyfriend?"

"Friends with benefits. Your boyfriend?"

"Jump off."

"He's fine as hell. Damn, Nia. You have jump offs that look like that? You better jump on that jump off tonight. Jump, jump, jump."

In the next breath, I was pulled to the side and introduced to another one of Lola Mack's associates, Attorney Carmen Jones. We shared a few words. Then I shook hands with her teenage daughter, Destiny Jones. Mrs. Jones made it known that she was of Caribbean descent, Jamaican, not one of the islands that I was fond of, not when it came to Jamaican women, but she was cordial and thanked me on behalf of the islands, especially Jamaica, where her mother had been born. Finally, we reached my mother and my stepfather.

My parents ended their conversation in French.

With a smile on her face, her unsmiling eyes hidden behind her Jackie O sunglasses, my mother had been chastising, and arguing with her former husband. I smiled a nervous smile. Dad returned it, uncomfortably. Mom nodded, telling me that she was under control.

I said, "Mom. Dad. I would like to introduce you to my dear friend who has just flown in from London. This is Prada Rambachan. Prada, this is my mother, Mrs. Hazel Tamana Bijou-Wilson—"

She corrected me, "*Miss* Hazel Tamana *Bijou*. Surely you haven't forgotten the horrible divorce."

"And this is my stepfather, Francois Henri Wilson, who just flew in from France."

My stepfather stepped forward and extended his hand. "So what are you to my daughter?"

"We are presently dating, have been dating for quite some time, and I am trying to persuade her to love me as I love her."

That shocked me and paused us all.

My stepfather grinned. "You love her? That is a very bold statement, one that leaves me feeling uneasy."

"We have known each other for a while. Four years. But I live abroad and I travel on behalf of my company. I apologize for us never having met. But I am here in hopes that we can become acquainted."

Dad said, "Then we must chat. Let's excuse ourselves and have a seat and talk man-to-man."

I said, "Dad, believe it or not, I'm not a little girl nor am I in high school anymore."

"No matter what your age, you will always be my little girl. Every man has to be vetted. If you are sixty and I am still alive, he has to be vetted."

"You don't have to do the fifty-question drill."

In French my mother said, "*He likes to drill. Usually a younger Italian woman, but let the man drill. No one invited him anyway.*"

I said, "Stop it, Mom. Don't embarrass me."

My stepfather smiled at my mother. Then he nodded.

She nodded in return. She remained vexed.

Francois Henri said, "Just a few questions, Nia. Simple questions that should be easy to answer, Mr. Rambachan. Like what is your purpose in dating my daughter? What are your spiritual beliefs? What are you doing to protect the purity of my daughter? How do you provide for yourself? Have you ever hit a woman? Can you protect my daughter if another man becomes violent? Easy questions."

Francois Henri needed to exert his power as a man. Like Prada, he was a man of business, a man who was used to being in charge. Yet I knew that he was a man and had a fragile ego. A man was a boy who grew up and absorbed culture and became what he thought a man should be. On behalf of culture, on behalf of what he believed, I submitted to Dad. Because he was my dad. Before the pain, before the divorce, he had been my god. And he had left. That's what gods did. My mother was silent. She didn't know Prada, didn't approve of a man just showing up and being so brazen that his first words were how he was in love with her daughter. Four years. Sixteen seasons. If I had never told her about him, his words of flattery had not flattered her. She hated my stepfather, but in this moment they were in agreement.

My stepfather kissed my cheeks, then put a hand on Prada's shoulder and pulled him to the side. They spoke in French. It didn't matter how powerful Prada was abroad, not to the man who saw me as his daughter. The moment Prada was pulled away, a crowd again descended on my mother and me. My mother gave a look, accompanied by a smile that was as sharp as the claws of a wolverine.

THIRTY-ONE

Nude, her chest heaving, breasts beautiful and round, skin flushed from three sequential oral orgasms, each orgasm grander than its predecessor, she remained splayed across the bed, a cat squirming in her own heat, purring and smiling as she watched us follow her command, as she watched us kiss. Her husband and I kissed for the first time. There were one hundred times more nerves in the lips than fingertips, each nerve a desire stimulator. The kiss became heated, desperate. My nipples ached. His lingam stood strong, pressed against my belly. We emoted. Then as we became physically acquainted, as he became aggressive and sucked my earlobe, as he traced the outline of my ear with the tip of his tongue, she eased off the bed, pulled the white covers down to the carpet with her, and lay back on the floor. While he stimulated my yoni with his mouth, teeth, tongue, throat, and chin, she spread her legs and played with her sex, the tips of her fingers rubbing circles, pulling at her fleshy folds as her eyes tightened and her mouth made an *O*, then grinned and bit her bottom lip as her hips moved up and down. He stopped tasting me and raised his head. We looked at his wife and she nodded the nod of permission, owned the intense expression of heightened sensitivity. He put me on my back for a moment, thrust his lingam between my thighs, engaged in interfemoral intercourse for a moment, then turned over, he too was severely aroused.

I straddled her husband, his lingam craving, ready, but not inside of me. He owned the ideal-size lingam, a wonderful length with an impressive circumference. Perfect. He was on his back and the way that I straddled him, when I glanced down it looked like I had grown a lingam, looked like his lingam was part of me, sticking straight up in the air. I wondered how many women had sat on their lovers and for a moment imagined themselves as men. We all started out as women, as females, then some of us changed into men, that was a simple fact of science, and another wonder of the world. With a rapid heartbeat and academic eyes I studied that human phallus, looked at that peculiarly shaped part of a man, his tool, his device, his manhood, that instrument of internal fertilization, and grinned, felt shy, almost snickered for being so curious. I reached and masturbated his penis, pretended I was a man masturbating, imagined him as a woman. His wife came to me and kissed me, took his penis from my hand, and masturbated him, then leaned over and took the mushroom of his erection into her mouth, sucked his long rigid shaft, regarded me and smiled, saw my delighted expression, and sucked him, took more of him inside of her mouth, the wetness, the sounds causing me to touch her hair, stroke her face as I watched. Again it looked like she was sucking my upside-down lingam. It aroused me. He looked at me as she sucked him, looked at me with glazed-over eyes. My hips moved. My itch was strong. As she sucked and licked his lingam, I moved against where he and I touched, moved like I was feeding her my upside-down lingam.

My cellular buzzed again. And again. And again.

We changed positions; the master became the willing slave. She did the same to me. Soon she and I were on our knees, asses up high, severely aroused, our thighs touching, sides of faces in the soft white pillows so we could look at each other, be with each other on this journey, holding hands, and as we held on to each other, her husband owned us, went back and forth, first eating us, then fucking us doggie style, fucking one while he fingered the other, fucking one while he slapped the other on the ass. He teased his wife and made her moan to Jesus, then he teased me, their unicorn, and made me call out to God, went from her to me, from me to her, gave both of us measured strokes, both of us singing that hour like orgasms were rising, then he left me empty, left me crazy and returned to her, did the same to her and returned to me, then back to her, to me, to her, to me, to her. She kissed me as he stroked her, tongue soft, her kisses smooth yet intense, nibbled my lips as his erection thickened, as his control waned, his need to come clawing at him, making him strain, making him pant and grunt and growl. We kissed. Our kissing excited him to no end. I enjoyed kissing her, enjoyed her tongue on mine, and loved the way she sucked my tongue, made me chase her tongue, and responded when I sucked her tongue. We ebbed and flowed, sometimes I was the one more aggressive, the one with masculine energy, and then I was submissive, become the über feminine one. Soon I was high on kissing, high on feeling, tasting, hearing, on the visual, on our blended aromas that created a unique erotic fragrance. Hated the way he made me come. Hated the way my body was made, how it relished this type of pleasure. She squeezed both breasts, then let one go and grabbed my hair, grabbed it roughly, pulled my face to hers. I chewed her lip, I sucked her lip, I growled. We devoured each other. She bit me and I bit her in return. She shuddered. He slapped my ass. Singsong moans and weeping sounds rose from my mouth, and my sounds were mirrored when I pinched her nipples.

I pinched her harder.

She wailed.

He grunted.

We all owned the same fire.

My cellular buzzed again, back-to-back, like a chain of orgasms.

Moments later came the back-to-back calls that aroused the *Sex and the City* ringtone.

THIRTY-TWO

My garments and jewelry had been removed before we engaged in the sharing of pleasure, before we loaned one another our bodies, everything I wore was folded or hung up. I didn't want any stains, no baby gravy on my attire. It would be a tell of my bad behavior. I hurried into the bathroom; left both of my lovers on the bed, spent, satisfied. Mouthwash. Toothpaste. Floss. All of those were lined up. After snowballing I would need to freshen up. After I smeared toothpaste on my teeth and tongue, I gargled as I turned the shower on and selected a big white towel and hand towel. After a while all centers of wickedness were the same. I showered, wondered how much time had elapsed since I had arrived here, since I had left everyone at the bar, since I had left Prada with my stepfather, had left my mother chatting with others, eased away from the conversation, snaked through the congratulatory crowd, and then come to this room. My cellular vibrated; my heart galloped. We'd gotten carried away. When luxurious self-indulgence was that good, space and time shed their meaning. I had disappeared for the better part of an hour. I touched my knees. Rug burns. I was always damaging my knees. No time to worry. Had to keep it moving. After I sprayed on a touch of perfume and began to dress I looked at the husband and wife on the bed. Even though it had been through a session of rigorous sex, her Afro was as stunning now as it had been at Decadence. I had owed her a debt of satisfaction. With my tongue, before I had gone to her husband, before the ménage à trois had commenced, I had paid my bar tab in full. In fact, I had overpaid and now she was indebted to me. Anaïs had taught me well, and I had paid that debt with enthusiasm and brilliance. My zipless lover was no longer zipless. I knew him. Ricardo was born in Curaçao. He was wrapped around Yesenia, her deep brown skin, her severe height, and extreme beauty in his arms, as if moments like these made their five-year union stronger. She was born in Geronimo, Oklahoma. Married for five years. And like me, I'd bet that she was surprised at some of the things that she had done. Feeling proud of myself, the dark side of Gemini grinned in victory. I had been to her what the Brit had been to me. Fair was fair and a promise was a promise and now that debt had been erased from my ledgers.

Those doctors snuggled like they lived in a world of communication, understanding, trust, support, and love. With a deep, rich plum lipstick I drew a heart and a happy face on the bathroom mirror. If I could have drawn a picture of a happy unicorn, I would have, but drawing unicorns wasn't in my skill set.

Then purse over shoulder and phone in hand, I eased out of the door and hurried down the empty hallway, trotted back toward the after-party. Rosetta and the rest of my friends might be in their connected suites now. My cellular hummed like a jealous vibrator. It was a text from Bret. That surprised me.

He asked,

HOW DID THE EVENT GO?

I typed my response as I walked, sensitive from the marvelous sex, knees stinging because I needed a pair of Band-Aids.

THE EVENT WAS ORGASMIC. PARTY IS STILL GOING ON. WISH YOU WERE HERE.

HOPE I'M NOT TEXTING YOU TOO LATE.

I paused.

YOU'RE NOT IN LOS ANGELES, ARE YOU?

ATLANTA.

I exhaled and sent a text.

OKAY. COOL. HOW IS THE A?

NOT MUCH FUN WITHOUT YOU. I WAS GOING TO GO TO BRUNSWICK LANES ON DELK ROAD, BUT I ENDED UP IN STONE MOUNTAIN OUT ON MEMORIAL DRIVE AT DUGAN'S BAR AND GRILL WATCHING THE WORST KARAOKE ON THE PLANET. THEY DO IT APOLLO STYLE AND EVERYONE IS GETTING GONGED. OLD WOMEN ARE ONSTAGE SHAKING THEIR ASSES LIKE THEY ARE TWENTY-ONE. THIS IS A TRAIN WRECK. OH, AND EARLIER I DROVE OVER TO MARIETTA AND ATE AT THE TASSA ROTI SHOP. THE TRINIDADIAN FOOD WAS EXCELLENT. I'VE EVEN PUT AWAY THE COUNTRY MUSIC AND I'M LISTENING TO MUSIC BY SY SMITH AND ALISON HINDS. ALL THAT TO SAY, WISH THAT YOU WERE HERE WITH ME.

A phone call. Now a long text. I shook my head. I didn't have time to process mixed signals. We had spent the night in Florida. Nude. No intimacy. And not even a kiss on the shoulder. Bret was calling and texting me now. I wondered what the fuck all of that meant.

I turned my cellular off.

I didn't want to start a back-and-forth text message exchange.

Inhaling air that lingered at the borders of the entertainment capital of the world, I exited the elevator to glitz and glamour, to music and chatter, to more congratulations and hugs in the land of boutiques, cafés, and movie houses. The rain had ceased and the night air had a sexy winter chill to it—the kind made for cuddling—Hollywood's finest were spread out amongst the bungalows. There were more people at the hotel, party seekers and potential social climbers who weren't here because of the premiere, but wanted to be here to hand out cheap business cards and rub shoulders with those they thought were either rich or were likely to become famous. There were several groups of women sporting super-short dresses and super-long front-lace weaves and they wore counterfeit fashion items like Jimmy Choo, Rolex, UGGs, Burberry, and Coach. Moments later I saw Panther and Driver near the front. They said my mother was inside and hadn't sent a text as of yet. I moved deeper inside of the W's party atmosphere, said hello to people

I had gone to high school or had acting classes with. I eased by socialites at the world-class restaurant, squeezed by others holding colorful and trending drinks as they grooved to house music at the iconic bar, then peeked in on tipsy lovers smooching in the vibrant Living Room. That's where I found Prada, in the dimly lit sexy area, where one-night stands were created over martinis, mingling with the beautiful, chatting amongst social alcoholics.

I felt evil. I felt as if I were now capable of doing to men all of the things that men had done to women. And it was exciting. It was thrilling. Empowering. Living on the edge was a new kind of high.

Prada saw me when I came into the crowded room. My mother was no longer in sight. My stepfather had set him free. I could only hope that my mother and stepfather weren't somewhere causing a scene that would end up on YouTube and being tweeted. But I smiled at Prada, waved. He motioned for me to come to him. I wondered if he had become liberal, if he had found a unicorn. Before I could get to him someone tapped my shoulder. Pushing my lips up into the practiced smile that ruled Hollywoodland, I turned around and faced a man who had a dazzling grill, gleaming eyes, full lips, and possessed the confidence and energy that Denzel did when he was in the movie *Glory*. Like mine, his mother had married a foreigner; only his stepfather had been a man of Irish, Italian, and German blend, then brought him here to the States when he was a child. I remembered that conversation, what we had in common.

In perfect Spanish he said, "*I just wanted to say congratulations. I enjoyed the film.*"

I responded in the same language. "*Hey, stranger. What are you doing here in Los Angeles?*"

His voice trembled and I heard his accent, heard the Dominican Republic rumble in his voice, heard the Caribbean that lived in his soul, and heard his motherland. "*I live here in Los Angeles.*"

"*Jesus. I went to USC for grad school. Have you been here since college?*"

"*I have only been here for a few months. I'm traveling the world. Will only be here for six more months. I played baseball abroad, for the Netherlands, only lasted two seasons, then went back to college. I went to the Netherlands and studied at the University of Amsterdam, then I lived in Willemstad a few years. Now I speak Dutch and Papiamento.*"

"You're a well-traveled polyglot now."

"Just like you. You inspired me."

"Never knew that I inspired anyone to do anything worth doing."

"You always inspired me to want to learn more. You always worked hard, were down-to-earth. Inspirational. And this evening, what you have accomplished only serves to inspire me more."

"Thanks. I'm speechless. And very surprised to see you."

"Your Spanish has improved."

"You were a great tutor."

Without warning, he leaned into me, kissed me on my cheek, gave me a soft kiss, a kiss that carried memories and emotion. Then he eased an envelope into my hands, in Spanish told me that for him it was now as it had been then, as it would always be. With that, he walked away, his high-fashion attire turning heads, as if he were nude walking the halls of Decadence. Prada watched us, then said a few words to the beautiful-yet-perpetually-unemployed talentless actress with whom he was chatting, a woman whose cleavage stood out as she held on to his arm. He finally freed himself from her grip and made his way over to me. As Prada walked away she looked pissed, until she saw that he was coming to me, then her bitchy expression changed immediately, became apologetic, became ass kissing and intimidated.

Prada asked, "Who was he? Another famous actor from your project? Or someone else that your stepfather will need to accost with one hundred questions regarding his intentions toward you?"

I slid the envelope that he had given me inside my purse, remembering so much that I had longed to be able to forget.

I said, "He's just an old friend . . . from college. Surprised to see him here. Hollywood events bring out people that you'd never expect to see. Actually he was the best friend of this jerk that I used to date when I was in college. I think that that guy's name is . . . Rigoberto. If I'd remembered that, then I would've introduced you. Rigoberto. Yeah."

"Latin?"

"Dominican. I don't remember his last name, but he and my ex were best of friends. Inseparable. Anyway. I see that you found the bar and right away beautiful women were keeping you occupied."

"Rigoberto. The way he looked at you, the way he was staring at you, the way that he was waiting, I thought that he was your lover."

"Again, he was the best friend of an ex from my college days."

"Were you intimate with him?"

"Why do you ask?"

"The look in his eyes. Your expression. Your body language."

In a state of mild shock, I looked in the direction that Rigoberto had walked, but he was gone. If only the past would do the same, greet me kindly, then walk away, vanish with ease.

My cellular buzzed again. I thought that I had turned it off, but it buzzed and saved me.

It was my mother. She was looking for me. I called her.

"Mommy, I'm down by the bar. Where are you?"

"I'm leaving. Shall I send Panther back for you?"

"No worries."

"You sure you have a ride?"

"I have friends here and taxis run all night. Where is Dad?"

"Probably with someone half his age."

"Are we going to meet and talk as a family, or will we keep avoiding what feels uncomfortable?"

"Maybe tomorrow for lunch, if he stays in Los Angeles and has the nerve to phone."

We ended the call.

As drinks were raised and chatter and music filled the room, I turned to Prada.

I asked, "How did it go with my stepfather?"

"The CEO of the Chevalier Group. You didn't tell me."

"Would it have mattered?"

Prada asked, "Where were you?"

"Turned out that I had to do junkets, which are a series of interviews. They are chatting up the actors as well but they pulled me in. Last minute thing. They dragged on. But my part of it is done for the night. I have paid my debts. Are you enjoying this elaborate ritual of self-congratulation? Hollywood loves to masturbate for the media."

"This is grandiose and with you being practically at the center seems like a lot of work. But since you are done, we can be alone."

I said, "Bad news. While I was gone, I got my period and didn't have any tampons, so I had to stop by a girlfriend's room and take care of that. I know, too much information, girl stuff."

"If you desire that I please you, there is always the shower."

"Would bother me. Hate blood, even my own. Plus I'm staying with my mother. You should've told me that you were coming and I could've made arrangements. Still, I would have loved to hear about your recent travels, the business side and the personal side as well."

"I should've had better timing."

"It's been forever. At least it feels that way."

"Same here."

"Well, look at the bright side; at least I'm not pregnant."

"I would love it if you were. Nothing would make me happier."

"Liar."

"I would marry you. We could marry first thing in the morning."

"I'd slit my wrists up, down, and sideways. Married because I was preggers. That's the last thing that I want."

He grinned, not thinking that what I said was funny at all.

His British accent was smart and stimulating, and smart and stimulating was an aphrodisiac. "Nia Simone, I have adored you since you were in Trinidad at Zen nightclub and I saw you walk into the room."

"You took your time. It took you years to get into my bed."

"You were worth it."

"Ha. Like you were not having relations with anyone while you waited. You tried to get me into your bed the night I met you, Prada, so that tells me a lot about you. You go to bars and pick up women."

"Were you not there to pick up a man?"

"Picking up men in bars in Trinidad is not part of my character."

"The night we met in Trinidad, I live that over and over in my mind. Sending you drinks. Reading your body language. Waiting for the proper moment to come introduce myself. You were closed off. I was surprised you let me take you to dinner. Was even more surprised that you came back to my room. I wanted you so badly that night. But you did the right thing. You made me want you like no other."

"That night I wanted you too. But the timing wasn't right."

"I haven't seen you in two months. There is a new energy. I sense the distance now that we are face-to-face."

"It can be like that, Prada."

"While for me absence, as the cliché goes for those in love, made the heart grow fonder."

"Unfortunately not being face-to-face, not being available can work both ways."

"It has not served to diminish what I feel for you. I'm in love with you, Nia."

"I know. I feel your energy. I know that you say that now, that you feel that way today."

"Madly in love with you as I have loved no other."

"But why?"

"You can't question what has no answer. If I knew then it would not be true love. It would have *because* attached. I love you *because* of this reason, or that reason. Real love has no *because* attached."

"How did you get to that point, Prada?"

"What do you mean?"

"I ask you that with envy. I have been there, but I have never been able to return to that place. How do you conquer the fear? I ask you that truly wanting to know how . . . how? Again, I have been in love before, a few times, not all of the same depth, but each affair ended. How do you get back to that point? How do you end a war, then go back into battle before the shrapnel marks have healed? How?"

"After all this time, after so many conversations, how did you not get to that point with me, Nia?"

"We've only had sex one weekend."

"Loving you is not about sex nor is it about the number of times we are physical."

"What is love without sex?"

"It is still love."

"That connection matters. The connection is what defines the level of the relationship. If we don't have sex, it's one type of relationship. If we have sex all of the time, it's another. If we have sex every now and then, then don't see each other for over two months after, yet another."

"But there is more than sex to life."

"If you're impotent or suffering from erotophobia or genophobia or tocophobia, sure, get off the field and let the big boys and girls have their fun while you kick rocks or go skydiving."

"Serious. More than sex to being in love."

"Love is love. Sex is sex. There may be things better than sex, there may be things worse than sex, but there is nothing exactly like sex."

"And there is nothing exactly like being in love."

I smiled. "You don't understand women. Maybe you do. You just don't understand me."

"Educate me."

"Love is my strength, and it is my weakness, where I rise, where I fail, my sole foible at this point in my life. During this season I am no good in love and I would be no good for you, Prada. But who is to say that each time I share myself, that each time I learn someone new, why can't that be a form of love? In those moments, during those connections, during that session of praise and giving and selfishness and pleasing and being pleased, I believe that there is love there. I crave love. I am human, and love I do need because love fuels us, but with the fear that resides in my heart, and now, not now but lately, very lately, realizing I have an unhealed wound, I can't cathect love, can't invest emotional energy into something so wonderful yet so destructive. And that does not mean that I don't believe in love. Sure it could work forever, but the odds are that it will eventually expire. I'm an artist. I am a writer. I am fickle. One day I am loved, the next I will be hated because I am uneven. I am like jazz, one long improvisation without an end in sight. I am no one genre. I am a funky mixtape and I am deeply felt and I am happy and I am bitter. I am underrated and yet people expect too much. I am restless. I am not a woman who feels that she is put on earth to seek out a husband, but one day I will and know that in the end he will suffer. I don't know if black will be the color of my true love's hair. I am outrageous in private and yet I am at times shy in public. Take me as I am. Accept me as I am. Take my fears. This is me. I told you that I was damaged. Most are damaged, so that only makes me normal. Without lies. Without pretense. Now I am free and I give you freedom and that is why this feels good. In love I would be too demanding. I would become like every other woman you have ever dated, then in the end couldn't wait to leave, couldn't wait to break up with, couldn't wait to jettison so that you could breathe again, so that you could exhale. I would lose my creativity and join mainstream society and become the woman that drove you to other women or made you seek noontime solace with a woman of the night. I would become intense, needy, my requirements would be many, my honey-do list never ending. Then I would be no one special. Then you would only abandon me in search of a woman who is like I am today, a woman who stimulates your mind and abuses your body with a sensation that feels like love then sends you on your way and gives you room to breathe and be as successful as you can be with your businesses. If I submitted to you, if you became the victor, your disposition toward me would change and I would resent you for your inconsistency. I would hate you for inspiring me to leave my career, to change my life and would remind you of all that I could have been. I would show you this film and yell and tell you that I could have created many more. You would fail me and I would fail you. When always looks like forever and it fails to last an eternity, I am disappointed. I'll be tired of your infidelities, and there will be infidelities, and not only by you because I am no saint nor am I interested in having the résumé of a nun, but then again during the course of things, as in life and based on statistics, there are supposed to be infidelities. We tire of each other and we desire strange. That life, your infidelities, my need to have indiscretions, it too will bore me. And then I will be sitting in a coffee shop and stare at a stranger, a man with dark eyes that dare me with excitement and danger. And I will remember who I am now, who I am at this moment, and I will want this back. And I will hop into a hand-me-down Mercury, or get on the back of a Harley or Ducati, and leave with a scarlet pimpernel and go wherever the road takes me. I'd leave you without a note, without a good-bye. I'd leave with a man but I would leave you for me. I wouldn't pack up my things. I would not leave a heart-shape image on a mirror, one with a frowny face in its center, nor would I leave a final billet-doux that would bring tears to your eyes. After the arguments and fights you will want to keep me. I will be in your blood. I would be the toy that you would hate to lose, despite all of your peccadilloes. You would be the toy that I no longer desired to play with. You would love me as much as you hated me. I would hate you as much as I loved you. You would go mad trying to find me. But I would be gone. I would be gone and trying to become who I am now, but it would be too late. My faith would be gone. Your relationship was what you believed in; became your religion. Then you found out that what you believed in was a lie. You found out that the relationship that you thought you were in didn't exist. And you lose faith. That's what happens to too many. We simply lose faith. I've been there before. God, my mother has been there before. Anyway. In the long run, you'd be good, but no good for me. God, I am going on and on and on. See what happens when you ask me things? I answer. I give detailed answers. Unlike you. I don't avoid. I have my own fears but I'm not afraid. I'm physically available for you, but not emotionally. Again I could be, I could give in to the light side of Gemini and put the dark side into a cage, but when the emotions are turned on, when I say that I love you, I would expect all that comes with love, the joy and the pain. And the pain would not be beautiful, not with me. I can care for myself financially but you would be responsible for my sexual and emotional upkeep. I would consume you. I would become a fire that burned and raged and gave heat and eventually destroyed. And call me selfish, but I don't want to let you go. I like knowing that you are there. I enjoy you in my life. Maybe that's why it took so long for me to bed you. Foreplay is always the best part. Sex is the beginning of the end."

"You don't love me, can't love me now, but you don't want to let me go."

After my diatribe, you respond with only one sentence."

"I am listening. Receiving. Not being rude and interrupting."

"I'm a swinger, Prada. But I am still a woman. I am still human. I understand why men have wives, but have other lovers. I understand why the cultures that allow a man to have more than one wife attract both men and women. I understand why mistresses prefer married men. I understand it all."

"I love you."

"As you have told many women before me. To how many women have you spoken those words?"

"I love you."

"As a few men before you have told me."

"I love you."

"As I have told only one man. Saying that is nothing I would do for kicks or as manipulation."

"I love you."

"You love me. How do you know for sure? How do you know, Prada?"

"When I'm with you time doesn't matter. All that matters is love."

"Can you love me as I am? Or would I have to change?"

He paused, then spoke in the softest voice, a voice of shock. "My beautiful Nia. My sweet, sweet Simone. You're a swinger? A libertine, a female philanderer . . . my intelligent, beautiful Nia Simone."

"A mermaid. A nymph."

"I am having a hard time processing this new information. You said that you are a swinger."

"I did say that. I am a swinger. I guess that my spirit has been that way awhile. Since a summer in Atlanta and North Carolina. After I left Memphis and moved to Atlanta, I had an experience a few years ago and it changed me. I did say swinger. Maybe I shed my skin at night and become someone new, or I am really a soucouyant from Trinidadian folklore. But I am not an old woman. I would rather consider myself a libertine. I prefer to think that I have evolved from the child that I was into a woman who is morally and sexually unrestrained, a woman who should be given the same level of respect as a dissolute man. An independent with politics and a freethinker in matters of sex and religion, liberated from all things unnecessary and undesirable. Libertine. Marquis de Sade with breasts. John Wilmot with a yoni. I work hard, then I seek out life's pleasures. Not a swinger. Maybe because most swingers have a partner. And they either share their partner or bring someone into the relationship. I haven't actually had a boyfriend or someone to share with a new lover. I am the free spirit amongst troubled souls. *Swinger*. Let me examine that word. That concept. *Swinger* is not an attractive word. Saying that you are a swinger can carry many negative connotations. Being a libertine implies both freedom and wanderlust. *Libertine* is a beautiful word. It flows from the tongue, challenges the mind, and reeks of both money and intelligence. It's not a slutty word. It rings of liberty. Of freedom. Being a libertine implies that you partake of . . . the decadence life has to offer. It sounds like it's a constitutional right to be a libertine. Ayn Rand would think that it would be. As would Anaïs Nin. There. I've said enough. More than enough. Are you still listening, Prada?"

"I want to hear more."

"There isn't more to say."

"Tell me more. I need to process this, for my own clarity."

"Let me be clear. Let me be very clear. Unbeknownst to you, since we last saw each other, I have evolved. During this season I am non-monogamous. I have chosen to be non-monogamous. Monogamy bores me. Monogamy is a prison. I am a woman with an unconventional lifestyle and even though I will never broadcast what I do, I am not ashamed of who I am. I am someone who lives an unconventional and hedonistic life. I will exchange sexual partners with others. I belong to a club. I am part of a beautiful society where singles or partners in committed relationships are liberal, engage in sexual activities."

"I figured that you had had another lover. Especially the last fortnight when you were missing."

"I assumed the same about you. In the plural. A woman in every port. Or the number to an escort service. I guess that if I were a man, if I were you, with your wealth, I would be that way, in Yoniville."

"Love the way you see me."

"Back at you. You assumed I had another lover. As in a steady lover. As in a boyfriend."

"But I had assumed it was the soldier."

"Have you had other lovers? Has someone sucked your lingam? Have you tasted yoni? Have you fucked anyone since you met me in Trinidad? Have you had lovers, girlfriends, whores?"

"Let's finish exploring this first. Let's remain focused."

"You ask me questions, many queries, which I answer, then you dodge my inquiries. Like the CEO of a company who is used to giving out orders and becomes riled when his authority is questioned."

"Nia Simone, I have been questioned extensively, have been questioned as if I were a hostile in a foreign country, and I would rather be the one obtaining a few answers at the moment, if that is acceptable. I want to focus on you. I want us to focus on you. Is that acceptable, or should I run it by your father as well?"

"We will focus on me, for the moment. But I will want answers as well. I will want the truth, not pretense. I want to hear about you. You are an industrialist, but from the night I met you I sensed that you were a philanderer, Romeo, Lothario, seducer, adulterer, satyr, stud, player, whatever term you want to use, whatever romantic label or euphemism they have given men."

"We will chat about me. After we conclude this interesting and possibly heartbreaking conversation regarding you."

"Suddenly so serious and businesslike. Are you perturbed?"

"With the long flight to get here, the long evening, and the questions, I am a bit irritated."

"Take the lead. I shall play the role of the dainty female and allow you to be the man."

"Tell me the truth about you and Captain America."

"Captain America?"

"The soldier who you find a reason to see several times a week."

"Men and their insecurities."

"Women and their deceptions."

"If we are deceptive it's only because you're insecure."

"We are insecure because we know more about the mendacities of women than we care to admit."

"If you say so. I'm not a man so I will not pretend to know how men think or what they feel."

"He's your lover. He's been inside of you. He knows you as I know you. I met you years before him and he makes love to you."

"Once."

"You bedded him the night that you came to know him."

"I still haven't slept with him again."

"The first time? That sounds very anticipatory, don't you think?"

"Six months ago. At the W Hotel in Midtown Atlanta. For me there is definitely something about the W hotels that . . . never mind. Six months ago we did it. I left before the morning. Before the sprinklers came on. No breakfast. No cuddling. Not even a hug since then. No kisses. No intimacy. He was asleep. I left him without saying good-bye. It was over. Then we met again. We don't mention it. I think that we have only alluded to that moment once. But nothing in detail."

"So there was an immediate sexual attraction that was acted upon."

"And I have to tell you that night I was with him, the only night that I have ever been with him, it was a ménage à trois."

"So. The other person, male or female?"

"There was another woman involved."

"You were with him and another woman."

"It was like that. So that tells you that it was all about fun and exploration."

"Are you attracted to him?"

"Very. But there is no sex, not since that one night."

"The woman?"

"I have no idea who she was. I'm not a lesbian, if that's what you're wondering. I don't wake up craving women. I don't dream of being with women. But I love to feel a woman's touch, love to experience her sensibility and texture every now and then. Because in some ways it feels like I am exploring myself. I get to be a virgin all over again. The woman that I met, the woman who was with Bret and I, she was a foreigner. I don't know her name. We all needed the same thing that night. We all had the same energy, the same liberalism, and were open to fantasies. I didn't know Bret's name until I ran into him again. It was a zipless night. A night of laughter, dancing, foreplay, and much-needed sex."

"You say things that are so outrageous, I never know when to believe you."

"Here. Take my cellular. This is his number. Push send. Ask him."

He pushed my phone back toward me. "I'm not calling him."

"Then drop it and stop asking me about him unless you're trying to be his friend."

"You're a swinger. You don't look like what I would consider a swinger would look like."

"Since the rumor is that most are fat, old, and unattractive, I take that as a compliment."

"But why? With all that you have accomplished, as beautiful as you are . . . why?"

"When the need arises, when my mind, body, and soul need stimulation and satisfaction on a corporal level, I answer my body's calling, and I prepare myself. I go out into the world and I seek satisfaction, make love to other people. I have enjoyed making love with you, but you are not available in my times of need, will not be available as you have responsibilities. I have responsibilities as well. And this might sound contradictory but if you were available, I'm not sure that I would like that. I will not wait for you. I can't be owned by you. I can share myself with you. But I will want to experience others."

"Other men."

"And women as well. I am exploring my sexuality, my limits, my likes and dislikes."

"Women are now featured on the list of those you desire to be intimate with."

"Yes. That door has been opened and I am not ready to close it, not yet. I surrendered to a curious moment a few years ago. It was exciting.

But a woman can't do for me what a man does. A woman could never be more than an entrée, where a man is the main course."

"You belong to a hellfire club."

"Hellfire club. I haven't heard that term in aeons. That was a wonderful era in literature."

"Is it not an accurate description of such an organization?"

"I belong to an exclusive club for high-society rakes and rakettes, an Order of the Friars of Saint Francis of Wycombe. I am a very recent member of a hellfire club. But that is all that I can say about that."

"And to be clear, you have joined and gone to your hellfire club."

"I have joined. And I have gone."

"How many times?"

"Does my wickedness disgust you? Does knowing that my yoni is not pristine piss you off?"

"Often? How many times?"

"This is where I feel the harsh judgment begins, so this is where the interview ends."

"*Fais ce que tu voudras*. Do what thou wilt."

"That French phrase pretty much sums up the philosophy of the club. Of all hellfire clubs."

He nodded.

I said, "You're angry."

"You anger me. But anger is a form of love. Without love, there would be no anger."

"Anger is part of love. Both invade the brain like meningitis. Too bad we can't look inside the brain, into the organic and see what happened, what happens to all brains, to the organic wiring and ripples of light. I digress. I'm starting to sound like . . . someone that I . . . find objectionable. That was his logic back in college. So. Then what is the opposite of love? When are you truly free?"

"Indifference. Indifference is freedom from love. From the politics of love."

"Yes. When you don't care, when you no longer give a fuck, then you are free from madness. But when you don't give a fuck, you are dead. You feel nothing and care about nothing."

"That mouth of yours."

"I was told that I had a beautiful mouth made for blow jobs."

"So ladylike, brilliant, then you speak vulgarities in the softest, sweetest voice that makes vulgarities become poetry, make each crudity sound like a flower. That mouth, that mouth makes your intentional uncouthness feel like a warm summer rain. All from your mouth."

"The mouth that you love to feel sucking you. The mouth that makes your toes curl, the mouth that makes you ache and moan."

He paused. "Where are the beautiful roses that I gifted you?"

"When I left, things became hectic and I hurried to fulfill an obligation. I had to leave them in the care of a dear friend. If you promise to not be judgmental, to be quiet, I'll take you to them."

"Where are they?"

"With my friends."

"Which friends?"

"The libertines. They are here. The hellfire club is here."

THIRTY-THREE

Sex.

The word *sex* was invented in 1382. The word *sex* is not in the Bible, not in the King James Version. Adam *knew* his wife. And Cain *knew* his wife. Some say that one night while he was drunk, Noah's son *knew* him. There was a lot of *knowing* going on. The word *fuck* showed up around 1475. Some think that it was derived from Middle English *fucken*, which came from German *ficken*. Others believed the urban legend that it meant "fornication under consent of the king." Or "for unlawful carnal knowledge." Dozens of variations of that word as an acronym. The kinder term *booty call* showed up in the 1990s, thanks to comedian Bill Bellamy and a song by an R & B group called Blackstreet, and it became what we called midnight rendezvous.

I used my key to open the door to the primary suite. Holding his hand, I led Prada inside.

We walked into one of the rented suites; this suite had five scented candles lit, the scent of ginger and pumpkin. Shadows on the walls, music down low, and lovers in the throes. Three couples. One was on the bed. The next couple used an armless chair. The third pair of lovers was on the floor. We walked into a room of knowing. Prada tensed. Shocked. Embarrassed. Ready to hurry from the room. But I took his hand, let him know it was okay to be here. We watched the couple on the bed. We watched Rosetta and her husband. Rosetta wore a golden negligee and red high heels, her hair down, tousled enough to prove that she had been making love awhile. He took over, took the lead. Her back arched. Her face tensed. His buttocks clenched with his every thrust. She wrapped her legs around his waist, pulled him into her harder and harder, again and again. She was wet. I heard her wetness. It made me tingle. I knew that move, understood how it changed the shape of her vagina, and knew how it gave a new massage, a new sensation. Soon they both moved, danced their dance, a beautiful dance of give and take and give and take and give and take, of emanating the feeling of euphoria and joy, of flooding the room with dopamine.

I left Prada by the door, stepped over the couple that was writhing on the floor, and went to the bed, went to Rosetta. I touched the side of her husband's face. He smiled. I waited while they changed positions, rested on their sides, in a very romantic spoon. Not performers. Lovers. Husband. Wife. While I traced my fingers over her skin, while I traced my fingers over his skin, they kissed for a while, Rosetta's neck craning to meet his face, accept his tongue as he too rubbed her body. I squeezed her breast, pinched her nipples, made her coo. She drew her knees up, a signal that she was ready for him to be inside of her again. He worked his lingam inside of her. She was wet. He went in with one smooth stroke. My hand was on her. I wanted to feel her energy at that moment of intrusion. I wanted to feel what she felt like when his energy became part of her. She sighed upon penetration, released the sweetest sigh and her face changed and she lost control and became someone else, as we all became someone else during rapture.

Rosetta's voice trembled as she asked, "Who is your friend?"

"His name is Prada. He flew here from London."

"Where are your manners? Proper introduction, please?"

"Rosetta, I would like to introduce you to Prada. Prada, I would like for you to meet Rosetta."

She said, "Hi, Prada. Nice to meet you. I would hug you but I'm a little occupied on the inside."

He nodded.

She said, "Prada, this is my husband, Jeremy. Jeremy, I would like for you to meet Prada."

The men waved at each other.

Jeremy adjusted his angle, and he thrusted. Rosetta trembled. She clamped her hand over her mouth to hide her moans, to eat her moans. A moment passed. I grinned and watched her.

As Rosetta shuddered in orgasm, Jeremy looked at me and said, "Enjoyed the film."

I kissed Jeremy on his cheek, and then I leaned and kissed Rosetta on her forehead. Her fingers traced the side of my face, my lips, her husband stroking her, her expression that of a profound bliss.

She whispered, "You made it. Thought you had gone with your parents."

"Has anyone ever told you that you look very beautiful with a dick inside of you?"

"I feel beautiful when a dick is inside of me. Especially my husband's dick."

"I should sit on your face."

"You are one nasty bitch."

"One day I will."

"Not before I sit on yours."

We laughed.

Then I sucked her nipple. I did that and absorbed their conjugal energy, their sexual energy.

She came again. While he stroked her, while I bit her nipple, she arched her back, trembled, moaned. He stroked her harder. I took my mouth away from her softness and looked at Prada.

Prada was still by the door. He hadn't fled the room. He stood with his hands in his pockets. He saw me, revealed. I felt like a vampire exposed, a nightwalker caught feeding. I stepped over the couple on the floor, stepped over the woman's long legs, and returned to him.

I asked, "You're okay with this?"

"This is a different version of you."

"We are all different behind closed doors. I have invited you behind mine."

"Never imagined you . . . like this."

"Shall we leave? Have I disgusted you?"

"No. Let's stay. Let's see where this takes us."

I kissed him. He put his arms around me, held my ass, and gave me his tongue. I stood next to Prada. Felt his discomfort wane as what was abnormal become normal. Then I held Prada's hand and watched the other couple. The man craved to be on top, facing away, one of the positions popular in the club. He asked her to lie down with her legs lifted and spread. He changed his position, eased down on her, had his head going toward her feet. For a moment it looked as if they were about to ninety-six, but this was something different. Muscle man lowered himself between her long legs and entered her that way, in reverse. He found leverage, and thrust backward as she held his ass, as she held his ass and moaned and pulled him toward her, pulled him deeper inside of her. While he thrust she spanked him, slapped his ass over and over. Then she teased his chocolate star and slid her middle finger inside. He fucked her while she finger-fucked his ass. With her long arms she reached down and played with his balls, squeezed his ass. Soon, as they moved, they finger-fucked each other in their chocolate stars at the same time. She stimulated his prostate. He thrust harder, and she did the same with her finger, behaved like the man, continued finger-fucking her lover, and each time she put her finger in his ass to her knuckles, he slapped her ass harder. She stopped fingering his chocolate star, then slapped his ass harder and harder, and he stroked her harder and harder, and as his toes curled, as her beautiful shoes slipped from her feet, they moaned and moaned and moaned.

I regarded Prada. He stared at them, then looked at Rosetta and her husband. One couple made love like a fairy tale come true. Another couple fucked like savages. Prada shifted a hundred times. I ran my hand across his crotch. He was aroused. Severely aroused.

I asked, "Where is everyone else?"

As the basketball player panted like she was in heaven, she raised a trembling hand and pointed at the door. Holding on to Prada's crotch, I led him to the door that separated this room from the next suite.

A pink sign was on the door that led to the adjacent bedroom.

☺ ANNEX OF DECADENCE. THE RULES OF THE CLUB APPLY. ☺

Below the sign was a titillating oriflamme, an image of a ménage à trois.

Prada asked, "There is more?"

"There is more."

We opened the next door and stood amongst many libertines. Unbeknownst to me, four connecting suites had been rented. There was plenty of space for creative Doers. There also was food, wine, and other alcohol. She didn't see me enter the room. The woman who had informed me of this club months ago when we were on the movie set in South Carolina; Lola Mack didn't see me. She was in rapture, focused. She climbed on top of her tall, dark, and handsome lover, held his lingam, smiled down on him as she squatted, amalgamated bodies, raised, lowered, did it with no hands, with a smooth and sweet rhythm, like a ballerina up on her toes, then down on her feet, then back on her toes.

Her friend, the attorney Carmen Jones, the Jamaican, was at this party as well. Her daughter wasn't here. The attorney was on the bed, seated on top of her lover, leaning back in slow motion, gently easing back until her back touched the bed. The next couple was just as hot. It was Chandra. She was with a dark-skinned man who was not selfish. She sat on him with his face to her back. Like Carmen had done, she eased backward until she was on top of his strong chest. He squeezed her breasts while she played a song on her clitoris. Lola Mack, Carmen Jones, Chandra, most of the women wore exciting negligees. A few were nude, but most wore lingerie. They were adorned in high heels and jewels. They were hungry socialites. Their sounds were beautiful, moans that blended like the musical instruments of the Danish National Concert Orchestra & Choir playing at Ledreborg Castle, sixteen vestal virgins with amazing voices, soft, seductive sounds that rang like mandolins, violins, flutes, clarinets, and alto saxophones. A few were like opera singers; lipstick-painted mouths stretched open wide, as exotic notes rose. We watched women and men, married couples, boyfriends and girlfriends *ficken* with love.

Prada held my hand as I moved through the crowd.

I asked him, "Want to have sex?"

"Yes, let's go to my suite."

"No. Here. Now."

"In front of everyone?"

"I can have a beautiful woman suck you while you eat me. Or we could both suck you at the same time. Ever had two women give you head at once? One sucking your shaft, the other your balls."

"You would like that."

"I would like that, but you would love that. Or we can ask two women to do that while you lick me to orgasm. We could love that."

"Is that what you and the soldier did?"

"You can call him and ask him. He might even draw you a few pictures."

"Is it?"

"It is what we did. Let me find a woman and I can show you everything that we did."

"I want you but I want you to myself for now."

"You want to fuck me."

"Yes."

"Then say it."

"I want to fuck you."

"Say it louder."

"I want to fuck you."

"Scream it."

"I'm not going to scream it."

"Please."

"No."

"Then let's sneak inside of the bathroom. I'll make you scream."

"Your period."

"I lied."

"Why?"

"For practice."

He followed me, taking in this glorious annex to fantabulust world. But the bathroom was occupied. It was a black couple. I had no idea who they were. They were in the shower, him behind her, her bumping into him over and over, him trying to keep his footing. The bathroom held humidity, the mirrors steamed as water fell over their hard bodies. Two more couples entered the bathroom and watched the show. I kissed Prada again. I was on fire. My lust was strong. His dick was a brick. I wanted to rape him. We stopped kissing and I stood in his arms, my back to his chest, my ass against his erection, my ass wagging against his distressed lingam, moving up and down on his hard-on, one of his hands on my breast, the other between my legs. We watched the joy of sex as if we were at a concert at Queen's Hall.

I asked, "Can you love this part of me? Can you love the mermaid, the nymph, the dryad?"

He pulled my hair back and sucked my neck, bit my ear, sucked my ear, growled. The couples next to us were making out too. Soon one of the women put hotel towels down on the tiled floor and eased down on her knees. When she started giving her lover an intense blow job, the other couple, the man put the petite woman on the counter, opened her legs and he gave her sex his tongue.

I looked at Prada, asking him to do the same, or to let me do the same. He shook his head. He saw my fire, my need, my out-of-*controlledness*, and denied me, used that to establish his moment of control. I rubbed his erection. Then I unzipped his pants and hurried my hand inside. He tried to move my hand away, but I grabbed his lingam, held it, refused to let him go. Prada kissed me. I stroked him as I kissed him, sucked his tongue, felt his strength wane, and now I was back in control. I took his lingam in my hand and I stroked him, stroked him as he watched the lovers in the bathroom. I pushed him back into the wall and I raised my skirt and I made him be still, gave him a stern face, a dangerous face, a challenging face, and he submitted, and that submission made me drip, made the blood rush to my yoni, made me swell, throb, ache, and he allowed me to ease him inside of me.

He was very self-conscious. I found that arousing, corrupting him, making him uncomfortable, angering him, and introducing him to something that pulled him from one compartment to the next. He sounded like he had died a thousand little deaths a thousand times.

I said, "You have wanted to be back inside of this sweet Caribbean yoni for so long. You waited years to get a taste. Now you have flown for twenty-four hours to feel me again. If you want it, take it. Take it."

"Why do you do this to me?"

"Take it now. Take it."

His breathing in snorts, like a bull, he began stroking me, mean-stroking me, but he stopped. Now breathing like he was suffocating, he held me so tight I knew my flesh would be bruised. I moved against him, wined like my ancestors from Trinidad, a mild dance that changed into the wilder *wukkup* they do in Barbados, danced on his sex. It was too much; he pushed me away. I laughed. I ran my hand through my hair, leaned against the towel rack and laughed. The other libertines in the bathroom, they laughed too. Laughed and applauded me.

Prada didn't laugh.

I eased my dress down and smiled at him, a well-dressed man with his lingam engorged. I had expected him to rush it back inside of his pants. He didn't. He left himself exposed. Straight. Long. Veins like ropes. Thick head. He inhaled and exhaled over and over; hands opened and closed. The industrialist who ruled many people, he was suffering. He was in purgatory, not in heaven, too close to hell, in the heart of misery. The others looked at his suffering, studied his arousal.

One of the women said, "You have a remarkable tool. It looks like a piece of art."

The other woman said, "My God. Are you a porn star?"

He didn't hear her. His skin was flushed. He was on fire, every nerve in his body alive, tingling. That was how I woke up so many mornings, how my sleep was interrupted so many nights, feeling as Prada felt now, in distress, in severe need. The shower turned off. The couple stepped out soaking wet, exhausted. One of the couples took off their clothes and went inside of the shower and began.

I touched the side of Prada's face, whispered, "Are you okay?"

Eyes closed, he touched my face gently, ran his fingers through my hair tenderly at first, then without warning his hand became a fist. He grabbed a fistful of hair and pulled my face to his and he kissed me. He was rough, dangerous, delivered a powerful kiss. He grabbed at the skirt of my outfit, became more than rough, and pulled it up. He lifted me, and my legs wrapped around his hips. With the absence of guff, he forced himself back inside of me. He had never felt this large before.

He held my weight, held my ass, and as I reached out a hand and held the wall, he bounced me up and down, forced me to take all of this overengorged lingam, forced me to bite his shoulder to keep from screaming. Others came inside of the bathroom. Others watched us. I opened my eyes long enough to see Lola Mack and her lover standing in the crowd. Then I closed my eyes and gave two angels their wings.

But Prada didn't finish. He refused to finish. Refused to come for me. Refused to come in public. He put me down, eased me down, each of my legs now feeling like a stick of jelly. Hardly able to stand, breasts rising and falling, sweating, I leaned against the wall. He forced his erection back inside of his pants. It was a battle he refused to lose.

Then he looked at me as if I were the devil.

Still struggling to stand, I smiled at him as if I were.

He turned around and walked out of the bathroom.

Women in the room made comical comments, chortled, shook their heads. A long moment later I followed. Chandra and her lover were on the bed kissing, tongues dancing, flavors being shared as he finger-fucked her. She was close to orgasm. She announced that she was coming. Prada wasn't in this room. I moved by the Watchers and Doers, went to the next suite. Others were there. Now Lola Mack and her lover were there as well. She straddled her lover, facing his feet. Her friend was in the same room. Carmen Jones was on her knees and her lover was behind her. She and Lola Mack had swapped partners.

I moved by the few people in this suite and ventured into the next.

Prada was there. He sat on the edge of the bed. I approached him as if he were a wild horse. Took easy steps. Made sure that he saw me. I kissed his dank neck. Kissed his lips. Sucked his tongue.

Hand sweaty, hair wild like the wind, I whispered, "I'm not done. So we're not done."

I undid his pants, pulled them down to his shoes, then I raised my beautiful skirt and I sat in his lap, sat facing away, sat looking at the others, my heels on the carpet. I put my hand between our legs, my fingers where two became one, then I touched his testicles, rubbed his balls. My spot. He was back on my spot. He held my waist and my hands moved to his thighs. I put a palm on each thigh, moved up and down on him and I couldn't stand it. I leaned forward, my head between my legs, my chest close to my knees, and he held my waist, pulled me back into him over and over. He went deeper. I pulled myself back up and he held me, held me tight, bit my shoulders, touched my breasts, put his hands all over my body. Again he stopped moving. It was feeling too good to him. He didn't want to come in public. I took control, I wined on him, moved up and down, squeezed my yoni around his lingam. He surrendered, worked his hand between my legs, fondled my clitoris while I danced, while I bounced and set free singsong moans. He came. He came hard. He came choking on his own saliva. He came drooling. He came telling me how much he loved me.

The room applauded.

THIRTY-FOUR

Back in his suite, when we were alone, when he had ripped away his clothing, after he had pulled away mine, Prada grabbed me by my neck, manhandled me, accosted me in the bathroom door frame, fucked me standing, my hands pushing the frame, my body bumping into his. I hadn't been choked in a long time. Alone, he was once again a sexual beast. It turned me on. It made me come. Soon he held my ankle, dragged me across the room, gave me carpet burn on my backside, panted and forced me onto my knees in a chair. He took me from behind, and again I challenged his every stroke. It was a beautiful battle. It was a glorious fight. It was a test that I refused to fail.

There was a rule, a rule called Ericsson's 10,000-hour rule, a rule that said to become one of the elite in any field you didn't repeat what you knew, but you engaged in deliberate practice, you constantly stretched yourself. That was how you became an elite musician. That was how much time an athlete had to spend to become an Olympian.

Or that was how you became as good in bed as a man like Prada. He had put in the time. He had challenged many women. He had experience, and not from repetition with the same partner. Making love to one person would be like playing the same team over and over. He had played many teams. He had been to championships. And he had won. It showed. He was a sexual outlier.

He said, "When I tell you I want to make love to you, you refuse."

"I did. I lied to you. You lied to me about being abroad. You played some silly game, so I lied to you. I give you what you give me."

"And now you want to have me, so when it's your desire, I should follow."

"Shut up and make me scream. Stop talking and fuck me."

He sat on the edge of the bed, forced me to straddle him and took me that way, and when I leaned forward, when I became weak and almost fell off his lap, my hands reached for the floor, my body balanced on my palms. He didn't stop. He stood up and made me walk on my hands, made me wheelbarrow and walked across the room like I was a child in a game. He kept me like that, on my hands, kept me in a position where I couldn't challenge his thrusts. He walked me, fucked me, walked me, did that until I sweated, until my arms began to burn. He remained strong, lifted me up by my pelvis and I gripped his waist with my legs. I tried to walk to a table, but I couldn't get that far. I went back toward the bed with him dancing inside of me, making me want to come. I was going to pull myself up on the bed, rest that way, let him do the work while I recuperated from having sex on the run. I struggled to keep my balance while he held my waist and grunted and continued his madness. He fucked me down into the carpet. When I couldn't hold myself, when I eased myself down, he followed me, never stopping, never slowing. His body was on top of mine and I pushed back into him. He slapped my ass a thousand times. He spanked me as if I were a rebellious child. I still moved. Hands on my waist, my ass in the air, he went into me up to his balls. His eyes were closed and I imagined that was his face of masturbation, as if he were calling upon erotic memories. He was so urgent with me, so rough with me, as if he were trying to destroy me by making me come over and over, my refractory period seemingly nonexistent because as one orgasm ended, a better one began. He went fast, hard, deep, panted, growled, sweated, paused, slowed down, caught his breath, then picked up the pace again, fast, hard, deep. I covered my mouth to muffle my moans and he moved my hand away, as if he wanted the world to hear me being punished, fucked, loved, pleased. He loved me. He hated me. He grew. He pounded me and grew. My orgasm was loud and dramatic. And that giving of wings aroused him more. The Leo in him roared at the Gemini that lived inside of this body. He roared and owned me. I couldn't move. All I did was accept and beg him to come, beg him to free me from this magnificent cruelty. He grunted and swelled inside of me. He lengthened. I was so loud. I was so fucking loud that it sounded like I was on the brink of death. And in response my insides grew, opened up, and lengthened to accept his elongation. He spewed. I loved the feeling. This was the way we were designed.

We rested an hour.

Until his refractory period should have ended.

So I crawled to him again. I gave him soft kisses. He returned soft kisses. Gave me bottled water before he hydrated himself.

And again he began making love to me, arousing me, fucking me, touching me, and making me feel extremely sexy.

He sat facing me as I sat facing him. We scooted toward each other and I put my legs outside of his. He eased himself inside of them, wriggled toward me, and leaned forward. I leaned back, used the palms of my hands to brace myself. I was slick like ripe papaya. He moved in and out of my body, took my wetness, my heat like that, stirred me with the tip, the head, then gave me a little more. I used one arm to hold myself up and touched myself, masturbated myself while he moved in and out of me. He bucked, and held my hair, and came growling, a dignified man set free from his conservatism. He collapsed and lay in bed in silence for a long while. He held me in his arms. Held me tight.

I said, "Ready to answer me, to tell me about all of your women."

Sweaty, his breath hot, he said, "None compares to you."

"At least you are admitting that there have been women."

"None compare to this night."

I lay with my legs crossing his. "I still want to know. In detail."

"Why?"

"Because I am a woman. Because I am not a fool. Because it might arouse me. Because I might actually feel envy. Because I need to understand my id and ego and I want to understand the id and ego of a man like you. Cognitive behavior interests me. Because group behavior intrigues me. Because I want to know how much of what we do is instinctive, if seeking new lovers is innate and if culture is getting in the way of nature and creating an unwinnable conflict and if that imbalance and fear is what makes us engage in deception and extraversion, if that is why so many sneak from wonderful relationships and continue looking to the outside world, to other people for stimulation."

"You have deep thoughts and a rich vocabulary."

"I guess."

"Vocabulary can be a key to success. Americans seem to take that for granted, shun it even."

"My mother and stepfather made sure I was prepared."

"You have a vivid imagination. Your film proves that."

"Thanks. That imagination lives inside of me. If I rejected it, I would not be creative."

"You have excellent ideas. You are quick to understand things."

"I'm not as quick as you. Not as brilliant as you are. The world of business doesn't interest me. If it did I could've gone to Yale or Harvard and graduated and stepped into the offices of my stepfather's well-oiled company. I have never lived in his shadow. As I have avoided living in my mother's shadow."

"At times you use difficult words. Words that are even difficult for me, I must admit."

"The words that I use are not difficult to me. I love words and I choose my words, change my vocabulary, change languages to fit my mood, move from French to Spanish to slang to proper English, dress my speech the way a woman dresses herself to suit her mood. Words are my wardrobe and my closet isn't near being full. Intellectual. Profound. Angry. Silly. Whimsical. Or ready to engage in a battle that I will refuse to lose on a mental level. I use words that are accurate to describe a moment. The problem with being educated at times, and I don't mean this in an arrogant or boastful way, is that you assume most of the world is the same way. If the government keeps the masses uneducated, they can appeal to people on an emotional level, on racial levels, on divisive levels, and that's why they have won. The last thing the government wants is a country filled with people capable of thinking on their own."

"Do you reflect on things?"

"All the time. It's part of my design. I think too much."

The winter rain returned. The winds blew through the night. I dragged my fingers across Prada's skin. He kissed me and went to sleep. Jet lag. Sexual exhaustion. But I refused to let him sleep.

Prada had assumed that he was done coming, assumed that he was finished, assumed that I was done stealing his power, but I took him inside of my mouth. The oral massage I gave him was a settling of scores, a sucking for the orgasms that he had given me, my need to show superiority. He went insane. He came like the Susquehanna. His orgasms were amazing, powerful enough to river across the room. I felt his reluctant orgasm in my nose, in the back of my throat. I choked. I choked like I had done in college, as I had done with Chris, memories of that moment of failure engraved in my mind. But I didn't stop. I recovered, mastered my breathing, my gag reflex, and continued. Never in my life had I devoured a man in that way. Never had I felt a man go insane and come that ferociously under the power of my hands, lips, tongue, mouth. I never would have thought that I would have loved sucking lingam as much as I did.

I enjoyed the power. I enjoyed making a man weak.

This time I didn't ingest his nectar. I snowballed. I gave his nectar back to him. As I kissed him, I force-fed him the drink of Greek and Roman gods and goddesses, fed him his own sweet liquid. He was surprised that I had done that. His eyes told me that it was something that no other woman had dared to do. I could tell. After a mild battle of the egos, where making love was a romantic competitive sport, after he had once again displayed his sexual showmanship, I was surprised that he had accepted that offering. But I had made him do so many things. I had made him partake of fleching. I pushed him to a new limit.

He swallowed what had been returned. I swallowed that which had been left over. That was what he got for choking me, for dragging me across the carpet like he was a caveman. He raised the bar. I raised the bar even higher. Then I stood on my head, again like I was dancing the headtop, my back against the wall as support, and he gave my sex his tongue, the blood rushing to my head as I came, as I almost lost consciousness. He caught me before I fell to the floor, held me as I trembled. He picked me up as if I weighed nothing. He carried me to the bed. I hadn't realized how strong, how powerful he was.

Then silence.

I was satiated. Hooks couldn't keep my eyes open.

In a sexually drunken voice I whispered, "You're quiet."

"I'm reflecting on things."

"Which things?"

"Everything that has happened since I entered this hotel."

More silence. We were in the spoon position, his arm around me.

My cellular sang. It was my mother sending a text. She asked if I was coming home tonight. I told her that I wasn't. I told her that I was with Prada. She told me that she was going to send me clothing.

I thanked her.

I put the phone away and whispered to Prada, "Tell me you love me."

We spooned again, then he did. He told me over and over and over. He said it once for each season that we had known each other.

I whispered, "Time flies."

He had judged our affair by the days we had known each other.

I had judged it by the number of times we had been face-to-face.

Or conjoined the parts that made him man and me woman.

He nodded. "I wanted to bring you a fantastic ring that I had seen."

"A ring?"

"From Dubai. But first I wanted to meet your parents. Well, your mother."

"You're joking about a ring, right?"

"I am not one to joke. Meet your mother. Ask you to marry me. That was what I wanted to do. It's time to enter the next phase of life."

"Under pressure to take a bride."

"This is my decision. But it is time to consider having a family."

"You need a woman with good breeding and good eggs."

"You should want a husband. Like me. A man who respects you and doesn't fear you."

"What would you expect from me as a wife?"

"To be faithful. I would expect honesty."

"Honesty is not the friend of love."

"My love would require honesty."

"And what would you give me as a husband? Would you give me the same?"

"Would you continue to partake in the hellfire club?"

"We could. We could be monogamous and partake. We could enjoy. Many of the libertines are married. Happily. Like Rosetta."

"Would we have to share?"

"Up to you. But I would be the greatest gift that you have ever received for even if I didn't get to relish in the pleasure of other lovers, it would excite me and bring me joy to give you other women, to bring women into what we have, to give you a level of stimulation that made you realize how wonderful sex can be when you open the door to other possibilities. We could make beautiful women our whores. We could tie them to beds and make them wait and see what we would do to them. We could praise and defile beauty."

"You could be faithful."

"I could be as loyal as you would be. I would follow the leader."

"What does that mean, exactly?"

"Your actions will set the standard. You would be the rule maker."

"My heart wants you forever. And with you I have a selfish heart. A very selfish heart. When you love someone so deeply, it's that way."

"I want that, maybe need a man who wants me that way. A man who wants me, only me."

"I don't want to share you with any other man."

"I will be the same way. If I give myself to you in that way, I will want the same. You will not be entitled to a mistress; there will be no woman with a Janet Rossi apartment waiting her turn. We're talking about settling on our religion, seeing where our spirituality lies, and having separate yet equal finances. And we are saying that this yoni and this mouth and this ass will be the last orifices you will experience from now until one of us breathes no more. And I will be an administrator on your Facebook account. I will approve your friends and be able to see all of your communication and delete anyone I disapprove of."

"I love you. I think I have loved you from the moment I saw you in Trinidad at Zen."

"And I still want to know about the women you have pleased since you met me."

"In the morning. I will tell you anything you need to know, all that you ask."

"Our accountants will have to meet. I'll need full disclosure. We need a starting point. And I am not as concerned with how much money you have, as I would want to know how you budget what you have. I'm not a helpless girl whom you will have to take care of, but I don't need any surprises either. I am a one-woman company. I have dreams. All I can ask is that you realize that I am your equal and respect that."

"Of course."

"We will have to take photos and issue a press statement."

"Why?"

"So that it will be on the record that we are dating. So if anyone googles my name, yours will appear and let all men know that I am taken. Same for you. All women will know you are off the market. And of course I will update my status on Facebook. I will send a tweet and let the congratulations pour in. But if you change my life, then yours has to be modified as well. I am not going to be like, say, R. Kelly's wife, and I know you have no idea who she is, but I am not going to marry a man and no one knows that we are married. I could choose to become someone's mistress, as that would be my choice when it started and it would be my choice when it ended as it would all be under my terms, but I will not be anyone's secret wife. Character is behavior. Change behavior, and character changes. If you are seeking to change my behavior, to tame me, then yours has to be modified as well. We have to be equally yoked, committed in that sense."

"You're remarkable. The way you think, how you process things, it's astounding."

"I am impulsive, but I am a thinker. I am a deep thinker. You may see me as wild, or may want to slap some unfavorable label on my behavior, but that's your issue. You can't define me. Ayn Rand. Anaïs Nin. Scarlett O'Hara. Anne Boleyn. My mother. I have great role models. Henry Miller. Salvador Dalí. I have read about the peccadilloes of many men. And I have read them without judgment, without becoming biased and bitter and devaluing the human condition. For every man who has a mistress, there is a woman involved who is behaving as a man. Women hunt too. Married men are the sexual conquests of many women, some foolishly seeking a seat at a throne that is already occupied. Men are selfish and women are selfish therefore we are all of the same cloth. I live in reality, but I have hope, and my hopes are not based on the fantasies of a fool."

"Nia Simone Bijou."

"Sorry. I was rambling."

"I like it when you ramble. Tell me more."

"From the man who tells me nothing."

"Tell me more."

"I think I want to have a baby. I'm getting older. Not old, only older. The thought of it terrifies me, but it intrigues me. My mind is changing. After I am married for a while, after I see what that feels like, being married, after I accept that change, after I see who that makes me become, after the psychological changes that it brings, I want to feel what it is like to carry a child, to be pregnant, to have life inside of me, and to make love to you while I am pregnant, to accept the love and lingam of the man who has impregnated me while I am with his child; for me, my unborn child, and the father to be bonded in that physical way, as I gestate. I want you to be there with me when the child is born. I want what my mother never had. I want what she deserved, what she was entitled to, but was denied. My father was dead before I was born, so my mother had to give birth to me alone. I wondered how torn apart she was to hear my father had been killed, how terrified she was to have me inside of her and be alone living in the dangerous parts of Trinidad. She was alone. There was no man to comfort her, hold her, make love to her, and tend to her needs. Pregnant women are very horny, so I have heard, just have to say. Moody and horny. Anyway. I am not faulting my father because by then he no longer existed. We have never truly existed at the same time. He was gone. His soul was gone but his memory remained. But he no longer existed. We like to say that as long as people exist in our minds they are alive, but that is a lie we tell ourselves. Gone is gone. I have never been in that part of Trinidad. I have passed by, but my mother forbade me to ever go in there. Taxi drivers refuse to go in there, like it's the favelas in Rio or the slums in Argentina. She went back to Trinidad, when she had made her money, and she bought us a family home in the land where we were born, a home that is paid for and there are no property taxes down there, not yet, so it is truly ours, but she never goes back to Laventille, never visits the ward, never returns to Hell Yard, that section of the Beetham Housing Estate, one of the most depressed areas on the island. My mother is strong, brilliant, but I don't want to do it the way she did. I will expect you to be there. Listen to me. I'm telling you what to expect. You have been warned."

"You would give me a son."

"If you promise to give me a daughter. I will be with her the same way my mother and stepfather were with me. God, I couldn't listen to N.W.A or 2 Live Crew or any music like that, or see movies like *Boyz n the Hood* or *Menace II Society* or watch *Def Comedy Jam*. But if it's a son, it will be your call. A real man is supposed to raise his son."

"Compromise at its best."

"Yes. Compromise at its best."

He kissed me, long and soft, and then he let me go and smiled.

I said, "I want to have sex over twenty-one times."

"In a month?"

"Over a weekend."

"Twenty-one times?"

"No. *Over* twenty-one times."

"More than."

"Yes."

"Why?"

"To see what that is like. Let's meet in Paris. Or Switzerland. Or Dubai. We could vanish from the world for a weekend and make love."

"Are you trying to break a record?"

"Yes. I suppose that I am trying to break a record."

"Whose?"

"Can you accommodate me?"

"Have you done that before?"

"No. But I want to know what it is like. To be with someone in that way."

"I can try."

"Don't try, do."

"In that case I will."

"Whatever pills or magic potion you need to make it happen is fine by me."

"Just have plenty of orange juice and water."

The light side of Gemini would've driven to Vegas and married him at that moment, would've let the windows down at a drive-through chapel, said our vows, then pulled over in Barstow and commenced our honeymoon at whatever motel was closest to the highway. The dark side offered no objections. The dark side bowed out. Submitted.

I said, "Prada, to be understood. You're my boyfriend."

"Yes."

"We're exclusive."

"Yes."

What I felt was what I imagined women felt when they were finally engaged. I understood that rush of emotion. The games were over. The chase was over. No more living day to day in the unknown. She could rest. She could build a real world. I was a whisper away from telling him that I loved him. One whisper away from singing him a love song that thanked him for his patience and told him I was ready to play for keeps. I wanted to erase all memories before him and leave the pain and fall into him, let him be everything I needed in a lover.

I said, "Trust me. Tell me about your women. Tell me of your whores. Tell me now while we are in this moment, not in the morning."

"Why?"

"Because I want to know. Because I want to know right now."

"That is not something a man tells a woman."

"I won't stop asking until I know. We will not rest tonight."

"You want to know."

"*I want to know*."

"Why?"

"I want to know the things that men do, what it's like to do them so freely with no consequence to character. I need to hear of your freedom. I want you to be human to me, not a shroud wrapped in a mystery. I want to know the things about you that will never be posted on your company's webpage, I want to know what can't be found out about you in newspapers or on Google or Wikipedia."

A moment passed.

He shifted.

He opened his mouth.

He told me. First he told me of his old girlfriends, of losing his virginity at the age of twelve to a girl who was three years older. Told me of a prior engagement, to a Turkish woman, an affair that had ended two months before I had met him. He didn't tell me why. Then he told me of the whores. His first encounter was when he was sixteen. A Hindu who had sex with him for what would have been the equivalent of buying one cigarette. He told me of the beautiful whores whom he had encountered, whores who were sent to his hotels when he was on business trips, the unasked-for perks that came with the business between men, the perks of powers, of the unnamed whores who gave him after-meeting blow jobs in taxis, in boardrooms, told me of one who traveled with him for a few months, paid for by a company that wanted his business, told me of being with women of the night in Dubai, Rio, and Monte Carlo. Stunning whores in Saint-Tropez, Cannes, Nice, Côte d'Azur, and even once Ezé. High-priced call girls were all over, especially in Monte Carlo. They were gorgeous, charming, clad in haute couture. Beautiful women impeccably dressed and flawless, women who reminded him of Audrey Tautou in the film *Priceless*, women who lusted for luxury and were very expensive.

I asked, "Have you bedded many?"

"I suppose that I have. I guess that I have bedded many models."

He told me of his adventures, some of his adventures, adventures that took place along the French Riviera, adventures in lesser-known towns, escapades in cities that were spotless and admirably maintained, cities that had self-cleaning bathrooms and delicious cuisine.

I said, "More. I want to know more."

"That's enough."

"More. Tell me of other places, of other women."

He told me of whores. He kindly referred to them as models. He called them models. Czech. Hungarian. Swedish. Jamaican. Nigerian. Indonesian. Bolivian. Models who accepted donations for time spent. Sex was free. He paid for the time. As I rested in his arms, he took a deep breath and opened that part of his world, of his life as a man, of his privileges of being a man, of the perks that came with being both drop-dead handsome and a rich man, a man of credentials and means.

His words took me around the world, took me behind his closed doors. Behind the doors of those who would never be judged. His words revealed one of his compartments. The things that I had done, even tonight, didn't compare to his conquests. His lovers had been amazing.

I asked, "How much money have you spent on yoni?"

"I'm feeling guilty. I feel uncomfortable telling you these things."

"You run a conglomeration. You talk in front of thousands. People bow at your feet. This is just you and I having an adult conversation."

"Sometimes it's easier to talk to thousands than it is to talk to one. It is easier to talk business with many than to communicate on this level with one. I prefer the former. That is what I have done my whole life."

"You hide. You hide behind your work. Your job is your shield."

"I have been with many, many models."

"No reason to be humiliated."

"I hadn't really given it much thought, not until this moment. I am ashamed. They have no names; barely have faces. I am feeling guilty."

"Paid for or gratis, each experience should be a celebration."

"But I did not love them. Each woman . . . there was no love. When you do not love someone they are not worth remembering. We forget those who are unimportant. We remember those whom we love."

I said, "We're alike, Prada. I struggle. I feel lost. Only I am not ashamed of who I am. I used to be when I didn't understand me, when I didn't understand that I wasn't alone, that there were many like me."

He was a beautiful man. What he had done before was irrelevant.

At some point, we could move on, marry, adjust, make babies.

I asked, "Are you okay?"

"I did love one. I did love one of them."

"One of the whores?"

"Years ago. I met a whore in London. I was walking the red-light district. I was on Berwick Street. There was a French whore and her friend was an African whore. The French whore was a smart woman. She was a polyglot. As was the African. I was with them. I would go to my meetings at the Gherkin, then return to them. I had them meet me at my hotel every evening. I was with both of them for four days. We went to the aquarium. We went to the theater. But one of them, I did feel love for. One I lusted for; the other I felt I could have loved."

"Which did you love? The French woman or the African?"

"This is starting to feel like a confessional. The room is shrinking and it feels like an enclosed booth for Sacrament of Penance."

"It's okay, Prada. Love does not have to be a totalitarian country that does not allow free speech. I ask to understand you, not to judge."

He shifted. "I am exhausted. I need to sleep."

"Then sleep. We can continue this later. It's fascinating."

His eyes remained open. He didn't blink for a long time.

I said, "Tell me that you love me."

"I love you. I love you as I have loved no other woman."

I smiled. Eventually, he closed his eyes. His breathing became heavy. His body was relaxed. I whispered his name. No response.

I used the bathroom. Took a quick shower. Rinsed my mouth with hotel mouthwash. I looked at my left hand, imagined it decorated with a ring. As I stood in the doorway, skin damp, hair pulled back from my face, I stared at him. I told him then. That was when I told him. I had not said that to any man in forever. As he slept like a man exhausted, a man thoroughly drained, a man suffering from jet lag. I said it then. I said the simple phrase that owned so much weight and power.

I said it to free myself from that old fear. To know that I could say it to someone else. To know that I could feel it take root and bloom. I said it while I felt safe. I said it softly, gently, nervously, like I was a Scaramouch. But I said it. What was important was that I said it. I had reclaimed my power to say it. As Prada slept, when he was no longer on this level, when he couldn't hear, that was when I said it.

When I could say it and not feel the burden of expectation, not hear it repeated because I had said it, or not hear it *not* repeated after I had said it, when I owned the moment, I let those three words free.

A weight had been lifted. The world was no longer resting on my shoulders. Then I eased back into the bed, the bed that many others had used for sleep and copulation, pulled his arm around me, absorbed his warmth, and I slept. The anxious, overbearing clock that ticked inside of me, it paused, gave me rest. For the first time in innumerable years, I slept like a woman who was finally satisfied. My journey had ended.

The fire had burned itself out. But like Gilsonite mines in the Utah wildlands, I smoldered. But there were no flames. Prada had all but extinguished my inner conflagration. My darkness had relinquished control to the emotions that lived inside of my heart. Tomorrow the fire would start anew. But tonight, there was a well-earned rest.

I woke up startled when a Spanish-speaking woman entered the room. I hadn't heard her knock. Hadn't heard her call out that she was from housekeeping. I didn't know where I was for a few seconds. It was close to noon. It was checkout time. Cocooned in come-stained, saintly white covers, wrapped in the exotic scent of a man who had flown the world to bring congratulatory flowers, I woke up alone, Prada's flavor on my tongue. He wasn't in the hotel room. There was emptiness in the room. The sound of *only* one heartbeat. I searched for him. His luggage was gone. Nothing had been left behind. No note. No text message. I had messages from others, from my mother, from my father, from Bret, from Rosetta, from my agent, from Lola Mack, from celebrities, from my underpaid-and-overworked New York editor, from my literary agent, from my agent at The Screenwriters Agency, from Regina Baptiste, even from high school and college friends, but nothing from Prada. Gone. He had left me the way I had left many men.

THIRTY-FIVE

Nia Simone Bijou,

First and foremost, congratulations on all of your success. I bet you're surprised to hear from me. I didn't expect that I would be compelled to write you after so long. One of my sisters and her boyfriend were married last month in the Dominican Republic and I was the best man for the ceremony. Being home felt strange, but I was happy to see my friends and family. I saw someone who looked like you. When I saw her, I didn't expect to miss you, but I did. The entire evening was filled with love and joy and for a moment I was sad because I was not with you. Does that sound stupid? We are strangers now. We have been for some time. I never had a chance to let you know why I left college without attempting to say good-bye to you, why I didn't call you after our last night in the hotel. Maybe you don't care. During that time, I couldn't tell. You weren't an easy woman to read. I left Hampton because I was in love with you and I couldn't take being in the same city with you and not being with you. I didn't want to be in the same state. I couldn't bear being in the same country. I know that after you broke up with Chris, we only had a few moments, but they meant the world to me. I had been on the sideline looking at you for years. Those moments that you were with me like you were my girlfriend, even though I knew that you weren't, were like a dream come true. I left to get away from the memory of us, a memory that was everywhere I looked. I left to be able to start over. What I didn't know was that the memories would follow me. I wanted to forget how much pain I was in. I wanted to forget how mad things had become, the cheating and the deception on Chris's part, a crime for which he had enlisted me to be his coconspirator. And I wanted to forget that I ever loved you. Most of all, day in and day out, I hated myself for lying to you on behalf of Chris. I couldn't stand to look at myself anymore. I had hoped that in the middle of all that we would become a couple. I had so much love for you and I had hoped that what I felt in my heart was real when I touched you. And then one day after that last night together, you didn't call. You never picked up the phone to even see if I was alive. You stopped talking to me. You left me without a good-bye. I was concerned about you. Graduation came and went. Not a call. Not a note. You just left Hampton and never looked back. And so many times, I would dial your number . . . just to hear your voice . . . not knowing what to say. So I eventually left Virginia. I went back to the Dominican Republic for two years. Then when I felt that enough time had passed I returned to the United States. Most days, Nia, I think about you. I wonder how you are . . . if I concentrate hard enough I can even smell you . . . that's the special thing about memory. There's no room for anyone else inside my heart because you're still there. Always there. I know you have someone else by now, but he will never love you like I did. My love was real, and I know this love I feel for you has carried us through many lifetimes. I know that we may not get it right in this life, but we will be together someday again as we should be. This I have never wavered on. I have always been clear about you and my intent to love you. Last night I had a dream about us. . . . I didn't want to wake up. I knew that if I woke up I couldn't touch you anymore. My dreams allow me to hold you. I told someone the other day that every love song that I sing, I sing to you, especially if it's a Mariah Carey tune. "Vision of Love," "Always Be My Baby," "We Belong Together," and "Don't Forget About Us" take me back to you without fail. It's sad, much sadness there. I have a great job now. Baseball is behind me. And I'm writing a book. What's inside of me refuses to leave so I will try and write it away. I think that I got the urge to write from you. I'm not good at it, not like you were. Not like you are. The book is about us. If I ever finish it, there will only be two copies. One for me. One for you. The reason I am not sure that it's over is that I don't know how to end it. Maybe if I end the story I'll stop wanting to be with you. It's damn good. You would be proud of me. I knew that we only had a few moments, but I knew you during my college life, those powerful years, watched you for countless semesters, and those were the best years of my life. If I could save time in a bottle, as it is already written, I would save every day that I have spent with you, even though there were but a few, even though you were crying over Chris. Every moment was important, every laugh, every tear, every time we made love, every time that I looked at you and dried your tears. I didn't care that you were in love with Chris, I didn't care that you were blinded by your love for him, because I was blinded by my love for you. That love that I had for you back then, I have it all with me still. I consider myself lucky to have experienced it, regardless of how it ended up. I always thought we would be friends at least, but I realized when people have loved as we did, when lines are crossed as we crossed lines, there is too much pain, and we would only serve to remind each other of a time in our lives we want to forget, so a friendship is impossible. I still humor myself with the idea. You are and always have been the one. It feels like you will always be the one for me, always, no matter where I am or whom I am with. No other woman has compared to you. You have my heart. I'm writing like I am writing a book. And I hope that enough of this rambling is clear. I hope that you have read this far. I don't know if any of this matters. It just mattered to me to let you know these things, to let you know how I feel about you still, to let you know that I love and miss you so much and that I am so sorry for everything. If you ever want to see me or talk to me, if ever you feel like we have a chance, please contact me. Hopefully this letter finds its way into your hands. Hopefully tonight I will have the courage to come find you and put it in your hands and see your face once again. And if I do find the courage, hopefully you will read it to the very end. As in life, it is funny how things turn out. I met you a few days before Chris. Maybe a week. At the student union. The AKAs were stepping. You were in the crowd, had on dark blue jean shorts, brown sandals, and a red, white, and black T-shirt from Trinidad. I had my favorite T-shirt from the Dominican Republic, one that had Sammy Sosa's image on the front, and on the back was the red, white, and blue flag of MI QUISQUEYA. That started our Caribbean conversation. You were passionate. You were funny. You were so innocent. Loved your hair short too. I told you that you were very *tierna*. I had called you ladylike and you thanked me. You asked me if I spoke Spanish. I said I did. Then you started speaking in Spanish, your pronunciation so good, and your vocabulary already so amazing that it was intimidating. You needed a little help in advanced Spanish, expressing opinions using concessive clauses. For a few sessions, I was your unofficial Spanish tutor and I had your attention, had you to myself two hours each Tuesday and Thursday for seven weeks, almost two months. I wish I could *69 those days. I think I learned more from you than you did from me. Every time I saw you, I wanted to ask you out. You were so passionate, so intelligent, and inside you lived the fervor of Ayn Rand and Hedy Lamarr. Hedy had beauty, but she had intelligence as well, intimidated many men. Then one afternoon *mi tigre* Chris came over to our table. Never will forget how you lit up. I smiled, but the way you regarded him devastated me. You ended up with him. Never understood that.

I keep trying to conclude this correspondence, but the words refuse to end. The finger has been pulled from the hole in my emotional dam. I remember your tears, your trauma. It's not my intent to remind you of the onslaught of problems or to loose a flood. But like the little Dutch boy who removed his finger from the hole in the dam, words pour out. I'll force the words to end, even though I'm long past making a fool of myself. It was great seeing you tonight. It was truly great being in the same room. Most importantly, even if I never see you again in this lifetime, I would love it if you consider me your friend forever.

Rigoberto Traveres.

P.S.—*Me encantó tu película muchísimo*. It was amazing.

P.P.S.—You were incredible on stage. Again you have motivated me.

P.P.P.S.—*Mi Quisqueya es, y siempre será mejor que el tuyo. Tenía que decirlo. No pude resistir.* ☺

THIRTY-SIX

Beverly Hills, California.

The conurbation of excess was bordered by Bel-Air, Santa Monica, and all areas that were so proud to be Beverly Hills–adjacent that they keep their real estate prices high enough that a single-digit millionaire was considered a broke man up here. Billionaires were the new millionaires in this country. The town of Los Angeles, California, was originally named El Pueblo la Nuestra Señora de Reina de los Angeles de la Porciúncula. The original name of the Beverly Hills area was Rancho Rodeo de las Aguas and was a lima bean farm until they started drilling for oil. Less than seven hundred people lived there a little more than one hundred years ago. Eventually, Hollywood came. Minorities were no longer welcome. Greed was planted and grew like trees. Dollar trees. More greed was planted. And the greedy were still coming. Presidents came here to have fund-raisers. Royalty came here, would visit 90210 but would never set foot in the area that houses the citizens living in 90220. For a few days I played the role and basked in the sought-after zip code of bourgeois television shows, real-life heirs and heiresses, dignitaries, television celebrities, movie celebrities, celebrities who were famous for doing nothing, executives, and media moguls who basked in a luxurious culture and did their shopping at the triangle along the cobblestone roads on Rodeo Drive, which in reality was a crappy version of the astounding Champs-Élysées in Paris. Nothing here was original. Not one single concept. They wanted to do a female version of *The Expendables*, and *The Expendables* was another version of *The Seven Samurai*. I'd never fit in here, not the way most did.

* * *

Six days later, the weather was dry and felt warm enough to wear shorts and a T. The warmest part of the morning was around eleven, when it reached the low eighties, but the temperature would drop thirty or forty degrees after the early sunset. But for now, considering we had taken a break from Hollywoodland and spent the last two days in Mammoth snow skiing, this dry warmth felt like summer in the islands. I wore a white, two-piece bikini and heels, along with wide Jackie O sunglasses. The outdoor sound system played music by Irving Berlin. "What'll I Do?" A cup of mango tea was at my side, as was a worn copy of Anaïs Nin's *Henry and June*, a novel that I had read more than a priest had studied a Bible. I sat poolside underneath clear skies, another rarity for LA. The letter that Rigoberto had given me was on the table. I read it ten times today. And I had read it just as many times yesterday and the days before. My cellular rang. I looked at the caller ID. It was a call from Chris's cellular. But I knew that it wasn't Chris. It was his humanitarian wife. It was a co-member at my hellfire club. It was my nemesis. She had dialed my number ten times a day for the last five days. Each time I had cursed her, used many dyslogistic adjectives to express my dissatisfaction with the audacity she had to call, cursed the walls and snapped out how I felt about her ringing my phone. The humanitarian hadn't left a single message. But I knew that it was she. Intuition. Expectation. I had been here before. Not with her. But I had been here before. I had been here with the Jewell of the South. It had been very ugly.

I wiped my face, looked at my hand, and expected to see spit that had been spewed like venom. With regret, I knew that when Chris touched his face he remembered my hands, remembered the moment that I had lost the plot and had become as irrational as the square root of the number two.

Again I looked at that emotional, moving letter from Rigoberto. I swallowed his pain.

My mother came out to the pool. She wore a red-and-black two-piece and high heels as well. My mother held two cellular phones. One was in her hand and as she walked, she typed a text message, a long text message. As she typed at the speed of light, my mood shifted. The other phone was being held up to her ear with her shoulder. Her tone was militant. It wasn't a Hollywood business call. It was personal.

"She and the farce for a government are a disgrace. I read online that they are trying to phase out the GATE program which made it possible for many blacks to get a university education. And the VAT they are promising to remove from certain food prices have been in place for years. Everyone already knows that. That's why she's a running joke. Black people need to wake up and stop being bought and sold so easily. She went into power and things for black people have worsened."

I tried not to, but I thought of Prada. I had whispered that I loved him. I was afraid, not heartless. I was filled with desire and fantasy, not without a soul. I did love him. Maybe not as he loved me, not at the level that he professed, but I did.

More than one thousand and seventy days had passed since I had met him at Zen in Trinidad. I ached for him now. I ached to be laughing and eating and dancing with him now. I ached for him as, based on his passionate words, Rigoberto had ached for me for many years.

He had desired me and I had cherished Chris and Chris had preferred Siobhán. Preferred. I refused to and never would see that union as a union of love. I searched but failed to see the humor in the cruelty that life brought to many.

Prada carried more weight at this moment. My heart was heavy for him. My mood hidden behind sunglasses and an expressionless face, I ached for Prada the way other men ached for me. I wanted to call him. I wanted to text him. Skype him. But ego would not let me.

My mother sat on the wicker recliner next to mine. She ended her call, put down both of her cellular phones, and right away she picked up the letter that I had been reading over and over. I didn't slap her hand. I didn't protest. She read it. She read my private life, read Rigoberto's confession of love. Then she put the letter back down and sat next to me in silence. Soon she picked it up and read it again. She shook her head as she put it back down. My cellular rang once more. The same phone number out of Florida. A number from a cellular from Miami. I turned my ringer off and put it down on the tile. I waited for her questions. I waited for the mommy voice and finger-pointing criticism.

She said, "The actors are in London doing *The Graham Norton Show* and a couple of them are in Paris for the French show *Le Grand Journal*, which I still think that you should have flown over to be on, but it was your call. You have a few more interviews, then we're done."

"The London interview. Radio. I have to talk to Angie Le Mar."

"She's brilliant. Comedian. Director. Simply brilliant. She understands what you do."

"It's going to be recorded and played the day of the premiere."

"The Leicester Square London premiere is in two weeks."

"I know. Time flies."

"Will Prada be there to escort you down the red carpet?"

"No idea."

"Have you talked to him since the premiere?"

"No."

"He hasn't called?"

"No."

"You haven't called him?"

"No."

"Something happen?"

"Honesty is not the friend of love."

"How long did you know him? Your stepfather said that he comes from a very powerful family."

"He does. They are on the level of Sabga."

"One of the top successful entrepreneurs in India and not just known in his parent's country or in London, but throughout the whole world. Petroleum, telecommunications, software, other things."

"I know."

"Did you love him?"

"Doesn't matter."

"Was it the cultural difference?"

"Mommy, please."

"Religious difference?"

"Let's not do fifty questions."

"You're okay?"

"Is there any other choice? Is there ever any other choice?"

She reached over and held my hand. She squeezed it three times, then held on. About twenty minutes later we turned over, were on our bellies facing each other.

She said, "That was a passionate letter someone wrote you."

"Very."

"Chris. That boy from Belize."

"What about Chris Eidos Alleyne?"

"I have a feeling that you are leaving a lot out. You have omitted much. That letter is from Rigoberto. That was Chris's friend."

"His best friend."

"I never heard about him. You have left a lot out, my daughter."

"Am I supposed to tell you everything?"

"Do you think that you should tell me everything?"

I shrugged.

She said, "It's not easy. What your stepdad and I went through. Not easy. My therapist said the most effective way to let go of anger was to forgive my ex-spouse. I told him that I had Caribbean blood and I'm not Jesus, plus I work in a very racist Hollywood, a town that thrives on revenge, so the concept of forgiving was a difficult one to comprehend. He told me that it was going to be an extremely difficult thing to do, especially in the case of unfaithfulness. So listen to me, it's very important to approach this in the proper manner."

"Which is what, exactly?"

"Decide that you are ready to truly forgive, and you mean it in your heart. Next you need to find a way to tell your ex that you've forgiven him. Can be face-to-face, on the phone, or even by e-mail."

"Can I just send a text or post it on Facebook or send a tweet?"

"Stop with your jokes. You might write or tell him that you know that you're not getting back together, but you want him to know that you forgive him. Accept that the past is the past, as I had to accept that the marriage was over. Had to let go of the anger."

"You haven't let go."

"We're talking about you, not me. You have to let go of the anger and become a better you. Remember both the good and bad sides of the relationship, as I have to do with the marriage. Make peace with yourself, as I have had to find a way to make peace with myself. Your stepfather wasn't perfect, but neither was I and I guess that I have to be realistic about how I contributed to the divorce."

"How did you?"

"He wanted more children. I guess that I was content with you. I denied him that right. He tells me that the resentment he had toward me came from that. I was never fully a wife for him, in his eyes."

"No one ever said."

"I know. I was busy working and I had, to be honest, lost your father. I didn't want to have another child and then end up divorced with two children by two men. I didn't want to stay at home and be taken care of like every other Botox-faced woman in this neighborhood. I was in the land of opportunity and I wanted to pull my own weight. Guess I was afraid. I didn't realize that then, not as I do now, now that I am able to clearly review my emotions. But I should've given you a brother or a sister, a sibling. Instead I remained stubborn, determined to succeed in my career, and I accepted his infidelity as if that were the true cause of our divorce, moved on and established a support network outside our marriage-related friendships. I moved forward and developed future goals that did not involve him. I fell into my work and made sure that you had what you needed. I allowed myself time, several years to heal before I even thought about another relationship. But the big thing was I planned my life as a single mother."

"Did you ever see Dad again? Had you seen Francois Henri before the premiere?"

"You know we talk off and on."

"That was not the question. Have you seen him?"

My mother paused. "What do you mean did I see him?"

"As a wife sees a husband. As a woman sees a man when she thinks no one is looking."

"Are you really going to ask your mother that type of question?"

"What's really been going on?"

"I saw your stepfather again. You were away in college. Your freshman year. We decided to talk without lawyers present."

"Well?"

"He came to Los Angeles. Stayed a few days, maybe a week. We went to dinner at Gladstones, to talk. Well, I went to talk and he came to listen to me tell him how he had made me feel, that affair."

"And?"

"Like I said, my therapist thought that it was a good idea that I said things to him face-to-face."

"So?"

"I was angry. Said horrible things. Told him that he had disappointed me, he told me that I had disappointed him as well. But it was my meeting so I took the floor and told him all that was inside of me. Said things that no lady should ever say. Whenever he opened his mouth in rebuttal, I did my best to emasculate him. He's French. He's expected to have a mistress. And when it happens, he expects that it will be dealt with privately. Or at least in his mind he felt that he was expected to. The problem is that I am not French, and if a French wife accepts her husband having other lovers, he married the wrong one."

"And?"

"We drank."

"And."

"We talked. Things calmed down and we talked in a normal tone."

"And?"

"We drank some more wine."

"And?"

"One thing led to another."

"And?"

"Afterward, he told me that he liked the sex that we'd had and wanted to do it again."

"Wow."

"He didn't say it that way. He said it in French, so it sounded . . . it sounded French."

"He liked it and wanted to do it again. He liked the sex? What does that mean?"

"He wanted me back in his life, but to me, since he had other involvements, that meant he wanted me to become his mistress."

"Did you?"

"No. And that's not funny."

"You sure that you didn't?"

"He's not a perfect man, but he is a good man."

"You did."

"No. It would've been like the song Sugarland sings, "Stay." He'd leave my home, then fly back to Paris, leave my bed and leave me in limbo. He'd be back in her bed and leave me wondering when he was going to come back. I'd be angry. Envious. How long does something like that last? I had gone through the madness and divorce with him and I had already exhausted myself of the foolishness. So I cut to the end of that script. She had already won. She had won. He belonged to her. So, I told him, married man, go home to your next wife."

"Talk about being in the dark. How many times did you see him?"

"He called whenever he came to LA on business, or if he was in Vegas or Seattle he would offer to fly me up to have dinner. Once a year. Maybe twice. And if I was available, I would answer his call."

"That's pretty vague. Anyway. Last time you saw Dad was . . . ?"

"After I broke up with this guy, the one who got married. Your stepfather came to town. I was pretty hurt. He was familiar. He has always been familiar. I couldn't bear being alone then."

"Same guy you mentioned when we were in the car with Panther?"

"Same guy. That was years ago."

"You really loved that guy."

"I did. Anyway, your stepfather was divorced from his second wife. And I wasn't seeing anyone at the time. We had a long history together. We have a long history. We know each other well."

My mother and I held hands. Like I was six years old. Like I was her Little Nia Simone. I wondered what our lives would have been like if Francois had never come to Trinidad, if he had never met my mother.

I said, "My father. My real father."

"What about him?"

"This interview that I did a few days ago was disturbing."

"The Quash bitch. I have advised you to leave it alone."

"Tried. Can't. Now it has me thinking."

"What does it have you thinking?"

"You remember the first time you saw my father?"

"Of course. I was on the Savannah. Late evening. Was buying doubles and he was getting bake and shark. He saw me walk by. I was with two friends and he came running up behind me."

"Well? What happened? Who saw who and said what?"

She smiled, laughed, and looked like a teenager again. Memories.

My mother said, "He run up to me, got in front of me, smiling. Ah hope yuh come wit a library card cuz ah checkin yuh out. I walked away. Gyul yuh parents hadda be retarded cuz ya special. I kept on walking. My name is Doug. Thas God spell backwards wit u in de middle. I shook my head. Baby yuh like table, ah jus wa ress sumting on yuh. I looked at him and rolled my eyes. Yuh lookin like a lobster, all de meat in the tail. I tried not to laugh. Gyul you have more form dan a secondary school. By then I had my hand over my mouth. Yuh fadda does cut cane? How ya smile sweet so? Stop laughing, Nia."

"Oh my God, Mommy. Yuh lookin like a lobster . . . all de meat in yuh tail. That is hilarious."

"That is what a Trini woman had to put up with from the Trini men. I heard that tripe so much I was often tempted to rip my ears from my head and put them in my pocket."

"All de meat in yuh tail. Mommy had a fat batty. Batty gurl."

"Stop laughing."

"Mommy, last time I was there this man come to me and he say, he say, *Yuh faddah is a terrorist cuz you is de bomb.* And when I blew him off . . . when I blew him off he said, *Yuh like a barbwire fence, ah cyah get ova yuh*. Oh my God, I had never laughed so hard. Those Trini pickup lines are horrible."

"Fah-ma-lay, oh gosh, ah go pay good money to fuck dat ass."

"Men still talk to you like that back home? Mommy, no."

"Oh gosh, gyul, ya man maybe does have a time with that ass."

I said, "Leh meh touch it nah."

"When I was younger, when I was out walking with your father it wasn't any better. He almost got into a fight on Frederick Street. Brotha man, you brave to let she out I wudda tie that to bed and fuck she right through. Every time she try to get up ah wudda breed she. That fucking ass boy oh gosh baby."

"Disgusting, Mommy. And you were with my father?"

"Your father was ready to cut the boy's neck off, but I handled it."

"How did you handle it, Mommy?"

"I told the boy that I would leave my boyfriend, your father, for him if he could spell the word *receive*. He walked way flailing his hands and cussing me out. You would've thought I cuss he momma."

My mother laughed too. We laughed until our sides hurt.

I said, "But out of all the Trini men who came after you, my father must've said something right."

"Yes, he did. Yes, he did."

"He was ready to fight for your honor."

"He was. Right on Frederick Street."

I let a moment go by before I asked what I wanted to know. "Did my father have other children?"

Then her expression changed. Her laughter ended. The smile went away. She glanced down. Her breathing changed. She closed her eyes.

My mother said, "Shit, shit, shit, shit, shit."

"Wow to the fifth power."

"Damn, Nia. How many years did it take for you to ask me the one question I have dreaded?"

"Swear jar six times over."

"You caught me off guard. I didn't expect a question concerning Derren Liverpool."

"He had other kids?"

She paused. "I think. I don't know. I can't say for certain."

"You don't know, yes, no, or you can't say for certain?"

"I have never seen them if he did."

"Don't be vague."

"There was a girl."

"A girl."

"Two girls actually."

"Who dey?"

"One lived in Chaguanas."

"Nice Anglican girl?"

"She was Roman Catholic."

"The other?"

"The other was a Laventillian. She was Lavantee like us. That one passed my house every day walking down the road to get a maxi or a taxi. She was old enough to be in secondary school. She was fifteen. She was terrified of me. Fifteen years old. We were all so young back then. I heard that when your father was found murdered, we were all pregnant for him at the same time. It was the girl from around the corner who came running to my house crying like she had gone mad after your father died. She came to tell me that he was dead. I had no idea when she ran up the streets pregnant and crying and came banging on my door. I was seven months pregnant and she was four or five. I thought the girl was about to have a miscarriage in front of my face."

"The other girl from Chaguanas?"

"Just heard about her. I guess that was nothing. When you have a very appalling childhood, things that come up, some things like those are just part of what you go through. It's as common as rain. My mother went through it. My grandmother and her first husband, my grandfather, he had babies all over Trinidad, the last one being made when he was over eighty. When she remarried her second husband, the Chinese man who gave her three more babies, she still had the same issue. I have an auntie young enough to be my baby. And don't let me start talking about incest. Lots of things happened. And a lot of things were accepted or swept under the rug and not really talked about outside of being back-porch gossip. I hear that I have an outside sister who is one week older than me. And an outside brother who is one month younger. I have no idea where they live, just know that they are in the islands, or maybe one or both of them are in London by now. Never liked talking about that. Never have. It's embarrassing. Many go through that, and when it's like that, to you it seems normal. You cope with it by not talking about it."

"Same here in America. It's no better here. This is the daytime-television pregnancy-test capital of the world."

My mother nodded. "Only they aren't trapped on an island. It makes you feel trapped."

"Here in America they spread the madness across the country, from sea to shining sea."

"There are a lot of weddings in America where the family of the bride and the groom can sit on the same side of the church. There are secret weddings between siblings."

"In the Genesis, Abraham and his wife Sarah were related. The fable of Oedipus speaks for itself. Myrrha and her father, Cinyras; she disguised herself as a prostitute and slept with her dad."

"God. When I grew up I knew men who slept with their brother's or sister's daughters."

I said, "America is just one big island. The rich commit the same sins that the poor people do."

"At least here it's spread out over three million square miles. On a small island, with all the secrets, you have to make sure you're not about to get into bed with somebody you don't know is your cousin or maybe your brother or sister. It has happened more than once."

"Gross, Mommy. Definitely good they can spread it from coast to coast here. At least they don't have to look at each other."

"True. They are not forced to see each other on the roads or at the market or on Frederick Street. After your father was buried I would see the other pregnant girls. They would see me. It was unnerving. Can't describe how I felt. Carrying the child of a man who has been eulogized, see the others, unnerving. But you have to remember that the island was much different back then. It's a lot more modern now than it was when I was a young girl. Back then I wore vests with flared pants, bracelets, rings, and earrings like Pam Grier, flip-flops and an armed forces bush coat, had on my Black Panther berets, might have had on one of my tie-dye jerseys, dashikis, and I never left home without an Afro comb. Head to toe I dressed myself in the symbols of the Black Power rebellion. Then I met your stepfather. The rest is history."

"Jesus, Mommy."

"You're crying."

"I'm fine. Back it up a little bit, please. Three pregnant women."

"That's not the way I wanted you to see your father. Or me. Or yourself. Or your island. I don't want you to ever see Trinidad that way. I'm going to stop talking now. Mommy doesn't want to go back to that part of her mind, not right now, not on a day like today."

A moment later he appeared on the other side of the pool. He had on swimming trunks, his skin pale, the hue of wintertime in Paris. The lean Frenchman dove into the far end of the pool and started doing laps. My stepfather was an excellent swimmer. He had been at my mother's home, his former residence, all week. He had stayed here while we went snow skiing, on vacation from his business and other obligations.

My mother said, "He's the smartest man I've ever met. Intelligent, cultured, extremely polite, caring. When I met him, I had never met a man like him. Not ever. Not in my life. He was different from all of the men I knew in Trinidad. It was like I had met a brand-new species."

"Love."

"Love. Yes. But I saw the reflection of who I wanted to be. My heart went crazy over him. He wanted me to follow him to America. I told him I had a baby. I wasn't a single woman."

"Then?"

"He asked me to marry him."

"Had you had sex?"

"You are pushing the envelope."

"Had you had sex?"

"Geesh. Yes. Over a weekend."

"Was it good?"

"I followed him to America. Answer your own question."

"Because of sex."

"No. Because of the way he made me feel."

"How did he make you feel?"

"Normal. I was feeling like an outcast in my own country. He made me feel normal. The sex was good. I was young. It was new. It was good. But the love he gave, that was what I needed."

"Okay. Now I'm crying."

"Me too."

We turned over again, reclined faceup. I took my sunglasses off, wiped tears from my eyes, and then put my sunglasses back on. My mother did the same. She kicked her feet like she was a little girl.

I sipped some of my cold mango tea and asked, "What about the young guy you're seeing?"

"He's just a friend. He'll be there when I return or he'll be gone. I'll be fine either way."

"You have put him on pause."

My mother took my tea from me and sipped. "I have put him on pause."

"Was he in Amsterdam with you?"

"He was. I didn't want to be abroad alone."

"International MILF."

"Well, Prada makes you an international DILF. So take that."

"Don't let good sex confuse your heart and make you think that it's love."

She put the teacup down on the small table next to her. "Hush. I do appreciate Francois Henri for what he is, and with his faults. I don't care what he does anymore. Is something wrong with me?"

"Life is as life is. Now whenever someone says life is short, what do you always say?"

Mommy recited, "'Tomorrow and tomorrow and tomorrow, creeps in this petty pace from day to day, to the last syllable of recorded time, and all our yesterdays have lighted fools the way to dusty death. Out,

out, brief candle. Life's but a walking shadow, a poor player that struts and frets his hour upon the stage and then is heard no more: It is a tale told by an idiot, full of sound and fury, signifying nothing.' "

I said, "Shakespeare. Macbeth's soliloquy. Act five, scene five."

"Life is short. It moves so slowly, yet it moves so fast."

"You and Dad."

"I would love to meet someone new. Someone else. Like it was back home, this is a place that only shows its surface. Hollywood is crowded, but it is its own island in that it's hard to meet people. Well it's hard to meet people who aren't befriending you to further their own agendas. It is an island of users. And if I do meet someone and the chemistry is not right, I don't try to pretend that it is right. I don't want to go through another divorce again. One of those is enough trauma for a lifetime. Yeah, I left an island to work on another island. Francois Henri is familiar. It's not that I want it, not this way. This was not how I had ever imagined that it would be. But this is how it is. I work hard and long, but when the smoke settles at times I do feel lonely and it's not as easy for me to open up on a personal level with the people in this pretentious town. I don't want to argue and fight. I want to have some enjoyment, to enjoy my life."

"Did you ever cheat on him?"

"While I was married? I had plenty of chances to."

"Did you?"

"No. How you make yuh bed is so yuh go lie."

"Do you regret not cheating on him?"

"Sometimes. After it was done, sometimes I did regret being so committed to the marriage."

"I'm glad you didn't."

"Why?"

"You're my mother. There are rules a mother must follow. Lead by example."

"Am I wrong for entertaining his desires now?"

"Do you desire him as well? Are you entertaining your own desires as well?"

"Yes."

"It isn't wrong. Only if you don't desire him and you give yourself to him, then it is wrong."

"The daughter becomes the teacher."

"Not even close. It's just that the eye can't see itself."

"Much easier to judge others than to see your own faults."

"You have to explore to see what fits you, and when that coat no longer suits the weather of your mood, shed it, or take on a different coat, one that warms the new mood. Sometimes others see us as we are not, and make expectations or demands based on that perception coupled with their own needs. You don't have to live up to their expectations, for their expectations are simply that, their expectations."

"My daughter, my daughter."

"So enjoy it. Go after whatever makes you happy. Seek what makes you smile. You decide if it is right or wrong. Don't ask if I agree. Dad is here. Don't ask me if I want him here."

"You sure?"

"You're smiling. I'm sure. I rarely see you in high spirits. Rarely see you unperturbed, not rushing, not in the middle of a call or in the middle of a major deal. Never relaxed. I'm very sure."

When I had come back from the W, after Prada had abandoned me in his rented bed, my stepfather had arrived here that same afternoon. With his luggage. He came in. I smiled and kissed him. Went to the game room and shot pool with him. Friends, celebrities, people who Mom considered her inner circle came over later that day and Mom turned on the popcorn machine and played the film again in the media room. Dad was there. I didn't ask questions. I loved her. I loved him.

I was starting to think that everyone had someone who could show up, married or not, if you're married or not, and take you back to a dark place, a place that was still hot, a place where unrequited love lived, a place of heat and remorse, a person who could irritate and ignite you, bring you back to their sex.

But I didn't like it when we were a fractured family, dysfunctional, emotionally far apart.

During the night, Dad slept in one part of the house and my mother slept in another. When my internal clock brought me restlessness and made me walk the hallways during the hours of writers, the hours when the world was at rest and our brains had clarity, wearing oversize sweats and a sweatshirt and big heavy socks, all that and a housecoat, I would go sit in the kitchen, on my computer, writing, thinking, missing Prada during one moment, thinking about Bret the other, and knowing that my stepfather wasn't in his room. He wasn't in the guest bedroom. I knew because he had left his door wide-open.

The door to my mother's bedroom was closed, a DO NOT DISTURB sign on the knob. It was as if they were in their own little Decadence, their own alcove with the curtains drawn. I knew the rules.

Loneliness was a bitch that taunted us all, especially after dark.

The same might happen tomorrow night. Then he would be gone back to Paris. And my mother would return to being one of those who ran Hollywood. They were adults. They had done adult things together. Things they would never admit. They had done things that a daughter should never know her mother had done.

Mothers were women who used to be little girls in pigtails.

A woman needed what a woman needed. And my mother was an amazing woman. So she deserved all things amazing. But even the amazing carried disappointment and pain.

My mother said, "The Production Company."

"What about it?"

"They accepted your original."

"My original offer? They rejected my original offer."

"You won. I reminded them of a few things. You won."

I smiled and felt the shadow of nepotism cover my existence.

My mother said, "We can go over it again tomorrow."

"How did the price go up in my favor?"

My mother grinned. She ran Hollywood. She made shit happen.

It felt good to win at something. It felt damn good. My occupation had never betrayed me.

My stepfather stopped breaststroking and treaded water.

He called out to me, "Nia Simone."

"Nope. Not gonna happen. I'm not getting in."

He swam closer and splashed water on me. "Nia Simone."

"Dad, seriously? Do I look like I came out here to swim? Let me be a girl for a moment."

"Swim with me."

"Dad."

"Daughter."

"Mommy?"

"That is between you and Francois Henri. And stop splashing water on me."

He laughed and splashed water. "Nia."

Dad was a typical man. What he saw in front of him were two women in bikinis, not women in high heels, not two Caribbean women basking in the sun, not mother and daughter bonding.

He splashed water and when he wet my shoes I yelled at him in French. He laughed and splashed more water.

I gave in and pulled my heels off, then put my sunglasses to the side. My mother's cellular rang and she took a call. Her expression changed. It was a personal call. It was a man. I smiled at her and winked. After I sipped the last of my tea I pulled my hair back into a ponytail and jogged toward the pool and did a cannonball. The cool water shocked my system when I landed next to the man who was the only father I had ever known. Not the best. Not the worst. He swam away from me and I chased him, caught him, and pulled his legs. We yelled back and forth in French as we played and had a water fight. The man swam like a fish. Then we swam from end to end of the Olympic-size pool. Soon my mother had ended her call and taken off her heels, pulled her hair back, and jumped into the pool.

The memories of the divorce lived within me. It had been difficult. It had been horrific. It had changed my mother. It had changed me. Now we all pretended that we were able to turn back the hands of time. We pretended that we were able to undo what had been done. Right now it felt good. Right now it didn't hurt. Right now we basked in an ersatz pleasure. We weren't stupid. We knew that fragile eggshells covered the well-manicured ground on which we walked.

For now we behaved as a functional family.

Like we used to do years ago.

Before innocence was lost.

When we entered our humble abode my cellular illuminated as it had illuminated nonstop since sunrise. The glow was beyond irritating, but I wasn't concerned. Not here. I was in a fully gated home, one fenced for privacy and security. I was in an area that was guarded and patrolled by the Beverly Hills Police Department. No one could simply walk onto the property, ring the bell, and spit in my face. After I had showered, the perpetual glow continued, my cellular a beacon for madness.

As I dried my hair, my cellular glowed; the name CHRIS EIDOS ALLEYNE lit up the display again.

While Mom and I wore battered Old Navy sweatpants and moved around the kitchen talking and arguing over recipes and cooking big pots of pelau, while my stepfather returned wearing sweats and began making sure we had what we needed for more than three dozen salads, Chris's phone number stayed alive on the display of my phone. In the evening we hosted more than thirty people and we played the film again for celebrities and people in the business and neighbors and people who had preferred to avoid the crowd at the theater. Everyone was Hollywood casual, meaning that they wore trendy clothing and sexy boots and Eddie Borgo bracelets and Elizabeth Knight earrings and Tory Burch boots or Zara heels and Linda Farrow eyeglasses and Chloé sweaters and carried Diane von Furstenberg handbags. I wore a USC baseball cap, runner's watch, wrinkled dungarees, and a sweatshirt emblazed with the phrase TEAM KRISTEN FOR LIFE. Tuna puffs, chicken puffs, cheese puffs, sausage rolls, croissants, currant rolls, cakes, accra, tamarind sauce, pastries, and dips and chips, paper plates and plastic cutlery were all laid out on a long table buffet-style. Deals were being made. In Hollywood every day was a day of business and no one wanted to miss an opportunity. I wasn't comfortable in that environment, in that world where once you were no longer lauded you were no longer well regarded, but I endured, I smiled, I laughed, I danced. Afterward we played the movie *Sparkle*. Then my mother and I pulled long colorful socks over our arms and danced for our friends, danced and lipsynced songs from the movie; this was our compartment of familial love. And almost everyone took a turn at karaoke. It was Hollywood and everyone was infected with either the blood of Watchers or Doers. All night, my cellular glowed. She was determined to make my phone ring from the age of Pisces into the Age of Aquarius. Siobhán. Chris's wife. That humanitarian bitch was crossing another line.

THIRTY-SEVEN

Prada sent me a text. His message arrived exactly at midnight, the start of a new day, as I boarded a Boeing 757 on Delta flight 1254, my red-eye flight for Atlanta. The flight was due to leave at five of midnight, but it was running behind. Except for that I would not have seen the message until I was on the other side of the United States of America. I had boarded coach with the third grouping of weary travelers toting books and computers and iPads, passengers who wore large winter coats and hauled too much luggage, as we all carried too much baggage. I had just stored my hand luggage, squeezed my frame into my designated compartment, stored my backpack underneath the seat in front of me, exhaled, sat down and buckled up and made myself comfortable at my window seat when my iPhone vibrated.

YOU'RE AN IMPOSSIBLE WOMAN. A DEMANDING WOMAN.

HEAR THIS; A MAN DOES NOT WANT TO BE CHALLENGED IN ALL ARENAS. WORK IS HARD. LOVE SHOULD COME EASY. I KNOW THAT MANY ARE RAISED TO BELIEVE THAT LOVE SHOULD BE DIFFICULT. I DISAGREE, NIA SIMONE. THE THINGS THAT LIFE BRINGS WILL ALWAYS BE UNPREDICTABLE AND TAXING, BUT I DO NOT WANT LOVE TO BE THAT WAY. I LOVE YOU. I LOVE YOU. I LOVE YOU. THAT SHOULD BE ENOUGH. THE PROOF IS IN MY ACTION. WITH THE ONE THAT I LOVE I WANT COMFORT AND I WANT TO GIVE HER COMFORT. I DON'T WANT TO SPEND EVERY DAY WONDERING IF I AM NOT GOOD ENOUGH FOR HER NOR DO I WANT TO WONDER IF SHE WILL BE WAITING FOR ME

ONCE I RETURN HOME FROM ONE OF MY MANY BUSINESS TRIPS.

And he ended the text with three words; three simple, powerful words.

ALL THE BEST.

I felt the lump in my throat. I took curt breaths to calm that globus sensation. Throat tight, face warm, I eased on my Jackie O shades and stared out from my seat in coach over the wing of the airplane, stared into the darkness, my pointer finger on the tip of my lip, touching my teeth as tears fell from my face in silence. A moment ago I was famished and couldn't wait to sit and nibble from the bag of trail mix that I had bought, but now I had no appetite. There was a fashion magazine in my lap, one that had Anya Ayoung-Chee's exotic Trini face on the cover. My right leg bounced. I turned my trembling body away from the world. As someone sat in the seat next to me, I battled, pretended that I was occupied getting something out of my purse. Swallowed emotion. Didn't want to cry. Lost the fight. The light side of Gemini mourned. As did the dark side. Many tears fell on Anya's face, on her eyes. She smiled up at me as if to say *Trini women we warriors*. I nodded. Loved Anya. Supported her. Always would. I'd slap anyone who spoke her name with a frown. But for now, as cabin doors were locked, as phones were shut off, as the plane rolled and took to the sky, the storm inside of my head made a hard rain fall from my eyes.

On Facebook he had changed his relationship status to single.

That did hurt. Iz a Trini. I strong. But I still woman. I still woman.

By the time my flight landed at seven in the morning, East Coast time, when I powered up my phone to send him a long thought-out message, he had both *defriended* me and blocked me.

Then I would send my thought-out message to someone who cared. I would send it to myself. I would send it to the explicit pages of *Abnormal Desires*, by Anonymous.

If only I had been a simpler woman, a woman who didn't act in her own self-interest, a woman who didn't think for herself, a woman who was not a threat to morality, a woman who didn't reach her own conclusions, a woman not afraid to take chances and walk the unbeaten path of enlightenment.

If only Prada had been a twin. Or was laissez-faire and had a liberal brother as handsome as he, as capable in bed as he, both willing to engage in adelphogamy, having the desire to share beautiful wives.

If only he had been more.

If only I had been less.

If.

If.

The shortest word with the longest meaning.

If.

THIRTY-EIGHT

M&M accepted my request for friendship on Facebook. My college roommate. It had been years. It had been too many seasons. I sent her my number and asked her to call me so that we could catch up.

"Nia Simone, it's Mona Marshall from back-in-the-day at Hampton."

"M and M, how have you been?"

She paused, then she laughed. "God, no one has called me that silly nickname in years."

"It took you forever to accept my friend request."

"I was so surprised when I saw that you had sent me one."

I asked, "Are you on Skype? Would be great to see your face."

She paused again, sounded a little nervous when she said, "I need to get my headset."

She told me how to search and find her. I was excited. Crazy with joy. It had been too many years. I was ready to see my former roommate, the Shakespeare-loving chemistry major, the rebel who wore natural hair and chastised all who didn't. Within five minutes, I buzzed her from my iPad and we smiled at each other from our computers. She saw me and laughed and smiled. I did the same. I was on my disheveled bed. She was in a modest kitchen; pictures of MLK, Obama, and Jesus adorned the bright yellow walls. I think that she was in the same home she had grown up in as a child. I was surprised to see that she had a lot of hair. It was long and massive. Her face, she wore a lot of makeup as well. The biggest surprise was that the woman I remembered with natural hair now had extensions down to her waist.

She said, "Look at your face. Your hair is long. I'll bet that you are so thin now."

"You're looking great."

She touched her voluminous mane. "Oh, please. I have put on so much weight since college."

"It's not showing."

"I gain all of my weight in my butt."

"Me too."

"Not like I do. Fried chicken and barbecue ribs and corn bread ain't no joke. And I'm about to have another baby. I'm three months, so I'm about to get real big in a minute, like I did the last time."

"I am so, so happy for you. Are you married now?"

"We're engaged. My husband-to-be is Italian. I met him at Verizon. He's a manager. Over the years I have expanded my options."

"Boy or girl?"

"Hope this one will be a girl. If not I'll have to try again in a couple of years."

"Where are you living?"

"I'm in Kentucky."

"Still in Lexington?"

"I was in Topeka, Kansas, for a while, then I moved to Arkansas, was in Houston and Missouri City, Texas, and Wewoka, Oklahoma, even slept on a few sofas up in DC, but I ended up coming back here to Lexington. I sell hair now. Virgin hair. Mongolian hair. Malaysian. Brazilian. Indian. Burmese. Indonesian. Custom lace weaves. Frontals. Yaky. Mink. Kinky. Silky. I told my new boyfriend that every day I wake up saying hallelujah and I thank the Lord that black women have been brainwashed and love to look like Barbie because it is keeping the lights on and the bills paid. And I can do most of my business online with PayPal. Business is booming. Hair sells faster than crack."

I didn't ask her about college, if she had ever made it back. That was obvious. She had changed a lot. She was no longer the forward-thinking girl who wore shorts and a T-shirt and turned heads when she walked by Ogden Circle. The Omegas were now dancing around someone else, were wagging their tongues for women a few years younger. She said a few things to her son. He was off camera making a lot of noise. The tone of her voice, her temperament had changed. She had evolved. She was a mother now. She was in the next season of her life. And she had made sacrifices. I smiled, happy for her.

In a mild tone of envy I asked, "So how do you like being a mommy?"

"What do you mean?"

"How is your son? I'll bet that he's a big football player like his father."

"Junior is fine." Her grin went away and her tone darkened. "You're calling me because of him?"

Her new tense expression startled me. She read the confused expression on my face.

I said, "That's . . . what was his name . . . the football player . . . that night at the dorm? The night we were . . . you know . . . all together."

"Eugene Williams?"

"Yeah. That's his baby?"

I said this not knowing if she had indeed had that baby, or if she had terminated and now the son she had was the son of some other man. I tried to remain politically correct.

She said, "You don't know, do you?"

"Know what?"

She called her son to the screen. I had expected that he had had a problem, maybe ADHD, or was autistic, or that he had Down syndrome. I prepared words of compassion and encouragement.

When I saw her child I had a familiar reaction. One that I had had not long ago, one that had stopped my heart when I had ripped open a box and stared into the eyes of an old love. The child had stunning eyes. He had a beautiful smile; his sea-green eyes bored into mine. His hair was in dreadlocks. He was a normal little boy. He waved at me. Sea-green eyes. That was all I saw. Blood drained from my face. My mouth opened wide. I didn't blink. He waved again. I waved at him.

Then he left the screen.

My old college roommate and I sat in silence for what seemed like an eternity. Her expression was apologetic, but she didn't cry. Maybe all of the weeping, sobbing, wailing, repenting, whimpering, and bawling had happened long before this call, long before her child had walked or talked. All she offered me now was a simple shrug.

Mona moved her long extension from her face and said, "Nia. I'm so sorry that you have to find out this way."

It took me a long moment, but I asked, "What is your child's name?"

"At first I named him Eugene Anthony Williams, Junior."

"You said at first."

"It turned out that Eugene Williams wasn't my son's father."

"Okay."

"Christopher. I changed the name on the birth certificate, named my son Christopher."

"Who is his father?"

"Chris is his father."

I paused. "Chris Brown, Chris Tucker, Chris Rock, Kris Kringle?"

She took a breath. "It turned out that Chris from Hampton was his father."

"My Chris?"

"Your Chris."

"Chris Eidos Alleyne is the father of your child."

My heartbeat muffled all words for a moment. There was a mercurial change in my attitude.

She took a breath. "Junior is his son. Christopher Eidos Alleyne, Junior."

Stunned, I repeated, "Chris Eidos Alleyne, Junior."

"The firstborn son should have the father's name."

"You and Chris hooked up? While we were roommates?"

"He had come to the room once, looking for you. You weren't there."

"You and Chris. In our dorm room."

"It was stupid."

"You and Chris Eidos Alleyne."

"I thought that you had found out a long time ago."

"Had no idea. No idea at all. This was a random call."

She said, "He came to the room and asked me what to get you for your next birthday. I told him books. Books were always a good present for you. You loved literature. I made him a long list."

"Plath. Rand. D. H. Lawrence. Henry Miller. Anaïs Nin."

"Yeah. I gave him specific titles to get. I knew what you liked and what you wanted."

I asked, "Were you with him on my bed?"

"We were on the floor. Ended up on the floor. I think we started off dancing to a song. Then we put a wet towel down at the bottom of the door and smoked a joint. Got high. The radio was on. 'Atomic Dog' or something. He came up behind me moving his hips and . . . teasing each other. Passing the joint. Blowing me a shotgun and putting his lips on mine. We ended up kissing. Then we were on the floor. It happened so fast. Then he left. I went to the shower and when I came back in the room, you were sitting on your bed, had earphones on, and were deep into doing your homework. If you had come back ten or fifteen minutes earlier . . . I jumped out of my skin when I saw you on the bed."

After the shock died down, I straightened my back, leaned away from my screen, and in a voice made for meetings and interviews with strangers I calmly said, "You and Chris made a handsome son."

"My son is my world now. He's a handful, but I wouldn't trade him for the world. He's definitely going to be a lady-killer."

"Glad you're happy and living such a blessed and prosperous life."

"I'm sorry."

"It is what it is. Everything happens for a reason."

"No matter how he got here, my son is my blessing."

"That's good."

"How have things been for you since college?"

"A struggle."

"I heard that things blew up between you and Siobhán."

"Several times. I was almost kicked out, but they worked it out."

"What kind of work are you doing? Schoolteacher?"

"Small assignments for a publishing company in New York."

"Like that little side gig you had in college?"

"Yeah. Nothing has changed. Same hustle."

"You know, hate to say this, but Chris had told me that he didn't think that you would ever amount to much. He thought that you were lazy and when he went to the pros you would be an unsuccessful writer. Writers end up being schoolteachers or living off their husbands and family, he had said that. Said you were used to living off your mother's money, then would try to live off his."

"I was on scholarship, just like he was on scholarship."

"Just repeating what he said . . . right before we had hooked up."

"From the man who never made it to the pros. Best he did was college ball."

"He lives off his wife now. Her inheritance."

"Her parents died?"

"They were in some country and they were kidnapped and killed by some dissidents. I guess that it was kind of like the embassy over in Libya only they were in Afghanistan. Wait. Might have been in Bolivia. Not exactly sure where they were. But the rebels killed everybody. That was a while ago. They marched them all out of the place and took them up in some remote area, lined them up, shot them all."

"Wow. Sorry to hear that. But you said Chris saw me as a slacker?"

"He did. He thought that you were needy too."

"Wow. Me? Needy?"

"Exactly. But when he met Siobhán he thought that she walked on water and that she was going to change the world. I don't talk to him anymore. Not since we ended up in court in Miami and forced him to do paternity testing. He sends money, but I don't talk to him. Don't want to talk to them and as long as the check gets here every month I won't bother trying to talk to them. Have no idea how they're doing."

"So, Chris assumed that I was going to be a failure."

"Just like he had assumed that he would be the next Jerry Rice."

"Shit. Then why was he with me?"

"You had no idea?"

"I wish that you had told me. I wish that you had told me years ago. You had a baby with him. None of this bothered you at all?"

"I prayed on it."

"Well, God never whispered it in my ears. When you do somebody wrong, sometimes you need to pick up a phone."

"Well, by the time that I found out, you weren't with him."

"It still mattered. He was my boyfriend while you were with him."

Swimming in awkwardness, while I maintained composure and yielded a smile as fake as her hair, I regarded the time on my phone. I gave Mona ten minutes of cordial conversation. Six hundred seconds. Long enough where I wouldn't seem rude. That would be enough flagellation. I tried not to react to being hit in the head with a brick. But I knew that it showed. My body language had changed, and my voice.

She said, "Life never turns out the way we have it planned inside of our heads."

"Rarely does it. It rarely does."

"But it's great to hear from you."

Struggling, I responded, “Great to see you too.”

“It’s like a load has been lifted from my soul. Praise the Lord.”

Despite being horned by my former roommate, I said a few polite things to her, asked her for her mailing address, for my records, and then I wished her well, wished both her and her son well.

“Nia Simone Bijou, since I have your ear, if you know anyone who needs some hair, send them my way. Virgin hair. Mongolian hair. Malaysian. I have it all and I have the best anyone can find. Like my page on Facebook and look for me on LinkedIn and you can follow my updates on Twitter. I’ll be in Atlanta in September for the For Sisters Only showcase. I’ll have a booth there. We should connect.”

“Seriously? I find out you have a baby by my ex and you ask me to send you customers? What kind of stupid bitch do you think I am?”

Again another awkward moment inserted itself. Denial had weight. She was in denial, or simply had thought that what had happened between her and Chris back then shouldn’t matter to me now. She had processed it for years. It was new to me. I regretted this call.

I said, “How could you sleep with him and smile in my face?”

“I tried to say no. He was the most important man on campus.”

“The risk. The adrenaline. And he wanted to test you.”

“I had no idea that he was attracted to me like that.”

“You were attracted to him.”

“I wasn’t attracted to him at all.”

“He was the most desired man on campus. Hands down, you had the nicest ass on campus. Not the biggest. The nicest. Five feet tall, very nice shape, intelligent, funny, energetic, Afro-centric, a DJ, a dancer, a chemistry major, a writer for the newspaper, a role model, a renaissance woman. What man could say no to you? And it had to be exciting. Opening your legs for the man of all men. Making love to your roommate’s boyfriend, then sleeping in the same room. You had him in our room. Then smiled at me knowing that you had just had Chris. I wish . . . I wish that you had reached out and told me.”

“I was tripping when I found out. I couldn’t tell you. Plus I was too busy dealing with it, dealing with Chris, his wife, my child, the court system. All of it left me with my hair falling out. I was stressed.”

“One phone call. I’m so disappointed right now.”

“I’m sorry. For what it’s worth, I am truly sorry.”

"You were my sister. We used to talk about you being in my wedding. We used to talk about me being in yours, if you married."

With a thin smile, she responded, "I didn't mean for it to go down like that. I was terrified when I was pregnant. I prayed that it was Eugene's baby. It is what it is now, Nia. But my son is here now."

Her son appeared on the screen once more, sea-green eyes, and his copper skin the same hue as Chris's skin. Her child asked me who I was. With a kind smile I said that I was an old friend of his father.

He asked, "You know my daddy?"

I said that I had known his father long before he was born.

He said, "Can you please tell my daddy to call me?"

"Does he call you?"

"No, ma'am. But I want him to."

"Has he ever called you?"

"No, ma'am."

"For Christmas?"

"No, ma'am."

"For your birthday?"

"No, ma'am. It would be cool if he picked me up on my birthday."

"Does he send you presents?"

"No, ma'am. I want a football with his autograph on it."

I almost choked up when he said that.

He didn't know his father, yet he worshipped the man.

He looked solemn, heartbroken, but soon he left the screen. M&M. Mona Marshall. Not until then did remorse cover her face.

We promised to keep in touch, knowing that we wouldn't, and we ended the Skype session. I would never contact her again, but as a gift I might send her son a football. Their illegitimate child was the innocent one. As I had been the innocent one once upon a time.

I would send Chris Eidos Alleyne, Junior, a football and a photo of his father from his glory days in college, a photo that had been given to me while we dated, the words *I love you* erased. All of those articles from days gone by. Maybe that was why I had kept them. Not for me. For that child. Soon, very soon, I would send him all of those as well.

THIRTY-NINE

The short French woman wore two coats of mascara, a glossy nude, and a sweep of light pink blush. She reminded me of Jean Seberg. Her flailing arms and hands revealed her disgust as she said, "Their sex tape was stolen from her boyfriend's computer, so he claims. I would have kicked his ass. And after I had kicked his ass from Moscow to Germany and back, I would have killed him with my bare hands."

"Should've called my office. I could still sue him. He'd settle."

They closed their lockers and we made kind eye contact. The second woman looked a lot like Jackie Kennedy, even had the same pillbox-perfect look, only her features were dusky, her figure curvy. Jackie Kennedy's face on Kim Kardashian's body. Both were curvy and had entered with their figures drenched in designer blazer dresses. Jewelry sparkled on them as it did on every woman, as it did on me.

The judge was here. The sassy adjudicator was here wearing beautiful Louboutins and nothing else, her personality strong as usual.

She said, "Since the weekdays can't be laid off, I'm starting a petition to rename the days of the week . . . Moanday. Tongueday. Wetday. Thirstday. Freakday. Sexday. And Suckday. I would be in church all day on Suckday. I would attend all three services. And I'd become a Seventh Day Adventist on the side and even go to Bible study. I hear the black churches have the best Bible study meetings."

The women laughed and many jokes were told.

The judge headed toward the main area. She waved and blew a kiss at me on the way out. Her name was Clara Parker. I waved at her and she moved through the dozens of vixens preparing for fun.

I had been standing at my locker staring at a folder that I had brought with me. I opened the folder. Browsed its contents. Then I closed the folder and put it back inside of my bag. I closed my locker. I regarded myself. A sheer pop of color on my cheekbones. A layer of nude gloss on my lips. I had been tempted to allow the makeup artists to add a few individual false lashes to enhance it all.

In English that carried the accent of France, the one who resembled Jackie said, "Good fucking."

I stopped inspecting my face in the full-length mirror on my locker and said, "Good fucking."

In the same powerful accent, her friend said, "Good fucking."

"Good fucking."

The one who had her hair nearly shorn, the one who resembled a very young Jean Seberg in the movie *Breathless* grinned, bit her bottom lip, and whispered, "You're yummy."

"Thanks. You're looking yummy yourself."

"Swapportunity?"

"I have made other arrangements. But thanks for the offer."

They looked at the monitor, took in the video from x-art.com, then they left, nude, in high heels.

Once again doctors, lawyers, born-again capitalists, educators, politicians, members of the clergy, speakers of many languages, and pilots surrounded me. I was in the undressing area of Decadence.

Siobhán was there. She had been six feet away from me for the last fifteen minutes. We ended up being assigned adjacent lockers. Siobhán and her scent of strawberries was one locker away. Her skin was tanned. Her hair was voluminous, flowing in the style of Lana Turner. Her makeup was understated, shades of peach, copper, and light brown paired with hints of dusky pink gloss. She looked like a movie-star beach goddess with red lips. She undressed and prepared herself, ignored me, made me invisible. She lived in my periphery. Music played and women danced and lived in joy around us. Erotic videos played. Drinks were served. Expensive chocolates were being given out. Mrs. Alleyne and I ignored each other. Eventually I stared. Looked at her until she looked at me. She paused. Stopped all that she was doing. Her wedding ring lit up the room like the sun.

Her nostrils flared. She was tense. I took a calm breath. At least I tried, but I felt flames leaving my body when I exhaled.

I said, "Mrs. Alleyne, did you sleep in the same bed with me last night?"

She blinked a dozen times. "What? Did I sleep in the same bed?"

"It's a Southern expression."

"I don't know what you mean."

"It's really silly of us to stand this close to each other and use this much energy pretending to ignore each other. We're adults. So I'm taking the high road. Good evening, Mrs. Alleyne."

"Good evening, Miss Bijou. It is Miss Bijou, right?"

"Yes, Mrs. Christopher Alleyne. It's Miss Nia Simone Bijou."

"You haven't married. I'd assumed that you had married."

"No ring. No stretch marks. No cheating spouse."

Her voice was the same, yet it was different. It was more mature. It was smarter. The way she said simple words told me a lot about her. She licked her lips. Touched her hair. Very self-conscious.

I stared at her without blinking. Stared until my eyes wanted to water. So much had changed because of her. And Chris. Because of him, because of the pain that he had brought into my life, I had made subsequent decisions to seek out a life that fulfilled my various needs. And it had been a wonderful life because I chose to make it that way, and I have had my needs fulfilled in ways I never would have imagined. Maybe I had unknowingly embarked on a very calculated and controlled approach to something that was supposed to be liberating. I had lost my balance in college. When you lost your balance, you fell. Not all falls were bad.

Siobhán cleared her throat and said, "Surprised to see you here."

Russians and Germans were on the other side of her. Italians and Romanians were next to me. We were the only English-speaking women in the area. It felt as if we were the only women in the room. It felt as if we were the only women in the universe.

I grinned. "For me it's just a phase."

"A phase."

"I go through phases. I go on personal journeys. I'm still single. I have made no promises to God therefore I had made no lies. While I am young and capable I choose to experience things. Take on lovers and discard them when they no longer fit my mood. When a new season arrives, I let those things go. We all have to know when to let go."

"Seems as if some of us take longer to let go than others."

"Seems some still think that they are entitled to the world."

Then the erotica on the monitors changed again. Provocative sex played on screens throughout the pristine edifice. A suntanned woman was celebrating her sexuality, sucking a young Jamaican boy.

Siobhán asked, "I want to ask you a question, need to ask you woman-to-woman."

"That's pretty hard to do with only one woman in the room."

"Okay, I'll accept that. You're bitter."

"I'm not bitter. Not at all. From what I've heard, I'm very sweet."

"You know what I mean, Bijou. The things you said to me and my husband while we were in Eros . . . bitter. They were rude, uncalled-for, and bitter. And since I had enough emotional maturity not to engage in such childish behavior, yeah, you're right, there is only one woman in this conversation."

"It's a new day. Actually I want to congratulate you and wish you the best."

"Did you sleep with Chris?"

"Did I sleep with my ex-boyfriend?"

"Were you with my husband?"

"Did he obey a particular commandment in the Sinner's Bible?"

"Did you sleep with my husband?"

She had called Chris her husband as if that were the most natural thing in the world. A reminder of who had won him. Inside of me lived the need to fulfill the desire for vengeance. I had to exist on this planet knowing that I was better than the bitch he had cheated on me with. And now, since my flavors had saturated the tongue of her husband, since he had entered me once again, the roles had changed. She was the fool. He had horned her with me. She was the deceived. I wanted to be able to scream *shah mat*, take that, bitch. Take that, *shah mat*, *shah mat*, *shah mat*, *shah mat*. But what happened at Decadence stayed at Decadence. Telling secrets was forbidden. The dark part of my psyche had achieved a Pyrrhic victory, the victory of an egotistical fool.

I said, "With Chris? After he slept with you and got my roommate pregnant? I guess that he had knocked up M and M before you. Or maybe he was juggling all three of us at once. He's an island man."

No reaction came from her when I mentioned M&M and the baby.

She knew. Like M&M, like my former roommate, my former friend had said, Siobhán knew, had known for at least the last decade.

She said, "So you didn't sleep with Chris?"

I laughed at her like she was mad.

She wasn't amused.

I said, "Do me a favor. Stop blowing up my phone. It's irritating."

"So that is your number."

"Stop calling me."

"Why does he have your number?"

"Draw your own conclusion. A very sweet conclusion."

It felt like we were as we had been. That night in Chris's room. The fight on the football field. And the unforgettable hamburger fight. Almost being expelled and losing everything. Still, she had sent me on a new trajectory. Only now we were in high heels. Only now we were as naked as we were nude. But it felt like she was wearing jeans and Timberlands and had her hair in a ponytail. And it felt like I had on jeans and trainers and a Hampton Pirates sweatshirt.

Again her nostrils flared. She tensed.

My nostrils flared.

I was ready.

I was ready, willing, and able to fight in high heels.

Others came into the area, laughing, dancing.

They noted the tension between us.

They stared at us.

Then I walked away.

I had wanted to get in her face and scream, "You think your life is so perfect now but I can fuck him whenever I want. I'm happy where I am. I wouldn't want to be you. If I were with Chris, if I had been his wife, he would have you in the background. M and M. You know that she and Chris made a baby and you're fine with that? You have what you deserve and he has what he deserves. Fucking slut monkey."

Anger, attitude, hate, it was all in my walk, in my body language, in my confidence. Those words never left my mouth. Not all thoughts should become words. I remembered my last fight with Siobhán. I heard the fading echoes from a Caribbean woman and a humanitarian screaming things as others held us to keep us from killing each other. My words had been rapid and emotional and my accent had been thick and only a Trini would understand a single thing that I had said. No one made out a word, but my body language had said it all.

I should have kept walking toward Eros.

But the dark side of Gemini made me turn around.

I said, "Fuck this shit."

Heels clicking, neck hot, I went back to her.

I wanted to spit in her face.

I went back to her prepared to spew venom in her face.

What I saw made me pause, made the light side of Gemini take control and slow me down. Siobhán was crying. She had sat down on a pink DECADENCE towel. Surrounded by foreign women, she was crying. In a crowded room she was alone. She looked up and saw me, then lowered her face and shook her head. I was the last person on this planet whom she wanted to see her looking weak. But it was too late. She cursed, tried to pull herself together, failed, looked embarrassed, and went back to crying. She put her face in her hands and cried like I had cried that day when I was in college. After Chris had thrown me out of his room, I had cried so hard. When Rigoberto had found me, I was broken down.

It was her turn now. It was her turn to struggle to breathe as tears fell.

She was unhappy. She was miserable with her life. The Cinderella story always ended at the wedding. No one knew what Cinderella had to endure once she married the prince, the man all admired, the man all women desired. For a princess or a queen, every day there was a new battle. Once upon a time, I had been the queen.

Once upon a time, I had been her friend. Once upon a time I had trusted her.

And for me trust was a form of love.

When I had befriended her, I had told her my personal demons, had revealed my weaknesses.

She had been a false friend then.

I was too real to be anyone's false friend.

She said, "What do you want, Bijou? What the hell do you want?"

I watched her for a while. I was a Watcher. A Watcher of misery.

I returned to my locker. I opened it and took out the folder that I had been browsing. I handed the folder to her. She took it, opened it, saw dozens of photos of us from when we were in college, from when we were friends. Photos of me tutoring her. Of us partying at the apartments across the street from the college. Laughing, smiling, drinks in hand. M&M was there too. But most of the images were of her and me. The Trini girl with the Halle Berry haircut sitting with the cheerleader wearing a ponytail. I wanted Siobhán to remember what we had had. I wanted her to imagine what we could have had as friends.

She said, "That was the day I met you. I was so skinny back then."

"You had on nice slacks, a blouse, and heels that day."

"We met underneath the Emancipation Tree."

"Emancipation Oak."

"Right, Emancipation Oak. I remember waiting, standing there thinking about how nervous I was. You were the best tutor. Your reputation had intimidated me before I met you. I had expected you to show up in a business suit or something. I had changed clothes five or six times before I came to meet you. And went super early. I'll never forget. You had on jeans. You had the coolest walk. You were walking toward me and all of the male students were breaking their necks to see you. It was like Natalie Portman at the end of the movie *Closer*. It was like you had some power over all of the men on campus."

"Wow. You're joking, right?"

"Serious. You were a star on campus. You had no idea?"

I shrugged. "We walked all over campus talking."

"This one, this was the first time you cooked and I was invited to your dorm. You cooked Trini food. You cooked for Chris too."

"You remember."

"It was a big deal. I was surprised that you had invited me to your dorm to eat. I didn't know how to cook, and that terrified me. I still can't, to tell the truth. It's never really interested me that much."

"Cooking wasn't your thing, but you showed up with enough alcohol to get the whole campus intoxicated."

"I had no idea what people might like, so I bought everything. I made drinks. I was the oddball. The new kid. I was really trying to fit in and be cool and make friends. I was the bartender and I made more drinks than I can remember. But I was nervous. I kept thinking, wondering if someone was going to snitch and get me kicked out."

"You did make some damn good drinks. I made Caribbean food and M and M made fried chicken and you made drinks that had everybody running up to my room with a plastic cup in their hand."

"M and M went on a rant about black women and hair. I remember that because I didn't really understand what the issue was. She was always so focused on hair and complexion and hated Barbie."

"That was her thing."

"She had a couple of drinks and shouted something like, 'Black people are always trying to do the black version of white people, and white people are never trying to do the black version of a damn thing black. Movies. Theater. Ever see the white version of a black movie? Or of a black play? Hell no, and you never will. But we imitate them. Know what that means? In the culture wars the white man has won.' "

"She was drunk as a skunk and looking at you."

"She was looking me right in my eyes."

"And you didn't flinch. Everybody thought that she would run you out of there."

"Never bothered me." Then she imitated M&M and said, " 'White people sing black music. Elvis. They sing R and B. And Vanilla Ice couldn't rap. If a black man sounded as bad as Vanilla Ice, he'd get booed off the Apollo. When a white man sings half as good as a black man, he makes ten times more money than a black man. When a white woman sings R and B, she makes more money than a black woman singing the same song.' "

"Had forgotten about that. She could be a bit extreme."

"She was a piece of work. Then someone brought up politics and welfare and she had a lot to say. 'All people on welfare are not illegal drug users, but those folks on welfare that are using illegal drugs shouldn't be on welfare. People who pay for the people on welfare to get a check, they take drug tests at their jobs, so people on welfare should do the same. I think that only those people guilty of using the illegal drugs would object to proving that they aren't. And for the record, listen up. Just because you can have a baby doesn't mean that you should have a baby. And if you are already on welfare and can't support yourself, don't have any more children. If you can't feed a baby, don't make a baby.' "

"You remember that day better than I do."

"M and M ended up dropping out of college and living off welfare for a few years. After all of that righteous talk, she was on food stamps."

"Had no idea that things had been like that for her."

"Well, I remember that day from my perspective. Everyone always remembers a different part of something, sees it a different way."

"That's true. When a crime has been committed, if ten people witnessed that crime, there are ten different ways that crime would have been seen. And maybe none of those versions is the truth. They are true, but they are not the truth. The truth is never in black or white; it's in the gray area of life. But to each person, what they think they saw, what they experienced, what they felt, that was their undeniable truth."

"I remember that day. It was a special day for me."

"It was the day that I introduced you to my boyfriend."

She pulled her lips in, looked the photos over, paused on some.

She said, "We had a lot of fun. All of us; we had so much fun."

"A lot of fun. Chris. Look at him. His dreadlocks were so long."

"His hair was something else. His hair and those eyes."

"Yeah. I had imagined he'd be in the NFL and those locks would be his brand."

"After the injury he taught high school physics for a while."

"He became a teacher?"

"For a while."

"He was one accident away from being great."

"You have no idea. When you're up that high and it all ends, it's a major readjustment. He was a mess, very depressed for a long, long time. Hard being married to a depressed man. Almost drove me mad."

"Sorry to hear that."

Then she closed the folder and slid those memories back to me. As haunting music played, I put the folder back inside of my locker.

Her voice trembled. "I want to know something, Bijou."

"Let me say this first."

"Okay."

I said, "I wanted to say that I was sorry to hear about what happened to your parents. They were good-hearted people, altruistic and role models for the world. I say that I am sorry and I grieve for your loss. Not as a friend, but as one human being to the other. Now, for the other thing. If you're crying over Chris, all I can say is that you get what you get. You get the love that you deserve. I deserve better."

"Did you sleep with my husband?"

"I used to be altruistic. Like your parents. I was so naïve. I fed you. I tutored you, taught you how to cook, introduced you to my friends, let you make my dorm your second home. And I introduced you to Chris. I had imagined that one day I would marry Chris and you would stand in my wedding. That's how I felt about you. We almost lost everything back then. So. Did I sleep with Chris? Your husband contacted me. He saw me here, followed me around, and as soon as you and your husband left he sent me a request on Facebook. He called me. He masturbated for me as I showered. He told me that he would leave you to come back to me. He wanted me to meet him here. He sent a limo for me. He paid my admission. I came here on your dime. We swam. We talked. We laughed. We went inside of a room. No one saw us. But they heard us. He still roars like a lion when he comes. Again he said that he would leave you for me. While he made love to me, I did fuck him. Twice. Two times. Then things got ugly. Very ugly."

"Things turned ugly."

"Extremely."

"Why?"

"Because I regretted it. Because I remembered when I walked in on one of my best friends and my boyfriend while they made love. Because he remembered I slept with Rigoberto. Chris remembered the fight with his *tigre*. Because I remembered all the fights with you."

There was a long pause.

She shed more tears. The truth spared no feelings.

Her voice splintered. "He's never gotten over you."

"But I am over him. He had an affair with you. He chose you. He knocked up my roommate. I had no idea. I didn't have all of the information. Now I do. You knew that and you married him."

She said, "Not before. After. It didn't come out until after. Four years into the marriage, it came up. It surprised me too. It's been hell. Seems like Mona has us in court every year. She lives off us. We had to pay for the kid being on welfare. She filed and gave Chris zero-percent visitation. He didn't fight it. She took the money and ran."

"In that case, better you than me."

"Marriage is forever. Marriage has trials and tribulations."

She was as emotionally dependent on Chris as he was financially dependent on her. That was my assumption. That was my hypothesis.

Only when a woman was truly independent and free of those things could she have the clarity to choose properly, if the desire remained to choose at all. Anything less was an act of desperation.

That was what I knew.

She asked me, "How did you end up here, Bijou?"

"I came to Decadence to study people. I did that at first. Mob behavior, group behavior, wanted to see what sexual energy did to the crowd. But for me it was like being in Plato's cave. Most of us live in dark caves and that darkness becomes all we know, what we adjust our eyes to. It is what we view as the truth. Darkness can be your truth and you can live fine that way, but that truth is not how things really are. You leave the cave and step into the sun. When you first leave darkness and step into the light it will be overwhelming, it will be blinding, it hurts. You're dazzled. Too much to process. Then your eyes adjust. When you return to the cave and try to describe the sensation of light to those who have lived in the cold, when you try to describe light to those who have only lived in the dark, when you try to explain enlightenment to the ignorant they will only laugh and criticize or chastise you for ever wanting to feel the sun and step away from darkness. They chastise what they can't comprehend. The egocentric and self-centered and terrified cannot understand or process what others see differently. But you have left the cave and now you don't want to go back inside because it is no longer where you belong. It's like leaving a small town for a big city. It makes it hard if not impossible to return to Mayberry for long. Mayberry is wonderful for some, but not all of us are cut out for skipping rocks on a lake and playing horseshoes and that nice, easy pace. I might go back to Mayberry. But it'll be a while. I'm enjoying the sun."

"That was beautiful."

"Most of that was bullshit. In reality, like everyone else here, I came for the sex, for pleasure. I came here to enjoy this part of life."

"It's amazing here."

"This could be a hard habit to break."

"Once you leave the cave, it is hard to go back inside."

"Decadence, for now, fulfills my desires. Going to bars, meeting random men, it can be exciting, daring, and fun because there is a rush, it's unpredictable, and I understand why men do what they do. The high that you get, everything that happens before the orgasm is a thrill ride. It can be thrilling but it can be dangerous. Decadence is safe and they embrace my desires here. Every need was nurtured."

"You did all that?"

"I've done a lot of wonderful things. And I have done things that I will regret forever. I have had . . . up to now . . . a pretty exciting life."

"I think I married too soon. There was a lot that I didn't do. I married so young. If I had known about this place before I married . . ."

"Then Mona would be living off of me."

"And I would be fucking so many sexy men up in here."

We laughed. She didn't palter, wasn't being deceitful. She was sincere. Envy danced and jealousy painted her face in bright colors.

It was a soft envy.

I asked, "Did you make it to graduate school?"

"University of Miami. Went immediately after Hampton. You?"

"USC. I went back home long enough to get my masters. Left all of the madness that had happened behind me."

"Congratulations, Bijou."

"Same to you. Congratulations."

"I'm not the writer. My thesis sucked. Writing has never been my strong point. I'm decent at articulating, at times debating, but when it comes to putting pen to paper, and spelling, not my strong point."

"I should've been a better tutor. But it was cut short."

"You were damn good. Despite everything else, I thank you."

"I should thank you. You've taught me more than I taught you."

She nodded, then said, "If you don't mind my asking, how did you end up here? Maybe not how, but why this particular club?"

"It wasn't because of Chris, if that is what you're thinking."

She looked relieved. I was being honest. I owned no attitude in body language or voice.

I said, "I was working on a film. Somehow this subject came up. Maybe because of the plot and characters in the film. They had multiple lovers and lived in harmony. And this actress, Lola Mack, said that she had heard of this place, she had heard of Decadence. She had always wanted to come here. Then I did my research. Eventually I joined."

She exhaled. "Totally random that you were here."

"Totally. My first night here and I ran into Chris; then I ran into you. I was speechless."

"No, you weren't. You were rude. You were a bitch."

We laughed a little.

I apologized for what I had done. She accepted.

Then she apologized for all of the pain that she had caused me. Her lip trembled and she wiped her eyes again. I accepted. Then I almost cried. She wiped her eyes over and over and said, "Thanks for the kind things that you said about my parents."

"They were good people. They had good character."

Again she nodded. "They were strict. While other kids were having parties on beaches and going to Paris and fun places for the summer, I always felt like I was being punished and dragged to some place where disease ran rampant. They were overbearing at times. They were über religious. But they had hearts filled with love and hope and forgiveness. They were the best parents in the world. And at the same time I could not wait to get away from them. I miss them now. I miss them every day. It hurts. Your mother is still alive, right?"

"She is."

"Enjoy her while you can."

"I do."

Not for Chris, maybe we would've been the best of friends, lifelong friends. Not for Chris, I never would have become a pariah, wouldn't have felt like a persona non grata at my own university.

I said, "Good fucking."

She grinned. "Good fucking."

I walked away and left her that way. She had robbed me then. I'd robbed her now. Like a thief in the night, I had broken into her marriage and burgled her. A woman stole a man from another woman and then was shocked when he horned her by cheating with another woman. Putting a wedding ring on him doesn't change his character.

Chris was in the greeting area. I walked by all of the nude men, moved through the forest of lingams and went to him. He saw me, was surprised that I was here, and he became uneasy.

He whispered, "I didn't report what happened. I just told the medics that the sex, that we sort of took the fetish too far. I've called you over and over. I care about you, Nia. Always have. Always will."

He told me he loved me. Said that he wished it had been only us. Said that he wished we had remained together. Said that the world would be perfect. He told me that it wasn't too late. He told me that we still had a chance to make it.

I stared at him for a moment. There were no erotic feelings. There was no Eros love, no erotic love. There was no Philos love, no love based on friendship. There was no unconditional love, no agape. Only happiness. I was happy that I had not been the one he had married. I was happy that I hadn't married him. Some dreams became nightmares.

I walked away from him and returned to the dressing room. When I came back out I was walking with Siobhán. I walked her to her husband. He had no idea what to think, or say, no idea what to do.

Siobhán said, "She told me everything. The phone calls. The masturbation. You brought her here. She scratched you. Not a cat."

I asked her, "Permission to speak to your husband, Mrs. Alleyne?"

"As long as I am present for the conversation, Miss Bijou."

"Out of respect for your marriage and the established rules of this fine country club for adults of various tastes and fetishes, I wouldn't have it any other way. From this moment I respect your ring."

Chris wanted to walk away, but she held his hand, tugged him.

He looked at her. He looked at his pissed off, vainglorious wife. A moment passed and he was able to look at me. I wondered how this felt for him. This moment. This truth. I wondered how powerless he felt.

I told Chris, "I had a long conversation with Mona Marshall from college. I saw your son. Chris Junior is handsome. Very energetic."

"You saw my son? That situation is very complicated."

"As complicated as a quadratic equation. That's something you might have said back in the day. But seriously, you should call your kid. Your wife told me about the visitation issues. Mona is difficult. But how can you not call your *son*? How can a man not call his *son*?"

That instant as the three of us stood there, it took me a moment but I understood what I felt. It was what someone felt when they no longer believed in something. Chris had been my religion, now I no longer believed. He had been a false god. He was not important. The same went for his wife. She no longer mattered. I wouldn't waste anger.

In a calm tone of indifference, I said, "Chris, don't call my phone or e-mail me ever again. Don't contact me on Facebook ever again. Don't follow me on Twitter. Don't follow me here. Don't call me and tell me how you felt like you made a mistake back then and that you will leave your wife to be with me again. Don't end up dead in a ditch."

Cheers and applause lit up the grand area. The sounds came from the wedding chapel. Someone had just married. Instead of the first dance, they would make love for the first time as a married couple.

I regarded Siobhán and with a curt smile I said, "Once again, good fucking, Mrs. Allyene."

She nodded. "Same to you. Good fucking, Bijou."

I moved through the crowd of beautiful people, smiled at members that I knew, and for a while I watched the orgy that had started on behalf of the erotic wedding. I watched a husband and wife take to the center of the room and kiss and make love. It was soft. It was tender. It was a love song composed of *oohs* and *aahs*. I joined in and applauded their first orgasms as a married couple, as husband and wife. Here comes the bride. Literally. Some women cried. Love made the hardest of the hard and the most cynical of us all cry. I cried too. It was an expression of how all women wanted to feel at some point. I saw other couples join in. No one shared. There were no ménage à trois. That was more than enough stimulation for them. It was beautiful. It was emotional.

Not long after that, I went to the library, sat on a red chair in a giant suite room filled with erotica. I found a leather-bound novel by Anaïs Nin. As videos of love played, I read parts of her journal.

As lovers made love, as a woman lay back on a sofa reading aloud as her lover licked the delicate folds of her yoni, as he praised her, I made myself comfortable, tuned them out, and read a hundred pages.

I read about Anaïs and her lovers. I read her works and searched for me on each page, in each situation, in every circumstance. Some pages I read a dozen times, each time feeling as if I were she.

But I was not. I wasn't Anaïs Nin. Nor Plath. Nor Rand. Yet I was parts of all of them. I gazed around the room; saw other women reading, some enjoying literature as they made love.

A kind server dressed in black lingerie came and offered us tea. I had peach mango with honey. The woman nearest me was reading as her lover pleased her, asked for tea and extra honey. She wanted extra honey. She filled her mouth with honey, and then sipped tea to melt the sweetness. She brought her lover's lingam to her face. She sucked his lingam with a mouth filled with melting sweetness. I eased down my book and I watched. When she was out of tea and honey, I offered her mine. She accepted, then continued. The server returned and brought her ice cubes. I smiled. She alternated between giving hot and cold stimulation. She drove him insane. She smiled at me and winked. I gave her the thumbs-up.

She stroked her lover, eased two Altoids inside of her mouth, and as she allowed those to melt she looked my way again, gave me a friendly grin and asked, "Which piece of literature are you reading?"

"*Delta of Venus*."

"*Little Birds* was my favorite."

"Really?"

"That and *Cities of the Interior*."

As she stroked her lover we said a few things about *Ladders to Fire*, *Waste of Timelessness*, *Nearer the Moon*, and *A Spy in the House of Love*. Her lover had his eyes closed the entire time, mouth slacked, in heaven. She returned to him, suckled him, and I watched as the heat from the mints drove him mad. She sucked and blew air, created a cool sensation that blended with heat, used her tongue to paint his erection.

It didn't look like sex. It looked like unconditional love. They were in the honeymoon phase of their relationship, as I was in the honeymoon phase with this wonderful country club for swingers. She wore Ferragamo heels and watches and diamonds and pearls, another woman who had fallen victim to the Sudden Wealth Syndrome. She sucked. She slurped. He moaned. As they continued, I returned to reading. When that cerebral part of me was fulfilled, my sensual side demanded attention. I closed the book, told the lovers to have a good evening, and I searched for Rosetta.

While I searched the edifice for my friend, I saw Chris and Siobhán on the monitors. She had him. She was happy. Yet she was as miserable as a woman could become. Maybe that was why tonight she was working on another man.

Sinner's Bible. Exodus 20:14. It looked like they were following those scriptures. But I felt that it was more like Matthew 7:12: "In everything, do to others what you would have them do to you."

I tried to imagine what that would have felt like, to have married him only to find out he had impregnated my roommate. Then to find out he had bedded the woman I had tutored. To have had Siobhán stand in my wedding, then for all the truths to come out. That flashed in front of me. That montage of possibilities flashed in front of me. The humiliation that I had suffered at Hampton wouldn't have compared.

No matter his faults, no matter how he fucked her over, she had to have him. When a man was seen as a hero, no matter what he did, he was forgiven. Love blinded us all. I had seen undying loving in his son's eyes. I had seen confusion sparkle in M&M's eyes. My head was no longer clouded. Chris was not a king. Not a warrior. He was the court jester. He was a Mensa, but he was a fool. Even a well-educated man could still remain a fool. Educated fools filled the world.

Rosetta asked me, "Are you sure?"

"I'm as ready as I will ever be."

I saw their beautiful faces. Three men who wanted to give me my final fantasy. Triplets. My ultimate fantasy had been arranged for me.

They assured me that it was okay, that I was in a world sans bigotry, sans hypocrites. With each touch, absolute arousal ignited and imprisoned me. We went slowly. A mouth on my neck. A mouth on my breasts. A mouth sucking my toes. Then. A tongue kissing me. A tongue inside of my yoni. Teeth nibbling at my nipples. Then. A tongue sucking my ear. A tongue swirling my chocolate star. A tongue dancing with mine. Then. A tongue deep inside of my yoni as both breasts were being suckled. There were so many combinations and permutations of stimulation and they walked me through them all. They gave me triple penetration and every nerve ending danced. I got it good, but I gave it better. As I panted, as my moans did a ballet with their moans and echoed like chamber music, as I owned them, as I owned all who were connected with me, as I saw the face of God and gave Her angels many, many wings, in the shadows, someone else was watching, her Cuban face becoming clearer and clearer, as did her red DECADENCE towel. It was Anaïs. It was my interviewer. I smiled and reached for her, for my friend, for my sister in hedonism. She dropped her red DECADENCE towel. She wore jewels and skyscraper heels that added eight inches of verticalness to her frame. She came toward the bed, was eager to join us, excited to help me. As soon as she became part of the loved, as soon as she was penetrated and sang, Chandra appeared, smiling, needing the pleasure that her husband had denied her. She joined our party. It became a daisy chain of exotic love, a provocative session of laughs and moans and Kama Sutra, everyone pleasing and being pleased, moving lightly, nimbly, orgasms rising, angels taking flight; a slow-moving exchange where the faulty design of man never arrived, never intruded on the bliss of a woman. Soon the Brit and Quince Pulgadas appeared and joined the chain of love, and so did my lover from Curaçao and his wife. As we pleased one another, I looked up and saw the room was crowded, filled with Watchers.

Soon I would find love. I would tire of this walk and search for that one lover. I wanted a husband. I wanted a child. One day. Not right now. Not too soon. But while my eggs were young.

While I was young. While my mother was young.

The perfect man for me, in all honesty, at this point in my life, would be a man like me. An adventurous man who wanted to please me and not limit my desires. A male libertine, the reader of Henry Miller and Sartre. But I knew that I would want the opposite. A man who was like me would be a man for fantasies, for fun, for my journals, a man who would help me verify that the Ericsson Rule was correct.

FORTY

Prada wasn't there. I didn't see him in the crowd when the movie premiered in Leicester Square. He lived in London. One of his homes was in Central London. I walked the red carpet. Large crowd. Flashing cameras. My mother at my side. I saw Margareta and her husband. I saw others from Decadence. But I did not see Prada. Nor did I see Prada in the assembly when the movie premiered in Trinidad. The home crowd was amazing. It rivaled the fête that had happened at the airport when the Olympians brought home the medals. I was a Trini, like my mother. But I sensed that Prada was there. He was watching me, wanting me as I lived in the spotlight, as I was blinded by its glare, as I frowned at its tawdry, ugly, oppressive, and inane nature, as it fed on us, this business of show made for sharks and piranhas. Every moment I wanted to flee, tried to get away. He watched. He saw many billboards featuring me holding the latest phones. He desired me. He loved and lusted for me. But he knew that I was no good for him. Women like me, in the end, only made men suffer. Anaïs Nin had made her husband suffer. So had Ayn Rand. We emasculated the strongest of men, made tigers become lambs, then we resented them for being so weak. Or it was the other way; they made us suffer, as Frida Kahlo de Rivera had suffered in her marriage with Diego Rivera. Maybe I was born a bitch. Maybe I was born a writer. I was born to make man suffer.

No, Prada wasn't in London, but he was in the Caribbean, in my shadows, on the island of Trinidad. When my plane landed, I knew he was there. I sensed his presence when I had run the Savannah with my mother. We had run by a limo that was parked in the driveway on the side nearest NAPA. I had passed that limo when I was collected from the airport. And as we ran, that same limo had remained behind us until we made it to the side with the upside-down Hilton. The next day I sensed that he was there as I bought coffee at the Rituals outlet on the ground floor of the Nalis Library on Abercromby Street.

At the movie premiere I had seen the same stretch limo with darkened windows. The following day, I had seen the black limo with darkened windows when I had stepped out of Rituals. The license plates were the same. Two days later, I had seen him again when I was near UWI, in the town of Curepe buying doubles at my favorite doubles spot. That time, I had paused and looked toward the car. I saw the driver, an Indian man with a goatee, but the passenger was hidden, but a silhouette in the backseat.

Curious, I took a step toward the limo, and the driver immediately pulled away from the curb.

My lover, my lover.

My capitalistic, billionaire, proficient, whore-loving lover.

The opposite of love was indifference. He was not indifferent. He was in pain. Men wanted what they couldn't have and fled what challenged them. If not for your jealousy; if not for your jealousy; but for your jealousy. If not for your jealousy, I would search for you, find you, give you flowers and a ring. With hot tea and honey, with Altoids, I would humble myself and bring you back to me.

But never for a jealous man. That was one trait I would never find admirable, be it in myself or in the hearts of others. I desired a good relationship. I deserved a great relationship.

If only Prada had Bret's personality. I would've been done; this journey would have ended. A great relationship was when someone accepted your past, supported your present, and encouraged your future. He had flown half the world to bring me a dozen red roses. He loved me. Yet he hated me; that I knew for sure, for we hate that which we cannot control. Frustration is a form of anger and anger is hate. He couldn't deal with me in the present. He couldn't deal with his own past. I was stronger than he. Truth didn't terrify me. My strength, my audacities made me smile. That was the way I saw it.

She who won the battle was allowed to pen the tale of the war.

That was the way it would be written, with me as the victor.

* * *

My stepfather showed up at every premiere. The Frenchman who had adopted me and made me his own was always there, here for me now as he had been there for me during my darkest hours during those college days. I loved him. He had broken my heart. But I loved him like I would no other.

Not for him, not for the man who had seen a beautiful Caribbean girl down by the Savannah and had fallen in lust, the man who had fallen in love with my mother and her rich brown skin that had been touched by the sun, I might be on the side of the road selling doubles. I might still be living in Trinidad. My mother would be at my side. Women who had wanted my father would be cutting her the side eye. And children who were my age, children who shared my father's bloodline would stare at me, their sister. Didn't matter. Our doubles would be the best doubles that anyone on the island had ever tasted.

Still. That wasn't my reality. That was the writer inside of me revising history. But still as we passed the Queen's Park Savannah I looked up into the hills, looked toward Laventille and saw the lights that dotted the slum where my mother was born, where my father was murdered, where I had never been.

I imagined my mother in intense arguments with other pregnant women. I remembered something that Siobhán had said to me. When we had first met in college she had said that she had been to Trinidad.

And she had met a girl who was about my age, a girl who looked just like me. We were in college, standing underneath Emancipation Oak when she said that. It was just now that I remembered that moment. I had siblings. How many, I had no idea. My father was a Caribbean man. I sensed they knew about me, that they had been in the crowd watching me as well. I sensed I had been watched for years.

FORTY-ONE

The stubborn romantic who lived inside of me encouraged me to contact Rigoberto. That part of me told me that I should have been with Rigoberto from the start. That part of me conjectured how different my life would have been. It showed me that if I had been with him since college, there would have been less pain. No relationship came without pain. None without trials and none without tribulations. I imagined how different I would have been if I had lived in the Netherlands with him. That could have been a wonderful season. Living there, loving, writing, maybe having a child. But the realist inside of me told me to refrain from playing once upon a time with my life. It was too late to travel down that road. I would look into Rigoberto's eyes and see the same thing; over and over I would see the same thing. I would remember his kindness. His energy. I might even remember his love letters. Especially the latest one, the last one. In an age when everyone communicated by Facebook and texting, he had taken the time to pen me a letter. A letter that had no errors. I would adore him for that. But more importantly, unfortunately I'd remember that horrible day. I'd remember being broken down. I would remember that day that I walked in on Chris and Siobhán. I would remember being kicked out of the dorms. Rigoberto had hugged me as I cried. He had found me inside of my dorm room crying, angry, confused, and in pain. He had taken me away from my dorm room, away from the embarrassment, away from the humiliation. Whenever I saw him I would remember that which I needed to forget. I would always live in the past.

Rigoberto sent me a request on Facebook. He asked for entry into my world. He asked for permission to reenter my life.

There were two choices: CONFIRM or DELETE REQUEST. Still I moved the mouse over CONFIRM. But I knew that he knew about Chris and Siobhán before I had. He might have known about M&M. He and Chris were best friends. *Tigres*. Men held the secrets of men as women held the secrets of women. With the mouse, I moved the arrow across CONFIRM and stopped over DELETE.

Rigoberto had been a beautiful dream inside of a horrible nightmare. I would not be able to be around him and not feel that nightmare again and again.

I engaged the DELETE button.

Rigoberto. My knight in shining armor. Chris. The king who destroyed my once-perfect kingdom. Best friends. I imagined that one day in the future their paths would cross again. I think that it was in their destiny to run into each other again. The world was not that large. They had much in common. They both liked sports. They were both intelligent. Maybe they would end up at some function.

That was too simple. Both loved sports, but had moved beyond that era in their lives.

They were worldly men, each in their own way. They would be in Europe. Off the beaten path. In Turkey. On the Turkish Aegean coast. İzmir province. In Dikili. At a remote location. Chris would be vacationing at the Dikili Sunset Hotel, a two-hour ride from the nearest airport. A long way from civilization as he knew it. He would have spent the day swimming at eight different beaches. If Siobhán were with him, she would have been swimming with the fish or engaging in a decadent mud bath. Or they would have been out on sea bikes. But I imagined that she wouldn't be there. It would be off-season.

Rigoberto would be out seeing the world, driving from Bulgaria to Bodrum, a port city in Muğla province, in the southwestern Aegean region of Turkey, a city of only a few thousand people. The Asian side of Turkey would be breathtaking. He would have been on the road for eleven hours and would see the four-story hotel, a hotel that had thirty rooms on three floors, rooms with balconies that overlooked the beach and allowed a view of the marvelous sunset behind the neighboring Greek island of Lesbos. Being a weary traveler, a romantic man, he would decide to stop and get a room with a sea view. And he would plan to see a crater lake in Merdivenli and the ancient caverns in both the

Demirtas and Delitas villages, all that and maybe the Merkez Mosque, a wooden structure that was built without using a single nail. He would travel as a man did when he had not found a love that would be returned. He would have had lovers along the way, but none would have touched his heart in a way that made him want to promise always and forever. Carrying a backpack he would enter the lobby and ask if any rooms were available.

It was off-season. There were plenty of rooms. The hotel would be practically empty. Chris would enter the hotel lobby, a place that he was planning to stay a fortnight. Rigoberto would be there, checking in. Maybe he was being handed his room key, or maybe he was asking the concierge for information about taking an excursion to Ataneus or Garip Island, possibly chatting about European Turkey, Bosphorus, the Sea of Marmara, and the Dardanelles. He would hear someone enter the nearly vacant hotel and turn and look and stop his conversation midsentence, mid-smile. Rigoberto would see Chris the moment that Chris saw Rigoberto. The man from Belize would see the man from the Dominican Republic. They would see each other at the same time.

And the world would stop rotating on its axis.

In one version I imagined them as I had seen them now, at this age.

In another version, I imagined them as older men, maybe middle-aged, both with hints of gray at their temples, maybe the same signs of maturity in their beards. Older men who had once been younger men, and as younger men, the best of friends. They were men who were supposed to be the best man at each other's wedding. Men who had known that one would be a pallbearer at the other's funeral.

Maybe Siobhán would be there. Maybe Chris's wife would be there. She would exit the elevator. She would be fat and wobble across the room looking like Miss Piggy on steroids.

Petty, I know.

But I was still a woman.

I was still of flesh and blood and emotions.

Maybe Rigoberto wouldn't be alone either. He would be with a beautiful woman. Brown skinned. She would have brown skin, the hue of an island girl. She would resemble me, would look the same as I had looked when I was in college.

No, this was about the men.

Their friendship.

No women.

Just the two men.

Just the *tigres*. Staring at each other. Remembering.

They would walk toward each other.

I abandoned the dream right there. I abated fiction and returned to reality. After I denied Rigoberto a chance at a reunion, I deleted Chris. After Chris was deleted, I deleted M&M. Denial. Anger. Bargaining. Depression. Acceptance. Five stages of grief had come and now they could be on their way to the next person. I had done my time. I had completed the cycle. The chains were gone. I stretched, yawned, and now I could move on with my life. The good. The bad. The memories. I left those days sealed in that tattered U-Haul box. I left that group behind, inside of its own compartment. With a black Sharpie I wrote large and bold letters across the top. PANDORA'S BOX. That part of my learning, that era of the education of Nia Simone Bijou, was finished.

FORTY-TWO

With Bret, I was not a woman, but a girl. I was not Louboutins and extravagant makeup; I was running shoes, lip gloss, and ponytail. He took me on another mud run, but the next one was more of a challenge. It was a triathlon that included hurdles, pole-vaulting, and an almost one-mile sprint. I went from being on red carpets around the world to being in a muddied world that existed on the other side of the barbed wire, running, crawling through filth, climbing over rocks, a 3.1 mile obstacle course. I finished first in my division. I hadn't been first at anything in a long time. It felt good. We went to the range and I learned how to use a firearm. When he had time we drove past Helen and hiked the mountain in Georgia. He was the father of two children, a responsible man, so his time was limited. I respected that. I respected him in a way that I would never respect Chris. Projects were due. I spent days writing, spent weeks working on multiple projects, spent weeks stressed, but when I was in Bret's company it all went away. Short lunches. Early movies. With him, I remained a girl who loved to have fun. I had been frustrated with him, was ready to dismiss him, but I realized that he allowed me to be me, and did it without asking questions. Sometimes he held my hand. Most of the time he didn't. It was fine. He didn't judge me. He wasn't jealous. He wasn't possessive. He appealed to me. I had been busy. I had traveled the world and returned and he still appealed to me. He had always appealed to a very important part of me. Part of me needed Decadence, but part of me needed Bret, and it needed to be nourished as well.

Time had marched on. My mother had come to Atlanta and gone.

She had spent a week helping me unpack. She hated me for that. My stepfather had come and stayed with me for a weekend, a weekend of speaking only French. I promised him that after the summer I would come to Paris and stay awhile. It had been too long since I had visited.

I had friends and acquaintances all over the world now.

It was almost summer, a transitional point of time, during the hours that existed between astrological signs, a division between houses, days before the season of my sign. Maybe I was on the cusp of love. Summer always made me feel the heat of love, always made my heat expand, and rise.

We were eight miles into a twenty-two-mile run on the Silver Comet Trail, the austral sun peeking through the trees that cast much-needed shade on the trail during the early morning hours. The pollen count wasn't as high as it had been the week before, but we endured both the pollen and the humidity.

Bret ran with no shirt on, running shorts, sweat draining over his heroic frame. I wore running shorts and a sports bra. I had added highlights to my hair, had given myself a new look for a new season. And my workout gear was cardinal and gold, the colors of USC, my grad school, and maybe where I would eventually obtain my PhD.

My blue and white days, my Pirate season was behind me.

I would always be a Pirate in my heart, but now I was a Trojan.

Bret said, "I'm going back into the military."

"Serious?"

"It's my best option at this point."

"When?"

"In about six months. If I re-up for Afghanistan, Iraq, or Kuwait, I can get a bonus of ninety thousand dollars. I won't have to pay as much in taxes. I can do more for my kids. I have the custody issue settled, for now. But things like that never end. It exhausted the money I had. Not a lot of good work for a former soldier and Uncle Sam is waiting with open arms. So, I'll leave in about six months."

"You'll be gone for a year. I'm going to be sad."

"Didn't think that you would care one way or the other."

"Why would you think that?"

"Just did. Nothing seems to faze you."

"Well, it matters. Everything matters to me, but I can't afford to let it show."

"It matters to me too. Hard for me to say that, but it matters to me."

"Will I get to spend time with you before you leave?"

"Of course. I'd like to see you every day, but I know that's not possible."

"You'd slit your wrists if you saw me every day."

"Probably."

We laughed.

He said, "To be honest, I enjoy your company. You send me places I have no right being."

"Wow. For real?"

"You make me feel things, make me think about things."

"All I ever do is run with you."

"You're powerful. I think that you know what I'm trying to say. Not good at this sort of thing."

"Well, you tempt me too. You make me feel things too. Thought about you while I was gone."

"When you were gone to LA and Europe and Trinidad, to be honest, I was pretty lonely for you. When you texted me that you were going to Hawaii for a week with some friends, then from there you went to Sweden for research, wanted to call you all the time. I've never been like that with any woman. It was really hard being around you for a while, to be honest. I guess my feelings were getting too strong."

"If that's the case, if you felt something, why haven't you tried to be intimate with me?"

"Wanted to. Believe me. I wanted to."

"What was wrong in Tampa? Was my body language wrong? Did my breath stink?"

"I knew that night changed everything between us. You distanced yourself after that."

"I did. I hated you for that. You know I wanted you. You rejected me."

"I didn't reject you. I thought that you were happy with us being a one-off in that department."

"I came to your room. Naked. I was in bed with you. Naked. I let my hair down. Do you know what it means when a woman lets her hair down? Naked. In your bed. Hair down. How do you spell rejection?"

"I opened the door between our rooms. I saw you had opened yours.

You looked so sexy when you were sleeping. Swear to God, I wanted to climb on top of you and get inside of you."

"What was the problem?"

"You have a boyfriend. If you're single and doing your thing, you see whoever you want to see and do whatever you do, and that's fine. Nobody can start a quarrel or have the right to engage in a personal war. But when a woman has a boyfriend, I'm not really comfortable crossing that line. That could be dark territory. That's a two-man war that usually ends with a man being put in the ground. I enjoy your company, but if there was ever a time that your boyfriend and I crossed paths, I would want to be able to look him in the eye and tell him man-to-man that I am attracted to you, but we are platonic. I want to be able to shake his hand and buy him a beer, if that's what needs to happen."

"You're honorable."

"To a certain degree. I'll take it outside, but only when I need to take it outside. I'll go man-to-man and toe-to-toe. But I have kids at home. I have to reconsider how I do things. I'm not eighteen, so I can't behave as if I am still eighteen. I have to grow up and look down the road before I do things."

"Where were you when I was in college?"

"Probably wishing that I was still in college."

"Look, Bret, I don't have a boyfriend."

"Prada? You've been seeing him, right? He flies in from London to see you, right?"

"Haven't seen him in a very long time. If he was my boyfriend, it lasted about three hours."

"While you were gone, I assumed that you were flying all over the world with him."

"Long gone. We ended that a while ago. We don't communicate at all."

We ran some more, our pace almost eight-minute miles, slow for us. We ran by Rollerbladers, bikers, and joggers. The world was green now. Everything was blooming, growing, coming back to life.

Bret asked, "What do you want to do for your birthday?"

"You remember my birthday?"

"I remember everything about you, pretty much."

"Wait. To be sure, was that an offer to take me out on a date?"

"It was. I would love to take you out. I'll pick you up at your front door, if you want. Just tell me ahead of time what you'd like to do."

"Anything I want?"

"Anything within my budget."

I told Bret, "I want to have sex over twenty-one times."

"More than twenty-one times?"

"Over a weekend. That's been on my mind for years. That fantasy is stuck in my head."

"With whom?"

"With you. Just us two. Just you and me. Unless you want to find a third party. But I would prefer for it to just be me and you. Just us."

He paused before he asked me, "Which weekend?"

"My birthday weekend. Or any weekend you're available and it works for me."

"Which hotel?"

"If it's just you and me, my place. We can be at my place. If we have a unicorn, then the W."

"You're serious?"

"Very. As a heart attack."

"Sure. It would almost be a year to the day that we met."

"Pretty much. I guess that we could celebrate our special friendship as well."

"Let me arrange a babysitter."

I smiled. "You should come by my townhome after we run. You've never seen my place."

"I'll need to go home and shower."

"Do I need to be direct with you? Is that what it is? We can't be shy and coy and get anywhere."

"I'm a soldier. We don't do indirect. We don't do shy. We don't do vague."

"I want you in my bed, soldier. I want to make you come, then send you off to have a good day."

"I still need to shower."

"I have water. I have soap. I have towels."

"Can't stay long. I'll have to get my kids soon. They're in Macon with their mother."

"I'll be quick. I just want to suck you."

He slowed his pace and wiped sweat from his brow. "We could always turn around now."

We turned around. Today would be the day that I broke the six-minute mile.

I had motivation. Today I craved normal things. I missed normal.

Altoids. Tea. Honey.

After I had tied his hands, after I had tied his ankles, after I had blindfolded my soldier, I whispered, "Lay back, Bret. Relax. Keep your eyes closed. Enjoy. Enjoy me as I enjoy you."

With Bret I was not a woman, but a girl. I was a naughty girl who loved to have fun.

As the woman had done at Decadence, first I filled my mouth with honey, then I sipped hot tea to melt the sweetness. I took him inside of my orifice of speech. Tried to take all of him. He jerked. He tensed. He panted. I sucked his lingam. Hot water and the stickiness of honey on his flesh made him weep and convulse and struggle to catch his breath like I had never seen a man weep and convulse and struggle to catch his breath before. He pulled at his restraints. He whispered my name over and over, then called to God and sweet baby Jesus. I took him too close to orgasm, backed away, took him to the edge, backed away, did that over and over and over. He was dying. Then I delivered him from his agony. His muscular contraction, his spasms, his facial contortions, his change in breathing, the contraction in his lingam, then the moment of inevitability, the point of no return, his orgasm. His orgasm sounded like stress leaving his body. I watched him as he returned to normal. I watched him and his smile of astonishment.

I said, "You taste good. So damn good. One more time, if it's okay."

"I'll be a little late and right now that's fine by me."

I touched him, kissed him, and massaged him until his refractory period had ended. When he was capable, ready to rise again, I used the Altoids. I crunched on four, let those dissolve as I grinned at him.

I told him, "This might take a while. There are one hundred Altoids in the box."

When I was done, when I had made him jerk and strain and come again, when I had freed my slave from his bondage, he came to me, kissed me, put me on my back, then he tied me to the bed.

He told me that I was a queen, a ruler, a sensual goddess walking amongst mere mortals. Once again the warrior told me that.

He whispered, "Bowl. Towels. Scissors."

"Oh God. Yes, yes, yes."

I told him where they were.

"Okay to cut your towels?"

I nodded. I didn't care if he cut slits in the best towels that I had. He filled a bowl with hot water. He put hand towels inside. He put me on my back with my knees bent, legs open. He wrung out one of the steaming washcloths. Bret found scissors on my dresser and cut slits in the towels like the slit of a yoni. I swallowed. I twitched. He put the hot washcloth on me, put its heat on top of my sex, lined the slit from the washcloth up with the opening that nature had given me. You didn't become a good writer by leading a bland, cookie-cutter life. At some point I will understand what drives me. And maybe as I take pen to paper and continue to write the honest and explicit pages of *Abnormal Desires*, as I pen my life and include this wonderful moment, as I include all of my experiences, my life until now *unbowdlerized*, as I include truths that may be shocking or unpleasant to some, as I refused to weaken my existence and my experiences to make someone like me more, maybe I will stop and count and see both the gains and losses I have incurred because of my chosen lifestyle, losses and gains that were small or large, obvious or subtle.

Once it had been written, only then could it be viewed deeply.

The eye could not see itself.

Bret blindfolded me. I wiggled. Anticipated. Craved. The steamy towels against my anxious sex felt amazing. Bret eased his organ of taste through the slit in the towel. He moved through the opening of the towel into my opening, held his tongue inside of me. I moaned, tensed, and pulled at my restraints. He took the tin of Altoids and chewed four. He chewed them until his tongue was saturated with the mint. Then he started over, moved his tongue across my sex, around my sex, up and down my sex. As it had been in my dream he painted from my glans clitoris across my labia minora to my meatus. He pushed his tongue inside of me, inside of my yoni. He ran his tongue up and down, painted me from my clitoris across my labia to my opening. I loved tongue. His tongue, his organ of taste moved like he had missed me. Up and down and up and down and then in circles. Soon his tongue opened me up again. His tongue moved back inside of me. Deep, deep, deep inside of me. I counted the ups. The downs. The ins. The outs.

I counted his tongue strokes. "Hundred . . . and seventy . . . one hundred and seventy-one . . ."

The heat from the towels. The uniqueness of his tongue. I remembered. I had missed his tongue. He tasted me and moaned an excited moan, a beautiful moan, an arousing moan. He licked me in circles. In eights. He held my trembling ass and licked me.

He sucked my clit.

My spot.

The spot.

He stayed on my spot.

He tortured me as I had tortured him.

Close to orgasm.

Back away.

Close.

Back away.

And he sucked.

Gently.

Hard.

Gently.

The heat from the towel. Altoids on his tongue. It was too much. I fought to get free.

He held my ass and sucked and refused to let me go.

My legs tensed. Singsong moans rose.

I shuddered, tears ran from my eyes, and I gave an angel its wings.

I came. I came. Damn, I came.

I have long, dry seasons of famine. Then I feast, become a glutton. I have fantasies, some extreme, some violent, some loving, and I act on them. Sometimes I need a day where I have a lover and all he does is please me. I have days where I really need to fuck a man, ride, suck a man. When I'm having sex I feel so alive, the world, my existence feels so wonderful. Sometimes I want the friendship of a man, but other times I only want his passion. Friendship can be false; passion never lies.

You have a right to experiment with your life. You will make mistakes. And they are right too. . . . Society is the one that keeps demanding that we fit in and not disturb things. They would like you to fit in right away so that things work now.

—Anaïs Nin

ACKNOWLEDGMENTS

Bienvenidos a los agradecimientos de este libro!

Hello, O ye faithful reader. I'll wait a moment, allow you to sip water and cool off. Cold shower? Sure. There. Better. Okay. Sure you're okay? Good. Once again we have made it to the end of another journey and I hope that you enjoyed reading *Decadence* from beginning to end, from foreplay to orgasm, from anger to resolution. There are only three types of stories and I think that Nia has covered them all.

Pardon all of the gunfire and shouting. Gideon never eases up. He's frustrated. He's an international killer. And I'm scared. So let me get through these acknowledgments so I can get back to his next adventure. Gideon. Shotgun. Konstantine. Hawks. Midnight. Raven. They are all screaming.

Lolita Files, my twin, thanks for reading the early pages. You are the best! And you are so friggin' brilliant! Hugs.

I have to thank my friends and fans in Trinidad. Once again I had fun jogging the Savannah, eating doubles, and hanging out at Movie Towne. Next time I hope to get down south as well as over to Tobago. I pretty much ended my book tour for *An Accidental Affair* there back in July. Nigel Khan Booksellers, thanks for everything. The tour was wonderful. You were the perfect host. You kept my belly full with doubles. Leslie Ann Caton, thanks for collecting me at the crack of dawn and getting me all over the island. Thanks for the Trini-to-English translations. We will have to make arrangements to go see the PM again. (ROFL! We can laugh about it now, right?) Dionne Baptiste (no relation to Regina) at TV6, thanks for arranging the twenty-one question interview with the

Trinidad Express. Two thumbs-up on that one. Tia Haynes (whassup!) and the amazing staff at the Carlton Savannah, thanks for the wonderful accommodations. I shall return. Tishanna Williams, it was great running into you in town. Thanks for the Trini-to-English translations as well. And thanks for arranging to get the locks done.

Hold on. I have to grab my laptop, bulletproof vest, and run like a gazelle. Being chased by the new and improved version of the Four Horsemen. Okay. Now I am so friggin' terrified. Siri too afraid to talk too. Whew. I'm in a ditch. Don't talk to loud. Where were we? Oh yeah. Thanking people.

Once again thanks to all of the hardworking people at Dutton. Brian Tart, I'll have to get back to NYC soon and stop by and shake your hand. Thanks for the support. Denise Roy, my wonderful editor, this was probably the largest book you've seen in a while. ROFL. We'll chop it up, down, and get it under control. If all else fails, we'll send it to Jenny Craig and make it lose a few chapters. To Liza Cassity and everyone in publicity, thanks. Time to send me back out on the road again. I'm packing as I type.

Sara Camilli and everyone at the Sara Camilli Agency, thanks for helping me get this one wrapped up. I have officially lost count. How far am I from book one hundred? How much wood can a woodchuck chuck?

DeMarMc, thanks for reading the initial, rambling version of *Decadence* back when it had many more words, hot off the pages of my second-generation MacBook Pro. Thanks for the info on Hampton, once again. I should've had you create blueprints for the club Decadence. Dammit. Next time. Farrah Gilyard from Florida, thanks for the input and I hope you enjoy reading about your AE once again. Hope you enjoyed TEoNSB as well. Corinne (TGIF!) Biagas up at Hampton, I must thank you for information on the university. It all came in handy. Ozlem Evans, once again thanks for sending me the information that I needed toward the end. Arleen Abhiram, my Trinidadian amiga, thanks for answering many questions via text. Leslie Quash, my Tobagonian amiga, thanks. Hey, Zola! Any bloopers made are mine. Same for cultural mistakes. Make sure you tell them all that this is fiction. Lynette, thanks for reading this as well. I'll make sure the advance copies arrive on time.

And you, special person, invaluable one, of course I'm not going to forget you. I would never forget about you. The best for last.

I want to thank ________________________________ for all of your assistance while working on this novel, be it real or imaginary. I had no idea what *colorful* showers, glory holes, and unicorns meant, but you seemed to be the expert on all things that happened after midnight, so I will take you at your word. No wonder you keep tea and honey in your purse and Altoids in your pocket. You rock, Gangnam style.

Feel free to stop by www.ericjeromedickey.com. From there you can find me on social media. And look for the Official Eric Jerome Dickey Fan Page on Facebook.

Hasta la próxima! Time for me to get on a flight to South America. Gideon time. Medianoche time. It's long overdue.

¡Chau!

Sunday, September 30, 2012. 9:31 P.M.
33.9936° N, 118.3469° W
73°F | 23°C
Wind: SW at 4 mph
Humidity: 68% Clear skies.
☺

FORTY-THREE

(Bonus Scene)

In a sleepy voice she said, "Hello. Yes, this is Rae-Jeanne Quash."

"Pardon the intrusion. Mrs. Quash, this is Nia Simone Bijou calling."

"Excuse me. Is this a joke? Nia Simone Bijou?"

"If it is okay I would like to have a word with you, Mrs. Quash."

"Lord in heaven, do you know what time it is?"

"Some time ago, months ago, you interviewed me for the *Trinidad Express*."

"It's the middle of the night. No sane person calls anyone at this hour."

"I'm the woman who was born in Port of Spain and you said wasn't a true Trini."

"It's three fifteen in the morning. You just woke up both me and my husband."

"Freshwater Trini, to be exact. That was the insult that you spat across the wire."

"This is my home. How did you get my phone number?"

"It's not a private number. I called information."

"What can I do for you? Is there some reason you are calling my home, Miss Bijou?"

"You interviewed me."

"If you have issue with the interview, don't ring my home, don't be unprofessional, follow the proper channels and take it up with my employer. Don't intrude into my personal life. How dare you."

"That was some review. It was but one of many, but that one has been a thorn in my side."

"Did you not like the results of the interview? Is that why you are stalking me?"

"It was harsh. It was page one. Above the fold. And it was cruel beyond belief."

"It was honest."

"It was mean-spirited. It was personal."

"Did you think that your little American movie was perfect?"

"Your opinion is your opinion."

"This phone call is out of line."

"I hated the review. But that is not why I called you."

"What can I do for you?"

"This is personal."

"Okay."

"Quash is your married name? What is your maiden name?"

Not until then did she pause. "Liverpool."

"And who is your father?"

"His name was Derren Liverpool."

"We have the same father. We had the same father."

"He was my father."

"He was my father as well."

"So I have heard."

"You knew all along."

"I knew. I know who you are. Your face is all over Trinidad. You Bijous are . . . inescapable."

"How old are you?"

"If you must know, we born same year, same hospital, and are the same age, more or less."

"More or less. You know of me and I know nothing about you. Which month were you born?"

"Why? Why would you need that information?"

"You're my sister."

"We have the same father. You are not my sister."

A moment later I said, "Thanks for your time, Mrs. Quash. Thanks for your time."

"Again, if you have issues regarding the interview from so many months ago, call my employer or send him an e-mail."

"Noted."

"You may be rich. You may be smart. But you eh no Trini. I grow up in the bowels of Laventille. No white man from Paris comes to rescue me and my mudda. Iz a true Trini. Remember that, bitch."

Then I took a slow breath and calmly I pressed the end button.

Another day. Another time. Another season.

Another chapter of my life.